T0046282

WHO CRIES FOR THE LOST

A Sebastian St. Cyr Mystery

C. S. HARRIS

BERKLEY
New York

BERKLEY
An imprint of Penguin Random House LLC
penguinrandomhouse.com

Copyright © 2023 by The Two Talers, LLC
Excerpt from *What Cannot Be Said* copyright © 2024 by The Two Talers, LLC

BERKLEY and the BERKLEY & B colophon are registered trademarks of
Penguin Random House LLC.

Poem excerpt on p. vii copyright © Charles Gramlich. Used by permission.

ISBN: 9780593197059

The Library of Congress has cataloged the Berkley hardcover edition of
this book as follows:

Names: Harris, C. S., author.
Title: Who cries for the lost / C.S. Harris.
Description: New York : Berkley, [2023] | Series: A Sebastian St. Cyr mystery
Identifiers: LCCN 2022037534 (print) | LCCN 2022037535 (ebook) |
ISBN 9780593102725 (hardcover) | ISBN 9780593197042 (ebook)
Subjects: LCGFT: Detective and mystery fiction. | Novels.
Classification: LCC PS3566.R5877 W47852 2023 (print) |
LCC PS3566.R5877 (ebook) | DDC 813/.54- dc23/ eng/ 20220808
LC record available at https:// lccn.loc.gov/ 2022037534
LC ebook record available at https:// lccn.loc.gov/ 2022037535

Berkley hardcover edition / April 2023
Berkley trade paperback edition / March 2024

Printed in the United States of America
1st Printing

For Aaron Cook,
real estate agent, fix-it man,
knight in shining armor, friend

Who speaks for the restless and the damned?
Who cries for the lost?

—CHARLES GRAMLICH

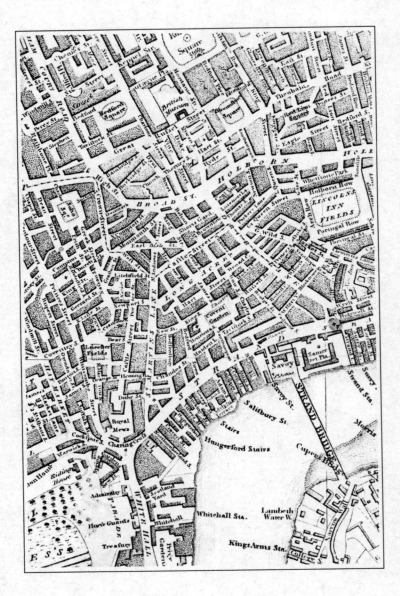

WHO CRIES FOR THE LOST

Chapter 1

London
Tuesday, 13 June 1815

*T*he dead man smelled like fish. Rotting fish.

Pale, bloodless, and faceless, he lay on the stained granite slab in the center of Paul Gibson's ancient stone outbuilding, filling the small room with a foul stench. But then, bodies pulled from the Thames did have a nasty tendency to reek of fish. Fish, brine, tar, and—if it was warm and they'd been in the water long enough—decay.

The outbuilding stood at the base of a newly planted garden that stretched out behind the medieval Tower Hill house where Gibson kept his surgery, and he paused now in the doorway to suck in one last breath of fresh, rose-scented air before entering the room. The morning was damp and chilly, the sky a low, menacing gray, the ache from Gibson's truncated left leg sharp enough that he winced as he limped forward.

Irish by birth, he was thinner than he should have been and

younger than he looked, his dark hair already heavily laced with gray, the long grooves that bracketed his mouth dug deep. Pain had a way of doing that to a man—pain and the opium he used to control it.

There'd been a time not so long ago when he'd served as a surgeon with His Majesty's 25th Light Dragoons, honing his understanding of the human body on the bloody battlefields of Europe. Then a French cannonball tore away the lower part of his leg, and though he'd tried to keep going, in the end the phantom pains from that vanished limb became too much. And so he'd come here, to London, to open this humble surgery in the shadow of the Tower, share his knowledge of anatomy at the city's teaching hospitals, and conduct postmortems like this one for the local officials.

But lately there were times, such as this morning, when the demands of even that simple routine could come close to overwhelming him. The lingering effects of yesterday's generous dose of opium had left him shaky and clumsy, and he found it took him three tries with a flint before he managed to light a lantern against the gloom and hang it from the chain suspended over the stone slab. The swaying golden light played over the ghostly flesh and shattered face of the unidentified corpse before him and cast macabre shadows across the room's bare stone walls in a way he did not like.

Tall, well-formed, and probably somewhere in his thirties, the dead man had been delivered just after dawn by a couple of constables from the Thames River Police. "An East Indiaman in the Pool pulled him up with their anchor," one of the constables had said when they heaved the half-naked body up onto Gibson's slab. "Otherwise he probably wouldn't have surfaced for another two or three days—if ever."

"Who took his clothes?" asked Gibson.

"Whoever tossed him in the river, I s'pose," said the older of the two men with a wink as they turned to leave. "That's the way he come up—wearing his shirt and that one sock and nothin' else."

It was a fine shirt, Gibson thought now as he put up a hand to still the swaying of the lamp. Expertly tailored of the best linen, with its long tails reaching halfway down the man's bare, well-muscled thighs. A shirt like that would fetch a good price from one of the innumerable secondhand clothing stores that filled the city. So why had someone taken the dead man's coat, boots, and breeches, yet left his shirt?

And what the devil had they done to his face?

A blunderbuss or even a pistol would do that, Gibson decided, hunkering down to study the ravaged features. A pistol fired at close range and at an odd angle, almost as if its purpose was to destroy the features rather than kill the man.

So what had actually killed him? Gibson let his gaze wander. The watery red stains on the lower part of the shirt looked ominous.

"The River Police pull dead bodies out of the Thames all the time," said a woman's voice from the open doorway behind him, her lilting French accent more pronounced than usual. "Everything from clumsy sailors and drunken wherrymen to desperate housemaids impregnated by their masters. They usually just haul them out of the water and dump them at the nearest deadhouse to be buried in the local poor hole. So why was this one sent to you for a postmortem?"

Straightening, Gibson turned to find Alexi Sauvage leaning against the doorjamb, watching him. She was a small woman, finely boned, with a halo of untamable fiery red hair and pale skin lightly dusted with cinnamon across the bridge of her delicate nose. Parisian-born and brilliant, she had been educated as a physician in Italy, where such a thing was possible for a woman, although she was allowed to practice only as a midwife here in England. She had lived with him now for over two years, and he loved her desperately. Yet there was still so much about her he didn't know. About her life before that night he'd found her wounded and near death on the mean streets of St. Katharine's. About why she refused to marry him.

About why she stayed anyway.

"Why?" she said again, and such was the wandering train of his thoughts that it was a moment before he remembered she spoke of the dead man.

"Because from all appearances, this one's a gentleman." He lifted one of the corpse's limp hands from the slab. "Not only are his fingernails carefully manicured"—he turned the bloodless hand over—"but his only calluses are such as a gentleman might acquire from riding or fencing."

She studied the man's ravaged face and the water-matted but obviously fashionably cut golden hair that framed it. "So what fair-haired young man of London's Upper Ten Thousand has been reported missing?"

"None so far, according to the constables who brought him."

"Interesting."

He laid the pallid hand back on the stone beside him. "Since you're here, how'd you like to help me take off his shirt?"

She stayed where she was, her gaze hard on his face. "Your leg's still hurting, isn't it?"

"Just a wee bit."

"I might be able to help you with that, if you'll let me."

"So you keep saying."

"And yet you keep refusing to let me try."

"We Irish are a stubborn lot," he said with a crooked grin, exaggerating his brogue.

"That's one word for it."

Their gazes met, and something flared between them, something filled with the echoes of much that had been said in the past and more that remained unsaid. Then she pushed away from the doorframe and stepped forward. "If you'll lift him, I'll strip off the shirt."

Levering his hands beneath the corpse's cold shoulders, Gibson raised the dead man's limp torso as she reached for the shirt's long tail and yanked it up.

"Jesus, Mary, Joseph, and all the saints," he yelped as the man's groin came into view. Whoever had shattered the unidentified corpse's face had also emasculated him.

Alexi paused with the shirt bunched at the man's taut stomach. "You didn't know?"

Gibson shook his head. "No. I was too busy looking at the ruin of that face."

Wordlessly, they finished peeling the brine-stiffened shirt over the dead man's head. She said, "Who would do something like that?"

"Someone who was either very angry or very sick. Or both."

Gibson was easing the dead man's torso back down on the slab when he heard Alexi's breath catch in a strange muffled hitch. Looking up, he found her standing with her elbows cupped in her palms, hugging her arms close to the shawl-covered bodice of her plain muslin gown as she stared down at a pattern of saber scars on the man's chest, left arm, and neck.

"What is it?" he asked, and somehow a part of him understood that what she was about to say was going to shatter his world.

Her head jerked up, her lips parting, her loamy brown eyes liquid with what looked very much like fear. "I know who he is."

"Who? Who is it?"

She had to suck in a quick, jerky breath before she could answer. "It's Miles." She hesitated, and Gibson felt the earth spin oddly around him as he waited for her to add, as he somehow knew she would, "Miles Sauvage. My husband."

Chapter 2

The last lingering wisps of the early-morning mist were drifting up from the river to cling to the leafy branches of the ancient elms and chestnuts overhead as two men cantered their highbred horses along the southern boundary of Hyde Park, the thunder of their hooves muffled by the soft surface of the nearly deserted Row. One man was older, in his seventies now, his eyes a deep, piercing blue, his once heavy shock of white hair beginning to thin even as his big barrel-chested body thickened more and more with each passing year.

His companion was younger, in his early thirties, lean and dark haired, his eyes a strange feral yellow, his seat on his elegant black mare that of a cavalry officer accustomed to spending long hours in the saddle. They were known to the world as father and son, although they were not. The events and painful revelations of the last several years had strained their relationship, but they were slowly working their way toward a new understanding. Lately they had taken to meeting frequently for these early-morning rides in the park—although every time they somehow ended up having what was basically the same argument.

"You're pushing that wounded leg too hard, too fast," said the elder man, Alistair St. Cyr, the Fifth Earl of Hendon. "And you know it."

His companion and heir, Sebastian St. Cyr, Viscount Devlin, swallowed the angry retort that rose to his lips and forced himself to keep his voice light. "I didn't realize you'd taken up medicine in your spare time."

"I don't need to be a doctor. I can see it in your face. It hasn't been three months since you nearly got that leg shot off, and I doubt there's more than a handful of surgeons in all of England who wouldn't have insisted on taking it off completely."

"Then I suppose I'm fortunate to have been shot in Paris," said Sebastian, and heard the Earl growl in response as they reined their horses in to a walk.

"You're fortunate Napoléon decided to let you go," snapped Hendon, "rather than holding you and Hero hostage."

"He was hoping for peace, remember?"

"So he said. But he's not getting it, is he?"

"That he's not."

They continued along in silence for a time. The air was cool and damp and heavy with the fecund smell of the wet tan mixed with gravel beneath their horses' hooves, but the sounds of the city stirring awake around them were beginning to intrude on the countryside-like calm of the park. Hendon said, "You do realize that it doesn't matter how hard you press yourself. You're never going to get that leg strong enough to rejoin your old regiment and fight Napoléon in July."

The words caught Sebastian by surprise, for it was the first time either of them had acknowledged precisely why he was pushing himself so hard. He found he had to pause to swallow the bitter taste that rose to his mouth. "I doubt it'll be July."

It had been over three months now since Napoléon Bonaparte had sailed away from Elba, the tiny island off the coast of Italy to which he'd been banished after his defeat in the spring of 1814. Landing on the southern coast of France, he'd been welcomed back by his people with joy, while the Bourbon King Louis XVIII—so recently restored by the armies of France's enemies—simply fled Paris before him in the dark of night.

Installed once more in the Tuileries Palace—without a shot being fired—Napoléon had issued a stream of proclamations, reassuring the people of France and the world that all he wanted was peace. But the bitter, frightened crowned heads of Europe—many of them only recently restored to their wobbly thrones—were determined to crush forever the dangerous philosophies of liberty and equality that the French Revolution had unleashed upon the world. Already gathered in Austria for the Congress of Vienna, the representatives of Russia, Prussia, Austria, and Great Britain had declared Bonaparte an outlaw and signed a series of new treaties in which they pledged to raise an army of six hundred thousand men and not lay down arms again until Napoléon was destroyed. The lesser states of Europe hastily joined them.

"It's the date Wellington has set for the invasion of France," said Hendon. "So what are you saying? You don't think it will happen until August?"

Sebastian shook his head. "We've already declared war, so Napoléon knows exactly what's coming. I can't see him waiting around for the Seventh Alliance to gather all of its armies and attack him at a time and place of their choosing. If he can't have peace, then he's going to need to strike quickly and decisively, and he knows it. I wouldn't be surprised if he's preparing to leave Paris for the frontier as we speak."

"Good God. You think he'll march against Wellington in Belgium?"

"Why wouldn't he? And if Wellington were smart, he'd spend less time in Brussels attending balls and picnics and seducing his officers' wives and daughters, and pay more attention to getting his troops in order."

"Then for God's sake, Devlin, why not give up this brutal regimen you've set yourself? If you're right, you'll never be fit in time to join the fight."

Sebastian clenched his jaw and stared off across the misty park to where a small dark-haired figure wearing a tiger's striped waistcoat and mounted on a familiar gray hack was galloping headlong toward them, heedless of the angry shouts that followed him. It was not the "done thing," galloping in Hyde Park.

Hendon's eyes narrowed as he followed Sebastian's gaze. "Isn't that the scruffy little pickpocket you insist on employing as your groom?"

"I'll admit he's still a bit scruffy and small, but Tom hasn't been a pickpocket for years," said Sebastian, and heard Hendon grunt as the boy reined in beside them.

"A message from Paul Gibson," said Tom, his breath coming hard and fast as he held out a grubby, slightly crumpled sealed missive. "The lad what brought it said it was important, so I figured ye'd want to see it right away."

"Gibson?" said Hendon, the displeasure in his voice unmistakable as Sebastian broke the seal. "You mean that Tower Hill surgeon?" Sebastian's involvement in murder investigations had never sat well with the Earl.

"Yes." Sebastian skimmed through his friend's message. But it was so cryptically worded and hastily scrawled that he could make out little beyond the words "mutilated corpse" and "Alexi."

"Something's come up." He tucked the note in his pocket and said to Tom, "Go back to Brook Street and get my curricle ready. I'll be right there."

Hendon swore softly under his breath as Tom galloped away. "You're doing it again, aren't you?"

"In all likelihood," said Sebastian, gathering his reins. "One might expect you to be pleased."

Hendon stared at him. "Pleased? Me? Because you're off to hunt down another murderer, like some common Bow Street Runner? Why in heaven's name would I be pleased?"

"Well, I suspect it will keep me out of the saddle so much."

"What I'd like to see is you resting beside your fire with your wife!"

"If I'm not mistaken, Hero was planning to spend the morning interviewing some wherryman for her new article. Or was it a dung boy?"

"Lord preserve us," muttered Hendon.

But Sebastian only smiled.

Chapter 3

$\mathcal{B}$y the time Sebastian reached Tower Hill, the strengthening sun was already chasing away the morning chill as the heavy cloud cover overhead shifted and began to break up. Reining in his pair of matched chestnuts at the doorstep of the ancient, low-slung stone building that housed Gibson's surgery, he took a deep breath and caught the unmistakable odor of rotten fish wafting on the breeze.

"'Oly 'ell," said Tom, scrambling up to the curricle's high seat to take the chestnuts' reins. "Stinks as bad as Billingsgate, it does."

Sebastian hopped down to the narrow cobbled lane. "Very nearly. Walk them, why don't you? I don't know how long I'll be."

"Aye, gov'nor."

Rather than knock at the front door, Sebastian cut through the narrow passage that ran along the side of the old stone house to a rickety wooden gate that led directly to the high-walled enclosure at the rear.

Once the house's ancient yard had been a neglected, weed-choked wasteland where Gibson quietly buried the remains of the cadavers he dissected by night in the same room he used by day to perform his official postmortems. By British law, only the bodies of executed criminals could be dissected, and there were never any-where near enough of those to go around. And so any surgeon or student wishing to expand his understanding of human anatomy or practice a new surgical technique was forced to turn to the Resurrec-tion Men or Sack 'Em Up Boys, as they were sometimes called: ruth-less, unsavory gangs who stole newly buried bodies from the city's churchyards and sold them for a hefty price. Gibson was one of their best customers.

But over the last two years, the enigmatic Frenchwoman who now shared Gibson's house and bed had been slowly transforming the space into a restful garden. Any bones she came upon were col-lected and then deposited in a grotto-like ossuary she'd built against one wall. Sebastian had never asked Gibson what he did now with the remains of the bodies he dissected. But as Sebastian followed the winding path that led to the outbuilding at the base of the yard, he noticed that Alexi Sauvage had added a wooden cross above the en-trance to the grotto and was burning a small candle there. He'd never thought of her as a practicing Catholic, but he realized now that she must be—at least in some sense.

As he neared the foul-smelling outbuilding's open door, he yanked his handkerchief from his pocket and held it pressed against his nose.

"Bit ripe, isn't it?" said Gibson, looking up from where he stood doing something Sebastian didn't want to think about to the body that lay on the granite slab before him.

"It's bloody stomach churning. I don't know how you stand it."

The Irishman's eyes crinkled with amusement. The skin of his face had a definite grayish tinge to it, the pupils of his eyes were suspiciously small, and he needed a shave, but he appeared unfazed by either the smell or the sight of the mutilated corpse before him. "You get used to it."

Sebastian drew up strategically just outside the entrance to the room. "I'll take your word for it," he said with a grin.

The friendship between the two men—the Irish anatomist and the Earl's heir—was an unusual one, dating back more than ten years to a time when both men wore the King's colors and fought the King's wars from Italy to the West Indies and beyond. They'd fought and bled together; laughed and cried; knew most of each other's deepest and most troubling secrets, and would give their lives for each other. There wasn't anyone besides Hero to whom Sebastian was closer, and it cut him to the quick to see his friend slowly killing himself one bloody grain of opium at a time.

Now Sebastian cast a swift glance at the dead man's gory face and mutilated groin, then looked pointedly away. "Where did this come from?"

Gibson reached for a rag and wiped his hands. "The Thames. From the looks of things, I'd say he was probably thrown into the river Saturday night or Sunday morning. The only reason he wasn't dragged quietly out to sea by the tides is because he somehow got caught around the anchor chain of a merchantman, and they hauled him in when they were getting ready to set sail."

"Surely the River Police don't expect you to identify him."

"No." Gibson tossed the rag aside. "But as it happens, I have."

"You have?"

Gibson nodded. "Meet Major the Honorable Miles Sedgewick, younger son of the late Third Marquis of Stamford and brother to the current holder of that esteemed title. I'm told he was once an exploring officer for Wellington in Portugal and Spain. Did you know him?"

"I knew him," said Sebastian. Then he wondered what his friend heard in his voice, because Gibson's eyes narrowed.

"I take it you didn't care much for the man?"

Sebastian forced himself to look again at what was left of Miles Sedgewick, searching that scarred torso and shattered face for some trace of the handsome, deceitful nobleman's son he'd once known. "He was brave to the point of being fearless, cunning and clever and very, very good at what he did. He could be gay and charming and almost irresistibly likable. But underneath it all, he was a treacherous, untrustworthy bastard who'd do anything to get what he wanted. And I do mean anything."

"Alexi says much the same."

Sebastian was aware of the sound of a woman's footsteps crossing the garden toward them. "She knew him?"

Gibson scratched behind his ear. "It seems he sometimes used aliases. One of them was Miles Sauvage."

Sebastian stared at him. "Are you telling me—"

"That's right," said Alexi Sauvage, coming up behind him. "He was my husband."

Sebastian turned to face her. He'd first met this woman five years before, in the rugged mountains of Portugal, when he—like Miles Sedgewick—was serving as an exploring officer for Wellington. It was there, in the shadow of the ill-fated Convent of Santa Iria, that he'd killed the man she loved and she'd sworn to kill him in revenge. He still didn't trust her—didn't trust her not to someday stick a knife in his back and didn't trust her not to hurt Gibson enough to destroy him.

Now their gazes met and clashed, and he said, "You told us your husband was dead."

Rather than answer him, she simply looked beyond him, to the mangled corpse on that slab. Her face was hard, closed; he could not begin to guess what she was thinking.

She said, "Did you ever wonder what happened to me after Santa Iria?"

"No," he admitted.

A faint smile touched her lips. "Of course not. Why would you?"

"So tell me now," he said.

She was silent for so long, he didn't think she was going to answer him. Then her slim white throat worked as she swallowed, and she said, "All right. I will."

Chapter 4

She'd been born on the Île de la Cité in the heart of Paris, the daughter of an esteemed French physician and surgeon named Philippe-Jean Pelletan. As a young girl she'd dreamt of becoming a physician herself, although such a thing was no more possible in France than it was in England. And so at the age of sixteen she'd traveled to Italy, where those of her sex were allowed to study medicine. It was there, at the University of Bologna, that she met and married a brilliant young French medical student named Antoine Beauclerc. At the end of their studies he joined the French Army to tend to the medical needs of the soldiers of the Republic, and Alexi went with him. When Beauclerc was killed, Alexi simply stayed with the regiment and took his place.

Sebastian had first encountered her in the spring of 1810, in a high mountain pass between Portugal and Spain. He'd been on a mission for a colonel he should have known better than to trust, while she'd been with the band of French cavalry who captured him. By then she was wearing rugged trousers, a wide-brimmed hat, and two bandoliers slung across her chest, and she had taken a new lover, a lieutenant named Jean Tissot. In a desperate, ultimately futile attempt to save the doomed women and children of the nearby convent of Santa Iria, Sebastian had escaped—killing the man she loved in the process. That was when she'd sworn not to rest until she killed Sebastian in revenge.

And even though she'd been with Gibson for over two years, Sebastian still wasn't quite certain she'd given up the idea.

"You remember Major Rousseau?" she said to him now.

The three of them—Sebastian, Gibson, and Alexi Sauvage—were seated atop the low, ancient sandstone wall that edged one section of the garden she'd spent the last two years making. The colorful riot of lilacs, honeysuckle, roses, and marigolds around them was drenched with the morning's clear light and abuzz with life; Sebastian could feel the sun warm on his back, breathe in the sweet scent of a gnarled old pink rose that bloomed nearby. But inside he felt cold, so cold. That dark, unforgettable night in the mountains of Portugal had altered him forever. And although he would find it difficult to articulate, he understood deep down within him that much of what he did now—his dedicated, unending quest to find justice for the innocent victims of murder—was in atonement for the events of that night. Or, rather, for the blood-soaked blur of days that followed it.

"I remember," he said, his voice rough. Of course he remembered; he'd killed that French major with his own bare hands . . .

Alexi gave a quick nod, as if she knew. And perhaps she did. She said, "I always knew Rousseau and his men could be vicious. But with Jean dead, and after what they did to the nuns and orphans of Santa Iria, I couldn't stay with them." Something flared in her dark brown eyes. "I know you don't believe me, but it's true."

Had he ever said such a thing to her? he wondered. In anger

perhaps, although if so, he couldn't remember it. He said, "So what did you do?"

"There was a village nearby, not far from the convent. Their doctor had been killed by Rousseau some months earlier for treating a wounded partisan. The people in the area needed help, and because of what Rousseau had done, I felt I owed them. So I stayed. I was still there the following summer when a British brigade came through." She paused, her hands spasming into fists against the rough stones beside her. Reaching out, Gibson quietly rested one of his hands over hers.

Sebastian said, "Captain Sedgewick was with them?"

"Not initially, no. When they first came, the men camped in the ruins of the convent and left the village alone. But the convent's wine cellar was still intact, and several nights after they arrived, they broke into it."

Sebastian understood then what was coming. He knew only too well what a drunken brigade—or even a small band of soldiers—could do to a town full of defenseless civilians.

"I was returning from delivering a baby down in the valley when a group of four or five soldiers caught me." She paused to suck in a deep, shaky breath. "Miles was out on patrol for Wellington and happened upon us by chance. He stopped them—killed them. All of them. But in the process he was badly wounded." She glanced toward the dark, shadowy interior of the silent stone building beside them, where what was left of Miles Sedgewick still lay. "Those scars on his arm, chest, and neck all came from that night. The wound to his arm was particularly severe, and I told him it needed to come off, that I was worried about septicemia. But he wouldn't let me take it—said he'd rather be dead. I thought he'd surely die within a week. He didn't, but it was too dangerous to move him. So when the Army moved on, he was left in my care."

She was silent for a moment, her eyes taking on a sad, distant look, as if she were gazing far, far away, to another time and place. "When he wanted to, Miles could be charming, so gay and full of laughter and an infectious kind of joy. We grew . . . quite close."

In other words, you became lovers, thought Sebastian, although he didn't say it. He watched her hand twist beneath Gibson's so that she could entwine her fingers with his, and after a moment, she continued.

"It was about six weeks later that word came through that his father, the Marquis, was ill and in danger of dying, and that Wellington had decided to have him sent back to England to recuperate. When he heard, Miles asked me to go with him. He was healing, but he was still far from well and we knew the trip would be hard on him. He was afraid that if I wasn't there, his wound would take a turn for the worse, and some British Army surgeon would insist on cutting the arm off."

"You agreed?"

"Not initially. I remember I said to him, 'And what will become of me, if I go with you and you die? I would be all alone in a strange land.'"

"And?"

"At first he laughed and said I wouldn't let him die. But when I simply looked at him and said, 'You might,' he sobered and said he'd marry me. That way, as his wife, if anything were to happen to him, his family would take care of me. So I said yes." She let out her breath in a soft huff. "Love can make us do foolish things."

Sebastian had a hard time imagining this brutally pragmatic and self-contained woman as either lost in love or foolish. But all he said was, "You were married before you left Portugal?"

"Yes, by the father in the village." For a moment, she paused again. "The voyage back to England was magical. I'd never been to sea before, and Miles was at his most gay and fun loving. But when we arrived in London, he didn't take me directly to his family's home. Instead, he rented rooms for me in Golden Square, using the name Miles Sauvage. He said that given his father's failing health, he needed to break the news of our marriage to him gently—that the old Marquis had been hoping Miles would marry the daughter of a wealthy acquaintance, so it might take some time to bring him around." Her lips curled into a sad, wry smile as she gave a faint shake of her head. "It was a lie, of course—although I didn't realize it at first. But as the weeks passed and nothing happened, I began to question him, and he didn't like it. That's when I realized there was another side to the man I'd married, a side that was neither charming nor easygoing, but selfish and spoiled and ugly."

Sebastian nodded. He knew that side of Miles Sedgewick only too well.

She stared out over the garden, watching a butterfly dance around a stand of hollyhocks; it was a moment before she continued. "It was almost a relief when he told me one day that he was being sent on a mission to Switzerland. I thought that when he came back, we could start over—that he'd finally tell his father and things would go back to being the way they'd been between us before, in the mountains of Portugal. But he'd only been gone a few weeks when one of his friends came to tell me he'd been killed." She gave a low, humorless laugh. "I believed him. Why wouldn't I? And I grieved—not for the man I'd caught glimpses of in London but for the one I'd fallen in love with in Portugal."

"Who was the friend?" Sebastian asked quietly.

"Montgomery McPherson. You know him?"

"I know him."

She nodded as if this didn't surprise her. But then, the three of them had all been exploring officers—Sebastian, Miles, and Monty.

Perhaps she knew that. She said, "It was less than two weeks later that I chanced to see him—Miles, I mean—from a distance. He was with a plump, fair-haired woman and two young children, and I heard one of the children call him Papa."

"Did he see you?"

She shook her head. "I thought at first that I must be imagining it, that it couldn't be him, that it must simply be someone who looked like Miles—perhaps even his older brother. But it wasn't difficult to discover the truth—that the Marquis of Stamford's younger son, Captain Sedgewick, was still very much alive and living with his wife, Eloisa, in Mount Street. He'd told me he was staying at his father's town house, but it turned out his wife's father had bought them a house when they married—four years before we even met."

"Did you confront him?"

"Not then—not that first time when I saw him with his family— but two days later, once I knew for certain I was right. He was coming down the steps of his house when I stopped him, and he looked me straight in the eye and denied even knowing me—said, 'My good woman, I don't know who you think I am, but I fear you are sadly mistaken.' He was so dismissive, so condescending, even faintly concerned—as if for my sanity—that for one mad moment I thought perhaps he was right, that perhaps I was somehow mistaken. But as he was turning away, I reached up to catch the edge of his cravat, and the scar from the neck wound I'd dressed myself was there. I wasn't mistaken."

"So what did you do?"

Her chin came up. "I told him that the Honorable Miles Sedgewick was obviously very much alive, but I agreed with him that my husband, Miles Sauvage, was dead. And then I just walked away."

"Have you seen him since?"

"No. Why would I?"

Sebastian wasn't sure he believed her. "Why did you tell us your husband was dead?"

She twitched one shoulder in a shrug. "Because he was dead to me. But—" She cast a quick sideways glance at Gibson, who sat silently beside her, his head bowed, his gaze fixed on their entwined hands. "But I couldn't be really, truly certain our marriage actually was bigamous. I mean, Miles was such a liar. I've never known anyone who could lie as easily and smoothly and without conscience as he. What if his marriage to the woman everyone considered his wife was somehow not valid? Then his marriage to me would be." Her hand was gripping Gibson's so tightly that her fingers turned white. "I knew I could never marry again, not as long as he was still alive." And then the blood drained from her face, as if she'd suddenly realized the implications of what she'd said.

Sebastian had a niggling feeling she was leaving something out, something important, but he couldn't begin to fathom what it was. He said, "As soon as they know who he is, the Thames Police will hand the case to Bow Street. And once Bow Street knows about you, you will in all likelihood be their prime suspect. You do realize that, don't you?"

It was Gibson who answered, his breath easing out in a long, pained sigh. "Aye, we know it. If it were up to me, we'd be keeping quiet about who that bloody bastard lying in there is. We'd just hand his mangled corpse back to the River Police and let them bury him in the local poor hole. But Alexi won't hear of it."

"Why not?"

Something blazed in the Frenchwoman's eyes. "Because he has a wife and children who have no idea what has happened to him. His father is dead now, but he still has a brother. They all deserve to know he's dead. How could I let them go on forever, wondering and hoping against hope that someday he might come home? Apart from which . . ." Her gaze drifted again to that open doorway and the mangled body that lay within. "It doesn't matter what manner of man Miles Sedgewick was. Whoever did this to him needs to be stopped before they do something like it again."

Sebastian looked at Gibson. "What can you tell me about how he died?"

The Irishman swiped one shaky hand over his unshaven face. "Not a great deal at this point. About all I know so far is that he was probably in the water a good forty-eight hours or more, and that the shot to his face didn't kill him. In fact, I'd say that in all likelihood it was done after he was already dead."

"You think it was done to prevent anyone from identifying his body?"

"Perhaps," said Gibson. "Although the scars on his chest and arm would be pretty telling to anyone who knew him. And why castrate him, too? I'd say it's more likely both were done in anger. Or maybe bloodlust."

Sebastian nodded. Their years at war had taught them both about the primitive, brutal urges aroused in some men by the act of killing. To Alexi, he said, "Where were you Saturday night?"

"Bloody hell," yelped Gibson, pushing up from the wall so fast he staggered slightly when his weight came down on his peg. "You can't be serious."

Sebastian met his friend's flaring, angry gaze. "It's a question Bow Street is going to ask, and you know it." He studied the Frenchwoman's seemingly calm, emotionless face. "So where were you?"

"Here," she said, her voice cracking unexpectedly. "I was here."

"All night?"

She nodded.

"Did anyone see you here besides Gibson?"

She shook her head, her face suddenly white, her nostrils pinched. "No. No one."

"And you have no idea who might have wanted Miles dead?"

"Besides me, you mean?" she said with a wry curling of her lips. "His real wife, perhaps? But beyond that, no; I have no idea at all."

ร.

After Devlin had gone, they stood silently side by side—Gibson and this awe-inspiringly tough, baffling, and sometimes infuriating woman he loved so fiercely. They listened to his friend's receding footsteps, to the rattle of harness and the clatter of hooves and iron-bound wheels over ancient cobblestones as the Viscount drove away.

It was only then that Gibson turned to look at her and said, "You didn't tell him everything."

She met his gaze squarely. "I can't. You know why."

Chapter 5

*A*n hour or so later, Sebastian stood at the window of his library, a glass of brandy cradled in one hand, his gaze fixed unseeingly on a team of snowy white shires pulling a heavy brewer's wagon up Brook Street. Thanks to his morning ride, his leg hurt like hell. He knew he should sit down, and yet he stayed where he was, lost in a succession of uncomfortable thoughts. Somewhere out there, far across the Channel, the armies of Europe were massing for what would in all likelihood be one of the most decisive battles in history. He could not agree with Britain's war aim—the restoration of the repressive Bourbon monarchy against the will of the people of France. But the pull of his allegiance to his old regiment was powerful. And it annoyed the hell out of him to know that they needed every last experienced officer they could get, while all he could do was stand here, drinking brandy, nursing a bad leg, and stewing in a toxic but ultimately useless brew of frustration and rage and endless regrets.

Draining his drink, he reached for the brandy carafe that rested on a table near the fireplace. Then he thought better of it and set aside his empty glass with a muttered oath. It had been some five years now since he'd sold out and returned to London, haunted by the things he'd seen as much as by the things he'd done . . . and not done. And it occurred to him as he turned back to the window that almost everyone associated with the tragic, blood-soaked events of those days in the mountains of Portugal was now dead. The innocent nuns and orphans of Santa Iria. The French major Rousseau and his men. The treacherous, conscienceless British colonel who'd set it all in motion. Of them all, only two still remained alive: Sebastian himself, and the Frenchwoman who called herself Alexi Sauvage.

A patter of light, quick footsteps on the front steps and a child's ringing laughter jerked Sebastian's attention to the entry hall. He heard the door open, heard the stately tones of his majordomo, Morey, and Hero's cheerful response. Then the library door burst open and two dark-haired, hot, and slightly grubby little boys catapulted into the room, bringing with them all the smells of London on a sunny June day. One was slightly taller and older than the other, but otherwise they looked enough alike to be twins.

"Papa!" shouted Simon, the younger lad, startling the big black cat that had been sleeping in one of the chairs by the hearth. "We been to see the soldiers paradin' in Hyde Park!"

Laughing, Sebastian caught the boy around the waist and swung him high. "Have you, now? And did you see any cannons?"

"Yup," said the older boy, Patrick, hanging back slightly, his eyes alive with excitement and wonder. Unlike Simon, Patrick was not in fact Sebastian's own child but the orphaned son of a man whose uncanny resemblance to Sebastian had never been adequately explained.

"Patrick is now torn between the artillery and a career with the light horse," said Hero, unbuttoning her dusky blue spencer as she came to stand in the doorway. She was a handsome woman just under six feet tall, with a Junoesque build, dark hair, and her father's aquiline nose and fine gray eyes.

Sebastian reached out to rumple the little boy's dark hair. "Your father was a rifleman, you know. I never knew a better shot."

"He was better'n you?" said the boy in wonder.

"He was."

"*Alors, mes enfants,*" said Claire, the boys' French-born nurse, coming to stand beside Hero. "Let's go see the parrot, shall we?"

"I thought we were finding a new home for that decidedly foul-mouthed bird," said Sebastian as the boys whooped and turned to tear off up the stairs.

"I'm working on it," said Hero with a laugh, untying the ribbons of her broad-brimmed feathered hat and tossing it aside as she walked into the room. "So, did you ever make sense of this morning's strange note from Paul Gibson?"

Sebastian reconsidered his decision not to have another drink and went to pour himself more brandy. "I did," he said, easing the stopper from the cut-crystal carafe. "The dead man is the Honorable Miles Sedgewick, younger son of the late Third Marquis of Stamford and brother to the current holder of the title. Up until three or four years ago he was an exploring officer with Wellington."

She peeled off her spencer and tossed it, along with her blue kid gloves, after the hat. "So you knew him?"

"I knew him," said Sebastian, and left it at that. "Most exploring officers simply ride around the countryside drawing maps and such, always being careful to stay in uniform so they don't get shot as spies if they're caught. But some have been known to undertake more clandestine assignments. It's frowned upon, of course, for a gentleman to engage in such underhanded skullduggery. But a few have been known to do it."

"As did you."

"As did I," Sebastian acknowledged.

"And Sedgewick?"

"He was a natural at it. His mother was Parisian, so his accent was impeccable. One of the aliases he used was the name Sauvage—with the French pronunciation. Miles Sauvage."

He watched as comprehension flooded Hero's face, her eyes widening before narrowing shrewdly. "Dear God," she whispered. "Not Alexi's Miles Sauvage."

"The very one."

"Did she know? I mean, did she know he was still alive?"

"She knew. It seems he went through a marriage ceremony with her—a bigamous ceremony, although she didn't know that at the time—while they were in Portugal, and she didn't find out the truth about him until weeks after they'd come to London."

"Good heavens. I always thought he was a bit of a bounder, but I don't think I realized just how bad he was."

"You've met him?"

She came to lift the brandy glass from his hand and take a sip. "Several times over the years, but never more than casually. His wife, Eloisa, is a year or two younger than I am. They have two—no, three children now. When was he killed?"

"Gibson says he thinks it was probably Saturday or Sunday."

"And they've kept it out of the papers? Why?"

"Because he's only just been identified—by Alexi. Whoever killed him mutilated the body."

"How?"

He told her. Another man might have sought to spare his wife the gory details, but Sebastian knew better than to even try.

"Why would someone do such a thing?" she said when he had finished.

"Revenge? Bloodlust? A desire to prevent the body from being identified, perhaps."

"So how did Alexi recognize him?"

"By his scars. She—"

He broke off as a fierce peal sounded at the front door.

"Expecting someone?" said Hero as Morey moved to open the door.

Sebastian shook his head. "No."

"The Marquis of Stamford," an imperious voice announced. "To see Lord Devlin."

Sebastian's gaze met Hero's as they heard Morey say, "Do come in, my lord. If you'll just—"

Quick, heavy footsteps sounded on the entry hall's marble tiles as the Marquis brushed past Sebastian's manservant. "Where the devil is he?"

"My lord! If you'll just allow me to—"

"In the library, is he?" growled the Marquis. "Never mind, I'll announce myself."

"But, my lord—"

Benedict Sedgewick, the Fourth Marquis of Stamford, drew up abruptly just inside the room, with Morey at his heels. "You know why I'm here," he growled, his gaze meeting Sebastian's across the room.

"I suppose I can guess," said Sebastian. "That will be all, thank you, Morey."

The majordomo hesitated a moment, then bowed and withdrew.

Sebastian studied the man who stood before them, his eyes narrowing as his gaze went from Sebastian to Hero. He was an older, paler, plumper, less handsome version of his dead younger brother, probably somewhere in his early forties, his straw-colored hair laced with gray, his silk waistcoat fitting snugly across the soft swelling of his belly. It was as if each of Miles's features was exaggerated in his brother, the Marquis's jaw too square, his nose too big, his eyes a pale, washed-out blue.

"If you'll excuse us, Lady Devlin?" he said gruffly, sketching the briefest of bows in her direction.

She raised one eyebrow in a way that reminded Sebastian forcefully of her father. "Thank you, but I rather think I'll stay."

The Marquis's full cheeks sagged, his nostrils flaring, as if the idea of a mere female setting her will against him was new to him. Then his face hardened. "As you wish." He swung back to Sebastian. "I've just come from seeing what's left of my brother lying naked and bloody on the stone slab of some common Irish-born surgeon in Tower Hill, of all places."

Sebastian leaned his hips back against his desk and fought really, really hard to keep a rein on his temper. "One must make allowances for the recent loss of your brother, Stamford, but I'll be damned if—"

"That's right," shouted Stamford. "Miles was *my* brother, and now Bow Street tells me you've taken it upon yourself to interfere in this. What the devil? I told them I want Miles moved elsewhere for whatever examination they require, that under no circumstances should he remain where he is. But that damned little upstart magistrate—Sir Harold or Sir Henry or whatever his name is—refused. *Refused.* Me! Claimed no one was better at what he did than that bloody Irishman."

"Sir Henry is right," said Sebastian, the desire to gather what information he could from this arrogant, abrasive man at war with the urge to slam his fist into that dark, angry face. "There is no better anatomist than Paul Gibson."

"The devil you say. He lives with *that woman.*"

"You know Alexi Sauvage?"

Stamford snorted. "She's still calling herself that, is she? Let's just say I know of her. She's the little French doxy Miles brought back from the Peninsula to nurse him. Then, when he was better and went to dismiss her, she tried to claim he'd married her! Raised quite a ruckus over it some three or four years ago. Wouldn't surprise me in the least if she's the one who murdered him."

The words twisted the knot of worry in Sebastian's gut, but he kept his voice low and even. "So was she his wife?"

"Of course she wasn't! It was all a ridiculous lie—just an ugly scheme to get money out of Miles."

"And did she? Get money out of him, I mean."

"Of course not."

"How do you know it was a lie?" said Hero.

Stamford glanced over at her, his heavy jaw tightening. "Of course it was a lie! He's been married to Eloisa these past eight years and more."

"Men have been known to go through a bigamous marriage ceremony in order to trick a woman into doing what they want her to do," said Hero, meeting the Marquis's angry gaze with a tight, faintly contemptuous smile.

The Marquis stiffened. "I'll remind you, madam, that you are speaking of my brother!"

"And I'll remind you that you are speaking to my wife," snapped Sebastian. "If you've seen the body, then you know that whoever killed Miles also mutilated his face and castrated him. Can you think of anyone angry enough with him to do something like that?"

"Good God, no!"

"He hadn't quarreled with anyone recently?"

"No."

Sebastian watched the older man's eyes shift away and knew it for a lie. "Your brother and I served together in the Peninsula. He was far from faithful to his wife then, yet you would have me believe he was faithful to her now?"

The Marquis's face had taken on a deep, almost purplish hue. "Enough of this. You stay out of my family's affairs, do you hear?" He raised one hand to point a shaky finger at Sebastian. "You let the authorities handle it, and you keep your ugly insinuations about my brother to yourself." He turned to Hero and gave her a swift, jerky nod. "Your pardon for the interruption, Lady Devlin. Good day."

And then he swept from the room.

"Well," said Hero as they listened to Morey close the door behind their departing visitor with a decided snap. "What a rude, unpleasant man. For a moment there I thought you were going to plant him a facer."

Sebastian took a slow sip of the brandy he suddenly realized he was still holding. "I was tempted, but I wanted to hear what the bastard had to say. For a man who just lost his dearly beloved younger brother, he strikes me as far more angry than grief-stricken. What do you think?"

Hero reached out to take another sip of his brandy. "He does, yes. But in my experience, anger is one of the few emotions most men are comfortable with. So when they feel frustration or anxiety or even grief, it all simply gets translated into anger."

"Oh, really?" said Sebastian.

Hero's eyes crinkled with amusement. "Yes, really." Her smile faded. "Somehow I don't think you're going to be able to get anything useful out of him."

"Somehow I suspect you're right. I might have more success with

Miles's wife if she'd agree to see me. But given that she's in mourning, I doubt that will be possible."

"There's a chance that she might agree to receive me," Hero said thoughtfully. "Not today, surely, but perhaps tomorrow. I wouldn't say I know her well, but we've met each other often enough over the last nine or ten years. And she's one of those women one might politely describe as 'socially ambitious.'"

"I wonder if she's come to regret her marriage to a mere younger son."

"I've no idea. I do know she's become quite religious of late. And I don't mean in a quiet, devout way, but in that smug, ostentatious, self-righteous fashion that so often teeters dangerously close to fanaticism."

"Interesting. I'm surprised she fell for a man like Sedgewick."

"Well, he was a very handsome man, and he could be charming. When she first came out it was expected that she would do quite well; she was pretty enough in a pale, unassuming way, and her dowry was impressive. She might not come from what your aunt Henrietta would call a 'good family,' but what the Platts lack in terms of ancient lineage they more than make up for in good, hard, filthy lucre. So when she married Sedgewick, no one could understand why her father let her 'throw herself away' on an untitled younger son—until she presented her new husband with an eight-pound pledge of her affection just six months after the wedding, at which point it all became clear."

"Imagine that," said Sebastian, smiling as he reached out to take her hand.

She shared his smile. "Shocking, isn't it?" Then she was silent for a moment, her thoughts obviously troubled. "I wonder if she knows. About Alexi, I mean."

"Probably not. Although after eight years of marriage, I'd be surprised if she doesn't have at least some idea of the manner of man she married."

Hero glanced toward the window overlooking the street. "You think Stamford told Bow Street about Alexi?"

"You know he did," said Sebastian, and drained his glass.

Chapter 6

London's police system was a never-ending source of puzzlement to visitors to the city from the Continent, mainly because there was no police system. The Thames Police patrolled the river, but they had no jurisdiction beyond it. The rest of the metropolitan area still hobbled along with an archaic patchwork of medieval vestries, unpaid and often corrupt county magistrates, and aged, underpaid constables and night watchmen, all combined haphazardly with a handful of underfunded and understaffed "public offices" that had been established by the Home Department less than twenty-five years before.

At the apex of this chaotic jumble stood—sort of—the Public Office of Bow Street, which was both the oldest of them all and the model for those established after it. Bow Street's three stipendiary magistrates and the famous Bow Street Runners they controlled had the authority to operate not only throughout the metropolitan area but throughout the land as well. Yet their small size—and the fact that the Home Office liked them to focus on things like social disorder and threats to national security—meant that they generally became involved only in London's most high-profile cases.

The mutilation and murder of a powerful marquis's brother qualified.

"I fear Lord Stamford is a man unaccustomed to taking no for an answer," said Sir Henry Lovejoy when Sebastian stopped by his small book-lined Bow Street office later that day.

"He does manage to convey that impression," said Sebastian, and saw a rare hint of a smile touch the magistrate's somber features.

Lovejoy was the newest of Bow Street's three magistrates, a sparsely built man barely five feet tall—if that—with a balding head, gold-framed spectacles, and a peculiar high-pitched voice. The two men had met shortly after Sebastian's return to London from the wars, when the Viscount had been accused of a murder he didn't commit and Lovejoy charged with bringing him in to face justice. The differences between the Earl's heir and the onetime merchant were many: Apart from the contrast in age, birth, and breeding, Lovejoy was a sternly religious man whereas Sebastian had long ago lost his faith on the battlefields of Europe. But with time the two men's respect for each other had only deepened. Lovejoy admired the Viscount's intelligence, ingenuity, and deep sense of honor, while Sebastian knew he had never met a more principled or determinedly honest man.

And yet Sebastian had also learned not to tell the little magistrate everything he might discover in the course of a murder investigation. And so he was very, very careful when Lovejoy said, "You've heard what the Marquis is saying about that French midwife, Madame Sauvage?"

"Yes."

Lovejoy looked at him over the tops of his wire-framed spectacles. "Did you know?"

"That she was married to Miles Sedgewick? No."

"Stamford claims it's all a lie, that his brother never went through any kind of sham marriage ceremony with her."

Sebastian thought about it a moment. "I suppose it's possible the Marquis honestly believes that—although if he does, then either he didn't know his brother very well or he is allowing his grief over Miles's death to distort his judgment now."

"You knew Sedgewick?"

"We were in the Peninsula together."

"Ah. And you think him capable of such a base deception?"

"Without a doubt. Miles Sedgewick was handsome, charming, brilliant, and clever. But he was also deceitful, treacherous, and totally untrustworthy."

"Sounds like a delightful fellow. When precisely did he sell out?"

"It's been several years, at least."

The magistrate started to say something, then glanced toward the outer office, staffed by his clerk, and said, "Let's go for a walk, shall we?"

🔖

They turned down Bow Street toward the Strand and the river that lay beyond it. Once, back in the seventeenth century, this had been a prosperous, even fashionable area. But those days were long gone. With the construction of first one theater and then another had come prostitution, gambling, and so many taverns and gin shops that virtually every other building on Bow Street was a drinking establishment. Today the entire district was synonymous with decadence and dissolution, all of it colored by the vast, tumultuous market that operated from the nearby Italian-styled piazza known as Covent Garden. Even this late in the day, the air was filled with the endless rattle of cartwheels, the raucous cries of the costermongers, and the pungent, earthy scents of their wares.

"We're told the anxiety and horror provoked by the manner of this murder has prostrated the Prince Regent," said Lovejoy as they paused at the kerb to let an ironmonger's wagon rumble past. "He's convinced that such a brutal killing could only be the work of revolutionaries who've been inspired by Napoléon's return and are now determined to murder us all in our beds."

"Sounds like Prinny," said Sebastian, stepping wide to miss a gutter overflowing with filthy water and garbage. He came down hard on his wounded leg and had to grit his teeth to keep from grunting.

Lovejoy glanced over at him. "Still bothering you, is it?"

"Just a bit."

Lovejoy's eyes narrowed, but all he said was, "The Palace has asked us to keep the details of the body's condition from the press— the idea being, I suppose, that it's bad enough to have the brother of a marquis murdered without the populace knowing that he was also savagely mutilated. I'm afraid it won't be long before we come under pressure to arrest someone. Quickly."

"Even if that someone isn't actually responsible?" said Sebastian dryly. They'd both seen it happen too many times in the past.

"Oh, my colleagues will settle on someone who's responsible for something," said Lovejoy. "Even if it doesn't happen to be this particular crime."

"And if the real killer strikes again?"

Lovejoy let out his breath in a sigh as they paused to stare out over the sun-dazzled river that opened up before them. "Let us pray to God he does not."

The two men stood for a time in silence, each lost in his own thoughts as they watched a barge make its slow, laborious way upriver. Then Sebastian said, "Did the Marquis have any idea as to who—besides Alexi Sauvage—might have wanted to see his brother dead?"

"Not really," said Lovejoy as they turned to walk on, the breeze off the river feeling surprisingly chilly. "It seems Lord Stamford only recently came up to Town from his estates in Devon and hadn't seen his brother for several months. So far, the last person we know to have seen Sedgewick was a simple acquaintance who encountered him by chance in Whitehall on Saturday night."

"Whitehall? What the devil was Sedgewick doing there?"

"We've no idea. It's odd, isn't it, given that the encounter took place at something like ten o'clock. At this point, all we know is that Sedgewick must have been killed sometime after that."

"That's something, at least. Gibson says he thinks Sedgewick was probably killed either Saturday night or early Sunday morning. When did his wife last see him?"

"Earlier that evening. She says he went out somewhere around half past six or seven and never returned. His valet confirms it."

"And yet she never reported him missing?"

Lovejoy's stern moral principles were frequently troubled by the behavior of his fellow men, and he cleared his throat now awkwardly. "She says she assumed he was busy with what she referred to as his 'personal affairs.'"

"What sort of personal affairs?"

"She didn't specify. But I gather he sometimes stayed away for several days at a time without warning her beforehand that he would be gone."

"Suggestive," said Sebastian. "Do we know the name of his mistress yet? Because I've no doubt he had one."

Lovejoy looked pained. "Not yet, but we are looking."

"And how is his wife taking his death?"

"Better than one might expect."

"Huh. I suppose one's expectations would depend on how well one knew Miles Sedgewick."

"Yes, I can see that," said Lovejoy. "Have you any idea as to who might have killed him?"

Sebastian shook his head. "Not really. But I thought I might try talking to one of our former comrades who knew him better than I did, a man named Monty McPherson."

"You mean Sir Montgomery?"

"That's right; I keep forgetting he's a baronet now. His brother was still alive when we were in the Peninsula. How do you come to know him?"

"I wouldn't exactly say I *know* him, but we have met. He's a member of the Royal Scientific Society, although I believe his main passion is folklore."

Sebastian nodded. "When we were in the Peninsula, he and Sedgewick spent hours recording as many of the local folktales, superstitions, and traditional ballads as they could find. Monty was always fretting that an entire rich oral heritage was being lost."

"And you say Captain Sedgewick took part in this venture? From what I've heard of him, it's not something I would have expected of the man."

Sebastian squinted across the water at the tumbling gray clouds beginning to re-form on the horizon. "Sedgewick was a complicated man. Just when you thought you knew and understood him, he'd say or do something, and you'd suddenly realize you didn't actually know him at all."

Lovejoy looked thoughtful. "Couldn't the same be said of many?"

"Perhaps," said Sebastian, meeting the magistrate's troubled gaze. "But some more than others."

Chapter 7

$\mathcal{S}$ir Montgomery McPherson, late of His Majesty's 25th Light Dragoons, was pushing his way into the crowded tavern known as Cribb's Parlor when Sebastian finally tracked him down. A solidly built man of average height somewhere in his thirties, he had thickly curling light red hair, ruddy cheeks, and a ready grin.

Like Sebastian, he'd been born a younger son—in McPherson's case into an old but not particularly prominent family with a rambling Elizabethan manor house on an estate in eastern Yorkshire. With his own way to make in the world, he'd bought a pair of colors at the age of sixteen with a bequest left to him by a maiden great-aunt. Over the course of the following twelve years he'd nearly died of fever three times, first in India, then in Flanders, and again in the West Indies; he'd been captured by the French but escaped twice, been shipwrecked, and once, in Spain, had his horse shot out from under him four times in three days. He liked to say he couldn't decide if he was very lucky or very unlucky, but he figured that as long as he was still alive with all his appendages and bits attached, he was happy with it. He was, in general, the kind of lighthearted, good-natured, cheerful soul that many had believed Sedgewick to be—without Sedgewick's dark side.

At the sight of Sebastian, his eyes crinkled into a smile and he shifted direction to come over and playfully punch his old comrade on the upper arm. "Devlin! It's been a long time. You'll let me buy you a drink?" The smile faded. "You've heard what happened to Sedgewick?"

"I have, yes," said Sebastian.

"Bloody awful, isn't it? Who'd have thought he'd go through all those years at war only to end up with a knife stuck under his ribs in *London*, of all places?"

"When was the last time you saw him?" Sebastian asked as they threaded their way through the crowd of fashionably dressed young bucks to an empty table near the back.

"Me? Oh, hell, it's been a while. Why?"

"Bow Street is still trying to figure out exactly when he was killed."

He was aware of McPherson studying him, his eyebrows drawing together in a frown as he took a chair. "I've heard you do this—help solve murders, I mean. Why?"

"What would you have me do instead?" said Sebastian, settling into the chair opposite him. "Take up a seat in the House of Commons, perhaps? I have a hard time seeing myself as a politician. And I seriously doubt Hendon would welcome my interference in the running of the estates."

McPherson laughed. "Not if he's anything like my sire was. I suppose there's always faro, vingt-et-un, and hazard."

"That was more Sedgewick's poison than mine."

"So I remember." He leaned forward and dropped his voice.

"They're saying Miles wasn't just killed—that his body was also muti-lated. Is it true?"

So much for the Palace's confidence in Bow Street's ability to keep that quiet, thought Sebastian. Aloud, he said, "I'm afraid so."

"Dear God." McPherson swallowed hard. "He really was castrated?"

Sebastian nodded. "And his face shot off at close quarters."

"Who would do something like that?"

"Can you think of anyone?"

"Me? Good Lord, no."

"He hasn't seduced anyone's wife lately? Run off with someone's daughter? Raped their chambermaid?"

An unexpectedly fierce light blazed in the other man's eyes. "I wouldn't know. Like I said, I haven't seen much of him lately."

Something about the way it was said pricked Sebastian's interest. "Any particular reason?"

McPherson leaned back in his chair, one hand swiping at the con-densation on his tankard. "If you must know, I found I simply couldn't stomach the way he treated women—particularly one young French widow he'd induced to fall in love with him. We didn't exactly have a falling-out, but he knew what I thought of him and, well, after that we rather went our own ways."

"I take it you mean Alexi Sauvage?"

McPherson's lips parted on a quickly indrawn breath. "You know about that?"

Sebastian nodded. "I understand you're the one Sedgewick sent to tell her he was dead."

A faint flush touched the other man's cheeks, and he looked away. "It's not something I'm proud of."

"So why did you do it?"

"To be honest, at the time it seemed the kindest thing to do. It was either that or tell her he'd lied to her, that their marriage was a sham and he was basically using her as his whore. And I wasn't cruel enough to do that."

"You didn't think she'd find out the truth?"

"I don't know . . . I suppose I thought she'd go back to France. Not sure why she didn't."

"There was a war on at the time, remember? It tended to make travel to the Continent a bit difficult."

"I suppose."

"You know she discovered the truth anyway?"

McPherson nodded. "Sedgewick told me. He was furious about it. Seems she tracked him down and confronted him in front of his own house. I said, 'Well, what did you expect?' He didn't take it well, but at that point I didn't care."

"And you haven't seen him much since?"

"Occasionally, but not often, no. I actually thought he was still out of the country. Last I heard, he was."

"He was? Where?"

McPherson shrugged. "I've no idea. I'm not in that business anymore, remember?"

There was no missing the man's meaning. "You're suggesting Sedgewick was?"

"A variation of it, at any rate. His arm was never right again after what happened in Portugal, you know. In the end he sold out, but it didn't take him long to grow bored with life in London. He missed the excitement of it all."

"I can understand that," said Sebastian.

"Mind you, he never actually *said* what he was doing, but there were hints. You know what he was like. He was very good at what he did in every way but one: He had a big mouth."

Sebastian waited while a barmaid dumped two more tankards of porter on the table, then said, "Do you know if he still maintained his interest in folklore?"

McPherson took a deep swallow of his drink and nodded. "If anything, I'd say he was more fascinated by it than ever. Truth is, it was about the only thing we had in common beyond what we did in the Army—well, that plus the fact that we both had French mothers, I suppose. Although I'd say that lately his interests had shifted more toward the occult. I heard he was spending a lot of time with the Weird Sisters."

"Who?"

McPherson laughed. "That's what people call them—the Weird Sisters, although their real name is Wilde or something like that. They've got a shop down in Seven Dials where they cast horoscopes and read cards and sell love potions and charms and such."

"So are they supposed to be Scottish witches?"

"Well, the witch part is all for show, of course. But the eldest one—Sibil is her name—is definitely Scottish. I understand she used to be on the stage at one time."

"Sibil Wilde, you mean?"

"You've heard of her, have you? I never followed the theater much, but I gather she made something of a name for herself at one time, especially for playing Lady Macbeth. Hence the 'Weird Sisters,' I suppose. They're said to be able to 'see' things, but the truth is they're simply very good at ferreting out everyone's secrets. Which means they might be able to tell you something useful if you're willing to venture down there."

"Sedgewick seriously believed in them?"

"I don't know if I'd say he actually *believed* in them, but they definitely fascinated him. Like I said, his interest in folklore had taken a strange turn lately, mainly toward the mythology surrounding witches—to the point I'd say they were becoming less of an interest and more of an obsession."

"Do you know why?"

For a long moment, McPherson simply stared back at him. Then he shook his head and said, "No, I don't. To be honest, it never occurred to me to wonder why. But it is odd, isn't it?"

"I'd say so, yes. Very."

Chapter 8

$\mathcal{B}$y the time Sebastian made it back to Tower Hill, a gentle, balmy darkness was falling over the city and the lamplighters were almost finished with their rounds.

He knew it was something he'd been avoiding—coming here again. He'd always felt awkward around Alexi because of what had happened between them in the past, and he wasn't sure if what he now understood about her would make that better or worse. But to his relief it was Gibson who answered his knock at the old house's heavy wooden door.

"Ah, there you are," said the surgeon, opening the door wider. "I was just about to send you a message." At some point during the day he'd shaved, made an attempt at combing his unruly hair, and tied a clean white cravat around his neck. But his eyes were still bloodshot, his skin sallow, his face sunken and haggard.

"Finished the autopsy, have you?"

"I have indeed. Come see."

Sebastian followed the Irishman down a narrow passageway to

the house's ancient, smoke-darkened kitchen, where Gibson paused
to light a lantern. "Alexi's gone off to deliver some costermonger's
baby," he said, thrusting a taper into the coals glowing on the hearth
and waiting until it flared.

"Had she told you about Sedgewick before?" Sebastian asked as
his friend turned to hold the burning taper to his lantern's wick.

Gibson shook his head. "No. I only just found out about him this
morning, after she saw the scars on the corpse's torso." He blew out
the taper, then picked up the lantern and turned toward the door.
"But I can now tell you what killed the bugger."

"Oh?"

Gibson led the way along the path that wound through Alexi's
garden, dark now with the shadows of the coming night. "There's a
wee slit in his left side. Doesn't look like much from the outside, but
it's there because somebody shoved a dagger up under his ribs, straight
into his heart."

Sebastian drew in his breath in a hiss. *Bloody awful, isn't it?* Monty
had said. *Who'd have thought he'd go through all those years at war only to end
up with a knife stuck under his ribs in London?*

"What is it?" asked Gibson, glancing back at him.

But Sebastian only shook his head and said, "So whoever killed
him got close."

"About as close as you can get."

"Any idea where he went into the river?"

"Somebody who knows the Thames might be able to tell you, but
not me." Gibson pushed open the door to the outbuilding and went to
hang his lantern on the chain that dangled over the naked corpse that
still lay on the high stone table in the center of the room, now bearing
a series of incisions that testified to Gibson's explorations. "But I did
find something else interesting. Look here."

Shifting to the end of the table, he gently cradled the dead man's left heel in his palm and turned the pale foot to one side. "See the abrasion marks there, and there? Somebody tied a rope around your captain's ankles—or maybe his own cravat, because I don't see any sign of rope fibers."

"Huh." Sebastian reached for one of the dead man's cold hands and turned it to the light, but there were no marks on the wrist. "Before he died, do you think?"

Gibson shook his head. "I'm almost certain it was after. It might have been done to keep the legs together while your killer was shifting the corpse. But given that he didn't bother to also tie the hands together, I'm thinking it's more likely he fastened something to Sedgewick's feet to weigh the body down when he tossed it in the river."

Sebastian shifted his gaze to the singed ruin of Sedgewick's face. "If true, that means that whoever killed him didn't intend for the body to be found. So why bother to obscure his identity by obliterating his features?"

"Insurance, perhaps, in case the body somehow turned up after all? Although that wouldn't account for the sexual mutilation."

"So, what, then? Rage? Revenge?"

"Maybe." Gibson turned to the row of wide wooden shelves that stretched across the back wall of the room, where a silent, oddly truncated form lay beneath a bloodstained sheet. "You might want to take a look at this," he said, and flipped back the covering to reveal the pale, naked shoulders and torso of a stocky male form.

"*Jesus Christ,*" whispered Sebastian. The man's neck ended abruptly in a jagged, raw mess of pulpy red tissue and torn muscle and gleaming white bone.

There was no head.

"Who the hell is that?"

"Not a clue. And look here," said Gibson, easing the sheet farther down the dead man's body to where the wrists ended in two bloody stumps. "He hasn't been identified, and I'm not sure he ever will be. It's rather difficult to identify a naked body that's missing both its head and its hands. And unlike in Sedgewick's case, there are no prominent scars on the parts of the body that we do have."

"Where was he found?"

"Washed up on the Isle of Dogs this afternoon. From the looks of things, I'd say he was probably in his late thirties or early forties. Well fed, and with nicely kept feet and toenails, so he's no pauper. Although he's muscled enough to suggest he's probably not something like a merchant or shopkeeper or clerk, either."

"No one's been reported missing?"

"No one who fits his description," said Gibson, reaching to draw the sheet back up over the headless corpse. Then he turned to face Sebastian, his arms crossing at his chest as he leaned back against the shelves. "Maybe we're coming at this all wrong. Maybe Sedgewick was the victim of some madman who's simply choosing his victims at random."

Sebastian met his friend's troubled eyes and saw there a tumult of disturbing thoughts that mirrored his own.

"Maybe," said Sebastian. "Or maybe there's a method to his madness, and we just need to find it."

Gibson sighed, his hands falling to his sides as he pushed away from the shelves. "Well, if you're right, then I pray to God you figure out what that method is. Before whoever he is kills again."

❧

Later that night, Sebastian lay in his wife's arms, his head nestled at her shoulder, one hand resting lightly on the soft swell of her belly where a new child grew. With the coming of darkness it had turned chilly, and a small fire burned on the hearth, filling the bedroom with its warm glow.

The birth of their first child, Simon, had come so close to killing Hero that the thought of this new child filled Sebastian with both joy and terror.

"I'll be all right," she said softly, somehow guessing the drift of his thoughts. "You'll see. And this one will be your girl."

"Promise?" He kept his voice light, although inside he was howling with fear. If he lost her . . . Dear God, he couldn't lose her.

"I promise," she said. "Have you come up with a name?" They'd made a bargain back in the early days of their marriage: She would name the boys, while he would get to name the girls.

"Not yet. There's plenty of time." He shifted to press a kiss against the soft flesh of her stomach. "How did your interview with the wherryman go this afternoon?"

For several years now she'd been writing a series of articles on the poor of the capital. It was an original and profoundly important project that endlessly enraged her powerful father, Lord Jarvis. But Hero simply smiled at his grumblings and went on with her interviews, for she was one of the few people in all of Britain unintimidated by the King's formidable cousin.

"We had to reschedule for tomorrow morning. Something came up." She paused, then said, "Given that no one knows the river better than a wherryman, I thought I might see if he has any idea where Miles Sedgewick's killer is likely to have tipped his body into the river."

Sebastian lifted his head to look at her. "It's certainly worth a try."

She moved her fingers, entwining them in the curls at the nape of his neck. "Are you going to ask Monty how he knew Sedgewick had been stabbed and mutilated when Bow Street has been at pains to keep the latter out of the papers and even you hadn't learned of the former?"

"I will, but not just yet. I want to look into some of the other things he told me first."

"I was under the impression you'd always had a favorable opinion of the man."

"Monty? I do like him. I was always a bit puzzled by his friendship with Sedgewick, but then, they did share that odd, intense interest in folklore. And people like Monty always tend to see the best in others. I assumed he simply thought Sedgewick as pleasant and easygoing as he seemed. It's a mistake enough people made—even clever, clear-eyed, hardheaded ones like Alexi."

"You think he could be the killer?"

Sebastian was silent for a moment. "I don't want to think it, but I also don't see how I can discount the possibility. At least, not yet."

"No," she agreed. "Except why on earth would Monty stick a dagger in his old friend's side and shoot off his face?"

"I've no idea. I have a hard enough time wrapping my head around the fact that I even need to suspect him."

"War can change people," she said quietly. "Or even destroy them."

"God knows that's true," said Sebastian. Hadn't his own experiences in the war come close to destroying him? "But I still have a hard time imagining Monty chopping off someone's head and hands."

"We don't know this new corpse is the work of the same killer." She paused. "Although the thought of *two* such killers roaming the city is rather disconcerting."

"Just a tad," he said, and saw her smile in the firelight. He shifted until he lay almost on top of her, his breath tickling a curl beside her ear. "Let's talk about something else, shall we?"

"Mmm." She reached up to entwine her arms around his neck and pull his lips down to hers. "Or we could not talk at all . . ."

Chapter 9

Wednesday, 14 June

*S*ebastian spent the next morning visiting a string of coffeehouses from Brompton to Piccadilly, places like the Scarlet Man on Cockspur Street and Yellow Dog near the Hyde Park Barracks that were the known haunts of military men. He was looking for veterans of the Peninsula, men who'd served with Sedgewick and might know what the former captain had been up to since his return to London.

The coffee shops were relatively thin of company, for many of the men typically to be found there were now in Belgium preparing for the coming attack on Napoléon. But he finally came upon Captain Martin Roche, a onetime exploring officer still suffering from a year-old wound to his side that was probably going to kill him. A tall, painfully thin man with lifeless brown hair and a drawn, haggard face, he talked about getting well enough to rejoin his regiment in Belgium and fight the "bloody Frenchies" again. But in the meantime he was subsisting on half pay and what he could scrape together by teaching Latin to small boys.

"Can't say it surprises me," said Roche when Sebastian bought the man something to eat and casually steered the conversation around to the murder of their former comrade. "Him getting himself killed, I mean. You know what Sedgewick was like; the more dangerous an assignment, the happier he was. He was always looking for trouble."

"Any idea what he'd been up to lately?"

"Not exactly, but I reckon you can guess as easily as me. Three trips to Switzerland, two to Italy, and another to Holland, all in the last few years? Hear tell he just got back from the Continent a day or so before he was killed, and it isn't likely he was taking a belated grand tour, now, is it?" He threw a quick glance over one shoulder and leaned forward, dropping his voice. "Is it true what they're saying? That someone chopped off his balls and doodle?"

"That's what I'm hearing," said Sebastian. News of the mutilation of Sedgewick's body had obviously spread far, far wider than Bow Street realized. He added casually, "But I haven't heard exactly how he was killed. Have you?"

"Nah, no one seems to know. All I heard was the bit about him being castrated."

"Any idea who might want to do something like that?"

Roche gave a throaty laugh that turned into a cough. "Some cuckolded husband, maybe? What do you think?"

"Are you referring to anyone in particular?"

"Nah. I just knew Sedgewick. It was like it was a game with him, wasn't it? Taking another man's woman, I mean. Just to show he could do it." He coughed again and this time brought up blood. "'Scuse me," he said, and turned his face away to wipe his lips with his handkerchief.

"You say Sedgewick just got back from the Continent," said Sebastian. "Do you know where he'd been this time?"

"Never heard." Roche paused. "You're thinking maybe that's why he was killed? Huh. Bloody hell; never thought of that."

"Do you have any idea who he might have been working with here in London?"

"I always figured it was either Castlereagh or Bathurst or—" He dropped his voice and leaned forward again, his eyes widening as he whispered, "*You know.*"

Lord Castlereagh was Foreign Secretary, while Lord Bathurst was Secretary of State for War and the Colonies. And the man whose name Roche was reluctant even to whisper was doubtless the King's powerful, Machiavellian cousin, Charles, Lord Jarvis.

Sebastian's father-in-law.

🥀

Sebastian decided to start at the Colonial Office in Downing Street.

An Old Etonian known for his learning, wit, and affability—at least toward those of his own class—Henry Bathurst, Third Earl Bathurst, was both High Church and High Tory, the kind of man who believed the first responsibility of government is not just to protect but to strengthen the established order at home and abroad. He might have been born the heir to an earldom, but Bathurst had made politics his passion and his life, first entering the House of Commons when he was just twenty-one years old. Over the course of a long career he'd been Lord of the Treasury, Master of the Mint, President of the Board of Trade, and, briefly, Foreign Secretary. Sebastian knew him through Hendon, who had for some years served in the cabinet as Chancellor of the Exchequer.

"Devlin," said Bathurst with a smile, coming around from behind his ponderous, heavily carved desk when a clerk ushered Sebastian into the secretary's personal office. It was an elegant chamber with dark oak paneling, red velvet drapes, and a collection of massive battle scenes painted in oils and hung in heavy gilt frames. "Good morning. How are you? And how is your father?"

"Excellent, thank you."

"Good, good." The smile widened, but Sebastian was aware of the older man's eyes narrowing, as if he were simultaneously assessing Sebastian and calculating his reason for being there. Now in his late fifties, the Earl was a slim, handsome man with a long face, high forehead, and good strong chin. He was dressed, as always, in the height of fashion, with an elaborately knotted cravat, a dark blue tailcoat with large gold buttons, and tight pale pantaloons. "How may I help you today?"

"I'm interested in Major Miles Sedgewick."

"Ah, yes." He shook his head sadly. "Such a tragedy." He retreated behind his stately desk and stretched out a thin, aristocratic hand toward a nearby red leather chair. "Please, do have a seat. I understand from Bow Street that you are assisting in the investigation of this shocking murder, although I'm not sure I understand in what way you think I might be of assistance. Sedgewick sold out two or three years ago now, you know."

"Yes. Except I understand he was traveling recently on the Continent. In fact, I gather he's made quite a habit of it the last few years. That wasn't in an official capacity, was it?"

"With the War Office?" Bathurst gave a light, practiced laugh. "Good heavens, no. Wherever did you get such an idea?"

"From someone who knew him quite well."

"I'm sorry, but they were mistaken."

"That's certainly possible. The thing is," said Sebastian, "he was last seen in Whitehall at ten at night. He wasn't by chance coming here, was he?"

"What? No, of course not. Why would he be?"

"Why indeed?" said Sebastian with a smile. "Is there a chance he could have been working with Castlereagh?"

"With the Foreign Office?" Bathurst picked up the quill he'd been using to write a letter and fingered it thoughtfully. "I suppose it's possible. But if so, I'm afraid I wouldn't know anything about it." He glanced at the heavy ormolu clock on the room's Carrara marble mantel and pushed to his feet. "I fear I must beg your pardon, but if I don't hurry, I shall be late for an appointment with the Prince. I'm sorry I couldn't have been of more assistance. Please do give my best to your father."

"Of course. Thank you; you've helped more than you know," said Sebastian, rising with him, and seeing the man's practiced smile freeze as he realized too late his mistake.

Chapter 10

*R*eckon I'm prob'bly one o' the oldest wherrymen ye'll find on the river," the gnarled old boatman told Hero. He said his name was Jeeper Jones, and that he'd been working the Thames since 1773. He was built stocky and strong, with long, wild gray hair and a heavily lined, weather-beaten brown face that made him look seventy or eighty. Except he said he was fifty-eight.

Hero sat perched atop an old stone wall near the wooden jetty where the man kept his wherry chained, her notebook balanced on her knees. London's wherries were basically the river's version of hackney carriages. Shallow skiffs rowed sometimes by one man, sometimes by two, they were built long and narrow with extended overhanging bows so that their passengers could step ashore at the river's various stairs and jetties without getting their feet wet. "I would imagine it becomes increasingly difficult to row against the river as one ages," said Hero, putting up a hand to catch the brim of her fashionably wide chip hat as a salt-tinged wind gusted up from the choppy, sun-sparkled waters beside them.

The wherryman cupped one palm around the bowl of his white clay pipe and gave a slow smile. "Nah, it ain't that. Most of us jist don't live very long. If ye don't drown, sooner or later the damp gets down in yer lungs and the river takes ye that way. But most of us jist drowns. Me sister's boy was pulled outta the Thames only yesterday, after tryin' to shoot the bridge, the young fool. It's why I had t' beg yer ladyship's pardon fer not talkin' t' ye when we was first supposed t'. Takin' it hard, she is."

"I'm so sorry. He was also a wherryman?"

Jeeper Jones sucked on his pipe and nodded. "Finished his apprenticeship last year. Takes six years, ye know, because ye gotta learn the river, and it's a wily one. His da was a wherryman, too; he was crushed by the ice back in 'fourteen when the river froze over."

"The profession tends to stay in families?"

"Always. Ye grow up around boats on the river, it gives ye a taste for a waterman's life so's ye don't want no other. Me da was a wherryman, and his da before him, and his da before him, on back t' before the days of Henry VIII—or so I've been told. Course, things was different back then. In them days, with all the mud and ruts and stuff on land, the Thames was London's main street—the only way ye could really get from one end t' the other. Time was, the only bridge over the river was London Bridge, and there weren't no theaters allowed in London, so's anyone wantin' to see a play had t' take a wherry to Southwark. I've heard tell there was more'n twelve thousand wherrymen on the river, back in the day. Know how many there are now?"

Hero shook her head.

"Three thousand."

"Good heavens," said Hero.

Jeeper Jones tightened his grip on his pipe and squinted up at the screeching gulls that circled overhead. "First they let theaters open up in the City, then they come up with sprung carriages, and now they're puttin' up all these blasted bridges."

The Watermen's Company had historically been large and powerful, and over the centuries they had fought long and hard to stop all of those changes, at one point even successfully bullying the Crown into passing a law that banned hackney carriages. That hadn't lasted long, but for years they had successfully prevented any new bridges from being built over the Thames. Westminster Bridge wasn't finally approved until the 1740s, with Blackfriars Bridge following soon after. And now three more bridges—one at the Strand, one at Vauxhall, and another they were calling the Southwark Bridge—were set to open in the next few years.

Jeeper Jones coughed up a mouthful of phlegm and spit into the muck at his feet. "I hear people sayin' that next thing ye know, we're gonna see steam boats on the river, that they're gonna put us wherrymen out o' business for good." He eyed Hero thoughtfully. "You think that's true?"

Hero stared out over the wide river to where the soot-stained brick walls of the barge buildings rose on the far side. "I don't know," she said tactfully, although she frankly thought it inevitable.

He didn't look as if he believed her.

"At least the bridges must cut down on the number of drownings," she said.

The wherryman let out his breath in a scornful huff. "Don't know about that. We still pull bodies out the water all the time. I reckon there's anywhere between a hundred and fifty to two hundred bodies fished out the river every year. Sometimes in a dense fog there'll be twenty or more people lost in jist a day or two—and those are the ones that're found."

Hero looked up from scribbling her notes. "Have you heard about the lord's son who was recently found in the Pool?"

"Oh, aye. They say somebody done cut off his pr—" The wherry-man broke off, his eyes widening as if he'd reconsidered what he'd been about to say. He swiped an open hand across his mouth and said instead, "Hear somebody messed him up real good, somebody did."

"Where do you suppose he went in the river? Is there any way to know?"

"We-ell." The wherryman pulled at his ear and stared thought-fully at a barge making its slow way up the river, the sun glinting off the water curling away from its bow. "It's hard to say, really. Some-place in Southwark is more'n likely, but there ain't no way to know fer sure. Things can churn around in that river real good when the tide comes in and goes out." He brought his gaze back to her face. "Was he somebody close t' ye?"

"No. A mere acquaintance only. He served with my husband in the Peninsula."

Jeeper's eyes narrowed as he regarded her in silence for a mo-ment. "I hear Old Hookey's gettin' ready t' invade France next month. Ye know anything about that?"

"Only what I read in the papers."

He looked out over the sun-spangled river, his throat working as he swallowed. "My youngest boy, Michael, is on HMS *Royal Anne*. Got impressed three years ago—him and his brother Micah both at the same time. But Micah, he died of fever after jist six months."

Hero sucked in a deep breath scented with tar and hemp and all the sun-soaked smells of the river. The Navy was always impressing wherrymen, largely because they were already familiar with life on the water. "I'm sorry."

The wherryman nodded his acknowledgment and blinked. "At first we heard Michael was bein' sent t' America t' fight the Yankees. But when Boney busted loose, the Admiralty decided t' keep his ship here. It's gettin' to where I'm wondering if he'll ever be let go."

"Surely he will be home soon," said Hero. "At least now the war with America has finally ended, and I don't see how this new conflict with Bonaparte can last long."

"Even if it don't, I reckon they'll jist start a fight someplace else. I was impressed meself back in 'seventy-six, and they got me da twice in his day. I know one wherryman impressed seven times, he was."

"Merciful heavens," said Hero.

But Jeeper Jones simply laughed.

3

It was after Hero had pressed several coins into the wherryman's hand and was climbing the worn stone steps that led up to the inn where she'd left her carriage that she felt it: that tingling at the back of her neck that told her she was being watched.

She kept walking.

Jeeper Jones's work base—assigned to him by the Watermen's Company—was the old Hungerford Stairs, at Hungerford Market near Charing Cross. The worn two-story stone building that housed the market was now nearly a hundred and fifty years old, and it was not prospering. As she passed the market hall's old colonnade, Hero paused beside one of the stalls to study a colorful display of ribbons. Then, as she turned to walk on again, she allowed her gaze to drift casually over the motley collection of stall keepers and housewives, cooks and housemaids, hawkers and porters, beggars and thieves, who crowded the square.

But if someone was watching her, they had obviously looked away.

Keeping her pace unhurried, she turned down the narrow street of squalid houses to where she had left her carriage.

"Everything all right, my lady?" asked one of her footmen, leaping forward to open the carriage door and let down the steps.

For a moment she paused again, her hands fisting in the skirt of her simple fustian gown as she glanced back toward the market. "Yes, thank you," she said, and turned to mount the steps.

But the sense of disquiet lingered even as the carriage swung out onto the Strand and the market was lost from sight.

Chapter 11

*I*t wasn't the "done thing" for one gentlewoman to call upon another in the morning hours. And so Hero waited until three o'clock that afternoon before setting out in her yellow-bodied town carriage to pay a formal call on Captain Miles Sedgewick's widow, Eloisa. In place of the plain dark fustian she'd worn that morning for her interview with the wherryman, she chose an afternoon gown of white muslin with a tiny border of embroidered primroses and short puff sleeves of yellow tiffany that matched her yellow kid slippers and the bunch of silk flowers fixed to her jaunty cap. She had little expectation that a woman so recently widowed would actually agree to see someone who was, after all, a mere acquaintance, but it was worth a try.

Miles Sedgewick's house in Mount Street, purchased at the time of his marriage by his bride's father, Edward Platt, was impressive, with rusticated stonework on the ground floor, Ionic columns, and an elaborate entablature decorated with swagged garlands. Once simple Manchester mill owners, the Platt family owed their meteoric rise to the first American War, when Eloisa's grandfather, also called Edward

Platt, secured a contract to supply the Army with cloth. The long, interminable war with France provided the second Edward Platt with a similar opportunity to increase his fortune, and it was this younger Platt who had then embarked on an ambitious campaign to raise the family's social standing. Purchasing first a sizable estate in Somerset, then an impressive London town house in Grosvenor Square, he'd determinedly set about marrying his two daughters and young son into the ranks of the nobility.

His son and heir—also imaginatively named Edward—had recently become betrothed to the only daughter of an earl whose massive debts had reduced him to marrying the girl off to the highest bidder, while Platt's elder daughter, Jane, had managed to catch an equally impoverished baron and was now officially Lady Lewis. With Eloisa, Platt had been forced to settle for a mere younger son, although Sedgewick was at least the son of a marquis.

Hero found the house shrouded in an ostentatious display of mourning, with black crepe draping the windows and a massive black wreath hung on the door. But to her surprise, Eloisa Sedgewick immediately agreed to see her.

She received Hero in an opulent drawing room that looked like a stage set for a performance of *Antony and Cleopatra*, with a profusion of straw satin-covered chairs and settees with crocodile legs and what she suspected were genuine painted wooden mummy cases propped up in several of the corners. A small, plump woman with very fair hair, blue eyes, and pleasing, even features, the young widow wore unrelieved mourning, from the black lace cap that covered her curls to the somber black slippers on her feet. She had been sitting on one of the crocodile-legged settees, deep in conversation with a gentleman in a clerical collar, but at Hero's entrance she rose to come toward her with both hands outstretched. "My dear Lady Devlin. It's so good of you to come."

Hero clasped the widow's outstretched hands and held them for a moment. Eloisa's eyes were puffy and glistening with unshed tears, her nose red. And Hero felt an upswelling of rage at the man who had been Miles Sedgewick. He didn't deserve this woman, didn't deserve her tears.

"I can't tell you how sorry I am," said Hero. "What a terrible shock."

"Thank you. You are so kind." She gave Hero's hands a squeeze, then turned to introduce the man in the clerical collar who was now rising to execute a neat bow. "May I present the Reverend Sinclair Palmer?"

"Lady Devlin," he said with a charmingly slow, vaguely roguish smile.

A tall, broad-shouldered man of perhaps twenty-eight or thirty, he had exquisitely molded, even features and golden hair, and he looked enough like Eloisa Sedgewick's dead husband to make Hero blink. *Interesting*, she thought, returning his smile. "How do you do, Reverend? My apologies for interrupting you."

"No, not at all," he said, reaching for the fashionable hat he had left resting on a nearby end table. "I truly was just on the verge of leaving." To the widow he said quietly, "Don't worry; everything will be all right. You'll see." Then he bowed again and took his leave.

"Sinclair and I grew up together," said the widow as she and Hero settled beside the empty hearth. "I don't know how I'd have made it through these last two days without him. My father and brother are both at present up in Manchester, and my sister—Lady Lewis, you know—is in Devon."

"You are fortunate indeed to have such a good friend," said Hero.

Eloisa nodded and produced a black lace-edged handkerchief she held for a moment to her trembling lips. "Sedgewick's brother, the

Marquis, has also been most supportive, of course. He tells me Lord Devlin has involved himself in the investigation of Miles's death."

"And did Lord Stamford also give you his decidedly less-than-favorable opinion of that fact?"

"Well, I'll admit that he didn't exactly sound pleased," said the widow with a hint of amusement warming her soft blue eyes. "But he knows that Lord Devlin and Miles served together in the Peninsula, so he must surely understand why the Viscount has taken an interest in what happened."

Do you know? Hero wanted to say. *Do you know that your husband contracted a bigamous marriage with the woman who saved his life in Portugal, and then abandoned her after she'd served her purpose?*

Do you know what manner of man he truly was?

But of course she couldn't say any of those things to this sad-eyed, grieving woman. "I can assure you that Devlin is most concerned," she said instead, then paused as a stately white-haired butler, assisted by a housemaid, entered bearing a massive silver tray loaded down with tea things. Hero waited until the servants had withdrawn, then said, "I understand Captain Sedgewick had only recently returned from the Continent?"

Eloisa lifted the heavy sterling teapot and began to pour. "Yes, just this past Saturday."

"It seems as if everyone is visiting Belgium these days."

"So true. My sister and her husband, Lord Lewis, returned from there just last week. Except that Miles wasn't in Brussels, you know."

Hero reached to take her cup. "He wasn't?"

"No. I suppose he had other reasons for going, but I believe his main purpose was to look into something called the Zaubererjackl trials."

Hero took a slow sip of her tea. "I'm not familiar with them."

"I'm not surprised. They were an obscure series of witch burnings that took place back in the sixteenth century—or perhaps it was
the seventeenth? I forget which. At any rate, they killed over a hundred witches, most of them children. Cut off their hands before killing them, and then afterwards they cut off their heads, too."

Hero stared at her. "I didn't know they did that sort of thing to
people they thought were witches."

"Oh, yes; it was a brutal time. I'll never understand why it fascinated Miles so."

"He was interested in folklore, was he not?"

"Obsessed with it, actually. He collected all sorts of disgusting
objects. He was particularly excited because in addition to visiting
the castle where those horrid burnings took place, he also somehow
managed to obtain a witch's ladder."

"A what?"

"A witch's ladder." Eloisa wrinkled her nose. "It's something used
by witches to cast spells or some such thing. He said that while he
was there, they were tearing down a house that used to belong to
one of the old women burned as a witch, and the workmen found it
in the attic."

"May I see it?"

Eloisa's eyes widened. "Are you serious? Do you truly wish to?"

"Yes. It sounds fascinating."

She reluctantly set aside her tea. "Very well, although I warn you,
it's not much to look at."

She led the way downstairs, to a rather untidy library that opened
off the entrance hall. The air here still carried the faint, lingering scent
of horses and leather, and Eloisa paused at the entrance, her chest jerking as she sucked in a deep breath.

The room was lined with dark shelves filled with old books and a
motley collection of objects ranging from a dirt-encrusted Bronze

Age dagger to a grinning human skull, its bones stained dark by the soil in which it must have once laid. Curled up at one end of a desk strewn with papers, open books, and a jumble of other objects lay a length of cord some three or four feet long, formed by what looked like brown string braided together with human hair and knotted every few inches with black feathers.

"That's it," said Eloisa, stopping just inside the doorway to point at it. "You'll excuse me if I don't touch it! Sordid, is it not?"

"How very curious," said Hero, going to study it closer. "What did you say it was used for?"

"Miles said they were used for binding spells."

"Any particular sort of spell?"

"I've no idea, but presumably something nasty. I must remember to ask one of the servants to burn the thing."

"Oh, please don't," said Hero, turning toward her. "There are societies dedicated to the study of folklore; surely one of them would be delighted to receive it."

Eloisa looked doubtful. "Do you think so? Miles did say there were several people he was interested in showing it to, but personally, I can't imagine wanting something once used in a sordid attempt to commune with Satan."

"No, of course not," murmured Hero, letting her gaze drift around the cluttered room, with its eclectic collection of strange and wondrous objects. "When Sedgewick went out that evening—the day he was killed—do you know where he was going?"

"He never said, no. But given that he'd only just returned from Austria and Bavaria, I assumed it was probably something to do with that."

"Austria?" said Hero, more sharply than she'd intended. The European powers had been meeting at the Congress of Vienna for nearly a year now. They'd been close to hammering out a final treaty when

Napoléon's triumphant return shifted their focus from the task of re-drawing the map of Europe to once again joining together to defeat the emperor who threatened their status quo so dangerously.

Eloisa looked surprised by the intensity of Hero's reaction. "Yes; didn't I say? That's mainly where he'd been: Salzburg and Vienna."

Chapter 12

*C*harles, Lord Jarvis, stood at the drawing room window of his town house overlooking the leafy expanse of Berkeley Square. He was a large man, well over six feet tall and fleshy now in his early sixties, with piercing gray eyes and an aquiline nose he had bequeathed to his daughter, Hero.

Although generally acknowledged as the most powerful and feared man in all of Britain, he held no government portfolio and never would, for Jarvis knew only too well how fleeting such positions could be. He preferred to exercise his power quietly from the shadows and had acquired a reputation for omniscience, thanks to the extensive network of informants, spies, and assassins under his personal control. His kinship with the poor old mad King George III and the King's self-indulgent, irresponsible son, the Prince Regent, was of course useful. But Jarvis's true strength lay in the rare brilliance of his mind and the ruthless cunning with which he employed it.

Raising his wineglass to his lips, he took a slow sip of fine burgundy and watched as his daughter's yellow-bodied carriage drew up before his house and Hero alighted. She was not, unfortunately, a pretty woman, although he would acknowledge that with her strong features and dark hair, one might call her handsome. Far too tall, of course, and far too outspoken and radical in her opinions. Her choice of husband was also a source of aggravation, although Jarvis had to admit that the marriage agreed with her. It had already produced a fine grandson, whom Jarvis most uncharacteristically but whole-heartedly adored, and soon there would be another.

She was Jarvis's only surviving child. His first wife, Annabelle, had been a silly, useless creature who found it nearly impossible to carry a live child to term. Amidst a seemingly endless string of mis-carriages and stillbirths, she'd managed to present him with only two living children: Hero, and a sickly, overly sensitive son named David. If the fates had willed it otherwise, Jarvis might in time have been able to make something of the boy, for in the end he'd proved to be surprisingly courageous and strong-willed. But David had gone to a watery grave years ago, while Annabelle had finally succumbed to one of the endless illnesses that always seemed to plague her. And so Jarvis had been left free to take a new wife—a wife who was not only young and beautiful but also brilliant and blessedly fertile. In a few days she would be brought to bed of their first child. And although Jarvis had never considered himself a superstitious man, he was nev-ertheless utterly convinced that she would present him with a worthy son and heir.

Now he listened to Hero's cheerful conversation with Grisham, his butler, in the hall below and then turned from the window at the sound of her quick steps mounting the stairs.

"Good afternoon, Papa," she said with a smile, crossing the room to kiss his cheek.

He caught her hand and held it for a moment, his gaze searching her face. "How are you? And how is my next grandson?"

Her other hand touched, briefly, the faint swelling of her belly, and she laughed. "I keep telling you, this one's a girl."

"So you do." He turned away to refill his glass. "May I offer you some wine? Or would you prefer tea?"

"No, nothing, thank you."

Carafe in hand, he glanced over at her. She was no longer smiling. "You're looking very serious this afternoon. I think I can guess why you're here."

"Can you?"

"Devlin's involvement in Bow Street's investigation of the Sedgewick murder isn't exactly a secret."

"I didn't expect you to admit that the captain worked for you."

"If you were listening carefully, you'd know that I admitted no such thing."

"So you're saying—what? That he was working with Castlereagh instead? Or was it Bathurst?"

He smiled and set the carafe aside. "I've no idea."

It was such a blatant, obvious lie that she laughed out loud. "Of course not. So do you know why he was killed?"

"I do not."

"But you have some idea."

"The authorities suspect that Frenchwoman."

He saw the flare of worry in her eyes and understood its cause, for the French midwife had delivered Simon, and Hero credited her with saving both their lives. But all she said was, "I didn't ask who the authorities suspect."

He took a sip of his wine and said nothing.

Hero's fist clenched around the strings of her reticule. "Did you see him after his return from Vienna?"

"Why would I?"

"That doesn't answer my question."

"It wasn't meant to." He was aware of a new sound of footsteps, these coming down the stairs from the bedrooms above, and said, "Let me put it this way: I have no idea who killed Sedgewick, or why."

She was silent for a moment, her gaze hard on his face. "I don't believe you."

He huffed a soft laugh but sobered quickly. "Enough of this. I've just received some far more important news: Napoléon has left Paris."

He watched the color drain from her face. "When?"

"June twelfth."

"Dear Lord," she whispered. "And Wellington?"

"Is presumably still in Brussels."

"Amusing himself at all the most fashionable dinners, picnics, and balls?"

"Hopefully not still."

They turned at the sound of the room's door opening. "Hero!" said his wife, Victoria, coming to grasp her cousin's hands and kiss both her cheeks. "I saw your carriage. How are you?"

She moved slowly, for she was big with child, and like Hero's dead mother, Victoria was a petite, dainty thing, with fair hair and blue eyes and a charming smile that she used most effectively to disguise the formidable extent of her intellect and learning and the strength of her will. She was, with perhaps the exception of Hero herself, the most brilliant woman Jarvis had ever known. But unlike Hero, she was more than content to hide it all behind the cheerful, gentle face Society demanded of the female sex.

"I'm well, thank you," said Hero, a faint hint of color touching her cheeks, for Jarvis knew she found it vaguely mortifying to be with child at the same time as her own stepmother. "And you? When do you expect to be confined?"

"Any day now, surely," said Victoria, easing her bulk down into a nearby chair. "Although it would be nice for the babe to wait until after the French Ambassador's ball on the eighteenth. Do you go?"

"Hendon particularly wants Devlin to attend, so I suspect we shall."

Victoria settled both hands atop her bulging belly with a smile. "And after that, young Master Jarvis may come with my blessings."

Jarvis went to stand beside her, one hand resting companionably on her shoulder. "If he's considerate, my son will wait at least one more week. I fear the next few days are going to be hectic, to say the least."

Hero let her breath out in a hard sigh. "When will the news of the French movement be made public?"

"It should be in all the morning papers."

"Will it create a panic, do you think?"

"I don't see why it should," said Jarvis. "We've known for weeks that a battle is coming; it's simply a matter of where and when."

"Except that up until now, Wellington has been confident it would be at a time and place of his own choosing."

"His mistake," said Jarvis. "Let's hope it's his last."

"You will let me know when you hear more?"

"Of course."

She took her leave soon after that, kissing them both again.

Victoria waited until they heard Grisham close the front door behind her, then said, "I assume she was here for the obvious reason?"

"Yes. But then, it was only a matter of time, was it not?" Draining his wineglass, he went to pull the bell, then said to the footman who appeared, "Send Major Drake to me."

Chapter 13

*H*ero was coming down the front steps of her father's house when a sporty curricle drawn by a pair of high-stepping matched chestnuts swept around the corner. It was driven by a down-the-road-looking man in a caped driving coat and a high-crowned hat; a diminutive, sharp-faced tiger perched on the seat at the rear.

The driver reined in behind her waiting carriage, his horses snorting and tossing their heads as Hero changed direction to walk toward him. "What are you doing here?" she asked, looking up at him.

"I came to see your father," said Devlin.

She laughed. "I think I know why."

He glanced back at Tom. "Hop down and meet us back at Brook Street—and tell her ladyship's driver to do the same, if you would?" To Hero, he said, "Fancy a drive in Hyde Park, my lady?"

❧

It was the fashionable hour for the promenade in the park, which meant that the roadways were clogged with a colorful medley of stylishly dressed young gentlewomen in barouches, turbaned dowagers in ponderous landaus, and gentlemen in high-perched phaetons, tilburies, or sporty curricles, all weaving their way through a crush of showy hacks controlled by riders with widely varying degrees of skill. They crawled up the crowded avenue.

"You think Jarvis was telling you the truth?" Devlin asked when she had finished telling him of her conversation with her formidable father.

"In part, at least," said Hero, wishing she'd thought to bring a parasol. The sun was only just beginning to sink toward the western horizon, its mellow light filtering down through the leafy branches of the rows of stately chestnuts and plane trees to cast a dazzling pattern of light and shadow across the fashionable throng. "But only in part. He claims Sedgewick was not working with him."

"In that, at least, I'm inclined to believe him."

She turned her head to look at him. "Really? Why?"

"Because Sedgewick was a bit of a loose cannon, and Jarvis is generally very careful about the men he employs."

"He has been known to make mistakes."

"He has. But when I saw Bathurst, he let slip that he's been discussing Sedgewick's murder with Bow Street. And I can't see him doing that unless the War Office's interest in his murder extends beyond the simple death of a former Army captain."

She thought about it a moment. "Yes, that does seem rather telling."

"Of course, it's possible Sedgewick was on a mission that involved both Bathurst and Castlereagh, but I haven't managed to see Castlereagh yet. They were all at sixes and sevens by the time I reached the Foreign Office."

"I'm not surprised," said Hero. "You were right when you said Napoléon wasn't going to simply sit around waiting for Wellington to attack him in July. Jarvis says they've received word that he left Paris for the frontier more than two days ago."

"*Damn*," whispered Devlin softly, the features of his face tightening as he stared out across the sunlit park toward the south.

She knew what he was thinking: that in just a few days, tens of thousands of men, including friends he'd known and fought beside for years, would face death. And yet because of his inability to regain the strength in his wounded leg in time, he wouldn't be there at their side. All he could do was sit and wait to hear the news of the momentous events that were about to happen.

Reaching out, she rested her hand, lightly, on his arm. But all she said was, "It makes the timing of Sedgewick's death particularly interesting, wouldn't you say?"

He brought his gaze back to her. "It does indeed. I wish we knew precisely why he was in Vienna. You don't think his wife knows?"

Hero shook her head. "She seems to think he went there mainly to visit some castle famous for a ghastly series of witchcraft trials. I suppose it's possible she was being disingenuous, but I don't think so . . . or at least, not in that."

"You think she knows about Alexi Sauvage?"

"I'm not sure. She was shocked and upset by Sedgewick's death, obviously—who wouldn't be when her husband's mutilated body has just been hauled out of the Thames? But I don't know if I'd say she is *grieving*, precisely. She may not know about Alexi, but I'd be surprised if she's entirely ignorant of her husband's habits. She doesn't strike me as particularly intelligent or learned, but she's not stupid. And I don't think she's still so lost in love as to close her eyes to the signs of his straying."

"Hence her failure to report him missing for days?"

"It would explain it."

"Do you know if Jarvis saw Sedgewick before he died?"

She shook her head. "He wouldn't say."

"Interesting. It suggests he's being less than honest when he says he doesn't know who killed Sedgewick, or why."

"Well, I noticed he didn't say he doesn't *care* who killed the man."

"That I can believe. If Sedgewick was on a mission to Vienna—whether at the behest of Bathurst, Castlereagh, or Jarvis himself—then I've no doubt Jarvis actually cares a great deal." He was silent for a moment, carefully maneuvering his curricle around a skinny, pimply youth in a phaeton with a blowsy black mare that was more interested in the grass at the side of the road than in her master's commands. Then he said, "The Bourbons have a well-earned reputation for sending their assassins to quietly stab—or garrote—those they want silenced, with the victims' bodies then being tossed into the Thames. If they saw Sedgewick—or the information he carried—as a threat, then I can see them ordering him killed. Although I'd be even more likely to suspect them if his body hadn't been mutilated. That suggests something more personal is going on here."

"Perhaps," said Hero. "Although to some people, all politics is personal, and that's particularly true of the Bourbons."

"It is indeed."

She stared out across the tops of the plane trees, their leafy green canopies shifting restlessly now with the growing wind. "What I don't understand is where the headless corpse Gibson showed you fits into all this."

"As you said, it's always possible the two killings are completely unrelated."

"Yes, but what are the odds?"

"Probably not good," he admitted. "But it is possible."

She brought her gaze back to his face. "Remember those Austrian witch trials Eloisa was telling me about—the ones Sedgewick was so interested in? She says that many of the victims had their hands cut off before they were killed, and then their bodies were decapitated."

Devlin reined in sharply and turned to face her. "I don't like the sound of that."

"No," said Hero. "Neither do I."

Chapter 14

*T*hat night, Sebastian dressed in a motley collection of old clothes culled from the secondhand stalls of Rosemary Lane and rubbed dirt from the garden onto his cheeks and forehead.

"Wouldn't it be safer to visit the Weird Sisters during the day?" said Hero, watching him disorder his stylishly cut hair.

He met her gaze in the mirror. "Perhaps. But I suspect I'll learn more after dark."

"Perhaps," she said. "Although you might also be less likely to come back alive."

Sebastian reached for his walking stick and, with a deft turn of his wrist, drew a small sword from its hidden sheath. "That's what this is for."

❧

Lying just to the north of the theater district of Covent Garden, the area known as St. Giles had its origins in a twelfth-century leper colony dedicated to St. Giles, the patron saint of lepers, outcasts, vagabonds, and cripples. It was an association that haunted the area still. For centuries St. Giles had been the last resort of those driven so low in life that they had no place else to go, particularly refugees from Ireland and France and what were known as "St. Giles blackbirds," servants from Africa abandoned by their former "masters" and forced to turn to begging to survive. Most constables refused to venture into the area's dangerous warren of mean alleyways, narrow streets, and dark courts, for those who did rarely came out alive. This was the haunt of pickpockets, housebreakers, and footpads, of murderers and prostitutes and pawnbrokers, a mean, stinking maze of crumbling gin shops and filthy "cadging houses," where multiple families lived packed into damp cellars, open sewers fouled the streets, and cesspits overflowed.

Pulling his battered old hat low over his eyes, Sebastian took a hackney to Long Acre, slouching in one corner of the aged carriage as he let himself sink into the role he was about to play. By the time he reached his destination, the confident attitude of the lord's son was gone; his posture and demeanor, his gait, the very way he held his head, were those of a poor man down on his luck. It was a trick he'd learned as a much younger man from a woman he'd once loved, a beautiful actress named Kat Boleyn, and it had served him well in the Army when he'd done the kinds of things gentlemen weren't supposed to do. Except of course that gentlemen did do them—they simply didn't talk about it.

He paid off the hackney, then slipped unnoticed through dark, noisome streets crowded with ragged, broken men; desperate, half-naked mothers clutching dying babies; and thin, ragged children with filthy matted hair and hollow-eyed stares. Not far from the ancient Church of St. Giles, the lane he followed emptied into what was known as Seven Dials, a mean circle where seven narrow streets converged to form a star pattern that had long attracted astrologers and alchemists. It was there, at the apex of one of the intersections, that Sibil and her sisters had set up a shop they called Wilde and Weird.

Pushing open the ancient building's warped, weathered door, Sebastian found himself in the low-ceilinged common room of what must have once been a pub. Now, narrow shelves crowded with dark vials and various other strange and vaguely ominous-looking objects hemmed the room, while pungent bunches of dried herbs and feathers dangled from the smoke-darkened beams overhead. Behind the former pub's counter stood a small, plump woman of perhaps thirty-five, her brown hair just beginning to fade to gray, her eyes small and dark and watchful. She was dressed in a heavy purple brocade gown from the previous century with ropes of thick, improbable pearls nestled in its lace-edged square neckline, and had one elbow propped on the counter's worn surface so that she could rest her chin in her palm. "May I help you?" she asked in a bored voice.

"Good evening," he said, making no attempt to disguise his cultured accent.

She straightened with a jerk as something flared in her eyes, a peculiar combination of avarice and interest mixed with what might have been fear. "Lose your way in the streets, did you, my fine sir?"

"Not exactly."

"No? So—what? Looking for a love potion, are you?"

He let his gaze drift again around that peculiar collection of objects on display, the skulls of various sizes and species, the strange crystals and waxen images and hideous, primitive-looking masks. Then a soft step and the swish of a curtain brought his gaze back to the counter, where a second woman now joined the first. This one was taller and thinner, with sculpted high cheekbones, unusual green eyes, and soft, sensuous lips touched by a knowing smile. A thin red scar sliced down one side of her cheek and chin to curl around her neck, but she was still strikingly attractive, even beautiful.

"I don't think it's love that's brought Lord Devlin to us, Astrid," said Sibil Wilde in a husky, ruined voice.

He met the former actress's gently mocking gaze. "You know who I am, do you?"

"Of course. I've been expecting you." Like her sister, Sibil Wilde wore a gown of the fashion of a different century. Except this was no relic from a secondhand shop but what looked like a finely made red velvet costume from a production of *Romeo and Juliet*. The front of the thinly padded bodice was styled with a low point and embroidered with gold thread; the wide sleeves were slashed and lined and ornamented with puffs at the shoulders, while the full velvet overskirt was trimmed with gold braid and fell open to reveal a figured silk underdress.

"Of course," he said, and she laughed.

Still holding his gaze, she took a step back to part the curtain behind her. "Won't you come this way?"

For a moment he hesitated, and she laughed again. "I won't murder you, I promise. At least not yet." Her accent was noticeably different from her sister's, shaded with a slight burr of the north but nevertheless the voice of a woman of the stage who, whatever her origins, has successfully learned to disguise them.

"And that's supposed to reassure me?" he said, his fist tightening around his sword stick as he followed her down the short, shadowy corridor to a surprisingly opulent chamber paneled in dark walnut, with an ancient carved sandstone fireplace surround and a particularly fine crystal chandelier overhead that filled the room with a soft flickering light.

"Well, that and the sword hidden in your walking stick."

He smiled. "Your sister doesn't sound Scottish. And yet, you do."

She circled around to the far side of the cloth-covered round table that stood in the center of the room. "We had different mothers—all three of us. My mother was from Edinburgh, while Astrid's mother was from Wiltshire. You haven't met Rowena, but her mother was a mulatto from Jamaica."

She settled in one of the table's heavily carved high-backed chairs, then gestured toward the chair that faced it. "Please, have a seat."

"Thank you, but I prefer to stand."

"As you wish." She drew a deck of cards from a pocket hidden in her voluminous skirts and cut it neatly. "I know why you're here."

"Do you?"

She shuffled the cards together with a neat, practiced flourish. "It's a peculiar interest for a gentleman of your station—solving murders, I mean. Why do you do it? I wonder. For the intellectual challenge? The excitement of facing danger? Or is it the thrill of solving a puzzle that appeals to you?"

"Nothing so complicated. I simply happen to believe that the victims of murder deserve justice."

She drew a deep breath that flared her nostrils, and it was as if the scar on her cheek darkened, became more menacing. "Not all dead men deserve justice."

"Are you suggesting Miles Sedgewick might be one of them?"

She let the cards fly in a professional shuffle, then sent them whirling back again. "I didn't say that."

"How did you happen to know him, anyway?"

"He used to come for readings."

"Of his stars? Or the cards?"

"Both, although he preferred the cards."

"So what did you see in his cards?"

Her smile firmly back in place, she gave a slight shake of her head. "My readings are like a Papist confessional: I don't reveal the secrets I learn."

"Even when the man you told them to is dead?"

"Especially then."

Sebastian found his gaze drawn to a hollow blue glass ball that hung over the mantel of the room's empty hearth. It was some six or seven inches in diameter, its lower half filled with a layer of salt strewn with what looked like lavender and marigold buds, bits of moss and cinnamon bark, and chips of amethyst and obsidian.

"It's called a witch's ball," she said, following his gaze. "Have you ever seen one before?"

"Not quite like that." He paused. "I understand Sedgewick had a particular interest in folklore—especially that involving witches. Do you know why?"

She shrugged. "Why not? It's fascinating, don't you think?"

He came to wrap his hands around the carved top of the chair facing her and leaned into it. "Who do you think killed him?"

She stared up at him, meeting his gaze openly. But she was an actress with years of experience, and he could not begin to read her. "I have no idea. Who told you to ask me?"

"A friend."

"A friend of Sedgewick's, or of yours?"

"Both."

She nodded. "McPherson, I assume." She paused, a slow smile curling her lips when Sebastian said nothing. "He has a very beautiful wife named Isabella; did you know?"

"Yes. I assume that's supposed to be relevant in some way?"

"You tell me. They say Sedgewick had his face shot off and his sex organs removed. Is it true?"

"Where did you hear that?"

"It's known."

"Not by many."

"Obviously by more than you think."

He couldn't argue with that.

For a moment, the room was silent except for the shuffling of the cards. Then she said, "So tell me this: Did you know Sedgewick well?"

"I knew him four years ago."

She shrugged. "I doubt he'd changed much since that time. Some men grow from the experiences they encounter in life, while others are diminished. Which it is sometimes depends on the character of the man, but not always. Sometimes it's the nature of the experiences that determines the outcome."

"And Sedgewick?"

"With Sedgewick, I'd say life didn't so much change him as . . ." She paused as if searching for the right word. "Accentuate him."

"In a good or a bad way?"

"I suppose that depends on your perspective." She set the deck of cards on the surface of the table before her, cut it three times, then looked up at him. "Shall I read for you now?"

He took a step back and dropped his hands to his sides. "No, thank you. Next time, perhaps."

She reassembled the deck. "Very well. But do be careful leaving here, won't you? The neighborhood can be . . . dangerous."

"And yet you choose to live here." Most of the residents of St. Giles were there because they had no place better to go, but that obviously wasn't true for the Weird Sisters.

"It adds a certain mystique—an aura of danger that people like."

"I can see that. Except the danger isn't simply a part of the mystique; it's real."

"Perhaps. But people around here are afraid of us. They leave us alone."

"Yet the same can't be said of your customers."

"Those who can afford it know to take precautions."

"And the others?"

She shrugged. "I suppose some of them might end up in the Thames with their throats slit."

"You're suggesting that might be what happened to Sedgewick?"

"Hardly." She leaned back in her throne-like chair, a smile touching her lips, the candlelight shimmering on what looked like a very real diamond that dangled from the gold chain around her neck. "When was the last time you knew a footpad to steal a man's privates?"

"I suppose it depends on what he wanted them for," said Sebastian, and saw her smile slip.

Chapter 15

A squall was blowing in from the North Sea, the brine-laden wind slanting a cold rain sideways when Sebastian left the Weird Sisters' shop to cut across the open expanse of Seven Dials. The storm had driven most of the district's wretched inhabitants to seek whatever shelter they could find, and as he ducked down the narrow lane of crumbling, soot-stained brick buildings that stretched toward Long Acre, Sebastian found himself swearing softly under his breath.

His hearing and night vision were both unusually acute. But even Sebastian could not see through driving rain, while the howling wind in combination with the roar of water sluicing off the broken gutters overhead would drown out the kinds of sounds that might otherwise warn of danger. He tightened his grip on his walking stick, wishing his leg didn't feel so damned unreliable but ready to whirl at a sudden rush of footsteps behind him even as he was alive to the potential threat of every man who came toward him.

The day laborer in stained canvas trousers and badly broken shoes.

The butcher with a bloody apron and a long, crooked nose.

The big drover in a torn oilskin and broad-brimmed slouch hat that hid his eyes in a way Sebastian didn't like.

The man was a giant, looming a good seven or eight inches taller than Sebastian and built broad at the shoulders, with a big, bony skull and a jutting jaw and powerful long legs that carried him quickly through the wind-driven rain. He turned his head away as he came abreast of Sebastian. But then, at the last instant, he careened sideways, slamming into Sebastian hard enough to send him staggering toward the dark mouth of an alley that yawned beside them.

In a searing wave of pain, Sebastian's weight came down on his bad leg and he felt it crumple beneath him. He landed on one hip, his right hand sinking into the fetid wet mud of the alley as he fought to keep from going sprawling.

Damn, he thought in a surge of impotent rage as he pushed up to his knees. *Damn, damn, damn.* His fingers slippery with filth, he was fumbling with the catch of his sword stick when the oilskin-wearing giant came up from behind to swoop down and wrap his massive arms around Sebastian's torso, squeezing the air from his lungs and lifting him bodily off the ground. Fighting for breath, his arms trapped at his sides, Sebastian felt the sword stick slip from his fingers.

"*Bon soir, monsieur,*" said a faintly mocking voice from the inner depths of the alley. "Having a good evening?"

"Not particularly," said Sebastian, his feet dangling several inches from the ground as the overgrown oaf swung him around to face the speaker. Unlike his companion, this man was of normal size, with overlong dark hair and a face mostly hidden by the folds of a black cravat. To his knowledge, Sebastian had never seen the man before.

"Don't struggle, hmm?" said the Frenchman, stepping forward to press the naked blade of a hunting knife flat against Sebastian's cheek and slide it up until the point hovered just inches from his left eye. "Otherwise, the blade might slip and steal your sight."

Sebastian went perfectly still. For one suspended moment, the only sounds in the alley were the drumming of the rain and the heavy breathing of the three men. Then the Frenchman said, "You picked a bad night to take a stroll through an unfamiliar neighborhood, *monsieur le vicomte*."

"So it would seem," said Sebastian.

A hint of amusement narrowed the Frenchman's eyes. "I have some advice for you, *monsieur*: Give up this investigation, now, or you will pay a price most dear. You do understand, yes?"

Sebastian blinked at the rain that ran down his face and into his eyes. At some point, he realized, he'd lost his hat. "Not entirely. What precisely are you threatening me with?"

"Use your imagination. Think of all that you hold dear, all that you could not bear to lose."

"*You bloody bastard,*" swore Sebastian on a harsh exhalation of air. "Who sent you?"

The man laughed.

Clenching his jaw, Sebastian arched back against the giant's massive torso, jerking his head away from the knife at the same time as he swung up both knees and kicked out to drive the heels of his boots into the Frenchman's gut.

The Frenchman stumbled back, his breath leaving his body in a *whoosh* as the overgrown oaf, thrown off-balance, staggered, momentarily loosening his grip on Sebastian.

Twisting to one side, Sebastian broke the oaf's hold and threw himself toward the mouth of the alley, landing in a roll. Snatching his walking stick from the muck, he brought the sharp double-bladed sword hissing from its sheath as he surged to his feet.

"*Non,*" said the Frenchman to his overgrown companion, reaching out to catch the man's arm when he would have surged forward.

The oaf drew up, his big hands dangling at his sides, his nostrils flaring and his jaw set hard.

"*Non*," said the Frenchman again, swiping one crooked elbow across his wet forehead. "Our message has been delivered." To Sebastian, he said, "Be wise, *monsieur*, and remember: all that you hold most dear."

The two men backed away from him down the alley, the Frenchman watching him carefully, the knife still in his hand.

Sebastian stayed where he was. His wounded leg on fire, the sword stick still gripped in one hand, he leaned back against the alley's soot-stained brick wall and felt the rain course down his bare face as he drew a long, shuddering breath.

⁊

"Calhoun might be a genius of a valet," said Hero, eyeing Sebastian's muck-smeared hat, "but I doubt even he will be able to salvage this."

Sebastian sank deeper into the water of the steaming bathtub set up before the fire in his dressing room. "You never know. The muck might help me to blend in better the next time I need to visit St. Giles."

She made an incoherent noise deep in her throat and tossed the hat atop the pile of filthy clothes near the door. "You're lucky Jeeper the wherryman isn't at this very moment fishing you out of the Thames—minus a few strategic body parts."

Sebastian tilted back his head and closed his eyes. His leg really hurt like hell now. "No, this was just a warning. They won't try to kill me until next time."

"Well, that's reassuring."

He opened his eyes and looked over at her. But all she said was, "Your leg is hurting, isn't it?"

"A bit."

She muttered what sounded suspiciously like an oath, then said, "You think the Weird Sisters sent those men after you?"

"It's possible. Except why would they?"

"Why would anyone?"

"I wish I knew. My friend with the knife was definitely French."

"A Bonapartist, a monarchist, or a Republican?"

"He didn't say."

"And the giant?"

"Who knows? He didn't actually say anything, although the French-man spoke to him in English, which rather suggests that he is not French. And the truth is, they could be working for anyone. One need not be English-born to hire oneself out as a thug to an Englishman."

"True."

He shifted his weight in a futile attempt to ease the pressure on his thigh, the movement sending the water sloshing against the copper sides of the tub. "Have you ever met Monty's wife, Isabella McPherson?"

"I have, yes. And Sibil Wilde is right: She is quite beautiful."

"She is indeed. Although I can't help but wonder why Sibil so very deliberately set out to make me suspect Isabella's husband."

"Well, McPherson did say the sisters have excellent sources of information. And I can see a cuckolded husband murdering and cas-trating the man who seduced his wife."

"Or a betrayed woman hiring a knife-wielding Frenchman and his large friend to kill and castrate her unfaithful lover?"

"That, too."

"The problem is," said Sebastian, "Sedgewick was involved with too damn many women, any one of whom could be holding a lethal grudge against him. If Sibil is telling the truth—which is unarguably an 'if'—we now know of three: Eloisa, Isabella, and Alexi. And there may well be more. Who would know?"

"Well, Isabella and Eloisa might," said Hero. "But no," she added quickly when he raised his head to look at her, "I am not going to ask either of them if they know who else the man they loved was sleeping with. I seriously doubt they'd be honest with me anyway."

"Probably not," said Sebastian, wrapping his hands around the edge of the tub to stand up, streaming hot soapy water. "I suppose I could try asking Aunt Henrietta. If there's been any gossip, she would know about it."

Born Lady Henrietta St. Cyr, the Dowager Duchess of Claiborne was Hendon's elder sister and thus not technically Sebastian's aunt. But she was definitely one of his favorite people. Bright, acerbic, and inquisitive, she knew everyone—and remembered every tidbit of gossip and rumor that had ever passed her way.

Hero reached for the towel that had been kept warming by the fire. "I think that's a brilliant idea."

"Huh. You just don't want to have to ask Eloisa who else her husband was screwing," said Sebastian, then laughed when she threw the towel at him.

Chapter 16

Thursday, 15 June

A grande dame now in her seventy-fifth year, the Dowager Duchess of Claiborne still lived in the sprawling Park Lane town house to which she had come as a bride many years before. Technically the house now belonged to her middle-aged son, the current Duke. But she had never surrendered it to him, and he knew better than to try to wrest it from her. He simply lived elsewhere.

The Duchess was famous for never leaving her bedchamber until twelve or one, for her regular attendance at the most fashionable of Society's balls, routs, and card parties meant that she rarely made it to her bed before three or four in the morning. But when Sebastian arrived on her doorstep the next morning shortly after ten, it was to find her already dressed in an elegant gown of dark blue peau de soie and seated at her breakfast table. A slice of half-eaten toast lay abandoned on the plate before her, and her tea was going cold. She had a copy of the *Morning Post* spread out on the table and was studying it carefully through the quizzing glass she wore on a gold chain around her neck.

"Devlin," she said, looking up when her butler ushered him into the room. "Have you seen the papers?"

"Not today, no," said Sebastian, going to pour himself a cup of tea.

She leaned back in her chair, her lips pursed, her face pinched with an uncharacteristically worried frown. Like Hendon, she was stockily built, with a broad, slablike face enlivened by the brilliant blue St. Cyr eyes. She had never been pretty, even when young, but she'd always had a stately manner, a regal presence, and an unerring sense of style. Sebastian was convinced she'd been born to be a duchess.

"Why?" he asked, coming to pull out the chair beside her. "What is it?"

"Napoléon has left Paris and is headed for the frontier!"

"Yes, I know."

She stared at him. "You knew? Since when?"

"Yesterday sometime."

"And you didn't tell me?"

He took a quick sip of tea and scalded his tongue. "I'm sorry; it didn't occur to me."

She folded her paper, then folded it again into a neat square, her attention seemingly all for her task. "You must know that both Alexander—Claiborne's middle son—and Peter—he's Emily's second . . . or is it her third? At any rate, they're both with the Army in Belgium. Alexander is one of Wellington's aides-de-camp. And it didn't occur to you that I might be interested in the fact that virtually the entire French Army is now marching against two of my favorite grandsons?"

"I truly am sorry," he said again.

She brought up a hand to rub her eyes with a spread thumb and forefinger. "Hendon tells me you've involved yourself in this ghastly murder of Miles Sedgewick."

"I take it he's displeased?" said Sebastian, wondering why the Earl—who must surely have known of Bonaparte's move—hadn't seen fit to notify his sister about that, rather than grumbling to her of his heir's shortcomings.

"What do you think?"

Sebastian simply took another sip of his tea.

"Frankly, I'm not surprised Sedgewick met an unpleasant end," she said. "He was a sordid man."

"But from a good family."

Henrietta sniffed. "The family is ancient enough, I'll give you that, even if the title is of fairly recent origin. And they've managed to hold on to their wealth better than many. But they've always been a bit *off*, if you know what I mean?"

"Oh? Do tell."

"It's not surprising, I suppose, when you consider that they got their start as robber barons back in the Middle Ages, kidnapping travelers to hold for ransom and blinding those who refused to pay up. And while that might be ancient history, they don't seem to have changed much on down through the ages. The current Marquis's grandfather—that would have been Robert, the Second Marquis— killed a man in a duel before he was eighteen."

"Well, that was rather more common in those days, was it not?"

"It was. Except there were rumors that, rather than besting his opponent in a fair fight, Robert actually ran his victim through with his sword when the man's back was turned. Some tried to discredit the tale at the time, but it was given more credence when first his valet, then his wife's mother, died violently under strange circumstances."

"Sounds like quite the rum character."

"He was, indeed. And his son, the Third Marquis, was no better. He kept a string of mistresses, but even that didn't keep him from seducing his best friends' wives and daughters. One of those friends finally caught him in flagrante and killed him."

"He sounds rather like Miles."

She nodded. "I've heard some try to dismiss Miles Sedgewick's exploits as those of a young man sowing his wild oats. But when you make a habit of ruining the daughters of tradesmen and innkeepers, you've passed a line."

"And he did?"

"It was as if it was a game with him."

Her words echoed something the half-pay officer, Captain Martin Roche, had said to Sebastian. "Do you know the name of his current mistress?"

"I don't believe I've heard. He had an opera dancer in keeping up until a few months ago, but I understand Lord Rockman has her now."

"Good God, where do you learn all this stuff?"

She gave him a level look. "People talk. I simply listen and remember. Or at least, I usually do," she added with a troubled frown. "There was a particularly sordid rumor making the rounds some years ago, shortly before Stamford bought Miles a pair of colors and he went off to the wars. But I wasn't particularly convinced it was true, and now I can't seem to recall the exact details." She sighed. "I must be getting old. Let me think on it a bit, and it may come to me."

"What do you know of his wife?"

"Eloisa Platt?" The Dowager sniffed again. "The father is a hopelessly pushing mushroom, of course. You've heard he's managed to get his son betrothed to Haskett's daughter? Of course, everyone knows that Haskett is all washed up, so I suppose he had no choice."

"Is it true Eloisa was in the family way when she married Sedgewick?"

"Of course she was. Platt would never have agreed to the match otherwise. She's much prettier than the sister who caught a baron, so he had set his sights even higher with her. Since then she's managed to cultivate a reputation as a levelheaded, sternly religious young woman, although she can't be too levelheaded if she allowed herself to be seduced by a younger son in search of a rich wife."

"Well, she would have been quite young, and Sedgewick could be quite charming."

"Oh, yes. His kind tend to make a study of it, wouldn't you say?" She paused for a moment, her expression thoughtful.

"What?" he asked, watching her.

"I remember hearing several months ago that the family's governess was let go rather hastily. Seems Eloisa dismissed her for allowing Sedgewick to seduce her."

"When was this?"

"When you were in Paris, sometime around February or March. Eloisa turned her off without a character."

"Do you recall the governess's name?"

"Good heavens, no; I doubt I even heard it." The Duchess fixed him with a level stare. "I understand that whoever killed Sedgewick also castrated him. Is that why you're so interested in the women in his life?"

"Was that bit of information in the *Morning Post*?"

"No, I heard it at Lady Sefton's ball last night."

"Ah." He drained his teacup and set it aside. "What do you know of Isabella McPherson?"

"Sir Montgomery's wife? Beautiful woman. Are you saying she was another of Sedgewick's conquests?"

"I honestly don't know. All anyone ever says of her is that she's very beautiful."

"Well, she is, isn't she? Not terribly bright, I'm afraid, but exquisite to look at, and sweet enough, I suppose, in that rather insipid way. If she's played Sir Montgomery false, then she's been very discreet, for I've heard nothing about it."

Sebastian nodded and pushed to his feet, being careful to take his weight on his good leg. "I promise if I hear anything more from the Continent, I'll let you know."

"Your wound is still bothering you, isn't it?" she said, watching him.

"It's healing."

"Hendon is worried about you. He says you're pushing yourself too hard."

"I'll be all right."

She gave him a look he had no difficulty interpreting, then said, "Will it be bad, do you think? This coming battle, I mean."

He wasn't going to lie to her. "I suspect so, yes. Both sides know how much is riding on it, so neither is going to hold anything back."

"When is it likely to begin?"

"By the end of this week, perhaps; the beginning of next week at the latest."

The Dowager pressed her lips together and nodded. "It's so dreadful to think about. All those handsome, gay young men with virtually their entire lives ahead of them. And yet in a week's time, so many of them will be dead."

"At least then it will be over, once and for all. If he's defeated, Bonaparte will never be able to come back again."

"And if he wins?"

"Then Europe will simply need to learn to live with him—in peace, for a change."

"Is that even possible?"

He met her troubled gaze. "I don't know. Hopefully we won't have to worry about finding out."

A gust of wind blew a chill rain in Sebastian's face as he descended the steps of his aunt's house. Walking up to Tom, he said, "It doesn't look like this bloody rain is likely to stop anytime soon. I want you to take the curricle back to Brook Street, then spend the rest of the day looking for a governess who was dismissed by Miles and Eloisa Sedgewick last February or March."

"Aye, gov'nor!" said Tom, his eyes shining with anticipation. "What's 'er name?"

"I have no idea. Sorry."

But Tom only laughed.

Chapter 17

*Y*ou've heard Napoléon is marching toward the frontier?" said Lovejoy as he and Sebastian sat at one of the round front tables of a small coffeehouse tucked away beneath the colonnade of the Italianate-style piazza that housed Covent Garden Market. A fire burned cheerfully on the nearby hearth and the sconces placed at intervals along the shop's mellow old wainscotted walls were lit, for the day had continued cold and wet. Outside in the square, the market's normally raucous activity was muted, the crowds of stall keepers and shawl-covered housewives, porters and ragged little pickpockets, all thinned by the rain and the cold wind that rippled the puddles of water collecting in the dips of the worn, sunken flagstones.

"I heard," said Sebastian, wrapping both hands around his hot coffee.

Lovejoy sighed. "I fear it's only a matter of time until we receive news of a terrible battle."

Sebastian nodded. "Napoléon isn't going to wait to launch his attack. The combined British and Prussian armies already outnumber his; he can't afford to give the Russians and Austrians time to get in place, too."

"I hadn't thought of that." Lovejoy stared out the paned front window at the gray, dismal scene, his expression that of a man who is forced by the realities of his age and circumstances to confront an unpleasant truth that fills him with regret. "It's difficult to sit here, safe and comfortable, knowing what others are facing just across the Channel."

"Yes," said Sebastian, and left it at that.

Lovejoy cleared his throat, as if belatedly remembering his companion's circumstances. "I fear that, so far, we haven't had any luck locating Captain Sedgewick's mistress."

"I gather he let his latest one go before he left for the Continent and had probably been amusing himself with the wife of a friend."

"Oh, dear," said Lovejoy, frowning. "We've had constables talking to boatmen and dockworkers up and down the river, but they've yet to locate anyone willing to admit having seen anything Saturday night. At this point, it's anyone's guess as to where Sedgewick's body was thrown into the river, and we've no idea at all where he was killed."

"What about the headless man? Any luck identifying him?"

"Not yet. No one has been reported missing." Lovejoy leaned back in his chair, both forearms resting on the table before him. "It's strange, don't you think? Although I suppose he could have come off a ship."

"It's possible. Although he looks far too soft, pale skinned, and pampered to have been a seaman or even a ship's officer."

"So a passenger, perhaps? Someone newly arrived in the city who was killed shortly after disembarking?"

"Or someone whose friends and family think he left town and don't yet realize he never made it to his destination."

"What a disturbing thought," said Lovejoy.

Sebastian swallowed the last of his coffee and set the empty cup aside. "I've been trying to trace Sedgewick's movements the day he was killed, but so far I'm not having a great deal of luck. Who did you say ran into him that night in Whitehall?"

"A gentleman of letters by name of Tiptoff—Dudley Tiptoff. I've met him several times at various lectures given at the Royal Scientific Society. He's something of an eccentric—lives alone in Bloomsbury and spends most of his time in the British Museum."

"I thought I'd try talking to him. He might be able to tell me something useful he doesn't realize he knows. What does he study?"

Lovejoy stared out the window at the torrent of water shooting off a torn, windblown awning. "I believe his specialty is folklore."

&

Dudley Tiptoff, Esq., lived in a narrow town house on Bury Street, conveniently located just around the corner from the British Museum. Sebastian's knock at his door was answered by a housemaid rather than by a footman or butler, for housemaids were considerably cheaper to employ than manservants, and Dudley Tiptoff was obviously not the kind of man who felt the need to ape the ways of the aristocracy. The Tiptoffs were a good old family, but as he was often heard to say, they'd never aspired to anything grander than simple gentility. He had a comfortable income from money judiciously invested by his father in the Funds and saw no need to fritter away on servants' wages what could be better spent on the books and artifacts that filled his modest Bloomsbury home. He had never married and had been known to confess that he tended to feel awkward around the fair sex, thanks to a birth deformity that had left him with a slight but unmistakable limp. But then wives, like manservants, were an expensive indulgence for a man with so many other interests.

"Sir Henry tells me you're working with Bow Street to try to solve this dreadful murder," said the scholar, receiving Sebastian in a bookcase-lined study where everything from corn dollies and a rusty iron cauldron to Stone Age battle-axes and an ancient bronze helmet jostled with a sea of books for space on the crowded shelves. "I don't know that I can be of much assistance, but I'm more than happy to do what I can to help."

"Thank you," said Sebastian as the two men settled into the comfortably worn tapestry-covered chairs drawn up to the room's crackling fire. "I understand you saw Sedgewick last Saturday night?"

"I did, yes," said Tiptoff, propping his elbows on the arms of his chair and bringing his fingertips together. He was an untidy man of average height and build, beginning to go soft around the gut as he crept toward middle age. His dark hair was already losing its luster and beginning to gray, and he wore a pair of gold-framed spectacles that caught the firelight as he turned his head. "I was walking up Whitehall when I heard someone hailing me from the other side of the street. I'm afraid I was rather lost in thought—I've been reading the *Kinder-und-Hausmärchen* by the Brothers Grimm, you see, and finding it quite thought-provoking. Are you familiar with the Grimms?"

"No, sorry."

"They're two German brothers who are making it their lives' work to write down the folktales of their people and save them from extinction. Some people mistakenly assume the stories are for children, but they're not. They're far too dark and gruesome, full of—" He broke off suddenly, as if realizing he was forgetting himself. "Well, never mind that. But as I was saying, I was rather lost in thought, so it was a moment before I became aware of the fact that someone was hailing me."

"Sedgewick?"

"Yes. Seems he'd just returned from Austria, and he'd brought something back that he thought I might be interested in seeing."

"Oh? What was that?"

"A witch's ladder. You've heard of them?"

"I have, yes," said Sebastian, remembering Hero's conversation with Eloisa Sedgewick. "But only recently."

Tiptoff nodded. "According to the old superstitions, they were used by witches to bind spells. To be honest, I've always suspected their existence was probably a myth. So needless to say, I was quite eager to see it. I told him I was planning to do some research at the museum in the morning, but I could stop by Mount Street in the afternoon. He laughed and said that would be splendid, that he rarely left his bed before noon anyway. Then he wished me good evening and continued on his way."

"In which direction was that?"

"Toward the Abbey."

"Where exactly on Whitehall did you see him?"

"Near the Horse Guards."

So before Downing Street, thought Sebastian. Aloud, he said, "Did Sedgewick happen to mention where he was going or where he'd been that day?"

"Not that I recall, no. Sorry."

"And what time was this?"

"Ten, perhaps?" He thought for a moment, then said, "Yes, ten; I remember now that the clock towers began striking the hour while we were speaking, and he remarked on my being out so late. I'd been studying examples of symbolism on the funerary monuments in the Abbey, and then stopped at a pub I know for something to eat before heading home. But I fear I had lingered rather too long—I was reading while I ate, you see—and forgot the time. He told me I should take a hackney, that it wasn't safe."

"Did he seem nervous in any way? Anxious? Angry, perhaps?"

"Oh, no; on the contrary, I'd say he was in excellent spirits."

"Did he happen to mention why he'd been to Austria?"

"I believe he was in the area mainly to visit Salzburg, the site of some rather horrific witch burnings in the late seventeenth century. He was fascinated by tales of witchcraft, you know. Witches and werewolves."

"Werewolves?"

Tiptoff cleared his throat. "Yes, it's from the Old English word *werwulf*, a compound of *wer*, meaning 'man,' and *wulf*, for 'wolf.'"

"I've heard of them. I gather they're something of a cliché in modern romance novels."

Tiptoff huffed a wry laugh. "Oh, yes; they're becoming quite popular now that we've quit burning them."

"I didn't realize we burned people for supposedly being werewolves."

"That we did—usually along with the poor souls who'd been tortured into confessing they were witches."

"Hence Sedgewick's interest in both?"

Tiptoff nodded. "In the sixteenth and seventeenth centuries, accused werewolves and witches were often burned together because both were believed to have received their powers from the devil. But that was actually a surprisingly late concept, you know—the idea that their powers came from Satan, I mean. Both Petronius and Herodotus tell tales of werewolves, as do Ovid and many, many others. And of course they appear in the medieval romances. In France they call them *loups-garous*, in Iberia they're *hombres lobos*, and in Bulgaria they're called *vrykolakas*. In fact it's quite astonishing how widespread the myths are, although there are always local variations, of course. Some of the legends say that werewolves can only be killed by a silver weapon, while others will only trust fire. In parts of Germany there is a belief that the only way to stop a man with the power to turn himself into a werewolf is to decapitate his corpse and throw the head into a river. Supposedly the weight of the werewolf's sins will cause the head to sink to the river bottom and stay there."

Sebastian was suddenly, acutely aware of the fire crackling beside them, of the ticking of the clock on the mantel and the cry of a street seller outside. He drew a deep breath. "Someone cut the hands and head off a man whose body was pulled from the Thames a few days ago."

Tiptoff's lips parted. "Merciful heavens," he whispered. "You can't think . . ."

"I don't know." Sebastian sat forward. "Have you ever heard of a folk story in which the victim has his face destroyed and his sex organs removed?"

Tiptoff looked troubled. "Well . . . there is an old French tale of a werewolf who once terrorized a village near Lyon. He would attack only the handsome young men, and after he killed them, he ripped off their faces and private parts."

"Do you know of anyone else in London with an interest in werewolves?"

"Yes, of course. As I said, it's a common, recurring theme in folk traditions, and folklore is increasingly being recognized as an important area of scholarly interest. Why? Do you think we might all be in danger?"

It was an angle Sebastian hadn't yet considered, that someone could have targeted Sedgewick because of his interest in werewolves and witches. He let his gaze drift over the scholar's strange collection of artifacts and curiosities. "Have you ever experienced hostility because of your interests?"

Tiptoff shifted uncomfortably. "Yes, of course. The world is full of bigoted, benighted people, I'm afraid. They see the ancient tales of such things as witches and werewolves as satanic and evil rather than as folklore to be studied and written down before such an important part of our heritage is lost. And they have a tendency to view any scholarly interest in that tradition as equally satanic."

"Have you had trouble with anyone in particular?"

"I've had crosses painted on my door—that sort of thing. But I don't know who's doing it."

"When did this start?"

"Some months ago. I don't think I could say precisely when. Why?"

"Do you know if Miles Sedgewick experienced anything similar?"

"If he did, he never mentioned it." Tiptoff paused, his nostrils flaring as he sucked in a quick breath. "You never said if you thought I might be in danger."

Sebastian met his frightened gaze and held it. "Let's just say it wouldn't hurt to be careful. I don't think I'd go out walking alone late at night again for a while."

Chapter 18

That morning, Hero spent some time writing up the notes from her interview with Jeeper Jones, then took the boys to the park. It was after they'd returned, when she was leaving the nursery, that she heard the distant peal of the bell, then met Morey coming up the stairs toward her.

"I beg your pardon, my lady, but I've put Lady McPherson in the drawing room. I told her you were not receiving, but she is quite distraught, and—"

"Thank you, Morey," she said. "Please tell her I'll be down in just a few moments."

She found Isabella McPherson pacing before the fire, her reticule clutched tightly in both hands, her eyes red and swollen, her cheeks flushed. The hem of her simple muslin gown was wet and mud splashed; her rain-splattered pink spencer buttoned askew; the brim of her fashionable straw hat bent and one of its pink ribbons torn. But even haphazardly dressed and with her face marred by crying, she was still a stunningly beautiful woman, tall and willowy, with enor-

mous velvety brown eyes, a perfectly sculpted nose, a full, short upper lip, and a small square chin. The only daughter of a comfortably
situated Kent baron, she had married Sir Montgomery in her first
season. It was said to be a love match, for with her beauty she could
have aimed much higher than a mere baronet.

"Ah, there you are," she exclaimed, drawing up sharply at the
sight of Hero. "I'm told Lord Devlin is looking into the death of Miles
Sedgewick; is that true?"

"It is, yes," said Hero. "Won't you please have a seat?"

Isabella tore the wet, crumpled hat off her dark hair and tossed it
aside. "No, thank you; I can't, I'm too wound up."

"You knew Sedgewick?" said Hero as the younger woman re-
sumed her pacing, a distraught cauldron of grief mingled with rage.

"Yes, of course. He and Monty were in the Peninsula together."

"Yes, I understand they—"

Isabella drew up abruptly and whirled to face her again. "I'm here
because Lord Devlin must know that I'm quite certain it's Bonaparte
who's done this—or rather, his agents. Miles had just been to Vienna,
you see, and he brought back a list of a dozen or so names—people in
London who used to secretly pass information to Napoléon."

Hero stared at her. "How do you know this?"

"He told me."

"You saw him? After he came back from Vienna?"

"Yes, yes. He came to see me Saturday—or rather, he came to
see Monty, of course. Only Monty wasn't there, so Miles stayed and
visited with me for a time."

"And he told you about this list?" It struck Hero as profoundly
strange for a man to divulge such sensitive information to a woman
he supposedly knew only as his friend's wife . . .

"Yes," Isabella was saying. "He was excited about it—you know
how he could get." Her lips trembled, her chest jerking as her breath

caught on a sob. "He said it would make quite a stir if it ever came out, and that he suspected there were some people in high places who would like to see him dead, if they only knew."

"Did he mention anyone in particular?"

"Not by name, no. But he did say there's someone in the cabinet who would be utterly disgraced, thanks to his association with some actress who passed information to Paris for years."

Dear God, thought Hero. *Hendon.* Hendon, whose Irish-born natural daughter had once used her position as London's most celebrated actress to acquire information she then passed on to the French—not because of any love for Napoléon but in the spirit of "my enemy's enemy is my friend." It had been years since Kat worked actively to help the French, even though she was still passionately devoted to her dream of an independent Ireland free from the onerous, oppressive boot of Britain. But Hero was quite certain that if such a list existed, Kat's name would be on it.

"When was this?" Hero said sharply.

Isabella's eyes widened. "That I saw him? I told you—Saturday."

"I meant, what time did he arrive? It could be important in determining what happened to him that day."

Isabella stared at her a moment, then blinked and looked away. "I truly don't see how it could be, but . . ." She thought about it a moment, then said, "He came just as I was sitting down to a nuncheon, so I suppose it must have been about one or shortly thereafter. I asked him to join me, and he did—said he'd just finished some tiresome meeting and was famished."

"How long was he with you?"

Isabella made a fluttering gesture with one hand. "I don't know precisely. Four hours? Something like that."

Good heavens, thought Hero. But all she said was, "Do you know how he was planning to spend the evening?"

"No, he didn't say."

Hero studied the younger woman's beautiful, tear-ravaged face. "Have you considered contacting Bow Street? They—"

"Oh, no. No!" Isabella took a quick step toward her, then drew up. "You can't tell anyone that this information came from me."

"Why not?" Hero knew precisely why not, but she asked the question anyway, simply to see her guest's reaction.

Isabella flushed and looked away. "I never told Monty about Miles's visit. We're just friends, of course—*were* just friends. Miles and I, I mean. But Monty . . . He doesn't understand. He gets . . . jealous. He can't know. He can't."

Hero kept her gaze on the other woman's face, her voice low and even. "Sedgewick didn't come to see Sir Montgomery, did he? He came to see you."

Isabella brought up one hand to shade her eyes, then let it fall. "All right, yes! I told you: We were good friends. But there was nothing more to it, I swear!"

"Did Sedgewick tell you how this list happened to come into his possession?"

"He said it was compiled by someone named Fouché. But I didn't ask how he got it, no."

Hero felt her breath catch. Once, Joseph Fouché had been the Minister of Police under Napoléon. A powerful, corrupt, brutal, and duplicitous man, Fouché had controlled an infamous network of agents and spies. He'd lost power even before the fall of the Emperor, but at one point before Napoléon's return from Elba, Fouché had been attempting to ingratiate himself with the Bourbons. Hero could see him having once compiled such a list in an attempt to work his way back to power with the newly restored regime.

"Do you know why Miles was in Vienna?" Hero asked.

"Yes, of course. He told everyone he was going to Salzburg to see the site of some famous witch burnings, but that was just a cover story. The government needed someone whom neither Napoléon's agents nor the Allies would suspect was actually there for a different reason entirely. He did that sort of thing, you see. He missed the excitement of what he used to do in the Army."

"He told you that?"

"Yes."

It occurred to Hero that Miles Sedgewick sounded like a man dangerously incapable of keeping a secret. But all she said was, "Precisely who sent him to Vienna?"

"I always assumed it was either the Foreign Office or the War Office, but I'm not sure he ever actually said." She sucked in a quick, shaky breath. "You will tell Lord Devlin about the list, won't you? But he can't tell anyone the information came from me. It's vitally important that my name be kept out of this." Her features hardened. "If it does come out, I'll say it's all a hum, that he simply made it up."

"I'll tell him. But you must realize that it may come out eventually, whether you wish it to or not."

"It can't! It simply can't!" she said, her eyes flashing and her jaw clenching with determination, as if she could somehow direct the course of events simply by the strength of her will.

꒰

Some ten minutes later, Hero was standing beside the drawing room window, her gaze on the gray, rain-washed street below, when Devlin came in, his face and boots still glistening with wet.

"I've just had a rather troubling conversation with a scholar named Dudley Tiptoff," he said, going to hold his hands out to the fire.

"Oh?" said Hero. "Well, wait until you hear about my visit from Isabella McPherson."

Chapter 19

Sebastian's relationship with the man he'd long called Father had always been complicated.

Of the four children born to the Earl of Hendon and his lovely, wayward Countess, Sophia, only two now survived: Amanda, their eldest child and only daughter, and Sebastian, the youngest son, who'd always been the least like the Earl. The son who'd grown tall and lean rather than big and stocky like his father and elder brothers; the son whose eyes were a strange yellow rather than the famous St. Cyr blue; the son whose very existence sometimes seemed to cause Hendon pain.

Sebastian was nearly thirty before he understood the reason behind any of it. But the truth behind Sebastian's paternity had never stopped the Earl from accepting him as his son and—after the death of Sebastian's last brother when Sebastian was eleven—as his heir. And it hadn't stopped Hendon from forming a deep and powerful affection for the brilliant, quicksilver changeling to whom he'd given his name.

But the bond between the two men had come close to rupturing more than once over the past several years. And much of the turmoil between them revolved around the beautiful Irish-born actress Kat Boleyn, whom Sebastian had once planned to marry and whom they now knew to be Hendon's natural daughter.

Profoundly troubled by the threat to Hendon implied by what Hero had learned from Isabella McPherson, Sebastian took his carriage to Hendon's town house in Grosvenor Square, only to be told that the Earl was out. He then tried to see Kat, but she was in rehearsals and he couldn't begin to have a private conversation with her. Frustrated, he considered trying to chase Hendon down, then gave up the idea and directed his coachman instead to Carlton House, the Prince Regent's overdecorated palace in Pall Mall, where private chambers were reserved specifically for the use of the Regent's powerful cousin, Lord Jarvis.

Ushered into his lordship's presence by an underfed, pale-faced, nervous clerk, Sebastian found his father-in-law seated at a delicate French desk, his quill scratching furiously across a sheet of paper. "One moment," he said without looking up.

Sebastian went to stand beside the window, his gaze on the rain-lashed forecourt below. He turned when he heard Jarvis set aside his pen and sit back in his chair.

"I presume you're here for some reason you consider extraordinarily pressing?" said Jarvis.

Sebastian leaned his hips back against the windowsill and crossed his arms at his chest. "I know why Sedgewick was in Vienna."

"You do, do you? And how do you come to know that?"

"Does it matter?"

"It might."

"You told Hero that Sedgewick wasn't working for you."

"Of course he wasn't. You knew the man. He was very good at

what he did, up to a point. But I prefer to use the services of those with a bit more . . . discretion."

"So he was working with either Castlereagh or Bathurst, was he?"

"I didn't say that."

"No, you didn't."

Jarvis pushed to his feet and went to pour himself a glass of brandy. He did not offer one to his visitor. "Just because I didn't send Sedgewick to Vienna does not mean, however, that I was unaware of his mission."

"Oh? And do you know the results of that mission?"

Jarvis took a slow sip of his brandy and swallowed before answering. "Seeing as how I was there when he reported, yes, I do."

"On Saturday? When?"

"Late that morning."

"In Downing Street?"

"Of course."

"Exactly when did he leave?"

"*Exactly?* I couldn't say. But probably somewhere around one."

Sebastian studied his father-in-law's bland, expressionless face. Jarvis never gave anything away that he didn't want to. "Why are you telling me this?"

"You suspect me of having an ulterior motive?"

"Actually, yes."

Jarvis smiled but said nothing.

Sebastian pushed away from the window, his arms dropping to his sides. "Sedgewick was last seen in Whitehall at ten o'clock the night he was killed. If he'd met with you, Bathurst, and Castlereagh earlier in the day, what was he doing there later that night?"

"I have no idea."

"You would have me believe it had nothing to do with the list Sedgewick brought back from Vienna?"

"What list?"

"A list compiled by Fouché of people known to have passed information in the past to Napoléon—and who presumably might still be doing so."

Setting aside his glass, Jarvis drew from his pocket a gold snuffbox decorated with an intricate inlay of mother-of-pearl, flicked it open with his thumb, and held a pinch to one nostril. "I fear your informant—whoever they might be—is misinformed. There was no such list."

"You're certain?"

"Of course I'm certain. Sedgewick was sent to Vienna to bring back correspondence from an allied state."

"It must have been extraordinarily sensitive correspondence if the government didn't want it going through the usual channels."

"It was."

"Sensitive enough to get Sedgewick killed?"

"Perhaps—if he'd been killed before delivering it. But since he was not, I fail to see how it's relevant to your inquiry."

"Actually, I can think of several reasons to kill a courier after he has delivered his message—particularly one with a reputation for failing to guard his tongue. For instance, you could have had him killed because you didn't want whatever he told you to go further."

"Don't be ridiculous."

Sebastian studied his father-in-law's hooded gray eyes. "What if you're wrong? What if, unbeknownst to you, Sedgewick did somehow manage to get his hands on such a list? If he didn't deliver it to you, what might he have done with it?"

Jarvis closed his snuffbox with a snap and shrugged. "I suppose that would depend upon whose names were on the list."

"Meaning?"

"Sedgewick had expensive habits, and his wife's father was clever enough to tie up her money in ways that kept his son-in-law from getting his hands on most of it."

"You're suggesting he might have been tempted to sell the list to the highest bidder, or perhaps blackmail some of the people on it?"

"I'm saying it's possible."

Sebastian didn't believe a word of it, but he still felt a vague stirring of uneasiness. "Why are you being so bloody cooperative?"

Jarvis huffed a soft laugh. "You're suspicious because I'm cooperating with you?"

"Yes."

"Perhaps you caught me in a benevolent mood."

"No," said Sebastian, and turned toward the door.

"If you find this list you claim exists, I want it," said Jarvis. "Do you hear?"

But Sebastian simply kept walking.

Chapter 20

$\mathcal{S}$ebastian was crossing the palace's forecourt when he saw Hendon turning in through the ornamental colonnade that faced onto Pall Mall. The rain had stopped, but the pavements still glistened with wet; heavy gray clouds pressed low on the city, and the air was unseasonably cold for June.

"Ah, there you are," said Hendon, pausing to let Sebastian come up to him. "I'm told you were looking for me earlier."

"I was, yes. Do you have a moment? There's something you need to hear."

Hendon's face hardened. "If it's related to this latest murder investigation you've involved yourself in, I can't imagine what makes you think I'd be the least bit interested."

Sebastian swallowed the inevitable spurt of irritation. "You'll understand when you hear it. Shall we go for a walk along the Mall?"

❧

They walked beneath the parallel alleys of gnarled, leafy plane trees that stretched along the northern edge of St. James's Park, toward

Buckingham House. The Earl's face showed no expression when Sebastian told him about the list Sedgewick was said to have brought back from Vienna and the actress's name that was supposed to be on it. Hendon had long known that Kat once passed information to the French, and while it troubled him, he also understood what had motivated her. And he knew, too, that it had been years since she'd severed her contacts with Paris.

"But no one knows Kat is my natural daughter," he said when Sebastian had finished.

"Perhaps not. But you spend a fair amount of time in her company. Do you think people haven't noticed and drawn the inevitable conclusion?"

Hendon's eyes widened. "Good God. You're not suggesting people think she's my mistress!"

"Would you rather they knew she's your daughter?"

Hendon was silent for a moment, his jaw working back and forth in that way he had when he was thoughtful or troubled. As unseemly as it might be for a man in his seventies to take over his own son's former mistress, that assumption was better than people knowing the truth of his relationship with Kat and thus concluding that her longtime liaison with Sebastian had been incestuous.

"You don't know that the actress on this list is Kat," Hendon said at last.

"No. But can you think of any other current member of the cabinet who has a known close relationship to someone in the theater?"

Hendon sighed and shook his head. "No." He stared off across the grove of trees to the gleaming waters of the park's long canal. "You think Sedgewick's murder was linked to this list?"

"I honestly don't know. It's been suggested that Sedgewick might have been planning to use the list for blackmail, although I find that hard to believe. But it is possible he hadn't yet decided what to do with it. The thing is, even if the list wasn't the motive for his killing, it's conceivable that the murderer found the list by chance and has taken it himself to use for blackmail."

"Have you told Kat about this?"

Sebastian shook his head. "I tried, but she was in rehearsals. I'll go back to the theater again tonight." He hesitated, then said, "Has anyone contacted you?"

"Good Lord, no!"

It was said with enough shock and indignation that Sebastian believed him. "You will tell me if someone does?"

"*Bloody hell.* Next thing I know you'll be thinking I killed the bastard."

"No. But others might, if this gets out."

"Oh? And precisely why am I supposed to have shot off his face and castrated him?"

"Heard about that, did you?"

"It's all over town."

"Obviously."

"If you ask me," said Hendon, "that smacks of revenge—perhaps the work of a particularly vindictive woman whom Sedgewick had unwisely betrayed."

"Perhaps. But while I can see such a woman shooting him in the face and maybe even castrating him, Sedgewick was a tall, strong man, and I doubt a woman could have managed to drag his body down to the river and dump it there."

"She could if she enlisted someone's help," said Hendon. "Or the murder could be the work of a man who loved a woman Sedgewick had seduced and then betrayed."

Sebastian simply stared back at Hendon without saying anything. So far he'd found two men who fit that description, and both were friends with whom he'd fought and bled and shared all the horrors of war: Paul Gibson and Monty McPherson.

"I can see a jealous man being enraged enough to destroy his rival's handsome face and cut off his privates," said Hendon, following his own train of thought. "But what about that other body they fished out of the Thames a few days ago? The one with no head or hands."

"You heard about that, too?"

"You think people aren't talking about all this?" said Hendon grimly. "Most people assume the two murders are related; are you suggesting they are not?"

"I have no idea." Sebastian decided to keep all speculation about the mutilations' possible connection to the execution of suspected werewolves and witches to himself. "But it's a lot harder to chop off a body's head and hands than it is to simply shoot off his face and emasculate him."

Hendon grunted. "I can't see someone interested in this list you say Sedgewick was carrying doing anything like that."

"No. But one of the things that bothers me is the fact that Sedgewick was only wearing his shirt. The mutilation would explain the removal of his boots and breeches, and I suppose the killer could have used Sedgewick's cravat to tie something to the corpse's legs when he dumped it in the river. But I can think of only one reason for removing his coat and waistcoat."

Hendon stared at him blankly. "What?"

"If Sedgewick was carrying a secret list of names, he wouldn't simply have shoved it in one of his pockets. It's far more likely he brought it from Vienna sewn into the lining of his coat or waistcoat, and someone interested in the list would know that."

"Bloody hell," growled Hendon, swiping one hand across his lower face.

"Of course, it's also possible the damned list is safely at the bottom of the Thames right now."

Hendon looked at him. "What are the odds?"

Sebastian met the Earl's troubled gaze. "Frankly? Not good."

❧

After Hendon had turned back toward Carlton House, Sebastian went to stand beside the sullen gray waters of the long canal, his eyes narrowed and his hat pulled low against the gusting wind. It had been two days now since Miles Sedgewick's faceless body had been hauled up from the murky depths of the Thames, and so far the only suspects Sebastian had been able to turn up were two of his own friends and the man he called Father.

"I found 'er, gov'nor!" A boy's shout floated across the park, scaring up a flock of pigeons that took to the gray sky above in a whirl of wings. "I found yer governess!"

Sebastian turned as the boy skidded to a halt beside him, his feet sliding in the wet grass and one hand flying up to catch his hat. "I found 'er! 'Er name's Phoebe Cox, and she's takin' t' sellin' oranges in the Haymarket!"

Chapter 21

The woman was dangerously thin, her bones painfully obvious through the pale, nearly translucent flesh of her bare wrists and hands, her face gaunt and drawn with cold and hunger and the kind of fear that has become habitual.

Sebastian found her leaning against the worn sandstone column of a building across from the Haymarket theater, a clutch of oranges cradled in her worn shawl, her shoulders slumped and her head bowed. She was dressed in a dirty, torn brown dress and broken shoes, and he thought at first that Tom must be mistaken, that this could not possibly be a woman educated and cultured enough to have served as governess to the grandchildren of a marquis. But then she stirred at his approach and stepped forward to say, "Oranges for sale. Fresh oranges, sir," and her flawless, precise diction gave her away.

"Miss Phoebe Cox?" said Sebastian, walking up to her.

He saw the horror that flared in her eyes, saw the shame that contorted her features as she shook her head. "I'm sorry, I don't know who you're looking for, but you've made a mistake."

She must have been pretty once, he thought, before months of starvation, ill health, and desperation wore her down. She had her lifeless dark hair pulled back in a way that emphasized the thinness of her face, and she'd obviously pawned whatever decent clothes she'd possessed.

"I simply want to talk to you," he said as she began backing away from him. "I'll buy all your oranges, and get you a cup of tea and some dinner, too, if you'd like. You only need to talk to me for a few minutes."

That stopped her, hunger, longing, and need warring with caution in her haunted gray eyes. Then she shook her head, her chin coming up. "I don't do that. I may be on the streets, but I don't go with gentlemen."

Not yet.

"All I want is to talk," he said again, wishing he'd thought to have Hero approach the woman instead; this was the sort of thing Hero did all the time. He nodded to a nearby coffeehouse, its paned front windows gleaming with a golden, welcoming warmth with the approach of evening. "We can sit in there."

Alarm flared anew in her eyes. "They have back rooms they rent out in that place. I know what they're for."

He cursed silently to himself, wondering how in the hell Hero did this. He decided to change tactics. "How long were you with the Sedgewicks?"

The question surprised her so much that she answered him. "Four years. Why do you ask?"

"You've heard that Miles Sedgewick is dead?"

Something he couldn't quite decipher shifted behind her eyes and she looked away. "I heard."

"I'm looking into his death, and I thought you might be able to help me."

She sniffed in disbelief. "You don't look like a Bow Street Runner. You don't sound like one, either."

"That's because I'm not a Bow Street Runner. The name is Devlin, and I promise you, I only want to talk to you. If you prefer, we can buy something from a street vendor and you can eat it sitting on the steps here while we talk." He paused, then said, "Please?"

The lure of warm food and drink overcame her fear and suspicion. He stood with his shoulder propped against one of the old stone columns while she sat on the steps and wolfed down massive quantities of sausages and bread and butter.

"Where are you from?" he asked while she ate.

"Lincolnshire," she said without looking up from her meal. "My father was the vicar in a small village there."

"Would you go back there, if you could?"

She paused, her head coming up as a look of painful longing suffused her face. Then she swallowed and shook her head. "They're dead now—my mother and father both. I have a sister—she married the local squire. But when I wrote her after I was dismissed, asking her for help, she said I'd made my own bed and must lie on it."

"I'm sorry," said Sebastian. "When exactly were you dismissed?"

Her gaze dropped to her food again, although she made no move to resume eating. "They turned me off last February. Or rather, *she* did. But Mr. Sedgewick didn't do anything to stop her. Afterward, I went to him for help—*begged* him to help me, or if he didn't care what happened to me, to at least think of his child. But he just turned away."

Sebastian sucked in his breath in a quiet hiss. "You were carrying his child?"

She nodded, her cheeks flaming with shame. "I hid it as long as I could. But then one day I fainted in the front hall, and one of the maidservants who'd guessed the truth let it slip."

"And that's when Mrs. Sedgewick dismissed you?"

She nodded again. "I begged her not to turn me out without a character—told her I had no place to go. But she said I should have thought of that before I got myself in trouble." Her voice cracked. "I was desperate, and she didn't care. She was *smiling*. It was as if she liked the idea of me suffering."

"Did she know Miles was the father of your baby?"

Her face hardened. "Oh, she knew. I told her. She called me a wicked liar, but she knew. She knew what he was like far better than I did. It's why she hated him."

"She hated him?"

Phoebe Cox chewed a mouthful of sausage and nodded. "I heard her tell her friend once that in a perfect world, Miles would just die and make everyone happy."

"What friend was this?"

"The Reverend Sinclair Palmer. He's the rector up in Marylebone." She huffed a soft, scornful breath. "A reverend. But that didn't stop him from lusting after another man's wife any more than it stopped her from encouraging him."

"Do you think they were lovers?"

"Truthfully? I don't know. But I heard him begging her to run off with him once. They were in the garden and didn't know I could hear."

"What did she say?"

"She told him she couldn't leave her children. That's when she said Miles should die and make everyone happy."

Sebastian watched as an overloaded cart made its laborious way up the crowded street. "When was the last time you saw Sedgewick?"

The fear was back in her eyes, and she glanced away again. "I haven't seen him since that time I told you about, when I went up to him in the street and begged him to help me after his wife turned me off."

"What did he say?"

She colored again, but this time Sebastian thought it was with rage as much as with shame. "He said I should have thought of the consequences before I spread my legs for every man who smiled at me. But it's not true! I never lay with anyone but him."

"How is your baby?" Sebastian asked softly.

Phoebe Cox brought up a shaky hand to press her fingertips to her trembling lips, her voice breaking on a sob. "She's dead. Her name was Amelia, and she was the sweetest, most beautiful little thing imaginable. But my milk dried up because I don't get enough to eat, and I couldn't find anything to feed her that she could keep down. So she died."

"I'm sorry." Sebastian watched as silent tears welled up in her eyes to roll down her dirty cheeks, and handed her his handkerchief. "You say you were with the Sedgewicks for four years?"

She clutched his handkerchief in her fist and nodded.

"Can you think of anyone who might have wanted to see him dead? Besides his wife and her friend the Reverend, I mean."

She thought about it a moment, then shook her head. "No. But I'm not surprised someone killed him. He could be so charming, so gay and *fun*. I'd never met anyone quite like him. But there was another side to him, too, although it took me a long time to see it. It's as if he were two different people, one lighthearted and cheerful, and the other quick-tempered, mean, and ugly. Afterward—after I realized what he was really like—I thought he was like Count Bacova. You know the character in Maria Carlisle's novel, *Bacova's Castle*?"

"Sorry, no; I haven't read it. Who exactly is he?"

"Count Bacova? He's a Hungarian nobleman known throughout the land for his kindness and generosity. But behind it all, he hides a terrible secret."

"What's his secret?" said Sebastian, although he had a nasty suspicion he knew exactly where this was going.

"He's a werewolf. Don't get me wrong," she added hastily. "I don't mean to imply that Mr. Sedgewick was a werewolf. It's only that he had these two sides to his character, and he could change from one to the other so quickly. I've often wondered if the tales of werewolves might have originated from that—the way some people seem to have two natures, one they normally show the world and another, darker side that they try to keep hidden." She paused, her eyes pleading, as if desperate for understanding, as she looked up at him. "Do you know what I mean?"

"Yes," said Sebastian. "I do."

Chapter 22

*A*fter Phoebe Cox finished eating, Sebastian managed with some difficulty to convince her to let him give her ten pounds. She still didn't trust him, still couldn't believe he didn't intend to exploit her in some way. But she was desperate, and in the end need overcame doubt. He then headed east, pushing his way through the gathering evening crowds of prostitutes and young bucks on the strut, to Covent Garden Theatre.

Stepping inside the theater's soaring marble-clad foyer, he breathed in the familiar scents of orange peel, greasepaint, and sawdust and found himself pausing for a moment. The sounds and smells of a working theater always sent him hurtling back in time, to the days when he'd been newly down from Oxford, young and idealistic and so very much in love.

The liaison between his heir and a beautiful young Irish actress had naturally alarmed Sebastian's father—or rather, the man he'd thought was his father. But in his youth and naive confidence, Sebastian hadn't cared. He'd asked Kat to become his wife, and she'd said yes. In a rage, Hendon promised to cut him off without a penny and make "damned sure" he didn't inherit anything that wasn't entailed. But Sebastian had simply laughed, and Kat had sworn she didn't care . . . until the day she told him she did care, that she'd changed her mind and decided she didn't want to marry him after all. That's when he'd bought himself a pair of colors and gone off to war.

He hadn't exactly been looking to get himself killed. But he'd thrown himself into battle with a recklessness that could easily have had that result. He didn't learn the truth of what had actually passed between Kat and Hendon for seven long years. And by then it had been too late.

He had no regrets. In the years since then he'd found a joy and love with Hero that he hadn't believed possible, while his friendship with Kat had gradually shifted into the kind of easy affection that exists between a brother and sister—which is what they'd once mistakenly believed themselves to be. But the mingling scents of greasepaint, sawdust, and orange peel still had the power to fill him with a piercing kind of sadness for the lost innocence of those halcyon days.

Pushing aside the memories, he worked his way backstage to find Kat in her dressing room, still struggling into her costume. Her gaze met his in the mirror, and she smiled.

"Wonderful timing," she said. "Make yourself useful and finish doing this thing up, will you? I know why you're here, by the way."

He set to work fumbling with her tapes and hooks. "I take it you've seen Hendon?"

"Are you surprised?"

"No. But you don't seem particularly alarmed by what I assume he had to tell you."

"About my name being on this list Miles Sedgewick is supposed to have brought back from Vienna?" She turned to face him as he did up the last of her fastenings. "You think I should be? Jarvis already knows what I used to do."

"Except it's not Jarvis who has the list—or so he says, and in this, at least, I'm inclined to believe him."

"Perhaps. But a list of names is meaningless without any sort of proof—unless of course one is willing to simply set about cold-bloodedly eliminating everyone on it. And while I wouldn't put that past Jarvis, he knows better than to try to move against me. We have each other in check, remember?"

Sebastian searched her beautiful, familiar features—the exotic tilted eyes, the childlike nose, the wide, sensual mouth. She was an actress and a good one, but he had a feeling she was more worried than she was trying to let on. "What other names are likely to be on such a list?"

"You know I can't tell you that. Besides . . ." She turned away again to pick up the brush from her dressing table. "I've been out of all that for years. I might know the names of some of the older players, but not the newer ones."

"What can you tell me about the Wilde Sisters?"

She drew the brush through her cascading waves of auburn hair, silent for a moment, as if choosing what to say. "Well, to begin with, they're not actually sisters."

"That doesn't surprise me." He watched as she set the brush aside and began weaving a green velvet ribbon through her hair. "I've heard that Sibil Wilde used to be the mistress of the Count d'Artois. Is that true?"

"It is, yes. He had her in keeping for years, until some crazed admirer went at her with his knife. The attack ruined her voice and left her face badly scarred. That's when she left the theater. She disappeared for a time, then I heard she'd set up shop in St. Giles with two other women. She was most famous for her work in the Scottish Play, so I suppose it's inevitable that people took to calling them the Weird Sisters."

He smiled. "Please tell me you don't believe that old superstition. You're not even onstage and you still won't say M—"

She moved quickly to press her fingers against his lips. "Don't. Don't say it."

"All right, I won't."

She turned away to finish tying off her ribbon, her gaze meeting his in the mirror. "Why do you ask?"

"Her name came up in relation to Sedgewick. And then when I paid her a visit last night, someone with a French accent and an overgrown henchman in tow jumped me in an alley and threatened me with all manner of calamities if I didn't quit asking questions."

She turned to face him, her arms falling back to her sides.

"What?" he asked, studying her suddenly solemn face. "What is it?"

"I've been told—don't ask by whom—that after the attack ruined her face and voice, Artois set her up as the Bourbons' London spymaster."

"How reliable is this unidentified source?"

"Very. Sibil gathers much of her information the way all cartomancers do, by adroitly pumping her customers for clues and bribing their servants or paying people to listen to their gossip in the markets. And she supplies women to gentlemen in sensitive positions and gets information that way. But I've heard she also works with one of Artois's assassins—although I understand she doesn't really *control* him, exactly."

Sebastian felt his mouth go dry. Just under a year ago, a man working to help Sebastian find his mother had been fished out of the Thames with a garrote around his neck. Sebastian had always suspected the murder was the work of one of the Bourbons' assassins, but he hadn't been able to prove it and hadn't even come close to identifying the assassin. "What do you know about him? The assassin, I mean."

"Not a great deal. As far as I can tell, no one knows much of anything about him. They call him Gabriel, but that's probably not his real name."

"Does he use a garrote or a dagger?"

"As I understand it, he's fond of both," said Kat.

"Lovely."

He saw a waft of fear wash over her features before she could control it. She said, "You think that's who killed Sedgewick? The Bourbons? To get their hands on this list?"

"Perhaps. Although it seems a bit excessive to kill him for it, let alone mutilate him. And none of this explains the headless man who was also pulled from the Thames a couple of days ago."

She shook her head. "I can't see Gabriel—or any other assassin working for the Bourbons—bothering to take the time to mutilate his victims."

"Not if his purpose is merely to eliminate them. But if his masters are intent on spreading fear or sending a message? Perhaps."

"A message to whom?"

Sebastian met her troubled gaze. "I can't begin to imagine."

❧

After Devlin had gone, Kat sank onto the stool before her dressing table, the candles in the small room flickering in a draft, her gaze on her reflection in the mirror.

It was never going to go away, she realized with a sinking kind of despair. This danger of being caught out, of being exposed and made to pay for what she'd once done.

At the time, she hadn't cared; a part of her had even found the danger exciting. And when she did know fear, it had still been a price she'd been willing to pay for the country she loved. She'd long ago made a vow that while she might feel fear, she would never allow it to control her life, and for many years she'd managed to keep that vow. But now the heady excitement and hopes of those days were both gone—the days when she'd thought that a French victory could lead to a free Ireland. But the fear—ah, the fear was still with her.

Maybe I'm getting old, she thought, leaning forward to study her reflection closer, looking for signs of telltale lines. But all she saw was a haunted, pale woman who stared back at her with wide, frightened eyes.

She'd spoken the truth when she told Devlin that most of the names on such a list would be unknown to her. But she had no doubt that she knew some of them—or at least one of them.

And that green-eyed, dimpled Irishman needed to be warned.

Quickly.

Chapter 23

That night, Sebastian dreamt of Paris. But the Paris of his dream was not the war-damaged, dismal city of today; it was the Paris he'd visited once as a child, when his mother was still alive, before revolution and the forces that sought to stop it had torn both the city and their entire world apart. In his dream, the sun shone warm and golden, the sky was a balmy blue, the gilded carriages of an age-old aristocracy the stuff of fairy tales as they whisked their privileged, powdered, and patched occupants from the grand mirrored halls of Versailles to the marble steps of the Comédie-Française.

Even as a child he'd been aware of the stark contrast between the extravagances of obscene wealth he could see around him juxtaposed with the unimaginable depths of poverty and despair of which he caught only glimpses. But those harbingers of the horrors to come did not intrude upon his dream. In his dream, a blossom-scented breeze played gently through the limbs of the leafy chestnuts along the Seine to cast a shifting pattern of dappled shadows across the sun-sparkled water. It was there, by the banks of the river, that he saw his mother, the sun warm on her golden hair, her lips parting in a smile as she watched a white swan shepherd her downy hatchlings across the grass toward the water. Then she turned toward Sebastian. And even though a part of him knew it for a dream, he felt a wild up-surge of joy at seeing her again, so young and carefree and alive. Her eyes gentle with love, the smile still curling her lips, she reached for him. Except when she touched his cheek, her hand turned blue and icy with death, and he awoke with a start, his breath rasping in his throat and his chest jerking as he stared through the darkness at the familiar satin of the bed hangings above.

He sat up, the cold of the night air biting the bare flesh of his chest and arms, for the fire had died down to mere glowing embers on the hearth. He went to feed it, then stood for a time watching the flames lick at the new fuel.

The people who killed Sebastian's mother had been French. Their motives and which of France's multiple murderous political and dynastic factions they identified with had seemed important at one time. But he'd eventually come to understand that it wasn't, that anything they might have once believed in had long ago been adul-terated or destroyed by twenty-five years of bloody internecine con-flict and the desperate struggle to survive it. All that mattered in the end was the shaft of cold steel they'd buried in his mother's back be-fore lifting her up over the worn stone parapet of an ancient Parisian bridge to send her hurtling toward the wasteland below.

She would have been conscious through it all, and Sebastian sometimes found himself re-creating in his mind what her last mo-ments must have been like. The mist cold against her upturned face; the sight of the cloud-churned night sky above; the silver sheen of lamplight glinting on the wind-ruffled black waters of the Seine as the ground rushed up to meet her. The breath-stealing thud of im-pact and the shrieking agony of splintering bones.

How long had she lain there in the darkness, alone and in pain and struggling to breathe as she felt her life's blood ebbing away? Had she been afraid when she heard the sound of approaching footsteps, only to turn her head and see the face of her last surviving son wavering above her? Had she known he was really there? he wondered. Or had she taken him for a mere figment of her imagination, conjured up by some alchemy of impending death to comfort her as she began her long journey into whatever lay beyond? And he wondered, *had* his presence comforted her? Or had he simply reminded her, painfully, of the choices she'd made, of the beloved people, places, and things she'd left behind long ago? Of the years he had lived without her in his life and of all that she had missed?

He heard the rustle of the bedclothes behind him as Hero came to slip an arm around his side and press her body close to his. He wondered if she knew where his dreams had taken him, because for a moment she simply held him, lending him the comfort of her love and presence. Then she said, "You're thinking it's them, aren't you? The French, I mean. Either Napoléon or the Bourbons?"

"It's certainly a very strong possibility, isn't it?" He turned to draw her into his arms and hold her closer. "But at the same time, I can't help but wonder if perhaps I'm coming at this all wrong. What if both murders were completely random—the work of some madman who has nothing at all to do with spies or assassins or one of the women Sedgewick seduced and destroyed?"

"Do you really believe that?"

"No. But I do think there's a tendency for the human mind to organize life into neat patterns even when none actually exist. And that means I can't discount it as a possibility." He held her in silence for a moment, his hand running up and down the strong curve of her back. "What if the killer stripped and mutilated his victims and hid their identities as a way to torment the men's loved ones even more? Since he didn't remove Sedgewick's shirt, the killer probably didn't even realize there were distinctive scars on his body that someone might recognize. So when he killed again, he tried to make certain that wouldn't happen."

"By stripping his next victim completely and then cutting off his head and hands, you mean?"

"It worked, didn't it? No one knows who the man is."

"Yes. Except why hasn't this second victim been reported missing?"

"That's the part that doesn't fit either scenario—either the one with a sick, random killer or the one in which the second killing is linked to the first by something we don't understand because we don't know who he is."

Hero pressed her forehead to his, her warm breath mingling with his. She said, "I keep coming back to the fact that Sedgewick told Isabella about Fouché's list—but he didn't tell anyone else. What if someone in the government—or one of our allies—thought he might sell or somehow betray the contents of the official correspondence he'd been dispatched to bring back?"

He met her troubled gaze. "Someone like Jarvis, you mean?"

"Well, I can't see either Castlereagh or Bathurst ordering one of their own men killed. But I wouldn't put it past Jarvis."

"Neither would I," Sebastian admitted. "Although if that were true, I wouldn't have expected him to admit so freely that he didn't trust Sedgewick's discretion."

"There is that," she said with a wry smile. "In which case, if this isn't simply the work of either a cuckolded husband or a madman, that leaves our dear allies the Bourbons."

"Or their enemy, Napoléon," he reminded her.

Or someone with a reason to worry about the names on that list. Someone like Kat Boleyn or Hendon. Neither of them said it, but the reality of it hovered in the air between them.

He said, "I think I need to have another conversation with the Weird Sisters."

"Oh, Lord. In the daylight this time, please?"

He laughed softly and kissed her warm, soft mouth. "If you think it will help."

Chapter 24

Friday, 16 June

*P*aul Gibson stood in the midst of Alexi's garden, his arms spread wide at his sides. It was the hour just before dawn, the vast city around him still quiet with sleep, the air cool against his hot face.

He smiled, feeling the warmth and relaxation spreading slowly through his body. It was like a balmy breeze on a sunny day or the rush of euphoric peace that comes in the moments after a man has pleasured a woman. It was heaven on earth.

He tipped back his head, eyes blinking at the universe of stars that whirled hazily above as he let himself sink deeper and deeper into that peaceful, pain-free place that beckoned like a calm refuge. He heard a door open behind him, but it only registered on the periphery of his consciousness, so that Alexi's voice came to him as if from out of a dream.

"You never finished the last autopsy, did you?"

He turned toward her, moving slowly, as if he were under warm water. "I can do it today."

"That's what you said yesterday."

He licked his dry lips and gave a faint shake of his head. A part of him knew he should worry. Worry about the work that lay unfinished, worry about Alexi leaving him, worry about the looming menace of the investigation into Sedgewick's death that threatened them both. But why worry? Everything was going to be all right.

For a moment he was aware of a distant, roaring fear that it wasn't going to be all right, that he and Alexi were both in grave danger. But then the fear receded beneath another wave of warmth and the stars above disappeared from sight.

٭

The sun rose on a cloudy day, with a fetid, oppressive atmosphere that seemed to press down on the rain-soaked city, the air heavy with the fecund odors of damp coal smoke, manure, and old, dank stone.

In the early-morning light, the narrow, wretched streets of St. Giles were populated mainly by ragged costermongers and an assortment of scavengers picking through the refuse left from the previous night. Pushing open the door to the Weird Sisters' shop in Seven Dials, Sebastian found an unknown woman behind the counter, her head bowed as she read the newspaper she had spread open there. She was younger than the woman he'd seen here before, tall and slender, with rich tawny skin, an elegant long neck, and a thick mass of tight dark curls that cascaded around her shoulders.

"You must be Rowena," he said, closing the warped door behind him.

She straightened slowly, her face unreadable. "Ah, it's his lordship, back again. Sibil told us about you."

"She did? What did she tell you?"

"I told them you're trouble," said Sibil Wilde, coming through the low doorway at the back of the room. Today she wore a Tudor-style gown of a rich green silk, with fitted sleeves and a kirtle bodice with a square neckline edged in petite white lace.

His gaze met hers. "Am I? Why?"

"You know why."

He gave a faint shake of his head. "I saw you at Drury Lane once; you were playing Ophelia. It was an amazing performance. I've never forgotten it."

She frowned. "How old were you?"

"Twenty-one."

"Huh. That was a long time ago." She glanced tellingly at Rowena, then said to him, "Follow me."

She led him to the same small, opulently furnished room he'd seen before, although this time the cloth on the round table was gold and a deck of cards already rested before the tall chair facing the door.

He walked around the table to pick up the cards and fan them open in his hands. It was a Marseilles deck, an Italian version of the tarot that had been popular in France for hundreds of years. "It's an interesting occupation for a woman with your talents—reading cards and studying natal charts, I mean."

Her nostrils flared on a quick intake of air. "I am very good at what I do. Or were you referring to my acting talents? What precisely would you have had me do after someone did this to me?" One hand flashed up to touch her scarred face. "Hmm? Dwindle into some pitiful wardrobe mistress, condemned to stand in the shadows and watch while other women play the roles I once loved? Or perhaps become a madam, finding protectors for the young women who have no real hope of ever succeeding on the boards?"

"Actually, I hear you do that, too."

That obviously surprised her. But then she huffed a soft laugh and twitched one shoulder in a shrug. "Men have appetites. I help them find the women to fill them."

"Is that why Sedgewick came here?"

"Hardly. From what I hear, he had more than enough success filling his own appetites. I told you before: He came for the readings."

He closed the deck of cards, then cut it in two. "So he believed in the cards?"

She watched him shuffle the deck. "I don't know if he believed in them, or if he was simply fascinated by the process. Does it matter?"

Sebastian cut the deck again, then turned over the first card. It was the nine of swords. "I was attacked by two men after I left here the other night. One of them was obviously French-born; the other didn't speak, but he could make a good living exhibiting himself at the local fairs as a giant. You wouldn't happen to be familiar with them, would you?"

"I did tell you it's a rough neighborhood."

"You did. Except the men who attacked me weren't after my purse; they were delivering a message—a warning, actually—to stop asking questions."

"A warning you don't appear to be heeding."

He turned over the next card: the four of cups.

She said, "Are you accusing me of sending them after you?"

"The possibility did cross my mind."

"If I had a message for you, I could have delivered it myself."

"Perhaps." He turned over the eight of swords. "I hear you collect information to send to Artois. That you were once his lover and you still work for him."

"Now, where did you hear that?"

Sebastian's eyes narrowed in a slight smile. "The implication was that your interest in Sedgewick—or should I say *Artois's* interest?—might have led to his death."

"You've surely discovered by now how Sedgewick amused himself when he wasn't wooing his friends' wives into his bed. Everyone from the Prince Regent and Lord Jarvis to their minions in Downing Street wants to see the Bourbons restored in Paris; why would Artois harm someone who was working with them toward that end?"

Sebastian turned over another card: the two of swords. "I don't know. If I had it figured out, I wouldn't be here."

She didn't smile. "Perhaps you should be directing your inquiries toward one of Napoléon's creatures in London."

"Now, there's an interesting idea. Do you have any names to suggest?"

"Me? I only tell fortunes."

"Of course." He laid one last card on top of the others, only facedown this time, then set the deck on the table and turned toward the door.

"Did they ever discover the identity of the man found without a head?" she asked, stopping him.

He paused to look back at her. "Not to my knowledge."

"Suggestive, don't you think?"

"Is it? Do you have any idea who he might be? Perhaps you could try reading his cards. It might tell you something."

"Not really. We already know how his story ends." Reaching out, she turned over Sebastian's last card. It was the ten of swords. She stared at it a moment, then looked up. "Who were you reading for?"

"No one. I was simply turning over cards."

She gave a faint shake of her head. "You had a question in your mind. The cards knew, even if you did not."

Chapter 25

I was wonderin' when ye'd be gettin' back," said Tom when Sebastian walked through the slowly awakening streets of St. Giles to where he'd left his tiger with the curricle on Long Acre.

Sebastian leapt up to gather his reins, then glanced back at the boy. "Never tell me you were concerned?"

The tiger pursed his lips and looked away to where a baker's lad was leaning against the wall of a carriage maker's, his load of hot buns tilting dangerously as he worked to shorten the strap holding the tray around his neck. "I was jist . . . wonderin'."

"Huh," said Sebastian.

He drove next to Paul Gibson's surgery on Tower Hill, hoping to learn the results of the final autopsy on the headless, handless corpse dragged from the Thames. But he arrived to find the surgery locked, and his knock on the house's unlatched front door was met with only silence.

He pushed on the door, the unoiled hinges giving a faint *creak* as the ancient wooden panels swung inward a few inches, then stopped. "Gibson? Anyone here? Madame Sauvage?"

Silence.

Sebastian pushed the door open wider. "Gibson?"

His own voice echoed back to him.

His hand tightening on his sword stick, he stepped inside, his footsteps light on the stone-flagged passage that led to the back of the old house. At the low doorway to the parlor he stopped, his hand clenching again on his sword stick.

Although it was not cold, a fire had been kindled on the hearth. Dressed only in his breeches and a rumpled shirt that hung open at the neck, Gibson half sat, half lay in one of the worn armchairs beside it, his gray-threaded dark hair plastered to his head with sweat, his chin sunk to his chest as he stared blankly at the flames before him. His face was gaunt and unshaven, his eyes bloodshot, his skin a sickly grayish yellow.

"You look like hell," said Sebastian, pausing in the doorway.

The Irishman looked up, his pupils so tiny as to be nearly nonexistent. "Devlin?" He struggled to push himself up straighter. "Come in. Have a seat. Pour yourself a brandy." He turned his head, his eyes narrowing as he searched the room. "There must be some around here somewhere."

Sebastian stayed where he was. "Did you ever finish the autopsy on the headless man?"

Gibson shook his head from side to side, the features of his face slack, his eyes unfocused. "No. But Alexi did."

"Where is she now?"

"In her garden. She . . ." He paused to draw a deep, shaky breath. "She doesn't like it when I get like this."

So why do you do it? Sebastian wanted to say. He wanted to grab his friend by the shirtfront, haul him up out of his chair, shake him

and shout at him and find a way, somehow, to stop him from destroying himself like this. Instead, he turned on his heel and walked out of
the house into the windblown morning. The high white clouds were
breaking up, allowing fitful gleams of sunshine to chase one another
across the dew-glistened beds of roses and honeysuckle and herbs.
Alexi Sauvage knelt in a bed of mint near the closed door to the stone
outbuilding. She was wearing an old gray gown with a broad-
brimmed straw hat tied under her chin by a fading blue ribbon to
keep the wind from taking it off, and had her hands deep in the dirt,
pulling weeds. She looked up when he paused on the stoop, then settled back on her heels, one hand coming up to shove a stray lock of
hair from her eyes with the back of her curled wrist.

"You saw him?" she said as he came up to her.

He was aware of the anger and frustration thrumming through
him, along with a sense of helplessness that he didn't quite know
how to handle. "You told me once that there's something you can do
that might rid him of his phantom pains so that he can get off that
bloody opium. Why haven't you done it?"

"Why?" Her hand flashed toward the house in a quick, angry
gesture. "Why don't you ask him why he refuses to let me even try
to help him?"

Sebastian looked away, toward the high wall at the base of the
yard and the simple stone grotto she had erected for the bones she
was collecting from this ground. He blew out a long, painful breath.
"I'm sorry; I shouldn't have said what I did."

He saw a glitter of what might have been unshed tears in her
eyes. But she simply nodded, swallowed hard, and went back to her
weeding.

He said, "Gibson tells me you finished the autopsy on the headless man."

She kept her attention on her task. "I did, yes."

"Did you find anything? Anything at all that might help identify him?"

"Not really. He was a Caucasian male much closer to forty than
fifty. At one time he'd led a more active life, but of late his days had
been filled with little physical exertion beyond enjoying his dinner
and a good bottle of brandy. But we already knew that, didn't we?"

"Any idea how he died?"

"No. He was healthy, and there's no sign of any wound on the
part of him that we have. Which means he could have been shot in
the face, bashed in the head, or . . ." She paused.

"Or what?"

"Or decapitated while still alive."

Jesus, thought Sebastian. "No scars anywhere on his body?"

"No. No scars, no birthmarks, no noticeable moles."

"I wonder what his hands might have revealed."

She looked up. "You think that's why the hands were cut off?
Because they could have helped identify him?"

"I can't come up with any other reason." *Beyond the history of what
we used to do to people after we tortured them into saying they were witches or
werewolves,* he thought, but he kept that to himself. "Can you?"

Her gaze drifted away, to a sprawling, ancient rosebush awash in
fist-sized, gloriously scented pink blooms, but he did not think she
was really seeing it. "The hands are a particularly human part of our
bodies, are they not? They're like the face and the eyes. Students of
anatomy frequently find dissecting them . . . disturbing."

"Yet this killer had no problem at all chopping them off."

"Perhaps the victim—whoever he was—used his hands to do
something that enraged his killer. A man uses his hands for many
things, yes? To steal. To wound or kill. To touch a woman."

It was an explanation that hadn't occurred to Sebastian, one that
might conceivably provide a link between Miles Sedgewick and this

unidentified victim—if only they knew who the hell the man was. And he felt it again, that upswelling of frustration and anger that was as useless as it was corrosive.

He glanced back toward the house. "When will Gibson be . . . better?"

"Tomorrow, perhaps."

"He's going to kill himself if he keeps this up much longer."

"Yes."

Sebastian brought his gaze back to the Frenchwoman beside him. "What can I do?"

"Help him find the courage to do what he must do—or at least try."

"How?"

But she simply stared up at him, her face pale and solemn, her eyes defiantly dry.

❧

That morning, Hero had arranged to interview a wherryman who worked Puddle Dock, just below Blackfriars Bridge. But when her carriage turned onto New Bridge Street, they found the way to the wharves blocked by a pushing, shouting crowd of fishermen and bargemen mingled with everything from costermongers and shopkeepers to beggars and crossing sweepers. The air was filled with excited voices and the barking of dogs.

Putting down her window, Hero stared out over the churning sea of bobbing hats and bonnets, but she couldn't begin to see what had attracted the mass of people. "What is it?" she called up to her coachman.

He shook his head. "I can't tell, my lady."

"I'll get down here."

His face went slack. "But, my lady!"

She gathered her skirts. "You heard me."

She waited while her footman let down the carriage steps, then descended to the pavement. A half-grown leatherworker's apprentice went to dart around her, but she reached out to snag his arm, swinging him around to face her.

"What is it?" she asked. "What has happened?"

Tall and skinny, the lad looked to be perhaps thirteen or fourteen, with sandy hair and a sunburned nose and a pronounced overbite. "They done found a man's body lodged up against one o' the piers o' the bridge!" he said, his thin chest jerking with his labored breathing. "And he's missin' his head, jist like that fellow they found down by the Isle o' Dogs a few days ago!"

"Only his head?"

"No," said the boy, his gray eyes wide with a combination of horror and excitement. "He ain't got a head *or* feet!"

Chapter 26

Sebastian arrived at the wharves below Blackfriars Bridge to find Hero's yellow-bodied carriage drawn up outside a neat redbrick eighteenth-century inn with white-painted double-hung windows. The door to the carriage stood open, and she was sitting inside drinking a cup of tea while scribbling in the black notebook she held balanced on one knee.

"Ah, there you are," she said, looking up. She was wearing one of the walking dresses she typically wore for her interviews, the color a soft silver that seemed to bring out the sooty sparks in her gray eyes; a tall, shako-inspired hat of the same midnight blue as the beading at the neck of her gown rested on the seat beside her.

"Have you seen him?" asked Sebastian, hopping up to take the seat facing her.

She finished her tea and handed the empty cup down to the inn's boy. "If you mean the latest mutilated corpse, no, I have not. The River Police aren't letting anyone near the wharf. But I have spoken to the two wherrymen who pulled the body ashore."

"And?"

"They confirmed what the leatherworker's apprentice told me."

"No head or feet?"

"To quote one of the wherrymen, 'Nuttin' but two bloody stumps an' a raw neck lookin' like somethin' ye'd see in a butcher's shop.'" She set aside her notebook and pencil. "But here's the strange thing: they said he's still wearing his clothes—or at least his shirt and pantaloons."

Sebastian drew a deep breath that smelled of the river and the climbing roses trained around the inn's doorway. "I don't understand any of this."

"Perhaps that's because you're trying to make sense of it, and there is no sense. Whoever is doing this is simply mad."

He shook his head, although he couldn't have said precisely what he was denying—that the killer was mad or that the killings were senseless and therefore unfathomable.

She said, "The body was lodged against the bridge's third pier when they found him. The younger wherryman told me he thought it had been in the water a couple of hours, but his uncle said no, it was probably more like twenty-four."

"How old is the uncle?"

"Forty-five, perhaps. The nephew is in the second year of his apprenticeship."

"Given the number of bodies he has no doubt pulled from the river over the course of his career, I think I'm inclined to believe the uncle." Sebastian stared out the carriage window at the crowds still milling around in the street. "Somehow I suspect the River Police aren't going to let me anywhere near the wharf, either."

"Probably not," said Hero, nodding to where a small man in spectacles with a high-pitched, squeaky voice could be seen determinedly working his way through the throng. "But I've no doubt Sir Henry will."

❧

"Lord Devlin," said Lovejoy when Sebastian threaded his way to him through the pushing, shoving mass of curious onlookers being held back from the wharf by the River Police. "How fortuitous. I hadn't expected the lad I sent to find you so quickly."

"He didn't," said Sebastian as the River Police stepped back to let them through to the wharf. "Lady Devlin was on her way to an interview when she came upon the disturbance, and sent me word."

"Good heavens. I trust her ladyship was not unduly alarmed by the spectacle?"

"She's fine, thank you."

Lovejoy cleared his throat. "Yes, well . . . Her ladyship is a truly remarkable woman." He drew up at the base of the steps that led down to the old wharf, his gaze fixed on the silent, formless lump that lay halfway down the stretch of weathered gray planks, the wind off the water flapping the corners of the worn canvas tarp that had been thrown over it like a shroud. "Have you seen him?"

"Not yet."

The magistrate nodded to one of the constables as they climbed down the stairs. "Let's see what we have here, shall we?"

Reaching down, the constable flipped back the tarp to reveal the headless body of a man dressed only in a waterlogged shirt and a fine pair of pantaloons; his legs ended at his ankles.

"Merciful heavens," whispered Lovejoy, groping for his handkerchief.

Sebastian found himself having to draw a deep breath, and then another. Once, his life had been filled with the mutilated remains of men strewn across more battlefields than he could remember. Sometimes they still came to him in his dreams, men missing arms and legs and jaws, the sides of faces, the tops of their heads. Men with bodies so shredded by cannon fire and grapeshot as to be nearly unrecognizable as human. He should have been used to it, should have long ago become inured to the sights and smells of carnage. Instead he found he had to look away from what was left of this unknown killer's latest victim. He was suddenly aware of the wind off the river ruffling the hair at the base of his neck in a way that sent a chill down his spine as he stared out over the choppy, sun-dazzled water.

"This one looks younger than the last," said Lovejoy, his hands braced on his knees as he leaned over.

Sebastian forced himself to look again at the headless corpse before them. Lovejoy was right; this man was obviously much younger than the previous headless corpse. Younger and leaner, his wet linen shirt clinging to the clearly defined muscles of his arms and chest. But it was the exquisite cut of his trousers that caught Sebastian's attention.

"We may be in luck," he said, hunkering down beside the dead man. "Whatever Bond Street tailor made these pantaloons will surely recognize his own work."

Lovejoy straightened, his troubled gaze meeting Sebastian's. "So why did the killer leave them?"

"Perhaps he wants us to know who this one is?"

"Then why take the head and feet?"

But Sebastian could only shake his head, the silence filling with the slap of the river against the wharf's pilings and the plaintive cries of the seagulls wheeling overhead.

Chapter 27

That morning, Kat Boleyn wandered the flower and live plant section of Covent Garden Market. The day was still cool and vaguely misty, the piazza a raucous, colorful swirl of brawling stall keepers and haggling buyers; of rumbling cartwheels and barking dogs and running, shouting children. She paused for a moment, breathing in the sweet scents of honeysuckle and jasmine and remembering another time, another place.

She'd been born in a small white cottage on the edge of an Irish green, to a beautiful, laughing, loving woman who'd died a hideous death at the hands of a troop of British soldiers. The sights and sounds of that misty morning—the fear and rage and gritty determination that had surged through her as she listened to the British soldiers' laughter while her mother and stepfather slowly died—would always be a part of Kat. It had helped form her into the woman she was now.

It's all right to be afraid, her stepfather used to tell her. *Sometimes fear is sensible. But you can't let fear control your life or stop you from doing the things you were meant to do.* She'd sworn to live her life that way. But now her fear wasn't stopping her; it was haunting her. She was being watched, and she was being followed.

Even before Devlin's warning, she'd been uneasy, although she couldn't have articulated why. But she now understood that what she had somehow sensed was a malevolence focused intently upon her. She'd never seen the man well enough to recognize him; only a shadow in the night, a nondescript, half-hidden face in the crowd that was quickly glimpsed and then gone. But he was out there and he meant to kill her. Of that she was certain.

It had been her intent this morning to contact a dashing, laughing young Irishman named Aiden O'Connell, who was something quite different from the careless, heedless younger son of an earl that most thought him. But she knew now that she was going to need to be very, very careful, lest in her attempt to warn him she inadvertently betray him instead.

Chapter 28

Sebastian spent much of the afternoon visiting the haunts frequented by gentlemen of means: the exclusive clubs of St. James's Street; Tattersall's and Cribb's Parlor; Manton's Shooting Gallery and Angelo's. But he finally came upon the man he was seeking walking across the forecourt of the British Museum.

"Devlin!" said Monty, his face breaking into a broad smile when he caught sight of Sebastian coming toward him. Then the smile faded. "Did you hear they've pulled another headless body from the Thames?"

"I did, yes."

McPherson gave an exaggerated grimace. "It's bloody ugly, that's what this is. What the devil do you think is going on?"

"I wish I knew." Sebastian threw a quick glance at a group of white-haired, stoop-shouldered scholars standing nearby, deep in conversation. "Walk with me a ways?"

"Of course."

The two men turned toward the portico to Great Russell Street.

By now the wind had blown all but a few stray wisps of fluffy white clouds from the sky, leaving it a pale, muted blue.

"So who is this new dead man?" said McPherson. "Does anyone know?"

"Not yet."

"Bloody hell," said the Scotsman on a harsh exhalation of breath. "I suppose when you think about it, it's a miracle Sedgewick was identified."

"It is," said Sebastian as they turned up the street. "I've discovered where he went when he was on the Continent, by the way."

McPherson glanced over at him. "Where?"

"Vienna."

McPherson sucked his lower lip between his teeth, his features looking oddly drawn. "I don't like the sound of that."

"Neither do I. From what I gather, he was on a mission for either the Foreign Office or Bathurst. But I'm hearing he also brought back a list of people in London thought to have sent sensitive information to Napoléon in the past. Have you heard about that?"

"Good God, no. Are you serious?"

"You don't know anything about it?" said Sebastian. *Your friend tells your wife about it, but not you? And then your wife tells Hero about it, but not you?*

"No," said McPherson. "You think that's why Sedgewick was killed? Because of this list?"

"It's obviously a possibility, although Sibil Wilde would have me believe it's far more likely he was killed by a jealous husband."

Sebastian kept his gaze on his friend's face. But McPherson was very good at hiding his thoughts and emotions behind an expression of bland innocence when he wanted to; it was one of the talents that had made him so good at what they'd all once done. "So you visited the Weird Sisters, did you?" he said, a gleam of amusement lighting his pale blue eyes.

"I did. And then got jumped by a couple of unsavory types when I left."

The amusement vanished. "You're lucky they didn't kill you. That kind will slit your throat for a penny."

"Except these weren't common thieves; they were messengers sent by someone who wants me to quit asking questions."

"About Sedgewick? That sounds rather telling." McPherson stared across the street at the leafy green swath of Bloomsbury Square, where a nursemaid was shepherding her three charges through the gates. "I've been thinking about what you asked me the other day—if I knew of anyone who might want to see Sedgewick dead."

"And?"

He brought his gaze back to Sebastian. "What do you know about Cabrera?"

The name stirred vague, dark memories, the kind that are all the more troublesome because you know deep down that the truth is actually far worse than anything you've heard. "You mean the island off Majorca where they sent the French prisoners who surrendered after the Battle of Bailén?"

McPherson nodded. "They say that altogether, somewhere between ten and fifteen thousand French prisoners of war were sent to the island. Did you hear how many made it back to France when they were finally released last year? Between three and five thousand."

"*Christ.* Why?"

"You dump thousands of men on a tiny desert island with no food, water, clothes, or shelter, what do you think is going to happen?"

"But those men were Spain's prisoners. What does any of it have to do with Sedgewick?"

"They were Spain's prisoners, yes. Except that under the terms of their surrender, the French prisoners were supposed to be repatriated to France. We're the ones who stopped the Spaniards from honoring their treaty obligations. We didn't want all those men being sent back to France to live and fight another day, but we didn't want them kept on the mainland either because we were afraid a French army would free them. So we basically told the Spaniards we'd blow their ships out of the water if they tried to transport the prisoners anywhere but the islands."

"I still don't understand what any of this has to do with Sedgewick."

"He was acting as a go-between at the time, shuttling back and forth between Admiral Collingwood and the various Wellesley brothers. Three of them had a hand in it, you know—not just Wellington but Henry and Richard, as well. And from what I understand, Sedgewick wasn't simply carrying messages; he also served as an advocate for Wellington, pushing London's demands. He was very good at that sort of thing, you know." Monty fell silent for a moment, his head tipping back as he stared up at the leaves of the plane trees shifting in the wind against the pale blue sky. "That island was the worst kind of hell, and it lasted for five long years—or at least it did for the few rare souls who somehow managed to survive it. I can see some poor bastard who went through that wanting to kill anyone and everyone he held responsible for what was done to him."

"Yes. Except there must be a hell of a lot of men who bear more responsibility for what happened at Cabrera than Sedgewick."

"Perhaps," said McPherson. "Except how many of them do you think are here in London now—and easy to get at? Castlereagh is so unpopular and afraid that he doesn't go anywhere alone these days."

Sebastian met his friend's gaze and simply shook his head, and the silence became something they shared, something filled only with the clatter of hooves and the rattle of cartwheels and the sweet laughter of the children playing in the distant square.

Chapter 29

That evening, Sebastian arrived at Hendon House on Grosvenor Square to find the Earl seated in his favorite armchair beside the library fire, a worn leather-bound volume of Marcus Aurelius open on his lap and a glass of tawny cognac at his elbow.

"Huh," grunted Hendon, looking up when Sebastian entered the room. "I hear you're still at it. Chasing after whoever's behind these ghastly murders, I mean."

"Did you think I'd quit?" said Sebastian, going to pour himself a cognac.

Hendon's jaw tightened. But there was a shadow in his eyes that belied his words. He set aside his book. "And have you discovered anything that might explain what the devil is going on?"

"I've found more than one person with a good reason to kill Miles Sedgewick. But are any of them responsible? I don't know. It's rather difficult to understand a murderer's motives when two of his three victims are still unidentified."

"Still?"

"Still," said Sebastian, coming to settle in the chair opposite the Earl. "What can you tell me about Cabrera?"

Hendon stared at him. "Cabrera? What the hell has Cabrera to do with this?"

"Perhaps nothing. Perhaps everything. I'm told some of the responsibility for what happened to those prisoners rests with Britain. Is that true?"

For a long moment Hendon simply stared at him, his face tight in a way that made him look older than his years. Then he drew a long breath and let it out slowly. "I suppose there are ugly episodes in every nation's past that ought by rights to stain their honor for eternity."

"You're saying Cabrera is one of ours?"

"Yes. But I suspect that in the end it will all simply be forgotten. The French don't want to remember the embarrassment of their defeat at Bailén, and the Spanish are, after all, the Spanish, while we like to pretend we had nothing to do with it."

"But we did?"

Hendon reached for his cognac and took a long, slow swallow. "Oh, yes. Spain was going to honor the terms of the surrender agreement until we stepped in."

"So it's true? We stopped them from repatriating their prisoners?"

Hendon nodded. "They'd marched them to Cádiz in preparation for loading them on transports and sending them to France. There were something like twenty-five thousand of them in all."

"That many?"

Hendon nodded. "Seventeen thousand from Dupont de l'Etang's army at Bailén, plus another five thousand of his troops that surrendered later and three thousand more from I forget where. Spain was going to send them all back to France. But then we stepped in. The regional commander of the Royal Navy at the time was Vice Admiral Cuthbert Collingwood, who'd basically been given the authority of a viceroy. He told the Spaniards that if they tried to honor their promise and repatriate the French prisoners, we'd blow their transports out of the water."

"So what happened?"

"At first, nothing. The Spaniards didn't know what to do. They couldn't send the prisoners to France the way they'd planned, so for a time they simply kept them in Cádiz. A few were being held in the castle there, but most were crowded onto hulks in the harbor, where conditions were appalling. Hundreds were dying every day, to the point the people of Cádiz were complaining because they couldn't deal with all the dead bodies."

Hendon drained his cognac and set the empty glass aside. "By that time, Napoléon himself had come to take charge of the French Army in Spain, and London was afraid he was going to march on Cádiz and free his captured soldiers. Just think: twenty-five thousand men—or, I suppose, more like twenty thousand by then—added to the French ranks. We told the Spaniards they had to get their prisoners out of there."

"But not send them back to France."

"Obviously not. The Spanish government—or what there was of it at the time with the King in exile—decided that if we wouldn't let them send the prisoners to France, and if they couldn't keep them on the mainland, then the only thing they could do would be to ship them to the Mediterranean, to Majorca or Minorca. Except the citizens of the main islands didn't want them, and Collingwood didn't want them there either because he liked to use the two islands for his fleet."

"So whose idea was it to send them to Cabrera?"

"I don't know. It's a tiny, wretched place about twenty miles from Palma, totally uninhabited and essentially uninhabitable. Basically it's just a small stretch of rocky cliffs and scrub-covered hills with only one freshwater spring that disappears in the heat of summer. I'm told there's a small medieval castle by the bay—more like a fortified tower, really—that could provide shelter for maybe twenty or thirty men. Not fifteen to twenty thousand."

"And we simply dumped them there?"

Hendon nodded. "With no food, no water, no shelter, and no means of building any. At least Robinson Crusoe had a wrecked ship from which he could salvage all sorts of tools and materials. Those poor bastards on Cabrera had nothing. *Nothing.*"

Hendon drew a pouch of tobacco from his pocket and reached for his pipe. Sebastian waited while he tamped a load of tobacco in the bowl and kindled a taper. After a moment, the Earl continued.

"Eventually the local government in Majorca hired someone to take over a small shipment of food from Palma every four days. But the rations were starvation level—a few ounces of bread and a handful of beans per man per day. And sometimes the ship simply didn't come, either because of the weather or because the officials in Majorca couldn't pay the bill. Then the men marooned on the island would starve. At first, when there were more of them, they were dying at the rate of four or five hundred a day."

"My God," whispered Sebastian.

Hendon was silent for a moment, his hand cupping the bowl of his pipe, his expression that of a man whose thoughts were far, far away. Then he sighed and said, "No one knows exactly how many died there. Some of the men eventually volunteered to join the Spanish Army simply to have a chance of surviving. At one point we took off a few dozen officers and brought them here to England. And the prisoners themselves tried to hide the real number of deaths because an artificially inflated number of survivors meant more food for the living. But it wasn't only the lack of food that killed them. Many died of thirst in the summer or of exposure in the winter. After a few years, they were basically naked, and they could never really build much in the way of proper shelters. More than a few of them despaired of ever leaving the island and threw themselves off the cliffs into the sea."

"I'm surprised any of them survived."

"I suppose it's a testament to the human spirit."

Sebastian lifted his cognac to his lips and took a deep drink that burned all the way down. "You say 'London' decided not to allow Spain to repatriate the French prisoners. Who in London?"

Hendon drew on his pipe, then let the smoke ease out slowly before answering. "Castlereagh was foreign minister at first and must bear a large measure of responsibility, along with Admiral Collingwood. But it would be wrong to put it all on those two alone. Wellington's voice was loud, as were those of his brothers. Richard Wellesley was our ambassador to Spain, then took over as foreign secretary, at which point their brother Henry was sent to Spain as ambassador."

"And Jarvis? What was his position in all this?"

Hendon met Sebastian's hard gaze. "What do you think?"

And yours? Where was your voice? Sebastian wanted to ask. Instead he said, "Who else?"

Hendon thought about it, then shook his head. "I honestly can't recall."

Sebastian decided to let it go. "I'm told Miles Sedgewick played a role, mainly as a go-between for the Wellesley brothers and Collingwood."

"You're suggesting that's why he was killed? But why would someone go after a mere messenger?"

"Because Collingwood is already dead, and men like Castlereagh and Wellington are essentially beyond reach, perhaps?"

"And the two headless bodies that have been pulled from the Thames? How do they fit into it?"

"I don't know that they do."

"God preserve us," muttered Hendon.

The two men sat in silence for a time, Hendon sucking on his pipe and Sebastian nursing his drink. Then Sebastian said, "Any news from Belgium?"

"Not yet. But it's coming."

Sebastian emptied his cognac and set the glass aside. "So tell me this: What happened to the men from Cabrera? The few who survived, I mean."

Hendon kept his gaze on his pipe. "After Napoléon was exiled to Elba, they were loaded onto ships from the French Royal Navy and taken to Marseilles. At first the Bourbons locked them up, intending to send them into exile in Corsica."

"Are you serious?"

Hendon nodded. "Except when word of it leaked out, the people of Marseilles stormed the barracks where they were being held and released them. After all, these were their brothers, fathers, sons, and husbands. At that point the Bourbons gave up and let them go. Most are so wrecked both physically and mentally by what they went through that they'll probably be invalids the rest of their lives and die young. But I've no doubt some of them found their way to rejoin Napoléon's army and are at this very moment marching against us in Belgium." He paused. "If I wanted revenge, I suspect that's what I'd do if I were one of them. Not come here to London to lop the heads off a few men who surely played only an incidental role in what was done to me." Hendon looked over at Sebastian. "Wouldn't you?"

"If I were still sane. Except . . . how sane do you think anyone would be after spending five years in hell?"

Hendon met his gaze and held it. "Probably not very."

Chapter 30

ow have I never heard of any of this?" said Hero later that night as they sat beside the fire in their room, Hero curled up in the armchair with Sebastian leaning back against her chair and sipping a glass of Burgundy at her feet.

"Who's going to talk about it?" he said. "I suspect even the men responsible for it aren't proud of it—although I've no doubt they long ago found a way to justify it to themselves. There's a certain kind of man who can justify almost anything."

She was silent for a moment, and he knew she was thinking of her own father. Then she said, "If McPherson is right—if this is all in revenge for what happened at Cabrera—how do you think the killer learned of the role Sedgewick played?"

Sebastian watched the flames lick at the coal on the hearth. "I don't know; that's a good point. The truth is, Cabrera could have absolutely nothing to do with what happened to any of those men. I mean, why castrate Sedgewick? Why cut off the other two men's heads? If the killer simply didn't want them identified, why not bury the bodies someplace where they'd never be found?"

She leaned forward to put her hands on his shoulders and massage his neck. "It's still possible the last two killings have absolutely nothing to do with what happened to Sedgewick. Yes, the bodies were mutilated, but in a dissimilar way. No one cut off Sedgewick's head, hands, or feet. Just his privates—which strikes me as a very different thing."

He blew out his breath in a long sigh. "There's no denying that what happened to Sedgewick does suggest a more sexual motive to his killing."

She reached for his wineglass, took a sip, then handed it back to him. "I thought I might try talking to Eloisa again tomorrow. I keep thinking about what that poor governess, Phoebe Cox, told you about Sedgewick's marriage."

"You think Eloisa and her reverend might have decided to make her wish that Miles die a reality?"

"I can see a woman whose husband seduced their governess under her own roof being so furious as to shoot off her husband's face and castrate him."

He swung around to look at her. "Even someone like Eloisa?"

"Yes."

"Interesting."

"And she would have had her good friend the Reverend dispose of the body for her afterward."

"I didn't realize you disliked her that much."

"I don't. I actually feel sorry for her, in a way. But excessively religious people tend to make me nervous. All too often, they're the kind who can massacre every Muslim in Jerusalem and burn witches at Smithfield and toss the heads of suspected werewolves into the Thames, then have a good dinner and go to bed to sleep the sound sleep of the proudly righteous." She reached for his wine again. "If you like, I could also ask her about Cabrera. She might know something."

"You think she'll agree to see you again?"

"I don't intend to give her a chance to deny me. She frequently takes her children for a walk in the park in the morning. I'll simply contrive to run into her there."

❧

Saturday, 17 June

The next morning dawned clear and sunny, with a light breeze that lifted the bright green leaves of the plane trees in the park against the blue sky and scattered the red and pink petals of spent roses across the grass like confetti. Hero and Claire took the boys to toss a ball near the round reservoir in Hyde Park and hadn't been there more than ten minutes before Hero spotted Eloisa Sedgewick with two of her three children and a middle-aged woman in a somber black dress turning in through the gate.

"Here," said Hero, throwing the ball to Claire. To the boys she called, "I'll be right back."

Eloisa had seen her now, and Hero caught the faint pinch of dismay that flitted across the woman's features before she smoothed it away.

"Mrs. Sedgewick, good morning!" said Hero, walking across the grass toward her. "How are you?"

Eloisa paused, one hand coming up to cup the crown of her black widow's bonnet as she cast a quick glance farther up the path. "Lady Devlin, what a pleasant surprise. I'm doing well, thank you."

The two children—a serious-looking towheaded boy of eight and a girl who couldn't be more than a year younger—stood a few paces away from their mother with the somber, pinched-faced woman who was surely their governess. Eloisa had obviously decided not to take any chances when she'd replaced Phoebe Cox.

"It's a lovely morning, is it not?" said Hero, coming up to them.

"It is, yes."

"How fortuitous, my seeing you like this. I've been wanting to ask you something: Did your husband ever speak to you of Cabrera?"

Eloisa looked at her blankly. "Who?"

"The island of Cabrera, just off Majorca in the Mediterranean. Did he ever mention it to you?"

The widow colored slightly, obviously embarrassed by her error. "No. Why do you ask?"

Hero kept her voice low out of consideration for the children. "Devlin thinks it might have something to do with his death."

"Oh," said Eloisa, casting another glance up the path.

"I'm sorry," said Hero, watching her. "Am I keeping you? Were you meeting someone?"

Eloisa jerked her gaze back to Hero's face. "What? Oh, no, of course not."

"Good, because I need to ask you something else. Let's walk apart from the others for a moment, shall we?"

"What is it?" asked Eloisa, accompanying Hero with obvious reluctance.

"It's about the governess that you dismissed last spring. I'm wondering, why was that?"

Eloisa's expression remained bland. But Hero could see the pulse beating in her throat, just above the narrow band of black lace that edged the high neck of her mourning gown. "I'm afraid she simply proved to be unsatisfactory."

"Oh? And how long was she with you?"

"Four years."

"Goodness. And you only just decided she was unsatisfactory?"

The widow's jaw tightened. "If you must know, I was forced to let her go because I discovered she was with child."

"Did she tell you who the father was?"

Eloisa gave a decidedly unbelievable laugh. "Good heavens, no. Why would I care?"

"She didn't tell you that your husband seduced her? That he was the father of her child?"

For a long moment, Eloisa simply stared at her, her face draining of all color, her chest jerking with her agitated breathing. "Who told you that?"

"Why? Is it true?"

"No! Of course not! The nasty little liar. She was desperate to stay—claimed she had no place else to go."

"And yet you dismissed her anyway?"

"Why wouldn't I? What do I care if she starves in the streets? Lying little strumpet, no better than she should be. She deserves everything that has happened to her."

"Are you quite certain she made it up? That Miles wasn't the father?"

"Don't be ridiculous." The widow gave a sharp, bitter laugh. "I heard just this morning that she's been remanded into custody."

It took Hero a moment to understand what Eloisa was saying. "Phoebe Cox is in prison? Why?"

"For murdering her own baby. And if there's any justice in this world, she'll hang." The woman cast another quick glance up the path, then said, "And now you must excuse me."

Signaling to her children and their governess, Eloisa turned away, her head held high, her eyes fixed straight ahead as she walked toward the fashionably dressed young gentleman Hero could now see waiting for them farther up the path.

It was the Reverend Sinclair Palmer.

❧

"I don't think dear Eloisa will agree to speak to me again," said Hero, taking off her chip hat as she walked into the library on Brook Street an hour later.

Devlin looked up from where he sat at his desk, cleaning a small double-barreled pistol. "Why? What happened?"

She told him. "Do you think it's true? That Phoebe Cox is in prison for killing her own baby?"

"Well, when I saw her, she did say the child was dead."

Hero went to stand beside the window, her arms crossed at her chest, her gaze on the housemaid scrubbing the steps of the house across the street with a brush and a bucket of soapy water. "I can't believe I actually felt sorry for Eloisa the last time I spoke to her. What a bitter, vile creature she is."

"But you already knew that, didn't you? You're the one who saw the fires of Smithfield in her eyes."

Hero turned her head to look back at him. "What prison would Phoebe be in?"

"I've no idea. But I can find out."

Chapter 31

Someone less familiar with the ways of his world might have been inclined to view what was happening to Phoebe Cox as a tragic but isolated incident. Sebastian knew better.

Sometimes, like Phoebe, a woman in service allowed herself to be seduced by her employer. But more often than not she was simply forced, by either her master or one of his sons or even a passing houseguest. English gentlemen of means were rarely held account-able for raping servants. After all, who would believe such a woman over her "betters"?

The lucky ones cried themselves to sleep at night and somehow found a way to live with what had happened to them. The unlucky ones fell pregnant.

Once her belly began to show, an unmarried servant "in the family way" would inevitably be turned off without a character. And if she didn't die of starvation or exposure but lived to birth her babe, she faced a new, even more terrifying danger, for a single woman

who gave birth to a child only to have that child die could be accused of killing it.

And then hanged for murder.

Driven by a heavy sense of dread, Sebastian went first to the
Haymarket, looking for Phoebe Cox. But her place across from the
theater was empty, and none of the women he spoke with would admit to knowing where she lodged. He told himself that for someone
who catered to the crowds of theatergoers, it was early yet; he would
need to come back again later. But on the off chance that what Eloisa
had told Hero was true, he set Tom to making inquiries at the city's
various prisons and sent a note to Sir Henry Lovejoy asking for his
help in locating the woman. London had a lot of prisons.

He then spent several hours making discreet inquiries into the
Reverend Sinclair Palmer.

Marylebone was a choice living, and it didn't take Sebastian long
to discover that Eloisa Sedgewick's childhood friend was related to
both the Duke of Newcastle and the Earl of Oxford. The Reverend
hadn't particularly distinguished himself at Cambridge, but he'd
more than made up for that by his ostentatious religious zeal. A conservative Old High Churchman in the mold of the new Bishop of
London, he was obviously an ambitious man. And it occurred to Sebastian as he turned his horses toward Marylebone that marriage to
Edward Platt's wealthy, recently widowed daughter would do much
to advance such a man's career.

꒱

The parish of Marylebone was an old one, once no more than a small
rural village to the northwest of London. Its original church, dedicated to St. John the Evangelist in the twelfth century, was long gone,
having been replaced in the fifteenth century by one built beside a
"bourne," or stream, and dedicated to Mary—Mary-by-the-Bourne.

That church, too, was gone, and its replacement was about to be supplanted by an even newer place of worship being built near Regent's Park, for the area had become increasingly wealthy and fashionable in recent years and would only keep growing.

It was at the site of the half-finished new church that Sebastian found the Reverend Palmer standing in a slice of golden afternoon sunlight and deep in conversation with the short, stocky foreman of the half dozen or so stonemasons working on a grand Corinthian portico that looked like it was modeled on the Pantheon of Rome. The Reverend was dressed in a long, plain black cassock, but this was not the rusty, threadbare garment worn by so many parish churchmen; the tailoring was exquisite, the cloth new and fine, and its black faille fascia ended in two long silk tassels. When Sebastian's curricle pulled in next to the kerb, the Reverend left the foreman and walked toward him, his handsome, even features smiling, his eyes alive with speculation.

"Lord Devlin," he said with a bow when Sebastian introduced himself. "This is indeed an honor. Have you come to view our fine new church?" He swept an expansive hand toward the building and raised his voice slightly so that he might be heard over the pounding and clatter of the workmen. "It was originally intended as a chapel of ease, you know, to accommodate our growing population. But then it was decided to make this the new parish seat, so it is being enlarged and reconfigured in a more impressive style."

Sebastian squinted up at the three-story stone spire that towered a hundred feet or more above them, surmounted by a miniature temple with eight caryatids and a dome. "It is indeed impressive."

The Reverend's smile widened. "The area was already becoming increasingly prosperous, you know. But now with the establishment of the Regent's grand new park, the rate of construction of fine town houses is frankly unbelievable. My mother feared I was making a mistake, taking up the living at a parish on the outskirts of London. But this is a new world we live in, is it not?" The smile faded, and he cleared his throat, his features becoming grave. "Mrs. Sedgewick tells me you're looking into the death of her late husband. Shocking business, that."

"You knew him?"

"Only peripherally; his wife and I are childhood friends. I fear this has all been a dreadful strain on Mrs. Sedgewick. She's such a good Christian woman, and she already had so much to bear."

"Because of her husband, you mean?"

The Reverend looked away toward the row of classically fronted houses that stood beside the church, his eyes narrowing against the westering sun. "As to that, I shouldn't say."

"Who do you think killed him?"

The Reverend brought his gaze back to Sebastian's face. "If you ask me, it's rather obvious."

"It is?"

"How well did you know the man?"

"I knew him in the Army. Why?"

"You know of his . . . interests?"

"To which particular interests are you referring?"

A loud clatter of lumber jerked Palmer's attention to where two of the workmen were moving a stack of boards. He lowered his voice and leaned forward. "I fear the man was attracted to the forces of darkness."

"By which I take it you mean his interest in witches and were-wolves?"

Palmer nodded. "Witches, werewolves, tarot, astrology, and good-ness knows what else. You know that he made a habit of frequenting the alchemists and cartomancers of Seven Dials?"

"I did, yes."

"Under the circumstances, I fear such a dark, violent end was inevitable, wouldn't you say?"

"You're of the opinion he was killed in St. Giles?"

The Reverend looked vaguely surprised by the suggestion. "As to that, I couldn't say. But his associates were evil. As the Good Lord says, 'Let not thy soul enter into their secrets nor join their assemblies, for in their anger they slew men, and I will divide them in Jacob and scatter them in Israel.'"

The quote didn't sound quite right to Sebastian, but all he said was, "Are you referring to any evil associates in particular?"

"I fear there are many who share his satanic interests. It's become almost an obsession in our modern world, wouldn't you say?"

"I don't know if I'd call an interest in folklore 'satanic.'"

Palmer looked at him with the patient, pitying eyes of one long accustomed to dealing with the delusional folly of sinners. "Ah, but that's how it often begins, is it not? By posing as an innocent 'scholarly' interest in the traditions and tales of our forebears? But whether such a one seeks to fool himself or only others, the sad truth is that he has simply found a cloak to cover his surrender to the seductive allure of darkness."

"I can see that this is something that troubles you a great deal," said Sebastian.

"These are troubled times, are they not?"

"But prosperous." Sebastian watched a workman begin to scramble up the scaffolding that still half obscured the portico's grand pediment. "And the other men whose mutilated bodies were thrown in the Thames? You think they were killed for the same reason?"

"It seems a logical assumption, wouldn't you say? Deuteronomy tells us, 'There shall not be found amongst you anyone who maketh his son or his daughter pass through the fire, or that useth divination, or an observer of times, or an enchanter or a witch, or a charmer, or a consulter with familiar spirits, or a wizard, or a necromancer. For all that do these things are an abomination unto the Lord.'"

"You're suggesting the men were killed by someone interpreting that passage literally?"

The Reverend's eyes widened in what looked very much like alarm. "Good heavens, no. Only that those who flirt with evil shall inevitably become its victims." He glanced back at his grand new church, its western front turned a deep gold by the afternoon sun. "And now you really must excuse me. I promised our foreman that I'd go over the proposed changes to the galleries."

"Of course. Thank you for your time."

"Always more than happy to be of service," said Palmer. Then he hurried away without looking back, his hands clenched into fists at his sides, the warm June breeze billowing the black skirt of his fine cassock out behind him.

After he had gone, Sebastian stood for a time on the pavement before the new church, his gaze on the leafy green expanse of Regent's Park spreading out to the north. The sun was warm on his face, the air fragrant with the sweet scent from a red climbing rose that tumbled over a nearby garden wall and the hot spicy tang of the gingerbread being hawked by a man near the corner with a barrel.

There were at least four good explanations for Sedgewick's murder. But the man's habit of seducing and discarding women did nothing to explain the deaths of the two unidentified dead men, while the dangerous list of names he was said to be carrying might conceivably explain all three deaths, although not the mutilation of their bodies. And when it came to Cabrera, Sebastian couldn't see how any of it fit.

But this troubling linkage of an interest in folklore to evil satanic forces did explain much of the mutilation, and it might conceivably explain the deaths of the other two men.

If only he knew who they were.

Chapter 32

*R*emembering what Dudley Tiptoff had said about the attacks he'd faced as a result of his research into the lore of witchcraft and werewolves, Sebastian decided to pay another visit to Bloomsbury.

He found the scholar at home, in an upstairs room that might once have been a bedchamber but was now lined with utilitarian shelves from floor to ceiling on all four sides and stacked with boxes in the center. The shelves were crowded with overflowing boxes and baskets, African masks and Native American beaded slippers jumbled together with red- and black-figure pottery from Greece and what looked like an ancient wooden statue of Quan Yin. Tiptoff was up on a ladder, rummaging through a box he had dragged half off one of the top shelves. When the housemaid showed Sebastian up to him, the scholar glanced over and said, "Don't mind me; I shan't be but a moment."

"My apologies for the interruption," said Sebastian, tipping back his head to look up at the man. "If you'd like, I could come back another time."

"No, no, seriously, I shan't be but a moment. Is there something you wished to ask me?"

"Actually, yes, I was wondering if you're familiar with a reverend named Sinclair Palmer."

Tiptoff paused in his search to squint down at him. "You mean that rector up at Marylebone?"

"So you do know him?"

"Shall we say I know of him? The man is quite vocally opposed to any scholarly interest in traditional folklore, but he takes a particularly violent exception to the study of the ancient tales of werewolves and witches. Why do you ask?"

"His name came up."

Tiptoff shoved the box back into place and climbed down his ladder. "I'm not surprised. Sedgewick loathed the man. He was particularly irritated by his wife's friendship with the fellow—which is rather amusing for a man with Sedgewick's habits."

"Sedgewick thought there was something between his wife and the Reverend?"

"As to that, I don't know," said Tiptoff, turning to rummage through a basket on one of the lower shelves. "Perhaps he simply grew tired of constantly tripping over the fellow in his own house. It's not as if Palmer's the type to keep his opinions to himself."

"Has he ever attacked you for your interest in folklore?"

"Not in person, if that's what you mean. But he wrote a particularly scathing attack on a paper I published in a journal last year. Accused me of doing the devil's work and all sorts of other nonsense."

"I gather he does have a reputation for zealotry."

"Oh, yes. Zealotry and hypocrisy. But then, the two often go hand in hand, do they not?"

"True," said Sebastian. "Although hypocrisy is hardly the private preserve of zealots."

"Yes, I fear it is a quite common human failing. We tend to justify our own evil acts as necessitated by circumstances or provoked by others, while refusing to acknowledge the role that provocation might play in the less-than-admirable behavior of our enemies. Wouldn't you say?"

"All too often," said Sebastian, his thoughts drifting, inevitably, to Cabrera. No nation could scream louder and with more righteous indignation than Britain when an opponent failed to honor their treaty obligations. "Is he capable of violence, do you think? Palmer, I mean."

"To be fair, I don't actually know the man, only his type." Tiptoff abandoned his search of the basket and straightened, his features grave as he turned to face Sebastian. "Tell me, my lord: Do you ever give much thought to the nature of evil?"

"Yes."

Tiptoff studied him in silence for a moment, then nodded. "Yes, I can see that." He sighed and turned away to paw through one of the boxes on a shelf near the door. "Men such as Palmer prefer to think of evil as something metaphysical, something caused by—or at least inspired by—the devil or some other force of darkness. I suppose it protects them from having to confront the age-old quandary presented by the thought of a benevolent God creating a human heart capable of evil."

"How do you see evil?" said Sebastian.

"Me? I see it as the result of selfishness—the elevation of self-interest and personal desires above all else. That, and a lack of any sense of our interdependence or the value of other living things."

"'Am I my brother's keeper?'" quoted Sebastian quietly.

Tiptoff nodded. "That's the first act of true evil in the Bible, is it not—when Cain gives way to his jealous urge to remove his brother as a rival? Or at least it is if we are talking about evil and not mere sin, which is distinctly different, wouldn't you say?" He stared down at the Celtic head of a bull in his hands, then set it aside to continue his rummaging. "I've sometimes wondered if the worldwide incidence of werewolf legends stems from our human need to explain evil. In most werewolf stories, a normal man—often through no fault of his own—becomes an animal. Sometimes he is bitten or clawed; sometimes he simply steps where he should not. But as an animal, he does great harm to others, committing unspeakable acts—murdering and devouring men, women, children, all without remorse. Then he goes back to being a seemingly normal man, although sometimes he bears some wound, something to show what he has been and what he has done."

"And witches?"

"Ah, yes, witches. There's a slight difference there, don't you think? The belief in witches seems less driven by the need to explain human evil and more by the need to explain natural calamities—the death of a cow, the sickness of a child, the destructiveness of a storm that comes out of nowhere." He paused, then said, "Or at least that was true until the fifteenth century, when churchmen such as your Sinclair Palmer began to equate witchcraft with Satanism. But in one sense I suppose both are the same: They're driven by the need to explain evil as something that comes from *outside* human nature rather than—" He broke off. "Ah, here it is!"

He stood up and turned, a small bronze statue of a boar held proudly in his hands. "Lovely, isn't it?"

"It is, yes," said Sebastian.

"Believe it or not, it's an ancient Norse symbol of peace. They saw the boar as a representation of Freyr, the god of peace, sunshine, and prosperity. He was the twin brother of Freyja, you know—rode a golden boar and ruled over the kingdom of the elves. Of course, he was also associated with fertility and virility, which is why he's sometimes represented by a phallus."

Tiptoff was silent for a moment, his gaze on the ancient object in his hands. Then he looked up, his features pinched. "I hear what people on the street are saying, that whoever is mutilating these men and throwing their bodies in the Thames must be some sort of inhuman monster."

Sebastian studied the man's earnest, bespectacled face. "You don't think so?"

Tiptoff shook his head. "What is more human than evil? Hmm?"

࿇

Sebastian came out of the house a few minutes later to find his groom, Giles, walking the chestnuts up and down Bury Street.

"Go ahead and take the curricle home, Giles," said Sebastian as the groom brought the horses to a stand before him. "I need to stretch my legs."

"Yes, my lord."

Sebastian stood for a moment watching his groom drive off toward Mayfair. Then he turned down Great Russell Street.

The afternoon was bright and surprisingly hot, and he tipped his hat brim lower on his forehead to shield his eyes from the westering sun. It had now been nearly a week since someone tossed Miles Sedgewick's mutilated corpse into the Thames; five days since Alexi chanced to identify him as he lay on Gibson's granite slab. If she hadn't recognized the scars she herself had once bandaged, the Marquis's son would by now be just another anonymous corpse covered with quicklime in the local parish's overflowing poor hole.

Was that what his killer had intended? Sebastian wondered. To rob Sedgewick and the other victims not only of their lives but of a decent burial? To deny anyone who loved them the knowledge of their ultimate fate? Is that why he mutilated them? Not in revenge for some unprincipled seduction or as part of an archaic religious superstition but simply to prevent their identification? How could he have been so certain none of his victims would be reported missing in time? Had he known them that well? Known them and hated them because . . .

Why?

If they could somehow discover the identities of the other two men, it might all begin to make sense. Was that another reason for the mutilations? Because by hiding his victims' identities the murderer also hid his own?

Perhaps if he hadn't been so lost in thought, Sebastian would have noticed the man following him sooner. Whoever he was, he was careful never to draw too near, but neither did he allow Sebastian to pull too far ahead. When Sebastian turned the corner onto Oxford Street he caught a glimpse of his shadow: Of medium height with slightly overlong dark hair, the man wore the neat, conservatively cut coat and trousers of a comfortably situated merchant or banker.

Sebastian knew it was more than possible that the man was simply, like Sebastian himself, walking toward Bond Street. But Sebastian found himself remembering another man of average height with overlong dark hair, a Frenchman dressed in a shabby coat and trousers that enabled him to fade into the background on the mean streets of someplace like St. Giles.

Damn, thought Sebastian. *Damn, damn, damn.* He was aware of the ache from his wounded leg growing more insistent and wished like hell he'd brought his walking stick—both for the sake of his leg and for the handy sword hidden within it. Without either the sword stick or the neat little double-barreled flintlock he sometimes carried, he would be forced to rely on only his wits and the knife he habitually wore hidden in a sheath in his boot.

He was suddenly acutely aware of his surroundings: of the stout woman in a lightweight bright turquoise pelisse and plumed turban walking a small white dog on the far side of the street; of the housemaid sweeping the steps of a house two doors down; of the boy of perhaps twelve washing the windows of a nearby greengrocer. Sebastian was looking for his French shadow's overgrown companion from St. Giles. But the giant was conspicuous enough that for the moment, at least, he was evidently staying out of sight.

Sebastian's attention shifted then to an aged hackney carriage rolling slowly up behind him. The carriage's windows were empty, but its body still swayed heavily on its springs.

"Oy, you there!" shouted the jarvey at the exact moment the Frenchman behind Sebastian broke into a run.

Chapter 33

Sebastian spun around as the near door of the hackney flew open, revealing the big overgrown oaf crouched awkwardly on the floorboards within. He felt the Frenchman slam into his back, sending him hurtling toward the open door, where the oaf, his craggy face breaking into a wide smile, was waiting to drag him inside. Gritting his teeth, Sebastian caught the edge of the swinging door with one hand and kicked out with his good leg, hooking his bootheel on the hackney's iron step so he could push back with all his strength.

The unexpected jolt caught the Frenchman off-balance, sending him reeling back. Sebastian felt his wounded leg buckle beneath him and staggered, but he didn't go down. Whirling, he grabbed the Frenchman by the front of his coat and threw him into the brick wall of the shop beside them.

With a roar, the overgrown oaf erupted from the carriage, his massive arms reaching out to enclose Sebastian in a deadly bear hug. Dropping to a crouch, Sebastian yanked the knife from his boot and came up in a lunge, stepping neatly between the oaf's massive reaching arms to drive his blade up under the man's ribs, straight into his heart.

Sebastian saw the big man's eyes widen, his features going slack with surprise as he staggered back. Jerking the knife free, Sebastian spun around just as the Frenchman pushed away from the shop wall and charged.

"You son of a bitch," swore Sebastian, slashing his knife's sharp blade across the other man's throat.

Without even waiting to see the man fall, Sebastian turned again to confront the hackney driver. But the jarvey was already whipping his horses, the carriage wheels rattling over the uneven paving stones as the hackney lumbered off.

The overgrown oaf was still on his feet, swaying. But as Sebastian watched, he took one step, two, after the departing hackney. Then, slowly, the big man sank to his knees, his mouth gaping open, one hand reaching out toward Sebastian before he pitched forward onto his face and didn't move.

Sebastian turned back to where the Frenchman lay crumpled and still on the pavement. He realized the boy washing the greengrocer's window had disappeared, while the housemaid and turbaned older woman were both screaming. Brushing one crooked elbow across his dripping face, Sebastian leaned back against the nearby shop wall and took a deep, shuddering breath.

❧

"It's not a sight one sees often on Oxford Street," said Sir Henry Lovejoy, his chin sunk against his chest as he stared down at the two dead men sprawled at his feet, their blood splashed up on the shop wall, across the pavement, and into the street. "What an extraordinary amount of blood."

"Yes," said Sebastian.

Lovejoy looked over at him. "You're not hurt?"

"No."

"Phenomenal. You're covered in blood."

Sebastian dragged a splayed hand down over the splatters on his face, but he suspected it didn't do any good. "Sorry. I didn't have time to be neat about it."

"No, of course not. Any idea as to who the men might be?"

Sebastian shook his head. "They're the same two who jumped me in St. Giles earlier in the week, but I can't say with any certainty exactly who they're working for."

"And you say the jarvey was in on it?"

"Little doubt about that."

Lovejoy's lips tightened. "I'll give the lads your description of the hackney. If we can find it, the jarvey may be able to tell us something."

"Maybe," said Sebastian, although he doubted it. Professional assassins like Gabriel rarely left potential loose links alive.

❧

Sebastian arrived back at Brook Street sometime later to find Aunt Henrietta's ponderous landau drawn up at the kerb and the Dowager Duchess of Claiborne herself, magnificently gowned in purple satin with a towering puce-and-purple turban, just descending the front steps.

"Merciful heavens," said the Dowager, groping for her quizzing glass as she looked him up and down. "Are you all right? What on earth has happened? Is all that blood yours?"

"None of it, actually." Sebastian swiped one crooked arm again, uselessly, at the blood on his face. "Won't you come in? Have a cup of tea?"

"I will come in for a moment, for what I have to tell you cannot be discussed on the doorstep," she said, following him into the library. "But I've already had tea with Hero, thank you, and mustn't stay."

"Please, have a seat."

She sank into one of the chairs beside the empty hearth. "This won't take long. You'll remember my telling you there was some sordid rumor about Miles Sedgewick from several years ago—something I couldn't quite recall?"

"Yes."

"Well, it came back to me when I saw Lady Brownfield at a rather boring soirée I attended last night. Her sister was Jane Stamford, you know—the current Marquis's first wife. Now, do keep in mind that I have no idea how much of this is true, but the on-dit some seven years ago was that Miles seduced his brother's wife."

Sebastian stared at her. "He did?"

"Who knows? But there was definitely a rift between the brothers, complete with a most vulgar public quarrel. Then Stamford bought his brother a pair of colors and sent him off to war. And I have it on excellent authority that Stamford was heard to say that if he were lucky, Miles would somehow contrive to get himself killed."

"Charming," said Sebastian.

"I did say the entire family has always been a bit 'off,' did I not?" She paused, then added, "It was perhaps two months later that Lady Stamford died."

"How?"

"No one really knows; she was found dead one morning in her bed by her maid. The inquest accepted the opinion of Stamford's physician that she must have had a bad heart. Except that the Marquis had refused to allow anyone to perform a postmortem examination, and everyone said she had never exhibited any signs of heart problems in the past, so naturally there were rumors that she must have been poisoned. But nothing was ever proven."

"How old was she?"

"Twenty-five. It struck me as odd at the time, for Miles Sedge-wick to go off to war like that when he'd only been married a year and had a new baby. But while the rumors do seem an obvious expla-nation, that doesn't mean they are true." The Duchess pushed to her feet. "And now I really must go."

Sebastian walked with her into the entrance hall. But at the door she paused and turned to him, her lips pursing with worry. "I don't like this, Devlin—what you're involved in here, I mean. And it has nothing to do with the sort of objections Hendon invariably raises to this sort of thing. It's because whoever is killing these men is evil. I generally see the use of that word as overly melodramatic, but in this instance I don't think there is any other way to describe it. And I'm not convinced that we can touch evil without somehow being contaminated by it."

"Someone was just telling me that he thinks of evil as the ulti-mate selfishness—the elevation of one's own needs and desires above all else."

She considered this a moment, then shook her head. "It's more than that, I think. It's a deliberate, conscious rejection of all that is good and right." For a moment her face seemed to go oddly slack, her eyes becoming cloudy as if she were gazing at something both private and deeply disturbing.

Then she shook it off and turned away. "And now I must be off. Do try not to get yourself killed, will you?"

❧

Later that evening, Jarvis was standing at the windows of his cham-bers in Carlton House, his thoughtful gaze on the shadowy fore-court below, when Major Drake was ushered into his presence.

The major was a tall, trim former hussar with hard gray eyes,

sweeping blond military mustaches, and numerous talents that combined nicely with a grim willingness to kill when necessary. He'd
been with Jarvis now for several years.

"So," said Jarvis, reaching for his snuffbox. "Does he suspect?"

Major Drake bowed. "I don't think so, my lord."

Jarvis nodded. "Good. And the other matter?"

"We're still working on that, my lord."

Jarvis raised his eyebrows. "Indeed?" He flipped open his snuffbox, his lips tightening into a thin line. "Work harder."

A faint flush rode high on the other man's cheekbones, and he
bowed again. "Yes, my lord."

Chapter 34

That night there was a strange quality to the air, a heaviness that had nothing to do with heat but was nonetheless oppressive. The moon was almost full, a fat silver orb ringed by a ghostly shadow. It was caused by mist, but it reminded Sebastian of the drifts of smoke that obscured both sun and moon after battle, and it added to the sense of urgency that stayed with him as he prowled the gentlemen's clubs of St. James's Street in search of the Marquis of Stamford.

He finally came upon Miles's brother crossing the vestibule of White's. Stamford's face hardened at the sight of him, and he was pushing past Sebastian without any acknowledgment when Sebastian stopped him by saying, "If I might have a word with you in private, my lord?"

"I have nothing further to say to you," snapped the Marquis and kept going.

"If you prefer," said Sebastian, raising his voice loud enough that one or two other men turned to stare, "I can ask my questions here and now. But for the sake of the late Lady Stamford, I thought—"

"You bloody son of a bitch," hissed the Marquis, turning back to him. "Keep your voice down."

Sebastian met the man's blazing gaze. "Shall we go for a walk?"

Stamford stared at him for a long moment, his face tight, his breath coming hard and fast. Then he pressed his lips tightly together and gave a curt nod.

⚘

They turned downhill toward the ancient brick palace of St. James's that lay at the base of the street. The pavements were crowded with boisterous well-heeled gentlemen of various ages and the laughing, richly gowned, considerably less-well-born females who hung on their arms. The scents of roasting meat and fine wine and spirits hung heavily in the air; golden light and music spilled from elegant windows and open doors.

"Say what you have to say and be done with it," snapped Stamford. "But I give you fair warning: Insult the memory of my dead wife and I swear to God, I'll call you out for it."

Sebastian studied the older man's cold, hard face. "I'm told you had a rather spectacular rift with your brother some years ago. You obviously don't need me to repeat the rumors it generated."

The Marquis stared straight ahead. "Family members quarrel. Sometimes brothers, sometimes fathers and sons." A gleam of malice showed in his eyes as he threw Sebastian a knowing look. "I doubt you need me to remind you of that."

"True. Although it becomes more of a concern when one of those family members turns up dead." Sebastian paused, then said, "Seven years ago I was in the Peninsula. I only know of the past rift with your brother because people are talking about it again. It might behoove you to set the record straight."

"Damn you all to hell," snapped Stamford, drawing up again. "If you must know, the quarrel was over Miles's debts. You know what young men new on the town can be like. He was bored and looking to amuse himself in any way he could, and I saw where things were going. So I called him on it, and then I bought him a pair of colors. It's what he'd been wanting for years—he'd been Army-mad from the time he was a young lad. I was the one who'd been standing in his way—he'd been my heir, you know. But by that point I had a son of my own who was a year old, and I realized I'd been making a mistake, stopping Miles from doing what he'd always wanted to do. So I let him go. . . . The rumors about my wife that followed were ugly and baseless, and damn your eyes for reminding me of them."

He drew a quick, angry breath. His face was stony, but fury had turned the flesh a dark, almost purple hue. "Why the hell are you poking your nose into something that occurred years ago, anyway? If you want to know what happened to my brother, I keep telling you to look at that French whore—the one who calls herself Alexi Sauvage."

Sebastian felt the warm night air gust damp against his face. "You're saying an incident that occurred two or three years ago must be relevant, whereas something from seven years ago is not?"

"Who said anything about two or three years ago? I'm hearing the bitch went after Miles the very night he was killed, in the middle of Charing Cross."

Sebastian was aware of a burst of laughter from an open window above them. According to Alexi, she hadn't seen her bigamous husband in years. "And where precisely are you 'hearing' this?"

"I've now had two different people tell me the tale."

"And did either of them happen to mention the subject of this quarrel?"

"One assumes it was more of the same mad nonsense she's been spouting for years."

Sebastian frowned. "You say this was in Charing Cross? At what time?"

"Sometime that evening. Why don't you try asking her?" Stamford drew back his shoulders, his chin held high as he ostentatiously readjusted the set of his coat. "And that's all I have to say to you. But mark my words, if I ever hear my wife's name on your lips again, I will call you out."

Sebastian let the man go. If Stamford was telling the truth—if his quarrel with Miles had in fact been over the younger man's debts, and if Lady Stamford had indeed died of some unsuspected heart disorder just months later—then the Marquis's anger was well justified.

Except that seven years ago, Miles had been a man of twenty-four, not a callow youth freshly down from Oxford. He'd also been recently married to Edward Platt's daughter, which meant that at that point he presumably still had money to burn. And then there was the matter of the Marquis's behavior after his wife's sudden, inexplicable death. A postmortem could have put to rest all the ugly speculations of foul play once and for all, yet Stamford had refused to allow one. And while families did sometimes balk at the procedure, Stamford's only objection to such an examination of his brother's remains had concerned the origins and social class of the surgeon involved, not the procedure itself.

For a moment Sebastian stood where he was, watching the Marquis stride angrily back up the hill. Then he turned to stare out over the dark, shadowy parkland beyond the palace.

Even if the rumors surrounding the events of seven years ago were true, they still didn't explain why a man who'd nursed a grudge against his brother for all those years would suddenly decide to murder him, blow off his face, and castrate him. It made no sense, unless . . .

Unless the handsome younger brother had set his sights on the Marquis's young, pretty second wife.

Of course, that wouldn't explain the two headless corpses that had also been pulled from the Thames. But while it was true that all three men had been murdered, mutilated, and dumped in the river, their bodies had not all been treated exactly the same.

Did that matter? It might.

And while Sebastian didn't want to believe that he was dealing with two different killers, he also knew that it was a possibility he couldn't entirely dismiss.

≈

Sebastian found Paul Gibson's surgery and the ancient stone house beside it dark and locked.

"If'n yer lookin' fer the surgeon," said a passing young lad as Sebastian was turning back toward his curricle, "I seen him just a few minutes ago down by the Tower."

"Thank you," said Sebastian.

The moon was nearly full, bathing the ancient stones of the looming fortress in a pale silvery light. Sebastian walked downhill along the banks of the old moat to where he could see a man's familiar thin figure standing near Tower Dock, his back to the massive medieval castle as he stared out across the wide moonlit expanse of the Thames. Gibson acknowledged Sebastian's approach with a nod, his gaze going back again to the south.

"Do you think it's started yet?" he said.

There was no need to ask of what he spoke. "Yes," said Sebastian, stopping beside him.

"I wish I were there."

"So do I."

Gibson glanced over at him. "But you chose to sell out."

Sebastian kept his gaze on a wherryman working his way across the choppy expanse of water. "I did. Because I didn't believe in what I was doing anymore, and because I didn't like what it was doing to me." He watched the wherryman ship his oars. "I still don't believe in what Britain is trying to do—putting the Bourbons and the rest of that spoiled repressive lot back on their thrones. But you and I both know that's not what's driving the poor bastards who're fighting and dying over there right now. They're fighting for each other . . . which I guess is why I feel like I should be there with them, too."

Gibson nodded, and the two friends stood in silence for a time, the wind off the river buffeting them with the scents of the sea and faraway places. Then Gibson said, "I was going to send you a note in the morning, about this new headless, footless corpse."

"You've finished the autopsy?"

"I have. Although if you're looking for answers to what happened to the poor bastard, I can't tell you. He wasn't stabbed—at least not in the parts we have. And while there are one or two things that make me suspect he was strangled, I can't say for certain. Your killer whacked the head off too close to the trunk."

"So what can you tell me about the man himself?"

"He was young—quite young, maybe twenty or twenty-two. Healthy, his hands nicely manicured. That's about it. Bow Street has his pantaloons and are trying to find the tailor, but if they've learned anything, I haven't heard about it."

Sebastian studied his friend's half-averted profile. Gibson's face was pale, his eyes dark bruises, his graying hair a windblown mess. But he seemed fiercely, almost brutally free of any signs of an opium-induced haze. "Is Alexi off delivering another baby?"

"No, she's got some other project she's working on. Why?"

Sebastian shook his head. "Just wanted to ask her something about Sedgewick. It can wait."

Gibson sucked in a deep breath. "She's got this idea that she can get rid of the phantom pains from my missing leg by using some crazy setup with a box and mirrors that tricks the brain. She keeps pressing me to try it."

"So why don't you? What can it hurt? If it doesn't work, it doesn't. But if you can get rid of the pains, you can quit taking that bloody opium. Before it kills you."

Gibson kept his gaze on the river. "That's just it. What if it does work? What if it does somehow trick my mind into realizing that the pains it thinks I'm feeling are just an illusion? Then I won't need the opium anymore. But what if—" His voice broke, and he had to swallow hard before he could continue. "What if I can't stop?"

Oh, hell, thought Sebastian.

"I started taking the opium to dull the pain," Gibson was saying. "But it's reached the point that a part of me is afraid to lose the pains because then I'll lose my excuse for taking the opium."

"And you don't think you can stop?"

"No."

Sebastian was silent for a moment. "God knows it won't be easy. In fact, it's probably going to be the hardest thing you've ever had to do. But if you fail, you fail; at least you'll have tried, and you can always try again. No one is going to fault you or judge you for it."

A muscle jumped along the Irishman's set jaw. "I'm afraid Alexi would leave me."

"If you can't stop taking the opium, you mean? You honestly think she might?"

Gibson dropped his gaze to his feet. "Why wouldn't she?"

"Because she loves you?" Sebastian suggested.

Gibson shook his head. "Who could blame her? Hell, I'd leave me."

"Do you want her to stay?"

Gibson looked up at him. "More than anything in this world and the next."

Sebastian met his friend's tortured gaze. "More than you want to keep taking the opium? Because that's what it comes down to, isn't it? Which do you love the most? The opium, or Alexi?"

But Gibson simply stared back at him, his dark green eyes glittering as if with broken shards of pain and fear and hopeless longing.

Chapter 35

Sebastian awoke the next day before dawn.

He was standing at the bedroom window, his gaze on the rich morning light striking the chimneys and rooftops of the houses across the street, when Hero came to rest her hand on the small of his back. "What is it?" she asked softly.

He shook his head, unable to put any of it into words. He felt as if someone had fastened a metal band around his forehead, a band that kept getting tighter and tighter. Part of it, he knew, came from his frustration over his inability to identify whatever sick killer had decided to make the Thames the dumping ground for his victims. But it was more than that. There was a hum in the air, as if all of London were holding its breath along with him, waiting for news from across the Channel.

After a moment, she said, "You feel it, don't you? Whatever is happening over there, I mean."

He looked at her. "You, too?" It was like a palpable turmoil in the atmosphere, born of the collective rage, agony, fear, and despair rising up from the tens of thousands of men who were surely at that very moment fighting, bleeding, and dying.

"Not as much as you, I suspect. But yes."

She was silent, her gaze on a milkmaid turning down the street, two heavy pails hanging from the yoke balanced across her shoulders. Then she said, "You can't suspect Alexi and Gibson of killing Sedgewick."

"Gibson? No. But I'm not so sure about Alexi. I'd say she's more than capable of killing—has done so, in fact, in the past."

"That was war."

He turned from the window. "We always make such a fine distinction, don't we? A man kills his nation's enemy in battle and it's a brave, noble, heroic deed. But if that same man were to kill the same Frenchman—or Italian or Russian—in a time of peace, we'd call it murder."

"Because then his motives would be selfish."

"His personal motives. But if the motives of his nation—or at least of his government or king—are selfish, it's all right?"

She tilted her head, her gaze hard on his face. "What if the man who dumped Sedgewick and the others in the Thames thought he was doing a noble, selfless deed? According to Dudley Tiptoff, would such a man still be evil?"

"I don't know. I'll have to ask him."

She reached to touch her fingertips to his temple, where he could feel that band of pressure squeezing tighter and tighter. "Your head hurts, doesn't it?"

He caught her hand in his and brought her fingers to his lips. "How did you know?"

"I know."

He found Alexi Sauvage in the surgery on Tower Hill. She was seated at a small round table in the front room, winding bandages, and looked over at him when he pushed open the front door.

"Gibson told me you were looking for me," she said, going back to what she'd been doing.

He braced one hand against the frame of the entrance to the room and leaned into it. "You lied to me. You told me you hadn't seen Sedgewick in years. Except now I discover you had a public quarrel with him the very night he was killed—in Charing Cross, of all bloody places. Did you really think I wouldn't hear about it?"

She went quite still, her hands resting in her lap, her face half turned away. But she didn't say anything.

"What time was it?" he said.

"When I saw him? Half past eight, perhaps. Maybe nine."

"Why Charing Cross?"

She gave a faint twitch of one shoulder. "I saw him there by chance. I'd been . . . visiting someone with a sick child and was heading home when I looked up to see him in a hackney snarled in traffic."

"And so you—what? Decided to accost him for old times' sake?"

Her nostrils flared on a quick, angry breath. "Something like that."

"And then what?"

"And then . . . nothing. He had descended from the hackney in the course of our conversation, and then he continued on his way, on foot. The last time I saw him, he was headed down Whitehall."

"When you first saw him, what direction had he been coming from?"

"Someplace in the east."

Except for the slight difference in timing, it fit with what Sebastian had learned from Tiptoff. But he had a feeling the rest of what she was telling him was pure garbage.

With a swallowed oath, he pushed against the doorframe and turned away, only to swing back and face her again, his hands hanging loosely at his sides. "You're in danger; you do realize that, don't you? The Marquis of Stamford is pushing Bow Street to have you taken up for murdering his brother at exactly the same time as the Palace is pressuring them to arrest someone—anyone—to calm the public's fear that we're all about to be chopped into bits and thrown into the Thames. Add in the fact that you're not just a foreigner, you're French, at a time when we are probably already fighting what many see as an apocalyptic battle against the French, and I'd say your chances of ever coming out of prison alive are not good."

She stared at him, her face now white, her nostrils pinched. "I wouldn't have thought you cared."

"God damn it! You're putting Gibson at risk, too. You know that! If you get taken up, he probably will be, too—as your accomplice."

A faint, ironic smile tugged at her lips. "Well, at least you're honest about why you care. It has nothing to do with me at all."

Sebastian took a deep breath, then let it out. "That's not what I meant and you know it. But even if you don't care what happens to you, I'd think you would at least care about him."

He could see the pulse that beat at the base of her long white throat. "I care."

"Then tell me the truth."

"I can't."

"Bloody hell," he swore, and turned toward the passage again.

He was halfway out the front door when she said, "Bow Street identified the body of the young man pulled from the river. Did you know?"

He looked back at her. "No. Who is he?"

"Some lord's cousin. He worked at the Foreign Office."

❧

"His name was Hamilton Evans," said Lovejoy when Sebastian drove up to Bloomsbury to see him.

He'd found the magistrate seated in his parlor with a cup of tea on the table beside him and some improving tome open on his lap. But he readily set aside his book at Sebastian's entrance. "The kinship with Lord Oakley is somewhat distant—second cousin once or twice removed, or some such thing. But his parents died in India when he was a young lad, and Oakley stepped in to pay his school fees, then secured him a position at the Foreign Office when he came down from Cambridge."

"How did you manage to identify him?"

"His tailor. The young man was supposed to be on his way down to Kent to stay with friends, which is why it was several days before anyone realized he was missing. But there is no doubt about the identification. Seems Evans broke his left forearm as a child and it healed a bit crooked. Paul Gibson had noted it in the report on his postmortem examination."

Sebastian found himself wondering if the break was actually discovered by Gibson or by Alexi Sauvage, although he kept the thought to himself. "His association with the Foreign Office is disturbing."

"It is, rather. Are you quite certain I can't offer you a cup of tea?"

"Thank you, but no," said Sebastian, going to stand at the window, his gaze thoughtful as he stared at the gray clouds beginning to gather overhead. After a moment, he said, "It could be irrelevant, but there's a reverend by the name of Sinclair Palmer it might be worth having the constables look into. He has the living up at Marylebone."

"We can do that. Incidentally," said Lovejoy, taking off his spectacles and rubbing his eyes with a splayed thumb and forefinger, "we located that woman you were inquiring about."

Sebastian turned. "Phoebe Cox? So she is in prison?"

Lovejoy nodded. "Her landlady reported her for disposing of her child, but it seems there is more to the story. According to the landlady, Phoebe had an emotional encounter last week with a man she kept calling 'Mr. Sedgewick.'"

"When was this?"

"Saturday afternoon. The landlady claims to have heard her threaten to kill not only Sedgewick but her baby and herself, as well."

Sebastian drew a deep breath and let it out slowly. "She told me the babe starved to death. What did she do? Smother it?"

"No one knows; it's disappeared." Lovejoy let out his breath in a long, sad sigh of resignation. "In all likelihood she dropped it in the river or down a privy somewhere. It happens all the time, I'm afraid."

"What prison is she in?"

"Coldbath Fields."

❧

Coldbath Fields Prison lay in Clerkenwell, on the north side of London. It was a miserable place, built back in the seventeenth century, freezing in winter and stifling and airless in summer, with cramped, overcrowded cells that were prone to flooding when it rained. Its prisoners were fed a meager ration of stinking water and stale bread and beaten with sticks or knotted ropes if they dared complain. Its death rate was shocking even by the dismal standards of London's other prisons.

A beefy, unshaven gaoler with massive hamlike arms and legs, a bald head, and a mouthful of rotten teeth escorted Sebastian to a room with bare stone walls, a high barred window, several crude wooden benches, and nothing else. He waited there for some time, the cold and misery of the place seeping into his bones as he breathed through his mouth in a futile attempt to keep from smelling the reek of overflowing slop buckets, unwashed bodies, damp, and decay. He was beginning to wonder if the gaoler had forgotten him when he heard footsteps coming back and the tearful, pleading voice of a woman.

"Where are you taking me? What have I done? Oh, please, why won't you tell me?"

Sebastian could see her now, one thin arm held fast in the gaoler's meaty fist. She looked as if at some point she had fallen—or been pushed—into mud and been unable to clean herself up: Her ragged dress was torn and stained, her cheap shoes gone, her hair matted and filthy, and her face streaked with dirt. She had her head bowed, her stringy hair hanging over her face as the gaoler shoved her into the room and then let her go so fast she stumbled and almost fell.

"Git in there," he told her roughly. "And mind you show his lordship the proper respect, ye hear?"

"That will be all for now, thank you," Sebastian told the man.

Phoebe had been standing with her shoulders slumped, her gaze fixed on the stone floor. But at the sound of Sebastian's voice, her head snapped up, her eyes widening with what looked like fear.

"If yer lordship will jist holler when yer done," said the gaoler, "I'll come and git the wench."

"Thank you," said Sebastian again.

The gaoler went to wait in the passage, his arms crossed at his chest, his expression blank as he stared into space.

"Sit down, please," Sebastian told Phoebe.

She went to sink onto one of the benches, her hands knotted in her lap, her face pale and trembling as she stared up at him.

He said, "You should have told me you'd seen Sedgewick."

She swallowed hard, her gaze dropping to her clenched hands. "I was afraid," she whispered. "Afraid that if anyone knew I'd seen him, they'd think I'd killed him. But I didn't! I swear to God, I didn't."

"I don't think you did." Sebastian studied the huddled, half-starved woman before him and wondered how anyone could imagine her capable of overpowering a man like Miles Sedgewick, killing him, mutilating him, and then somehow hauling his body down to dump it in the river.

"Why did he come to see you?" he asked.

She sucked in a deep breath that shuddered her thin chest. "I'd been to Mount Street that morning, to beg him to help me. I was actually standing outside his house, trying to decide how to approach him, when he came home. I didn't know he'd been away, you see. He was furious when he saw me—told me he would come talk to me later, but that I wouldn't get a penny out of him if I didn't leave right away." She dashed the back of one fist across first one eye, then the other. "I didn't really expect him to come, but he did. I suppose he was afraid that if he didn't, I'd go back to his house and make a scene."

"What did you want from him?"

"I was hoping he'd give me money for Amelia. I was desperate."

"And did he?"

She shook her head. "But I didn't kill him! I swear. Why would I? He was my last hope."

"And yet you threatened to kill him."

"No! I know that's what that old hag of a landlady told them, but it's not true. I only said I wished I'd died in childbirth and taken the baby with me, and it's true. It's true!" She flattened both her hands over her face, her voice a torn whisper, her body convulsing with her sobs. "Dear God, how I wish I were dead."

"What happened to your baby?" Sebastian said gently.

Her hands slipped down her face until they were covering only her nose and mouth. "He took her."

"Sedgewick?"

She nodded, her eyes two dark, pitiful bruises in a pale face.

"You gave him your child?"

"How could I stop him? He insisted it was his right, as her father. Said he would find a wet nurse for her."

"And you believed him?"

"What else could I do?" she wailed. "I couldn't feed her—my milk had dried up, and she couldn't keep anything else down."

"What time was this?"

"That I saw him? I don't know. Half past six? Maybe seven?"

Sebastian figured Sedgewick must have gone straight to her after leaving his house in Mount Street. Only, where the hell had he gone after that?

Aloud, Sebastian said, "Where is the baby now?"

"I don't know! Alexi told me I was a fool to trust him like that, that I never should have let him take the baby. But what was I supposed to do? I asked him to give me money, but he wouldn't."

"Alexi?" Sebastian stared at her. "You mean Alexi Sauvage?"

Phoebe wiped her running nose on the back of her wrist and nodded.

"How do you know her?"

"Alexi? She delivered Amelia."

"But how did she know Sedgewick had the baby?"

"I'd told her Amelia was sick, so she came that evening to

take a look at her. But by the time Alexi got there, Miles had already taken her."

"She knew who the baby's father was?"

Phoebe Cox stared up at him, her forehead puckered with confusion, as if she couldn't understand why such a thing would matter. "Yes, of course. I told her."

Chapter 36

*A*lexi Sauvage was at a street market near St. Katharine's when Sebastian found her. The sunshine was growing fitful, with gathering clouds that scuttled across the sky to send shifting patterns of light and shadow over the city. She had the handle of a market basket looped over one arm and was inspecting a pyramid of melons when he walked up to her.

"I've just seen Phoebe Cox," he said bluntly. "She tells me you knew Sedgewick had taken her baby."

Alexi turned her head to look at him, her dark eyes hooded, her features tense and wary.

He said, "That's why you confronted him in Charing Cross, isn't it? And what the quarrel was about."

Alexi hesitated a moment, then nodded. "All I wanted was for him to tell me what he'd done with the child. But he denied even taking it."

"Are you quite certain that he did take it? Phoebe could have abandoned the child herself and then lied about it."

"No. She'd spent weeks frantically trying to keep that child alive. She never would have abandoned her."

"Perhaps she simply gave up."

"No. I can't believe that."

Sebastian wasn't so sure. He said, "Why the bloody hell didn't you tell me this before?"

"How could I? To do so would only cast suspicion on Phoebe."

Sebastian looked away, to where a dirty little boy was playing with a kitten beside one of the stalls. "If Sedgewick did take the baby, what would he have done with her?"

Alexi let out her breath in a heavy sigh. "I don't want to even think. It isn't as if he'd had time to arrange for a wet nurse, and I can't see him walking around London with a ragged babe in his arms, can you? I wouldn't put it past him to have simply dropped the child in the river or down a well. I was hoping he'd given her to some gypsy woman to beg with, but I haven't been able to find any sign of one."

"You've been looking?"

"I have, yes. It's been over a week now, so unless he gave the baby to a woman who had breast milk, it's surely dead. But I'm still looking, because if I can't find out what he did with it, they're going to hang Phoebe for murdering her child."

"You think they will?"

"They hang women all the time when their babies are stillborn or simply die in their sleep. Of course they'll hang Phoebe." She gave a faint shake of her head. "Although the truth is, I'm not convinced she's going to survive in that prison long enough to even stand trial."

Sebastian squinted thoughtfully up at the thickening clouds. "You say you saw him shortly before nine? At Charing Cross?"

"Yes."

"Did he say anything at all to you about where he'd been or where he was going?"

"No. But wherever he was going, it couldn't have been far. Otherwise, why did he abandon his hackney?"

Why indeed? thought Sebastian.

⁊

Sebastian was beginning to have a clearer understanding of Miles Sedgewick's movements on the last day of his life. The problem was, given that several of his activities that day had been less than honorable, Sebastian couldn't help but wonder what else was still hidden.

According to Isabella McPherson, Miles Sedgewick came to see her shortly after one o'clock, which would fit with the time he had finished meeting with Bathurst, Castlereagh, and Jarvis in Downing Street. After spending the afternoon dallying with his mistress, he had then apparently gone home to change into evening dress before leaving again—according to both his wife and his valet—at around half past six or seven. It was at that point he'd gone to see Phoebe Cox. But where had he gone between the time he left her and shortly before nine, when Alexi saw him in Charing Cross? And what the hell had he done with Phoebe's child? It seemed unlikely that he had taken the infant back to his mistress, Isabella. But it was, surely, at least worth looking into?

Sebastian knew Hero would be more successful than he at getting the truth out of the woman, but when he arrived back at Brook Street it was to find Claire in the entry hall with Patrick and Simon, preparing to take the lads out.

"Papa," called Simon, running to him. "We's goin' to the park!"

Sebastian scooped the little boy up in his arms. "I can see that. Does your mother have an interview this afternoon?"

"Nope," said Patrick. "She's gone to Berkeley Square."

"Oh?" said Sebastian, looking over at Claire.

The Frenchwoman nodded. "She received a note from Lady Jarvis and left perhaps half an hour ago."

Sebastian let Simon slide back down to the floor, then bent to re-tie one of Patrick's shoes that had come loose. "*Lady* Jarvis, you say?"

"Yes, my lord."

🦢

He reached the McPhersons' house in Norfolk Street to find a town carriage pulled up in front and Lady McPherson herself, dressed in a demure gown of figured white muslin with a pale pink spencer and broad-brimmed chip hat, descending the carriage steps.

"Lord Devlin," she said with a wide smile when she saw him. "I fear you've just missed Monty; he's gone off to visit some old friends who've recently arrived in Town."

"Actually, I came to see you," said Sebastian. "If I might have a word?"

Her pretty smile slipped for just an instant before she fixed it firmly back in place. "Yes, of course; won't you come in?" She led the way up the front steps to where a middle-aged, sandy-haired butler was opening the door with a bow. "If you'll allow Richardson here to show you to the drawing room, I shan't be but a moment."

She disappeared up the stairs, tearing off her hat and gloves as she went. But Sebastian waited in her pretty pastel-colored drawing room for nearly half an hour before she finally reappeared. She'd changed her dress, and her hair was damp at the temples, as if she'd just splashed water on her face. But it had done little to disguise the fact that her eyes were red and swollen, as if she'd been crying. And that didn't make any sense at all.

"My apologies for taking so long," she said with a pretty smile that didn't reach her tear-reddened eyes. "I see Richardson has brought the tea tray; shall I pour you a cup? Or would you prefer a glass of brandy?"

"Tea is fine," he said. "Thank you."

"Won't you have a seat?"

"Thank you, but I prefer to stand."

She went to sit on the pink silk-covered settee beside the tea table, forming a conscious tableau of English gentility as she reached gracefully for the heavy silver teapot. "So tell me, my lord, how may I help you?"

He stayed where he was, beside the window overlooking the street, his hands clasped behind his back as he watched her pour. "Late last winter, Eloisa Sedgewick dismissed her governess because the woman had allowed herself to be seduced and impregnated by Miles. Did you know?"

Isabella McPherson's hand shook so badly that she had to quickly set down the teapot, her lips parting as she raised her head to stare at him. "No. Are you quite certain?"

"That the child was Sedgewick's? What do you think?"

She shook her head; she was no longer even trying to smile. "Last winter, you say?"

"Yes," said Sebastian, wondering exactly when Isabella's affair with Miles Sedgewick had begun. "The child was born in May."

She reached for a spoon to stir the cup of tea. "Why are you telling me this?"

"Because Sedgewick went to see his former governess the day he died."

She held the cup of tea out to him, her face hardening as he took it. "I don't believe it."

"Believe it," said Sebastian simply, holding the cup in his hands. "A week ago Saturday morning, the woman went to Mount Street, desperate for his help. He got rid of her by promising to come see her later that day, and he did. Except instead of giving her money, he took the baby girl away with him. Do you know what he did with her?"

She reached for the teapot again and began to pour a second cup, her hands now steady. "No."

Sebastian kept his gaze on her beautiful, closed face. "I don't believe you."

She looked up, tossing her head to shift a stray lock of hair from her face. "Indeed? How perfectly ungracious of you to say so. Personally, I'm not convinced I should believe anything you're telling me about this child. Why should I?"

"Miles saw Phoebe Cox that Saturday morning and again later that evening. You told Lady Devlin he came here early in the afternoon. Is that true?"

She nodded, her eyes wide, her face completely wiped clear of all expression.

Sebastian said, "How did he know Monty wouldn't be here?"

"But he didn't know. He came to see Monty."

"Cut line, Lady McPherson," Sebastian said impatiently, setting his untasted tea aside. "He came to see you. So how did he know Monty wouldn't be here? Did you send him a note?"

She hesitated, then nodded again, her cheeks coloring as her gaze slid away.

"And he said nothing to you about Phoebe Cox or her baby?"

"I keep telling you, no!"

"And you can't think what he might have done with the baby? That woman is in prison right now, accused of killing her own child. She could very well hang for it. *What did he do with her baby?*"

"I tell you, I don't know!"

Sebastian gave up and tried a different tack. "Did Monty know you were having an affair with his friend?"

She gave a high-pitched false little laugh. "Don't be absurd. I won't deny that Miles and I were enjoying a flirtation, but there was nothing more to it than that."

"Of course," said Sebastian dryly. "So did Monty know of this 'flirtation'?"

She looked directly at him, as if she could somehow compel him to believe her. "No. And I know what you're thinking, but you're wrong; Monty could never kill anyone. Never."

After their time together in the Army, Sebastian knew only too well what Monty McPherson was capable of. But he kept that thought to himself.

She sat forward, her hands coming together to rest in her lap, her own tea obviously forgotten. "I assume Lady Devlin told you about the list—the one with the names of people in London who've been in contact with Napoléon?"

"Yes."

She licked her lips as if they'd suddenly gone dry. "But the list wasn't the only thing Miles brought back from Vienna. He also carried official correspondence—Austrian proposals for the future governance of France in the event that Napoléon is defeated."

"He told you that?" *Good Lord; did he tell his secrets to all his women?* Sebastian wondered. Jarvis had been wise not to trust the man. Except why the hell hadn't Jarvis convinced Castlereagh or Bathurst to do the same?

She nodded. "The Austrians want Napoléon to be allowed to abdicate in favor of his son."

"Of course they do. His son is half Austrian and currently being raised at the palace in Vienna—which is only one reason why the British government will never agree to such a scheme."

"You don't think the controversial nature of those proposals might perhaps explain why Miles was killed?"

"No. If he'd been killed before he delivered them, then one might be able to make the argument—although I would still find it difficult to believe. But they had already been delivered."

"Yet it's still conceivable that someone in the government wanted to keep others from learning of the proposals, isn't it?"

If so, they should have chosen a more discreet courier, he thought. But he simply shook his head and said, "Did Sedgewick ever mention Cabrera to you?"

He didn't expect her to know what he was talking about, but to his surprise, she did. "You mean the island where all those French prisoners died?"

"So he did talk about it?"

"Yes, but it was months ago, back before he went to the Continent. Why?"

"What did he say about it?"

"Nothing much. He only brought it up because one of the Spanish diplomats involved in the negotiations leading up to sending the prisoners there was recently posted to their embassy here."

"Which diplomat?"

She looked at him blankly. "I don't know. If he said the man's name, I don't recall it. Why? What has Cabrera to do with any of this?"

"Probably nothing," said Sebastian. "What about a young man at the Foreign Office named Hamilton Evans? Did Sedgewick ever mention him?"

"No, but I heard he's been identified as the last body they found. He was so young—just twenty-two." Her face had taken on a pinched, frightened look. And he wondered if she really believed what she'd said about her husband—that he could never kill someone. Surely she must know that wasn't true.

"This is all so horrible," she was saying. "Who is doing it? Do you have any idea at all?"

Sebastian shook his head. "I wish I could say I did, but no, I don't."

The truth was, he had lots of ideas, but nothing to confirm any of them. And he felt as if a clock were ticking, that it was only a matter of time until the killer struck again. Because while Sebastian might not know who was doing this, he had no doubt at all that the killer was not yet finished.

Chapter 37

$\mathcal{D}$ressed in an elegant gown of sprigged lightweight silk with a fringed parasol tilted just so against the sun, Kat Boleyn strolled up Piccadilly, pausing occasionally to glance at the window displays of first a haberdasher, then a milliner. She could see the man she had come here to meet standing outside Hatchards, but she took her time approaching him. When she did finally come up to him, she greeted him as an old friend casually encountered, although the meeting had been carefully prearranged. Tall, lean, and powerfully built, with sparkling green eyes and two deceptive dimples, he was Aiden O'Connell, the younger son of Lord Rathkeale of Tyrawley. Fashionable London knew him as a lazy, heedless young man-about-town. Kat Boleyn knew him as Napoléon's onetime spymaster in London.

He held her hands and gave them a squeeze, an open, careless smile on his face for the benefit of anyone who might be observing them. "Walk with me," he said, drawing one of her hands through the crook of his arm. "Tell me what's happening."

She fell into step beside him as they turned up the street. "You've heard about the death of Miles Sedgewick?"

"I have. You think it should concern me?"

Kat kept her gaze fixed straight ahead. "You know what he used to do?"

"For Wellington? Yes. I also know what he was still doing for Bathurst and Castlereagh. Why?"

"He recently brought back from Vienna a list said to contain the names of those here in London known to have passed information to Napoléon. That list disappeared when he was killed."

He swore softly under his breath. "Where did this list come from?"

"It was probably compiled by Fouché when he was trying to ingratiate his way into favor with the Bourbons, before Napoléon's escape from Elba. I don't know why it was given to Sedgewick, nor do I know precisely whose names were on it." She searched his deceptively open face. "Why? What is it?"

"Two people whose names would in all likelihood be on such a list have disappeared in the last week—one a Frenchwoman, the other an elderly Scotsman."

Kat's hands clenched on her parasol, then relaxed to give it a casual twirl that was all for show. "Someone has been watching me. Following me."

"You don't know who?"

She shook her head. "No. What can you tell me about the Bourbons' assassin, Gabriel?"

"I don't know who he is, if that's what you're asking. But whoever he is, he's very good at what he does."

Before she could stop herself, Kat shivered.

He drew up and turned to face her. "I don't think I've ever seen you afraid before."

"I've been afraid before. But not like this."

He was silent for a moment, his gaze searching her face in a way that made her wonder what he saw there. "Why? Why now and not before?"

"I don't know. Perhaps I'm getting old."

A crooked smile curled his lips as he reached out to touch the backs of his fingers to her cheek in a gesture that was almost a caress. "You're not getting old."

Chapter 38

Sebastian drove next to Berkeley Square, meaning to confront Jarvis about what the powerful man really knew about Miles Sedgewick's death. But when he rounded the corner of the square, it was to find the cobbles spread with straw to deaden the clatter of hooves and the rattle of ironclad wheels over stone.

"What's this fer, then?" said Tom as Sebastian pulled in at the kerb. "'As somebody died?"

Sebastian handed the boy the reins. "Hopefully not. I suspect Lady Jarvis has been confined."

Hopping down, he took the front steps two at a time and was about to ring the bell when the door was opened by Jarvis's normally staid and censorious butler, Grisham. His hair was vaguely disarrayed, and a smile kept tugging at his lips. "My lord," he said, unbending more than Sebastian would have thought possible. "You've come to see the new babe, have you?"

"It's here, is it?"

"It is, indeed. And it's a boy!"

A soft step on the landing above drew his attention to where Hero had just appeared, a lavishly wrapped bundle cradled in her arms. "I saw you drive up," she said, coming down the stairs toward him. "Meet my little brother: Master Maximilian Charles David Jarvis." She held the babe up so he could see. "Isn't he beautiful?"

Sebastian gazed down at the red, scrunch-faced, sleeping infant and smiled. "He is, yes. And how is Cousin Victoria?"

"She's doing well. It was an amazingly easy delivery—especially for a first birth."

"Thank God for that."

"It's always magical, isn't it?" she said, looking over at him with a soft, joyous smile. And he felt his heart swell with so much love that it hurt.

"Always," he whispered, his gaze locking with hers.

A heavy tread on the stairs drew their attention to where Jarvis himself was coming down toward them. "Congratulations, my lord," said Sebastian, turning. "You have a fine new son."

"Thank you," said the big man. He paused beside Hero, his gaze on the child in her arms, his face so gentle, so filled with wonder and quiet joy, that Sebastian caught a glimpse that he'd rarely seen of a private side to this powerful, formidable man. Then Jarvis looked up, a speculative gleam banishing that brief moment of tenderness and vulnerability as his gaze settled on his son-in-law. "Did you wish to see me about something?"

Sebastian shook his head. "Nothing that can't wait."

※

It was some time later, when Sebastian and Hero were seated on the sunny terrace overlooking their rear garden while the two boys played with their big black cat, that Sebastian said to Hero, "How would you like to go to a ball tonight?"

She laughed and shifted the slant of her parasol so that she could look over at him. Then she said, "Oh, heavens, you're serious. Which ball?"

"The one being given by the French Ambassador."

"That's tonight? With everything that's going on, I'd totally forgotten it."

"Do you feel up to it?"

"Yes, of course. But why?"

"Because the Ambassador from Spain is bound to be there, and it's probably the easiest way to find out more about this diplomat who was involved in the negotiations that ended with the French prisoners being sent to Cabrera."

"What do you think he can tell you?"

"I don't know. But it seems a bit of a coincidence, don't you think? Such a man being posted to London now?"

"Coincidences do happen."

"They do," said Sebastian, watching Simon trail a length of string down a flagstone path for the cat to chase. "And sometimes their consequences can be deadly."

⁂

The French Ambassador to the Court of St. James was a blue-blooded aristocrat named Claude-Louis-Raoul de La Châtre. His father, the previous Marquis de La Châtre, had been guillotined by the revolutionaries in 1793, while Claude-Louis fled France to organize a regiment of émigrés loyal to the deposed Bourbons. He was in his late sixties now, with a long nose, a prominent, full lower lip, and fiercely dark eyebrows that contrasted strikingly with the thin white hair he wore hanging long to his shoulders. Sebastian had never met the man, but he was the representative of the newly restored—although now once again deposed—Bourbons, and the Bourbons were not fond of Sebastian.

"*Ah, monsieur le vicomte,*" he said when Sebastian and Hero were presented to him. "And Lady Devlin. I have heard Marie-Thérèse speak of you both." He paused, his heavy dark brows drawing together in a frown. "Often."

"Oh, dear," said Hero in a low voice after they'd turned away. "I get the impression the Daughter of France has not had nice things to say about us."

"Evidently not."

The roar of voices was so loud they could barely hear the music leaking from the ballroom as they worked their way through the press of laughing, gaily chatting members of London's moneyed elite. "Do you even know what the Spanish Ambassador looks like?" Hero asked.

"No," Sebastian admitted.

"Perhaps you can find Hendon and persuade him to introduce you to His Excellency while I stalk the Ambassador's wife."

"You're optimistic if you think Hendon will agree to do any such thing."

"Perhaps he'll surprise you. One would think he'd be in charity with you, given that we actually came here as he asked."

"Perhaps."

But when Sebastian finally tracked the Earl to the supper room, he glared at his heir and said, "What the devil are you doing here?"

"You sound like Amanda," said Sebastian, running his gaze over the rather meager spread the French embassy had provided for its guests. But then, funds did tend to dry up when one's monarch has been deposed. "You're the one who wanted me to attend tonight, remember?"

"Yes, but I didn't expect you to actually come."

"I need you to introduce me to the Spanish Ambassador."

Hendon fixed him with a steady gaze. "Why?"

"I'd like to ask the man some questions—and I promise not to create a diplomatic incident in the process."

"God preserve us," muttered Hendon, setting aside his plate.

⚸

In contrast to the French Ambassador, the Spanish Ambassador to the Court of St. James—Carlos Gutiérrez de los Rios y Sarmiento de Sotomayor—was quite young, still in his thirties. His family was also old and aristocratic—he was the Seventh Count of Fernán Núñez—but they'd never been either excessively powerful or excessively wealthy, and his long boyish face bore a habitual smile of almost impish goodwill.

"An honor, sir," said the Spaniard when Hendon introduced them and then withdrew with a warning glare at Sebastian. "I understand you fought in the Peninsula."

"I did, yes."

The Ambassador's smile lit up his features. He was a small man, slightly built, with bushy eyebrows, large protruding eyes, and a small chin. "Hopefully someday you will be able to return to Spain and enjoy your visit in a time of peace."

"I would like that," said Sebastian, watching out of the corner of his eye as Hero adroitly collided with a pretty young woman he suspected was the count's wife. "I wonder, did you ever meet my colleague, Captain Miles Sedgewick? He also fought in the Peninsula."

The Ambassador's genial smile faded. "I fear I never had the pleasure. He's the gentleman who was recently found murdered?"

"He is, yes. I understand he knew one of the members of your diplomatic mission—someone he met in Cádiz in 1808 or 1809."

"Ah, that would have been Francisco de la Serna."

"Is he here this evening?"

"Unfortunately, no. He was recalled to Madrid last week. His father has taken ill and is not expected to live long."

"I'm sorry to hear that. When did he sail?"

"Last Sunday, I believe."

For a moment, Sebastian could only stare at the Spaniard as a new and profoundly disturbing thought occurred to him. "I understand he was a young, slim man?"

"Francisco?" The Spaniard gave a soft laugh. "Once, yes. But after so many years and a great many fine dinners and bottles of wine, both youth and slimness are difficult to maintain, yes?"

"They are indeed," said Sebastian. "I'm sorry I missed him. Hopefully he'll be returning to London soon?"

"Once this flare-up of war is over—which, God willing, will be soon."

"God willing," said Sebastian.

❧

It was when Sebastian was working his way through the crowd toward Hero that he came upon his father-in-law.

"What the hell are you doing here?" demanded Jarvis, stepping in front of him.

"Everyone keeps asking me that," said Sebastian. "Why are *you* here?"

"You mean instead of staying home with my wife and newborn son? It was Victoria herself who urged me to come."

She would, thought Sebastian. Jarvis and his new wife were very well suited to each other.

Jarvis frowned. "Why were you talking to the Spanish Ambassador just now?"

Sebastian cast a quick glance toward the door, where something—or someone—was causing a commotion. "He invited me to visit Spain again."

There was a loud thump, followed by a curse.

"What the blazes is that racket?" demanded Jarvis, just as a small, skinny lad dressed in a tiger's striped waistcoat wiggled his way through the jeweled throng of silk-and-satin-clad ladies and their gentlemen.

"A message come for ye from Bow Street," Tom said breathlessly as he skidded to a halt beside Sebastian. "It's one o' them Weird Sisters. She's been murdered!"

Chapter 39

*A*strid Wilde lay slumped behind the counter of the room that had once, in its former life, housed a tavern. Her hands were curled limply at her sides, her head lolling awkwardly against one shoulder. The narrow cord that someone had used to kill her was still tight around her neck, embedded deeply in the flesh of her throat. Her wide-open eyes were bulging and bloody, her tongue so swollen it protruded from her mouth in a horrid grimace. A thin trickle of blood ran from one ear, and her bowels and bladder had let loose, soaking the skirts of her elegant old-fashioned gown of gold satin.

"Ghastly, isn't it?" said Lovejoy, holding his handkerchief to his nose and mouth.

Sebastian let his gaze drift around the shelf-lined room, ablaze now with light from the lanterns of the constables who stood huddled together in groups of two and three, their shoulders hunched and their faces wary. There seemed to be an extraordinary number of them. "Any idea when this happened?"

"Her sister says she found her just after ten."

"Which sister?"

"The Jamaican one."

"Ah. And the other one—Sibil?"

"Says she only came in shortly before we arrived."

"No one saw anything?"

"Nothing they're willing to admit to."

Sebastian jerked his head toward the somber groups of men crowded into the room. "Why all the constables?"

Lovejoy sighed. "It was the only way short of getting someone to call out the Army that I could convince anyone to accompany me here."

"St. Giles does have a nasty reputation."

Lovejoy dropped his gaze to the body at their feet. "It is well deserved."

❦

While Lovejoy was supervising the loading of Astrid Wilde onto the shell that would carry her body to Gibson's Tower Hill surgery, Sebastian walked down the shadowy passage behind the counter to find Sibil Wilde seated in her ornately carved high-backed chair. A glass with a healthy measure of brandy stood at her elbow and her tarot deck lay strewn across the surface of the table as if she'd thrown it down in anger or disgust. Tonight she wore a gown of dark green velvet that looked like something from the days of Charles II, with slit sleeves joined loosely with ribbons and a full skirt with a satin underdress. The small chamber was lit only by the candelabra she had set in the center of the cloth-draped table, its flames leaping up golden and bright but leaving the corners of the room in shadow. She had her rich dark hair flowing loose around her shoulders, and she looked both beautiful and, somehow, very, very dangerous.

She had been simply staring down at the spilled cards. But she looked up when Sebastian came to stand in the doorway, and for a long moment her gaze met his. Then she said, "You've seen her?"

"I have," said Sebastian, leaning against the doorframe. "Tell me what happened."

"You think I know?"

"I think you do, yes."

She settled back, her forearms resting on the carved arms of her chair. "Well, I don't."

He pushed away from the doorway to wander the shadowy recesses of the room. "Who would want to kill her?"

"I have no idea."

He paused on the far side of the table, his gaze hard on her face. "She's not really your sister, is she?"

Sibil hesitated a moment, then shook her head.

"So who is she?"

"An actress. Too old to be some rich man's mistress and never good enough on the boards to succeed once her looks began to fade."

"How did she end up here?"

Sibil twitched one shoulder in a casual shrug. "It was something to do."

"Spying for the Bourbons, you mean?"

Her expression didn't alter. "I never said that."

"No, you didn't. So what was her real name?"

"I've no idea. She used to call herself Astrid Burns, but I suspect that was only a stage name."

"When was the last time you saw her?"

"Earlier this evening."

"You were open when she was killed?" Most shops were required to close on Sundays. But such things were rarely enforced in places like St. Giles.

"We were, yes."

"But no one saw anything?"

"Business was slow; people were out in the streets, but all anyone seems to want to think about is either Napoléon or the bodies they keep pulling from the river. I don't know why we even bothered to open."

"Had Astrid quarreled with anyone recently?"

"No."

"Noticed anyone following her?"

"No."

"She didn't say anything to you at all about being nervous or afraid?"

"No. I keep telling you, I have no idea who killed her or why."

"You don't seem overly saddened by her death."

Sibil stared back at him, her eyes wide and dry. "I told you she wasn't actually my sister."

"Yet you knew her." He let his gaze drift around the room with its richly paneled walls and ancient sandstone fire surround. "So tell me this: Did you know Hamilton Evans?"

"Who?"

"Hamilton Evans—the young man at the Foreign Office whose headless corpse was pulled from the Thames a few days ago. Did you know him?"

"No."

"What about a Spaniard named Francisco de la Serna? Did you know him?"

"A Spaniard? No. What has he to do with anything?"

"Maybe nothing."

She cocked her head, the light from the branch of candles casting a golden glow over her fair skin and deepening the highlights in her rich dark hair. "You think what happened to Astrid has something to do with the murders of those men whose bodies were found in the river?"

"You don't?"

"No, I don't. People are killed all the time—particularly in St. Giles."

"You told me once that the people around here leave you alone, that they're afraid of you. But whoever killed Astrid wasn't afraid."

Again, that careless shrug.

He pressed his hands flat on the tabletop and leaned into them. "Tell me about Gabriel."

She kept her face completely blank. "Who?"

"Gabriel. The assassin working for the Bourbons. His preferred weapons are the dagger and the garrote. Sedgewick was stabbed. Astrid was garroted."

"I noticed," she said dryly.

"Gabriel," he said again. "Tell me about him."

Her head fell back as she stared up at him. "I don't know anyone named Gabriel, and to my knowledge, none of my acquaintances are also assassins."

Sebastian shook his head. She was doing her best to hide her fear, but it was there, in the flaring of her nostrils and the tightness around her lips. "You may not be grieved by Astrid's death, but you are frightened by it, aren't you?"

Her slim white throat worked as she swallowed. "Of course I'm frightened. In case you hadn't noticed, everyone in London is frightened. Who wouldn't be frightened by murder?"

"The person—or people—responsible, one assumes."

"Perhaps. Yet fear is sometimes a motive for murder, is it not?"

"Sometimes. So what is the person who killed Astrid afraid of?"

"I can't imagine. Perhaps I'm wrong; perhaps it has nothing to do with fear. Not all killers are afraid. Some are simply angry or filled with lust. Or greed."

"All the selfish motives."

"Yes." She stared back at him with hooded eyes, the scar on her face showing dark against her pale skin. "But then, what is more selfish than murder?"

Chapter 40

*I*t was nearly dawn by the time Sebastian made it back to Brook Street. He was standing at the library window, his gaze on a torn playbill blowing down the deserted street, when Hero came to lean against the doorjamb, her hair loose about the shoulders of her blue satin dressing gown, her arms crossed at the bodice against the morning chill.

"You could at least try to sleep," she said.

He shook his head. "I keep thinking, *why*? Why would this killer go after Astrid Wilde?"

She pushed away from the doorway. "You don't know her murder is linked to the others, or even to the murder of just Sedgewick. St. Giles is a dangerous place."

"It's linked," said Sebastian, going to kneel before the dying fire. "And Sibil knows it."

Hero watched him shovel coal onto the glowing embers. "You

think the headless, handless corpse they pulled from the Thames really was Francisco de la Serna?"

"Honestly? I don't know. It could be. I've asked Lovejoy to see if there's any way to find out if the man actually sailed with whatever ship he was booked on. But there probably isn't. Not at this point."

"The Ambassador's wife said Francisco was a former cavalry officer, roughly the same height as her husband, but he'd put on weight in recent years so that he is now something like two or three stone heavier."

"Which would fit Alexi's estimate. But then, I've no doubt it would also fit tens of thousands of other men out there."

She came to sink into one of the chairs beside the fire, her gaze on the flames slowly licking into the new fuel. "I keep thinking about Phoebe Cox's baby. Surely Miles Sedgewick couldn't be so cruel as to simply drop the child in the Thames. Could he?"

"I'd like to think he couldn't do something like that. But the truth is, even if he simply handed the child to some beggar woman, would it really be all that different? The child is unlikely to have survived."

Hero let out a long sigh. "Poor Phoebe. She lost her baby, and now the Crown is going to punish her for her poverty and her powerlessness by taking her life." She was silent for a moment, her gaze on the fire. "Will it ever change, do you think?"

"Perhaps. Although to be honest, I sometimes wonder."

She looked up, meeting his troubled gaze. "So do I."

❧

It was several hours later, when they were consuming a leisurely breakfast at the table on the terrace, that they heard the distant peal of the front bell. A moment later, Morey appeared with a bow.

"A personage here to see you, my lord."

"What sort of 'personage'?"

"She says her name is Rowena Wilde. She is . . . quite agitated."
Sebastian met Hero's gaze. "Show her back right away."

The woman Morey escorted out to them was dressed not in the costume of some past century but in a simple high-waisted muslin walking dress with a short red spencer. Her thick curly hair was wild around her face, and she clutched to her chest a bulging satchel from which protruded bits of lace and ribbon.

"You must help me," said Rowena, her eyes wide, her pretty features pinched with fear. "*Please*. If you don't, they're gonna kill me, too, the same way they killed Astrid."

Sebastian stood to draw back one of the chairs at the table. "Won't you please have a seat? How about something to eat? A cup of tea, perhaps?"

Rowena shook her head from side to side, her hands spasming against the satchel she held before her. "Are you gonna help me?"

"Who do you think is going to kill you?" asked Hero quietly.

"*Sibil!*"

"Your sister?"

"She ain't my sister."

Sebastian settled back into his own chair. "You're saying Sibil killed Astrid?"

"I ain't saying she did it herself, but she's behind it. I know she is."

"What makes you think that?"

"They had a big fight—Sibil and Astrid, I mean."

"About what?"

"About that fellow got himself killed—Miles Sedgewick. Astrid was sweet on him." Rowena's lip curled in derision. "She thought he was sweet on her, too, because he was always making up to her, and Astrid was too stupid to realize that's the way he treated all women."

"I still don't understand precisely what the fight was about."

"Astrid thought Sibil had him killed."

Hero said, "Why would she think that?"

"Because he came to see Sibil that night."

"You mean Saturday? The night he was killed?" said Sebastian.

Rowena nodded. "They had a big row. He accused her of tricking him—of using him. She doesn't really see stuff, you know. She likes to think she does, but the truth is, most of what she claims to 'see' really comes from information she gets from people's servants and the like. Or else she coaxes it out of her customers while she's doing a reading for them, but she does it so clever-like that they don't realize what she's done."

"I did rather suspect that," said Sebastian.

Rowena sniffed.

Hero said, "Did Sedgewick threaten her?"

Rowena nodded, her eyes wide. "Sibil, she told him to be careful, that he didn't know who he was dealing with. But he said he now knew precisely who he was dealing with."

"Did he say how or where he learned what she was really doing?" asked Sebastian.

"I don't know—I didn't catch everything they were saying. But Astrid did—she had really good hearing, you see; much better than mine."

"She confronted Sibil about what she'd heard?"

Rowena nodded. "Yesterday."

"And what did Sibil do?"

"She told her she'd kill her if she even thought about betraying her."

Sebastian and Hero exchanged glances.

"She does that, you know," said Rowena. "Kills people, I mean. Well, she doesn't do it herself, but she's got somebody who does it for her."

"Do you know who he is?"

Rowena took a step back, her nostrils flaring wide with fear as she shook her head from side to side.

"I can't help you if you don't tell me the truth," said Sebastian, his voice hard. "Who is he?"

"I don't know!"

"Sibil spies for the Bourbons, doesn't she?" Hero said quietly.

Rowena hesitated a moment, then gave a quick nod, her lips pressed tightly together.

"And this man she knows, he does the Bourbons' killing?"

She nodded again. "Sibil calls him 'Gabriel,' but I don't think that's his real name."

"What does he look like?"

"I don't know exactly. I've caught glimpses of him a few times, but he never looks the same. For a while there I thought he must be two or maybe even three different men. But then I realized it's all the same person; he's just really good at makin' himself look different. Sometimes he looks like a Bond Street beau, but other times you'd think he was a costermonger."

"Is he English, or French?"

"I don't even know that. Sometimes he sounds like one, sometimes he sounds like the other. And there was one time you'd have sworn he was German, listenin' to him. I reckon maybe he used to be an actor."

Either an actor, thought Sebastian, *or someone with experience adopting disguises.*

Aloud, he said, "I still don't understand what makes you think Sibil had Astrid killed. Why would she?"

"I told you! Because Astrid was that mad at Sibil for killing Sedgewick, and she said she was gonna tell you."

"You mean, she was going to tell me she thought Sibil had Sedgewick murdered?"

Rowena nodded. "And tell you that he was there right before he was killed."

"You saw him that night?"

"Yes."

"Did you see him leave?"

"Yes." She frowned. "Why?"

"What time was it?"

"When he left? I dunno. Maybe somewhere around eight or half past?" Rowena looked from Sebastian to Hero and back again. "Are you gonna help me or not?"

"Precisely what is it you want us to do?"

"Hide me from Sibil and Gabriel!"

"Who knows you're here?"

"Nobody! I slipped out this mornin' before Sibil was up and while the streets were all deserted. Ain't nobody followed me here. I'm sure of it."

Again Sebastian and Hero exchanged glances. He said, "I know a hotel where you can stay for now. But you mustn't leave your room or contact anyone you know. Do you understand?"

Rowena nodded, her eyes wide with the terror of a woman who'd long ago come to realize that her life was of value only to herself.

❧

Jarvis was still in his dressing room when Grisham—both his dignity and his profound disapproval of his master's son-in-law now thoroughly restored—showed Sebastian up to his lordship.

"I assume this is important," said Jarvis, still in his shirtsleeves. He glanced over at his valet. "Leave us."

Sebastian waited until the man had gone, then said, "You knew the woman who called herself Astrid Wilde?"

Jarvis reached for one of the cravats left by his valet and began to wrap the length of linen around his neck. "Not personally, no."

"But you knew she worked for the Bourbons."

"Technically I believe she worked for Sibil Wilde."

"And Sibil Wilde works for the Bourbons." Sebastian watched the King's cousin set about the important task of tying his cravat. "I've just spoken to someone who has very good reason to believe Astrid was killed because she knew Sibil Wilde was behind Sedgewick's death."

Jarvis kept his attention on his reflection in the mirror. "Now, that I don't believe. Why would the Bourbons—or, more specifically, Sibil Wilde—want to kill Sedgewick?"

"Perhaps because, unlike you, Sedgewick had only recently discovered—presumably from someone in Vienna—that she was working for the Bourbons. Or perhaps because the Bourbons knew he was carrying correspondence from Austria proposing that Napoléon be allowed to leave his half-Austrian son on the throne of France?"

Jarvis looked at him sharply. "Who told you that?"

"Does it matter?"

"Not really." Jarvis returned his attention to his cravat. "Sibil Wilde is smart enough to know that the Prince would never seriously entertain such a proposal—apart from which, the correspondence Sedgewick carried had already been delivered, remember?" He paused to carefully set a fold into the starched white linen. "Did it ever occur to you that the man's recent trip to the Continent had absolutely nothing to do with his death?"

"It has occurred to me, yes. But I can definitely see the Bourbons killing Sedgewick to get their hands on the list he also brought back from Vienna, although you claim to know nothing about it." Sebastian watched his father-in-law turn away from the mirror to reach for his waistcoat. "I've asked you several times now if you know the identity of the Bourbons' assassin."

"And I've told you several times that I do not."

"I don't believe you."

Jarvis shrugged into his waistcoat. "I understand you've developed an interest in Cabrera."

Sebastian studied his father-in-law's faintly smiling features. "Why do you ask?"

Jarvis went to work fastening his white satin waistcoat's row of tiny pearl buttons. "You know, of course, that Alexi Sauvage had a close relative who died there?"

"On Cabrera? Who?"

The amusement in Jarvis's eyes deepened. "Ah, so you didn't know."

"Why the bloody hell should I believe you?"

"Ask her. I understand they were exceptionally close—virtually raised together."

"How do you know this?"

"I make it my business to know such things."

"And yet you would have me believe you don't know who shot the face off Miles Sedgewick and dumped his body in the Thames?" said Sebastian, and had the satisfaction of seeing the big man's smile slip.

Chapter 41

$\mathcal{G}$ibson was leaning over a female cadaver on the elevated stone slab in the dank outbuilding behind his Tower Hill surgery, a butcher's apron tied over his rumpled clothes and what looked like a butcher's knife in his hand, when Sebastian came to stand just outside the building's low doorway. The surgeon's cheeks were unshaven, his eyes bloodshot, his skin the color of something long dead. But he was fiercely sober.

"If you're here looking for answers to help solve the riddle of what maniac is doing this," he growled, looking up from what Sebastian now realized was Astrid Wilde's eviscerated corpse, "I can't help you."

Sebastian let his gaze wander over the crude shelves on the surrounding walls until he found a shallow, chipped enamel basin containing a thin braided cord with a dowel knotted at each end. "That's the garrote that was used to kill her?"

Gibson nodded. "Professional, isn't it?"

"Very."

Setting aside his knife with a clatter, Gibson reached for a rag and wiped his hands. "You're thinking this is the work of the Bourbons' assassin?"

"I'd say it's more than likely. But it doesn't necessarily follow that he's responsible for all the other killings."

Gibson frowned. "How do you figure that?"

Sebastian had to force himself to look again at the contorted features of the dead woman between them. "I'm told she had it in her head that the Bourbons were responsible for Miles Sedgewick's death, and she was threatening to come to me about it. So even if they had nothing to do with any of the other deaths, I can see them deciding she was becoming a dangerous liability that needed to be silenced."

"Yes, I can see that," said Gibson. He tossed the rag aside, then fixed Sebastian with a steady stare. "People are saying the fighting has started in Belgium."

Sebastian blew out a long, troubled breath. "I'm hearing the rumors. But if the government has received anything official from Wellington, I don't know about it."

"Well, hell. I was hoping you might have at least heard something." Gibson scrubbed his hands down over his haggard face. "It's hard, just sitting here, holding our breath and waiting."

Sebastian nodded, his gaze drifting back up the hill toward the medieval stone house. "Is Alexi around?"

Gibson shook his head. "I think she said she was going to the St. Martin's workhouse to see if Sedgewick left Phoebe's baby there."

"She's still looking?"

Something flared in the Irishman's bloodshot green eyes. "Last year, one of the babies she delivered died in his sleep. The authorities accused the mother of smothering him and hanged her for it. So as long as there's a chance of finding that babe, then I'd say, yes; Alexi is going to keep looking for it."

❧

Alexi was just leaving the grim, soot-covered brick workhouse when Sebastian walked up to her.

"Any sign of the baby?" he asked.

"No. Nothing." She studied him in silence for a moment, her face difficult to read. "But that's not why you're here, is it? Has something happened to Paul?"

Sebastian shook his head. "He's fine. But I had an interesting conversation earlier today with Lord Jarvis."

"That sounds ominous." She brushed past him to turn down St. Martin's Lane, toward the river. "And what did the King's oh-so-powerful cousin have to say that brings you here to me? It can't be good."

Sebastian fell into step beside her. "He tells me someone you loved died on Cabrera. Is that true?"

She looked over at him, her forehead creasing with what looked like a puzzled frown. "It is, yes. I don't know how he knew, or what difference it makes, but my cousin Celine died there. Why do you ask?"

"Because Miles Sedgewick was involved in the British decision to force the Spaniards to abrogate their treaty with France and send the prisoners to the island. Technically his role was that of a go-between, carrying messages from the Wellesleys to Admiral Collingwood and back. But I'm told he wasn't simply a messenger—that he advocated quite forcefully to prevent the transfer of the prisoners back to France." Sebastian paused, then said, "It's been suggested that's why he was killed."

She drew up sharply and turned to face him. "Because of *Cabrera*?"

"Yes."

"And now you're back to thinking that maybe I'm the one who killed him, are you?"

"You don't find it odd how everything somehow keeps circling back to you?"

"Does it? And precisely how am I supposed to have manhandled him down to the Thames? Or are you thinking your good friend Paul Gibson helped me?" She half swung away from him, one hand coming up to her forehead. "I can't believe this."

Sebastian kept his gaze hard on her half-averted face. "Did you know of Sedgewick's involvement in the decision to send the French prisoners to Cabrera?"

"For God's sake, no! You think I would have married him if I had known?"

"You could have found out later."

She shook her head, her lip curling. *"Mon Dieu."*

"You say your cousin Celine died there? I didn't realize women were sent to Cabrera, too."

"You know how many women move with an army—not only laundresses, canteen women, and prostitutes, but also the wives of officers and the men."

"And we sent them to Cabrera?"

"Of course. There were children, too. I don't think any of them survived." She was silent for a moment, her face stark as she stared out over the wretched street. "I'm told the first few years were the worst, like something out of hell. No shelter, almost no water, and frequently no food. There were times when they resorted to cannibalism." She glanced over at him. "Did you know that?"

"No."

"It's horrible even to think about, but who can blame them? The fault lies not with those forced to do such a thing to survive but with everyone who sent them there in the first place."

"How long did your cousin Celine survive?"

"Not long. She gave birth to twins on the ship out from Cádiz.

Her husband died about a month after they reached the island—he was giving her his rations so that she could feed the babies. But they both died anyway, and after that, she threw herself off the cliffs into the sea."

"I'm sorry," he said, although it struck him as a damned useless thing to say.

She stared back at him. "Are you? Ten or twenty years from now, who will even remember them, let alone cry for them? Certainly not the British or the Spaniards who sent them there. And the French? The Bourbons see anyone who fought for Napoléon—even the conscripts—as traitors, while those who support Napoléon would rather it all be forgotten lest he be faulted for failing to rescue them."

"Those who lost loved ones there will remember," said Sebastian. "They will remember, and they will cry for them. And someone could even be killing for them."

"You genuinely believe that?"

"Let's just say I see it as a possibility." He watched the Frenchwoman's tightly controlled features very carefully. "Do you know of anyone else here in London who lost loved ones on Cabrera?"

She huffed a disbelieving laugh. "You think I would tell you if I did? So that Bow Street can hang them instead of me?"

"Whoever is killing these men is not entirely sane. You do realize that, don't you?"

Alexi stared back at him. "You think any of us are truly sane? After twenty-five years of war?"

Sebastian met her gaze. "No. Probably not."

Chapter 42

*L*ater that morning, Kat Boleyn stood at the window of her house in Cavendish Square, her gaze on the street below. She could see a workman painting the black iron railing around the leafy garden in the square; a ragged woman selling ribbons from a tray; a costermonger in a flop hat and jaunty red kerchief flirting with one of the cooks from down the street. Kat studied each one carefully, even the women, for she knew now that the person watching her could change his appearance with the practiced ease of one of the world's best actors.

She'd seen him clearly twice. Once he'd been dressed as a costermonger, the second time as a clerk. But she was certain it was the same man, despite the difference in clothes, hair color, and body type, for the shape of his head gave him away to a practiced eye. A skilled actor could alter his clothes and his posture; add pounds and years; thrust out his jaw or hunch his shoulders; alter his walk and entire demeanor. But the shape of his head was immutable. She'd been trying to remember if she'd known an actor over the years with that head shape, but she couldn't think of one.

She turned away from the window with a smothered oath. "Stop it," she told herself, saying it out loud, as if that might somehow be more effective. "Just stop it. What is *wrong* with you?" She'd faced death before, had come perilously close to dying more than once. So why was she so rattled this time?

Drawn against her will, she went back to the window, careful not to disturb the curtain lest he be watching and know he was making her nervous. If he was there, she couldn't see him, but she could *feel* him. And even though she knew it sounded ridiculous, she thought she understood at some fundamental level what was so disturbing about this particular man. It was the animosity emanating from him, a level of malevolence such as she'd never before encountered.

Life is full of scary things, her stepfather used to tell her. *The trick is to not let your fears get in the way of your living. Whatever else you do, Katherine, don't settle for a life half lived.*

"You're definitely one of the scary things in life," she whispered now to the unseen man out there, somewhere, who intended to kill her. "But I'm not going to let you destroy my life. You hear me?

"I'm not."

Shortly after midday, Hero took a wherry from Parliament Stairs all the way down the river to Three Cranes Wharf, just above London Bridge. She had never before done such a thing, and she found it a magical experience to glide silently past sights at once familiar and—from this angle—totally unfamiliar. The breeze rising off the water was cool and sweet, the sky a soft blue filled with wind-scuttled white clouds, the June sun bathing the world in a warm, intense light.

"Look there," said her wherryman, drawing her attention to a pair of snowy white egrets rising from the mudflats before Somerset House.

The wherryman was a big man named Devon Clark, built tall and broad across the shoulders and chest, with a massive head and powerful jawline. He wore a broad-brimmed hat with the typical pilot jacket and canvas trousers of a waterman, and he told Hero he'd been impressed twice—and had the stripes on his back to prove it.

"Ye'd be hard put to find a wherryman wasn't impressed at some point," he told her as they slid past the leafy chestnut trees and sweetly scented roses of Temple Gardens. "The Lord High Admiral has the power to demand a certain number of watermen serve in the Navy, ye see. Ye can try hidin' when there's a press in progress, but the press masters know where to look 'cause they're members o' the company themselves."

"They are?"

"Oh, aye. An' they always make sure they take apprentices when they can, rather than freemen. But then, who'd want an old stager in the Navy, hmm? It's hard enough on a young'un." He stared off down the river, his eyes narrowing against the glare off the water, his features tightening in a way that told her his memories of his time as an impressed seaman were not fond ones. "At least the Watermen's Company looks after those who come back too broken to work, which is more'n ye can say about His Majesty and that lot." He hawked up a mouthful of phlegm and turned his head to spit into the water.

"Do they resent it? The fact that so many wherrymen are impressed, I mean."

He looked at her, his face utterly blank. "What would be the point? It's just . . . life on the river. I reckon ye'll find more wherrymen riled up about these new bridges than about the press masters. Time was, the closest bridge after London Bridge was at Kingston, twenty-five miles upstream. But look at it now. Next thing ye know, they're gonna have a dozen or more bridges over the river. Ye ask me, instead o' buildin' all these new bridges, what they ought to do is rebuild London Bridge. The thing's a bloody hazard—beggin' yer pardon fer the language, me lady."

Hero stared down the river to where the crumbling old thirteenth-century bridge was just coming into view. With its narrow arches and thick piers, London Bridge acted essentially like a weir, holding back so much water that at times there could be as much as a six-foot difference in the height of the river above and below its medieval arches. Passage under the bridge was dangerous at all times, but it was particularly deadly when the tide was flowing. Most wherrymen refused to go anywhere near it; their passengers had to disembark at the Old Swan Stairs above the bridge and go on foot to hire a new boat below. But every month or so, a group of young bucks eager to test their mettle would find some wherryman desperate enough to take their money and try to shoot the rapids.

"Reckon there's somewhere between twenty-five and fifty fools killed there every year," Clark was saying. "They call it 'shootin' the bridge.'"

Hero nodded. "I heard there was a young wherryman killed just the other day, trying to shoot it."

"Ye heard about that, did ye? I'm surprised. Wherrymen die on the river all the time, and most folks don't usually give it a second thought. I'm still hearin' about that grand lord's son they pulled out o' the Pool a week ago. A week ago! Wouldn't nobody 'ave heard o' him if he'd been a wherryman."

"Except he didn't simply drown," said Hero. "He was murdered."

"Aye, so he was. And there was a wherryman murdered that same night—stabbed in the back, he was. But ain't nobody talkin' about him."

Hero looked up from her notes, the wind catching at the brim of her hat so that she had to put up a hand to steady it. "Where did this happen?"

"Who knows? They found his body down by the Isle o' Dogs, although his wherry was just knockin' against the dock of that old tannery by Jacob's Island what shut down a few years back."

"When did you say he was found?"

"Tuesday. He disappeared Saturday night, but they didn't find him till just a few hours before that lord's son come up with the East Indiaman's anchor."

Chapter 43

The remains of the McGuire Tannery lay just downriver from Jacob's Island, on the south bank of the river in a wretched neighborhood laced with tidal streams from the Thames. At one time it must have been a lovely place, with hedgerows and lush green meadows and lazily grazing cows. Now it was a hellscape of abandoned tan pits and dye pits, the earth blasted bare of all vegetation and stained various shades of red, blue, yellow, green, and pink. The tannery's tall smokestack was crumbling, the brick walls of the finishing shop and warehouse smothered in vines, the windows broken. The shattered remains of old drying racks lay strewn about, jumbled together with pushing poles and what looked like pieces of old wooden wheelbarrows.

"Why exactly are we here?" said Hero, picking her way carefully between deep pits half filled with foul-smelling water.

Sebastian looked over at her and grinned. "Because it seemed like a good idea when we talked about it in the comfort of Brook Street?"

She huffed a laugh but sobered quickly. "We don't even know that this murdered wherryman had anything to do with Sedgewick's death."

"No. But you must admit the timing makes it a curious coincidence."

"You keep using that word."

"I know. And I don't like it." He paused at the top of the high riverbank, his gaze scanning the refuse-piled waterfront. "There," he said. "There's the stairs down to the old wharf."

They worked their way over to the broken stone steps, then climbed carefully down to the weather-beaten dock. The narrow old arches of London Bridge lay just downstream.

"The wherryman's body might have ended up down by the Isle of Dogs," said Sebastian, "but if his boat was found here, then I suspect he was killed here."

Hero turned to stare up the river to where they could see the towers of St. Paul's rising on the far bank. "Or the wherry could have drifted here from upriver someplace."

"Perhaps, but I doubt it. The currents are all wrong to bring it ashore here."

He was silent for a moment, his gaze fixed on a nearby pile of rubbish.

"What is it?" said Hero, watching him.

Reaching down, he shifted a worn timber and some brush, then came up with a boot—and not just any boot but a fine Hessian such as a gentleman of the town might wear. Except for a bit of mud on the heel and its somewhat bedraggled silver tassels, it looked new.

"Good heavens," whispered Hero. "Do you think that could be Sedgewick's?"

Sebastian turned the boot in his hands. "I don't know. But I suspect his bootmaker would recognize it, if it is."

Hero looked back up the bank at the blighted landscape of the old tannery. "Why here, I wonder? Because it's a good place to kill someone?"

"Either that, or because it's a good place to strip and mutilate your victim's body and toss it in the river."

Hero brought her gaze back to his face. "So why kill the wherryman?"

"I suppose that depends on the role he played," said Sebastian. "And whether Sedgewick—or whoever this boot belonged to—was alive when the wherryman brought his passengers here."

※

"This is troublesome," said Sir Henry Lovejoy when Sebastian stopped by his Bow Street office. The magistrate sat back in his chair, frowning as he turned the fine leather boot in his hands. "You think it belonged to Miles Sedgewick?"

"I think it's worth asking his bootmaker about it," said Sebastian.

Lovejoy nodded. "I'll put one of the lads on it right away—and send a couple of constables out to take a look around this tannery, too."

Sebastian went to stand at the window, his gaze on the turbulent white clouds gathering above the city. "*Was* there a wherryman found stabbed last week?"

"To be frank, I've no idea. The River Police handle that sort of thing, and they only inform us if it seems pertinent." Lovejoy carefully set the boot aside. "The truth is, the entire metropolitan area needs a centralized, *coordinated* police force."

"It will never happen," said Sebastian.

Lovejoy sighed. "Well, probably not in my lifetime, at any rate." He peeled off his glasses and rubbed his eyes. "Remember how you asked us to look into the background of Reverend Sinclair Palmer?"

Sebastian turned from the window. "Yes?"

"It seems he didn't take up holy orders immediately after coming down from Cambridge."

"He didn't?" No one Sebastian had spoken to earlier had mentioned that. But then, they might not have known.

Lovejoy shook his head. "No. He spent two years as a cornet in the 40th Foot. He sold out after being wounded at Roliça and was ordained some six months later—just in time to take up the living at Marylebone."

Sebastian had fought at Roliça himself, but all he said was, "Interesting."

"Mmm," said Lovejoy, his worried gaze meeting Sebastian's. "I thought you'd think so."

❧

Sebastian spent the early-evening hours making the rounds of places like the Scarlet Man and Yellow Dog, looking for men who'd once served with Palmer. He spoke to a broken-down former corporal, a blind sergeant, and a one-legged lieutenant on half pay. Then, as the sun was sinking slowly in the western sky, he turned his horses toward Marylebone.

❧

He found the Reverend Sinclair Palmer in the small, fastidiously tidy parlor of his rectory. His hair was vaguely disarrayed, as if he'd only just come in, and he was in the act of pouring himself a brandy when the housemaid showed Sebastian in.

"Ah, Lord Devlin," said the churchman, looking up from what he was doing. "Splendid to see you again. Have you heard? Word on the streets is that the fighting has begun."

"Any official confirmation yet?"

"None that I'm aware of. But it must surely be so."

"Most likely," said Sebastian.

Palmer raised the carafe invitingly. "I was just pouring myself a brandy. Won't you join me?"

"Thank you, yes," said Sebastian, going to stand beside the empty hearth. "I'm told you served in the 40th Foot."

The Reverend gave a strange, startled laugh. "A long time ago, yes. Took a bullet in the shoulder in Portugal."

"That's when you sold out?"

Palmer set aside the carafe and turned with two glasses in his hands. "It was, yes. Although if truth be told, I'd realized by then that I would be far better suited to a life in the church than in the military." He handed one of the glasses to Sebastian and raised his own as if in a toast. "Here's to better days ahead, when we can focus on bringing solace into the lives of our fellow men rather than killing them, aye?"

It didn't exactly fit with what Sebastian had heard from the men who'd served with the then Cornet Palmer. "Yes," said Sebastian, raising his own glass. "Here's to peace."

The Reverend took a deep drink of his brandy. "So, have you made any progress in finding Sedgewick's killer?"

Sebastian wondered if the phraseology was significant—*finding Sedgewick's killer* as opposed to *finding the man who's doing these killings.* "Not as much progress as I'd like, I'll admit."

Palmer took another deep drink. "I should think a man known for seducing the wives of his friends must have made any number of enemies."

"Last time we spoke, you said you thought Sedgewick's death had something to do with his interest in witches and werewolves."

The Reverend's eyes widened. "Ah, yes, well . . . That was before I knew about Lady— Well, let's just say it was before I knew about a *certain* lady."

"Do I take it Eloisa Sedgewick knew her husband was having an affair with this 'certain' lady?"

"Of course she knew. The woman isn't stupid."

"She must have been very angry and hurt, if she spoke to you about it."

"What woman wouldn't be?"

"And what about this 'certain' lady's husband? Do you think he knew of his wife's affair?"

"As to that, I couldn't say. Some men are very good at deceiving themselves, are they not?"

"Up to a point, perhaps."

Palmer drained his glass. "Well, you would know that particular man better than I. You did serve together in the Peninsula, did you not?"

"We did."

"Then you should know what he is capable of."

"Meaning?"

"Meaning no offense, to be sure." Setting aside his empty glass, the Reverend went to stand at the window, his gaze on the slowly fading day. "It's hard to think that somewhere out there, at this very moment, the future history of the world is being decided, is it not? And yet here we are and we don't even know what's happening now, let alone what the eventual outcome will be."

Sebastian studied the man's handsome, chiseled profile. "You never thought of rejoining your old regiment when you heard about Napoléon's return? As a chaplain, perhaps?"

Palmer turned toward him with a self-deprecating smile. "No. Sadly, my responsibility now is to my congregation here. But 'they also serve who only stand and wait,' hmm? May I offer you more brandy? Ah, I see you've hardly touched yours."

Sebastian set aside his half-empty glass. "Thank you, but I must be going."

The Reverend walked with him to the door. "You still think the same killer murdered all three of the men whose bodies were pulled from the Thames?"

"Actually, I'm not sure what to think at this point."

Palmer nodded, his lips tightening into an upturned grimace even as his eyes wandered elsewhere.

❧

That evening, Hero worked at mending the torn flounce of one of her gowns while Devlin stood by the drawing room window, his gaze on the darkness beyond. There was a tension about his shoulders, mingled unmistakably with an air of profound sadness.

"You're afraid it's Monty who killed Sedgewick, aren't you?" she said quietly, watching him. "Because of what Palmer said today?"

He turned his head to meet her gaze. "It isn't as if the possibility hadn't occurred to me before. I can't see Monty killing Hamilton Evans or Astrid Wilde or whoever that unidentified corpse might be. But he would hardly be the first to kill a man who was cuckolding him."

"You're back to thinking the deaths are the work of two different killers?"

He scrubbed his hands down over his face. "Half the time, yes. The other half of the time . . ."

"Did you ever ask Monty how he knew even before you did that Sedgewick had been stabbed?"

"No. He'd probably claim it was just a lucky guess—and then never talk to me again for thinking he's a murderer. And while I won't hesitate to turn him in if he is the killer, I've no desire to lose an old friend if he's not."

She tied off her thread and set the mending aside. "If it were me, I'd put my money on the good Reverend Palmer of Marylebone. He eliminates the philandering husband, excuses it by telling himself he's doing the Lord's work in removing someone with a satanic interest in witches and werewolves, then marries the rich widow and thus leaps far, far higher up the social and economic ladder than he could otherwise dream of."

Devlin smiled. "That's because you don't like him."

She gave a soft laugh. "No, I don't. But then, I have an ingrained aversion to hypocritical churchmen."

"Oh, he's nothing if not hypocritical," said Devlin. "All three of the men from the 40th Foot I spoke to today told me Palmer was infamous for having twice executed French prisoners—put the muzzle of his pistol against their heads and blew their brains out."

"Dear Lord," she whispered. "So we know he can kill."

"Oh, he can kill, all right. But then, so can Monty." He paused, his head lifting, then said, "I wonder who that is."

"What—" she started to say, then broke off as a knock sounded at the front door below. "The acuity of your hearing is unnerving."

"Still?"

"Still."

Their gazes met as the sound of Hendon's voice mingled with Morey's drifted up from the entry hall. A moment later the Earl himself appeared at the entrance to the drawing room, his face set in unusually grave lines.

"What is it?" asked Hero.

"The Palace has received news from Wellington," said the Earl. "Napoléon has attacked the Prussians at Ligny. Seems he managed to put his army in the gap left between Wellington's men in the west and Blücher's to the east."

"And Wellington?"

"Was at a ball given by the Duchess of Richmond when word came through—as were many of his officers. They're saying some of them headed to the front in evening dress."

"When was this?" said Devlin.

"The first skirmishes started on Thursday. Then Napoléon absolutely routed the Prussians on Friday, while Wellington was forced to fall back before Marshal Ney from a place called Quatre Bras. According to the messenger he sent, our troops have retreated to some little village halfway back to Brussels. The city is in a full-blown panic, with the French expected to overrun the place at any moment and everyone who can scrambling to find some way to get to the coast. It will be in the morning papers that the fighting has started, but the government is being careful not to release just how bad things are looking."

"Have you told Aunt Henrietta?"

"Not yet, but I will. I know she's anxious."

"And you say this messenger left Wellington on Friday?"

"That's right."

"That was days ago," said Devlin as Hero quietly reached out to take his hand in hers. "Whatever the outcome, it's surely happened already. We just don't know about it yet."

Chapter 44

*B*uffeted by an eerie wind, a bank of clouds scuttled fitfully across the almost full moon overhead, casting shifting, ominous patterns of light and shadow across the haunted recesses of Alexi's garden. Paul Gibson stood on the small back stoop of his ancient stone house and breathed the cool night air deep into his lungs. His chest and arms were bare, but he still felt hot, his body riven by pain and burning with a shameful need. Wrapping his fists around the railing, he gritted his teeth, his body shaking as he fought against the hellish siren call of desire he was determined to resist, at least for tonight. He was dimly aware of the door opening softly behind him, Alexi's presence only on the periphery of his consciousness until she slipped her strong arms around his waist and pressed her warm body close to his.

"Hurting?" she said.

"A bit."

"I know what you're trying to do, and I admire you for it. But trying to stop the opium while you still have the pain is . . ." She paused.

He gave a ragged laugh. "Torture? Foolish? Doomed to failure? All three?"

She didn't answer. A silence fell between them, a silence filled with the night wind and the echoing memories of all the harsh, accusatory words they'd spoken to each other in anger over the years.

She said, "I also know why you don't want to let me try to fix your phantom pains."

He turned to look at her. It never ceased to amaze him how small and delicate she felt in his arms, and yet she was so fierce, so strong and capable. "How can you?" he said hoarsely.

A sad smile lit up her eyes. "Because I know you. You're afraid my mirror trick will actually work, only then you won't be able to stop taking the opium. And without the pain as an excuse, you're afraid I'll despise you for being weak and turn away from you in disgust."

He sucked in a ragged breath, and then another, and still he found he couldn't seem to say anything.

She said, "It will be easier for you to get off the opium if you don't have the pain from your leg to deal with at the same time. But I know that doesn't mean it will be easy. It's going to be god-awful."

He pressed his hot forehead to hers, their breaths mingling together. "You're right," he whispered, his body trembling. "I am afraid. I'm afraid I won't have what it takes to stop. And I'm afraid you'll leave me once you realize that."

"I won't leave you."

He gave a faint shake of his head. "I understand now why you would never agree to marry me. But I'll never understand why you'd want to stay with some broken-down one-legged Irish opium eater."

"You don't? I can tell you why. It's partially because you're brilliant and truly amazing at what you do. But you're so much more than that. You're good and kind, funny and giving, but also courageous and honorable and everything that's noble." She bracketed his face with her hands, her palms pressing flat against his cheeks as she smiled into his eyes. "And as it happens, I also really, really like the way you look."

Tilting her head, she kissed his lips slowly and lovingly. "Now come to bed, and let's take your mind off that pain."

Chapter 45

*T*he next day dawned cloudy and sullen. Sebastian awoke early, aware of a strange lassitude, a sense of palpable anxiety that seemed to hang in the air, as if the inhabitants of the city were collectively holding their breath, waiting for word from across the Channel.

He was in the midst of shaving when an urgent message arrived from Sir Henry Lovejoy. A wherryman on his way home at the end of his shift had discovered another body, this one at Rotherhithe.

❧

Sebastian could see Lovejoy standing at the water's edge, his features grim, his hands thrust deep in his pockets as a cold, briny wind lifting off the Thames whipped at the hem of his greatcoat. A constable and two men from the deadhouse waited nearby with a shell, their gazes, like that of the magistrate, on the dead man sprawled on his back at their feet, the gray waters of the river lapping against his legs. As he drew closer, Sebastian could see the man's dark, wet hair and the pale, waxen flesh of his vaguely familiar face. His clothing was sodden and disarrayed by his time in the water, but otherwise intact. If the killer had mutilated this victim in some way, it wasn't visible.

"My lord," said the magistrate, turning as Sebastian worked his way down the steep, slippery bank toward them. "My apologies for disturbing you so early."

"I was afraid we weren't finished with this," said Sebastian, a cascade of small stones rolling beneath his feet as he slid to a halt at the water's edge.

Lovejoy drew a deep breath. "At least this time there doesn't appear to be any mutilation. But his purse is still in his pocket, so it's obviously not the work of footpads."

"I didn't think it was," said Sebastian, going to hunker down beside the body. The man was young, probably no more than thirty, his clothing that of a gentleman of fashion and tailored in a style popular with the French. A neat slit was just visible on the left side of his waistcoat, the white silk marred by what looked like a watery bloodstain.

"He was stabbed?" said Sebastian.

"So it appears. Presumably an autopsy will tell us for certain."

Sebastian nodded, his gaze drawn back to the man's face. "I've seen him before, although I couldn't put a name to him. Any idea who he might be?"

"We've no official identification yet, but a French émigré by the name of André Ternant was reported missing yesterday morning by his wife. The description she gave fits."

Sebastian nodded. "Yes, that's who it is; I've met him. He fled Paris with his family in the first years of the Revolution, as a child." He stared down at the dead man's even, bloodless features. "Hopefully you can find someone besides his poor wife to officially identify him."

"Surely there must be someone," said Lovejoy with a sigh. "Do you know if he returned to France last year when the Bourbons were first restored?"

"No. He stayed here."

"Ah. It makes sense, I suppose. If he'd lived here most of his life, one would suppose London felt more like home than Paris."

"Perhaps," said Sebastian, although he could think of another reason for Ternant's decision not to return to France with the Bourbons.

Lovejoy said, "You saw the news in this morning's papers?"

"About the fighting in Belgium?" Sebastian pushed to his feet. "Yes."

"I suppose it was only a matter of time. Now the question becomes, how will it end?"

Sebastian turned his head to stare off across the wind-churned gray waters of the river. "It sounds as if the French caught Wellington and his men absurdly flat-footed, but I think we still have the advantage. If ever Napoléon needed his best commanders, it's for this fight. But most of his old marshals are honoring their oaths to the Bourbons and simply sitting this out."

Lovejoy nodded. "Yes, I was surprised to hear just yesterday that Maréchal McClellan is still in Vienna."

Sebastian drew a deep breath that did nothing to lessen the sudden constriction in his chest. "Yes, a surprise," he said, although he was careful to keep his face turned away when he said it.

Kat Boleyn was at her breakfast table when Sebastian was shown up to see her. She was wearing a simple white jaconet muslin gown, embroidered up the front with delicate double rows of entwined ivy, and had a cup of tea growing cold beside her as she bent her head over the newspaper she had spread out across the tablecloth.

"You've heard about the fighting in Belgium?" she said, looking up.

"Yes."

She was silent for a moment, her gaze searching his face as she waited for her maidservant to withdraw. "But that's not why you're here, is it?"

Sebastian shook his head. "The body of a young man was pulled from the Thames a few hours ago. It's André Ternant."

"Oh, no," she whispered, her lips parting on a quickly indrawn breath.

"How well did you know him?"

"Well enough."

"So tell me this: Is his name likely to be on Fouché's list?"

She hesitated a moment, then nodded. "Was he mutilated, like the others?"

"Not that I could see."

"I wonder why the difference."

"I suppose that would depend on why the bodies of the others were mutilated."

She stood abruptly, her back held painfully straight as she went to stand at the window overlooking the rear garden. He watched her, watched the way her hands clenched against the sill and her throat worked when she swallowed. After a moment, she said, "I'm told there are two other people—one an older man, the other a woman—who have disappeared in the last week and whose names could very well be on that list."

"I don't like the sound of that."

She turned to face him. "No, neither do I."

He said, "You need to leave town. Now. And stay away until I figure out who the hell is doing this."

A strange smile curled her lips. "Run away and hide, you mean?" She shook her head. "No. I won't live my life in fear. It's a promise I made myself long ago, and I'm not about to break it now."

"I know," he said. "So don't be afraid. Just . . . be careful. Will you leave town? Please."

"No. But I will be careful. I can promise you that."

"It might not be enough."

She met his gaze, her brilliant St. Cyr blue eyes glittering with both her fear and her fierce determination not to give way to it. "It's the best I can do."

Chapter 46

The murder of André Ternant and the disappearance of at least two other people whose names were likely to have been on Fouché's infamous list sent Sebastian east again, to St. Giles. But he found the shop at Seven Dials shuttered, and his insistent pounding on the front door and ringing of the bell went unanswered.

"Ain't nobody there now," said an old man's voice.

Sebastian looked over at the aged knife grinder sitting cross-legged against one of the shop's canted walls, the tools of his trade arrayed around him. "One's dead and another run off yesterday morning before she thought anyone was up to see her."

"And the third?" said Sebastian.

The old man sniffed. "She left maybe half an hour ago."

"She left town?"

"Her? Nah. Gone to St. Giles, she has."

Sebastian's first thought was, *But this is St. Giles.* Then he looked beyond the old man to the soaring stone spire that rose above the wretched rooftops and understood what he meant.

❧

The Palladian-style Church of St. Giles-in-the-Fields stood in the center of a vast ancient graveyard, not far from the junction of Oxford Street and Tottenham Court. There had been a chapel here since the days of the early twelfth century, when this was a leper colony, although that building was long gone. Sebastian had heard there were so many plague victims buried in and around the last church in the seventeenth century that rising damp undermined that structure to the point that it, too, needed to be replaced. It was hard not to think of those lepers and plague victims now, as he wound his way through the thicket of worn stone monuments and rusting iron fences to where Sibil Wilde, dressed in a Renaissance-era gown of celestial blue satin trimmed with cream lace, stood with her head bowed.

"Surely she hasn't been buried yet," said Sebastian, walking up to her.

Sibil looked around, her eyebrows twitching into a puzzled frown that cleared suddenly. "Oh, you mean Astrid. No; last I heard, her body was still with the surgeons, although I don't understand why. It isn't as if we don't know precisely how she died."

Sebastian nodded to the simple headstone beside them, which he now saw bore the name Alice Crowley. "Who was she?"

"A friend." Sibil hesitated a moment, then added, "A dear friend. When I was attacked, Alice tried to stop the man. He killed her."

"But he didn't kill you?"

She shook her head, her hand coming up to touch her fingertips to the scar on the side of her face. "He wanted me to have to live with this."

"What happened to him?"

"Someone blew his head off."

"You?"

She smiled with her eyes. "Perhaps."

Sebastian looked out over the sea of lichen-covered headstones and crumbling tombs. He could see a hunched old man in a tattered greatcoat winding his slow way through the thicket of ancient tombstones, but otherwise they were alone. "A wherryman pulled the body of a French émigré named André Ternant from the Thames this morning. From the looks of things, someone stuck a dagger in his side, but they didn't mutilate his body. Do you have any idea who might have killed him?"

"Why would I know such a thing?"

"Because Ternant used to pass information to Napoléon, which would have made him your enemy."

"Your enemy, too, surely? Or so one would assume."

"Personally, I prefer to meet my enemies face-to-face on the field of battle rather than jumping them in some dark alley."

"How very gallant of you," she said dryly. "What precisely are you accusing me of? Murder?"

He searched her beautiful, scarred face. "Actually, yes. I've discovered that Miles Sedgewick came to see you the night he was killed."

"Who told you that? Rowena?"

When he didn't answer, she huffed a soft laugh and shrugged. "It's true, of course. He did come to see me that night."

"Why?"

"He'd learned something in Vienna that . . . disturbed him."

"You mean he'd discovered that you were working for the Bourbons?"

"Yes." She looked at him, a smile still curling her lips. "You didn't expect me to admit it, did you?"

"As a matter of fact, no. What time was it when he left you?"

"Eight, or thereabouts. Perhaps closer to half past. Why?"

"Someone told me they saw him elsewhere at about that time." It wasn't true, of course; in fact, what she'd told him dovetailed well with Alexi's encounter with Sedgewick in Charing Cross. But he was interested in seeing her reaction.

She shrugged. "So they were mistaken. Or they lied."

"Or you could be lying now."

"Why would I? Do you know when Sedgewick was killed?"

"Not exactly."

"Then what would be the point in my lying about when I saw him?" She tilted her head to look up at him with an odd, quizzical expression. "Apart from which, why would I have him killed?"

"For the same reason you've had so many others killed: for the Bourbons. Or perhaps because he was a personal threat to you."

"To me? Hardly. And as for the Bourbons . . ." She gave a faint shake of her head. "As long as Jarvis lives, no Bonaparte—especially not Napoléon's half-Austrian son—will be allowed to remain on the throne of France."

"Heard about that, did you?"

"The Austrian proposal? I did—although not from Sedgewick, if that's what you're thinking."

"And did you learn about Fouché's list from this same source?"

"What list?" she said with a smile that didn't touch her eyes.

"Cut line," said Sebastian sharply, beginning to lose what little patience he had left. "Did he offer to sell it to you? Did you not want to pay his price? Is that why you had him killed? So you could simply take it?"

The smile was gone, her eyes sparkling with anger. "I told you before, I don't know what you're talking about."

"Yes, you do."

"Enough of this nonsense," she said, brushing past him.

She'd taken one step, two, when the man Sebastian had noticed earlier appeared from behind a crumbling mausoleum, raised the muzzle of a long rifle, and fired.

Chapter 47

Sibil staggered, then pivoted slowly to face Sebastian, her eyes wide with shock and surprise, her features contorted in agony, the bodice of her blue satin gown a wet sheen of dark red.

"*Hell*," swore Sebastian, leaping forward to catch her as she crumpled and drag her back behind a nearby table tomb. He was aware of the shooter running away, his movements quick and agile, not those of an old man at all. The urge to give chase was strong, except Sebastian couldn't leave the dying woman in his arms.

"I didn't do it, you know," she said hoarsely, her agonized gaze locked with his. "I didn't send Gabriel after Sedgewick."

"And me? Did you set Gabriel against me?"

Her head moved restlessly from side to side. "No. The people on Fouché's list, yes. But not you. Why would I?"

"Did Sedgewick sell you the list?"

"No."

"So how did you get it?"

She coughed, sending a torrent of blood flowing from her lips. "Gabriel . . ."

He raised her shoulders and head higher so that she wouldn't choke on her own blood. "Who is he? What is his real name?"

She stared up at him, her eyes swimming with pain and fear, her breath coming in ragged gasps as she brought up one hand to clutch at the sleeve of his coat.

"Damn it, he's just killed you! *Tell me.*"

"No," she whispered, her eyes sliding shut.

"Tell me!"

But she was beyond answering him, perhaps even beyond hearing him. He cradled her in his arms, conscious of the rush of the damp wind against his face and the hum of the bees buzzing around the gnarled red rosebush beside them. He listened as each agonized, gasping breath shuddered her ruined chest, her breaths coming farther and farther apart until at last they came no more.

"Damn," said Sebastian, easing her down into the long, rank grass. *Damn, damn, damn.*

Sir Henry Lovejoy stood with his shoulders hunched against the growing wind, his gaze on the dead woman at their feet. "And you have no idea who the shooter might be?" he said after a moment, looking up at Sebastian.

"At this point, the only thing I know is, he's not old," said Sebastian, remembering the nimble way the man fled through the graveyard's jumble of tombs and ancient headstones. "But he's obviously very good at sinking his real self into an assumed persona. I found the rifle and his tattered old greatcoat abandoned on the far side of the church."

"So it was a disguise?"

"Gabriel is said to be a master of disguise."

"Like you."

Sebastian took a deep breath and said nothing.

Lovejoy dropped his gaze again to the dead woman at their feet. "Why kill her?"

Sebastian shook his head. "He must have decided she was a threat to him in some way. But why, I don't know."

Lovejoy stared off across the churchyard to the lych-gate, where a couple of his constables were holding back a crowd of curious onlookers. "We've heard from Sedgewick's bootmaker, by the way, that boot you found out at the old tannery was his. And there was indeed a wherryman who was stabbed that same night, although of course we've no way of knowing if the two deaths were in any way connected."

"Any idea where or when the wherryman was last seen?"

"Actually, yes. Another boatman saw him picking up two men from the Whitehall Stairs shortly after nine o'clock. The waterman says he remembers hearing the bells of the Abbey tolling the hour."

Sebastian stared down at Sibil Wilde. In death, the anger and aura of danger had both eased from her face, leaving her looking peaceful, almost childlike.

Lovejoy said, "That's important. Why?"

"I'm not sure. It may mean nothing. Or it could be the key that unlocks this whole bloody tangle."

Chapter 48

$\mathcal{S}$ebastian was seated at his desk in the library, a blank piece of paper before him, a half-forgotten quill balanced in his hand, when Hero came to stand behind him, her hands on his shoulders. "Do you think Sibil was telling the truth?" she asked.

"When she said she didn't set Gabriel to kill Sedgewick, you mean?" He tilted back his head to look up at her. "She was dying. I can't think why she would lie. Can you?"

Hero shook her head. "You think it was Gabriel who shot her?"

"It seems the obvious explanation, but that doesn't mean it's right. For one thing, I keep thinking, why would he?"

"Because she was about to turn against him?"

"Perhaps." He tossed aside the pen. "When Sibil said 'Gabriel,' I assumed it was because she thought he'd shot her. But it occurs to me I'd just asked her how she got Fouché's list, so it's conceivable that what she meant was she got it from Gabriel."

Hero considered this. "It's possible. But she also knew about the

Austrian proposals, so she could have been given Fouché's list by the same source."

"Yes, I can see it playing out that way, too."

Standing up, he went to the game table near the front window where a wooden chessboard stood, its well-used pieces neatly aligned, ready for the next match. "If we ignore the Weird Sisters for a moment, there have been four people murdered—six if we include the man and woman Kat says have disappeared and are probably dead." Reaching out, he picked up one of the white pawns and held it up. "The first was Sedgewick. And while there is much that can be said to the man's discredit, I don't see how anyone could convincingly accuse him of working for Napoléon."

He set the first pawn on the table, just to the right of the chessboard. "Initially I assumed he'd been killed because of his nasty habit of seducing other men's wives. And if he were the only victim, I'd probably still be inclined to believe that. But he isn't the only one."

Sebastian reached for a second white pawn. "Then comes our nameless, headless middle-aged man, who may or may not be the Spaniard Francisco de la Serna. If he's someone else, I suppose he could have been working for Napoléon, so he's still a bit of a question mark." He set the second pawn near the first, although back a bit.

He picked up a third white pawn and put it beside the first. "Next is Hamilton Evans. He didn't even come down from Cambridge until after Napoléon abdicated last spring, so I seriously doubt his name could have been on Fouché's list."

He hesitated a moment, then picked up three black pawns that he set in a row on the other side of the board. "Over here we'll put André Ternant, plus the two others who have disappeared and whose names are probably on the list. Only Ternant has been found, but he wasn't mutilated like our three white pawns over there—

although obviously we don't know about the two people who are missing."

Hero walked over to stand with her arms crossed at her chest, her gaze on the disarrayed chess pieces. "What precisely are you suggesting?"

Sebastian looked up at her. "What if Gabriel killed Sedgewick for his own reasons, perhaps the same reason he also killed Hamilton Evans and No Name here"—he picked up the second white pawn and put it in line with the other two—"but when he was stripping Sedgewick's body, he found Fouché's list. He realized what it was and gave it to Sibil."

"And then, with her blessing, set about killing the people whose names are on the list? Except because those were professional kills rather than driven by whatever the original personal animus was, he simply killed them without mutilating the bodies?"

"That's the idea, yes."

"So why kill Sibil—and presumably Astrid, too?" She nodded toward the two rows of pawns. "You've left them out of your lineup."

"I need a third color of pawns."

"Here." Hero reached for the two queens, one black, one white, and set them by themselves in front of the board. Then she picked up a black knight and set it in front of Sebastian. "And this is you. Because if you're right about all this, Gabriel is now trying to kill you, too. And what I don't understand is, *why?*"

"That's easy: because he thinks I'm close to figuring out who he is."

"But you're not."

He turned away from the chessboard and went to pour himself a brandy.

Hero watched him in silence for a moment, then said, "You're not, are you?"

He paused, carafe in hand, and glanced over at her. "When Sedgewick was forced to sell out because of his damaged arm, he grew so restless and bored with life in London that he started working with Bathurst and Castlereagh."

She let out a slow, painful breath. "You're thinking about Monty, aren't you? You're thinking he could be Gabriel."

Sebastian replaced the stopper in the carafe and set it aside. "It fits, doesn't it?"

"Would he do something like that? Become a cold-blooded killer for hire?"

"Not for hire, no; he certainly wouldn't be doing it for money. But because he missed being a part of something larger? Missed the excitement and thrill of danger? I can maybe see that." He walked over to pick up the first white pawn. "What if he killed Miles Sedgewick because the man was having an affair with his wife? Then he found Fouché's list—completely by chance—and took it to Sibil?"

"That works for Sedgewick and Ternant, and for the two missing people. It might also work for our headless man if his name was on the list, although it doesn't explain his mutilation." She picked up the third of the white pawns and held it out to him. "And it doesn't explain Hamilton Evans."

He took the pawn from her outstretched hand. "What do we know about Evans, other than the fact that his parents died in India and he was raised by Lord Oakley?"

Hero met his gaze. "Obviously not enough."

❧

Dressed in a gown of deep blue satin trimmed with rows of beading and fringe and topped by a richly embroidered shawl, the Dowager

Duchess of Claiborne was coming out of her front door when Sebastian pulled up behind her waiting carriage.

"Sebastian," she said, pausing on her doorstep as he tossed the reins to Tom. "You've heard something from Belgium?"

"Sorry, not yet," he said, hopping down from the curricle's high seat. "I just have a couple of questions I need to ask you."

"Good heavens, not now. I'm on my way to a card party."

"This won't take but a moment, I promise."

"But I've already told you everything I know about Miles Sedgewick."

He ran up the front steps toward her. "It's not Sedgewick I'm interested in. What can you tell me about Hamilton Evans?"

Aunt Henrietta drew a deep breath. "Oh, dear."

"What? What is it?" said Sebastian, searching her face.

She glanced over at her wooden-faced butler, then said to Sebastian, "Come inside."

❧

She drew him into a small chamber just off the front entrance hall and closed the door. "What do you already know about Evans?" she said.

He shook his head. "Not a great deal. I know that he was twenty-two and recently down from Cambridge, that he worked in the Foreign Office, and that he was raised by Lord Oakley after his parents died in India."

She fixed him with a hard stare. "What I'm about to tell you must go no further. That's understood?"

"Of course."

She nodded. "It's a disturbing tale. Oakley and his wife had one son and three daughters. I presume you know the son; he's a ridiculous creature who basically spends his time dressing himself and kicking his heels while he waits for his father to die. The eldest daughter, Margaret, married Lord Selkirk, while the youngest, Beatrice, married Mr. Jeffrey Burns. But the middle girl, Grace, drowned twenty-one years ago under circumstances that were rather murky."

Sebastian's gaze met hers. "Are you suggesting she killed herself after giving birth to an illegitimate child?"

"Do I know for certain? No. But there were whispers. Grace was about a month into her second season when the family abruptly withdrew from London and went back to Ireland. And Oakley was always decidedly vague about which of his cousins Hamilton was supposed to have come from."

"Any guesses as to who might have fathered the child?"

"Given the timing and the brevity of Grace's second season, it's assumed the child's father was one of their neighbors in Ireland."

"Where are Oakley's estates?"

"County Meath. Near the village of Summerhill."

Sebastian felt his heart begin to pound. "Near Dangan Castle?"

"The two estates march together."

"*Oh, Jesus,*" whispered Sebastian.

Once, Dangan Castle had been the home of Garrett Wesley, the Earl of Mornington. He was such an improvident man—as was his father before him—that his eldest son and heir was forced to sell the family estates around the turn of the century. Yet so ambitious and ruthless were Wesley's sons that they had succeeded—brilliantly— despite the family's financial embarrassments. Of course, by the turn of the century the family had changed the spelling of their name to Wellesley. The eldest son, Richard, had been the British Ambassador to Spain before becoming Foreign Secretary and was now Marquis Wellesley. A younger son, Sir Henry, was the British Ambassador to

Spain after his brother. And a third son, Arthur, was now the Duke of Wellington.

"Which one?" said Sebastian. "Which of the Wellesleys was likely the father of Hamilton Evans?"

"No one ever knew for certain. Why does it matter so much?"

Sebastian shook his head. "Perhaps it doesn't."

Chapter 49

$\mathcal{S}$uspicion is an insidious thing.

Sebastian knew he could be wrong; in fact, he had no doubt that he surely was wrong in some way. But the pieces of this complicated puzzle were finally beginning to align in a clear pattern, and he didn't like where it was pointing.

He had three sets of victims. It now appeared conceivable that the first set—Miles Sedgewick, Hamilton Evans (because of his connection to the Wellesleys), and the headless possible Spaniard—were linked to what had been done to the prisoners of Cabrera. The second set—Ternant and the two missing people presumably named in Fouché's list—had passed information to Napoléon, while the third set—Astrid and Sibil Wilde—were known associates of the Bourbons' London assassin. The first set of victims had been horribly mutilated; the others were cold, professional kills.

That could mean two different killers: one the Bourbon assassin, the other someone determined to wreak his own personal revenge on those he held responsible for the horrors of Cabrera. But the role played in all this by the Fouché list made that doubtful. Sebastian found it far more likely that the Bourbons' assassin had lost someone he loved on Cabrera and set out to exact a brutal revenge on those he held responsible. Was it only by chance that in the process of mutilating Sedgewick's body he'd discovered Fouché's list of names? It seemed increasingly likely. But however it had come about, Gabriel had then set about eliminating the people whose names were on that list. He killed Astrid because she was threatening to reveal his identity, and then he killed Sibil because . . .

Why? Because she objected to his murder of Astrid? Because she was beginning to find him dangerously unstable? Both?

Neither?

Sebastian had been trying without success to uncover the identity of the Bourbons' assassin for the better part of a year now, and yet he still knew frustratingly little about the man beyond a few simple facts:

He was comfortable with killing, preferring to use a garrote or dagger but more than capable of employing a pistol or rifle.

He was skilled at adopting disguises.

He spoke French and was, surely, a man who'd lost someone he loved on Cabrera. Yet he was capable of speaking English without a trace of any accent.

The latter was not particularly surprising. England was full of émigrés who'd fled France twenty-five years before as children and were now indistinguishable from the native-born. There were also any number of Englishmen who were at least half French.

It was about the only thing we had in common, Monty had once said of Sedgewick. *Beyond what we did in the Army—well, that plus the fact that we both had French mothers . . .*

Suspicion could be an insidious thing.

Monty McPherson was in the stables of Tattersall's inspecting a fine gray hack when Sebastian walked up to him.

"Devlin," said Monty with a wide grin. "So what do you think of her? She's showy, but I know someone familiar with her, and he says she's a sweet goer with good bottom."

"She's a fine mare." Sebastian smiled as the gray nosed his pockets for carrots. "Is there another auction this week?"

Monty nodded. "The last Thursday auction until fall, I suspect." He ran a hand down the gray's near shoulder. "You're looking rather grave this morning. You don't believe the reports the papers are all carrying from that fellow who's supposed to have just arrived from Belgium? He's saying our lads won a grand victory last Friday and have already chased Boney back to France."

"You mean Sutton?" Sebastian shook his head. He'd seen the breathless reports and quickly dismissed them. "I'd like to, but it contradicts the official report we've already received from Quatre Bras and Ligny—which said that Wellington had been forced to fall back toward Brussels and that the Prussians were soundly defeated."

"Well, hell. I was hoping you'd heard something official that would confirm it." His face pinched and drawn, Monty stared off across the courtyard to where a black-and-white cat was rubbing against one of the columns of the pump house. "Do you think this new battle—however it has actually turned out—will end it all? For good, I mean."

"If Bonaparte has been defeated, yes. Otherwise . . . probably not."

"Damn," he said softly. "I guess I should have taken Isabella to Paris last year when she was pestering me to go. I thought we had all the time in the world to see France."

"Your mother was French, wasn't she?"

"She was, yes. From Avignon."

"Do you still have many relatives there?"

"Some, although I can't say we've kept in touch."

"Any of them fight in the French Army?"

"Probably. Why do you ask?"

Sebastian kept his gaze on his friend's vaguely puzzled face. "Do you know if any of them were sent to Cabrera?"

"No, I've no idea." Monty's eyes narrowed. "What the bloody hell are you thinking, Devlin? That *I'm* the one who killed Sedgewick? Who's been killing them all?"

Sebastian gave a faint shake of his head, unwilling to put his suspicions into words.

"Bloody hell," said Monty again. He started to turn away, then swung back to face him. "Why are you asking about Cabrera? What have you learned?"

"There is a possibility it's the link between some of the killings, although not all of them. But what I can't figure out is how the killer could have discovered that Sedgewick was involved in the decision to send the French prisoners there."

"So that's why you suspect me? Because I knew? I can't believe this."

"Did you tell anyone about Sedgewick's involvement in it?"

"Me? No. Why would I?"

"Hell, I don't know. Did Sedgewick ever talk about it much?"

"He wasn't ashamed of it, if that's what you're asking. In fact, he brought it up the last time I saw him."

"When was this?"

"That I saw him? I don't know exactly. Not long before he went to Vienna. He was intrigued by a discussion on the nature of evil he'd just had with someone and wanted to know my thoughts on the subject."

Sebastian felt the blood rushing in his head hard enough that he could hear it. "Did he say with whom he'd had this discussion?"

Monty frowned with thought. "He told me, but I can't remember, no."

"It wasn't Tiptoff, was it?"

His frown cleared. "Yes, that was it. Dudley Tiptoff."

Chapter 50

$\mathcal{H}$ero was seated in one of the cane chairs beside the drawing room's open windows and writing up some of the notes for her article when Devlin walked in, bringing with him all the scents of the city on a warm summer's evening.

"What is it?" she asked as he tossed his hat and walking stick onto a side table and went to stand at the window, his gaze on the light drizzle that was beginning to fall.

He turned to face her. "How well do you know Dudley Tiptoff? I don't mean his research and writing, but the man himself."

"I've met him, but that's about it. Why?"

He told her.

"It might mean nothing," she said when he had finished.

"It might," he agreed. "But I keep remembering how quickly he volunteered to Bow Street that he'd seen Sedgewick walking down Whitehall toward the Abbey, complete with the exact time: ten o'clock. Except that Alexi says she saw Sedgewick at Charing Cross that night at least an hour earlier, after which she says he walked off down Whitehall."

"Why would Tiptoff lie about the time?"

"Perhaps in case anyone ever questioned his servants about when he got in that night? All I know is, I'm inclined to believe Alexi, both because it fits with when Sedgewick left Seven Dials and because we now know a wherryman who picked up two men from the Whitehall Stairs just after nine that night was later found stabbed."

Hero set aside her notebook. "But you can't suspect Tiptoff! He's harmless, surely?"

"Is he? Can you think of anyone who might be able to tell us more about him?"

She was silent for a moment. "Actually, I can."

꙳

Wednesday, 21 June

His name was Elwyn Millard Dunn, and he was a specialist in medieval monastic architecture whom Hero had come to know through some work she'd once done on the remnants of medieval structures still to be found in London.

A tall, skinny man with a protruding potbelly, a bony face, and wispy, very fair hair, he was somewhere in his late thirties. He received them in the cluttered study of his rooms in Gilbert Street at the unfashionably early hour of eleven o'clock and invited them to sit on his somewhat dusty sofa.

"I've known Tiptoff since we were up at Cambridge together eighteen—no, goodness, I suppose it's more like twenty years ago now," said Dunn, templing his fingers before him as he leaned back in his chair. "Of course, he never finished his degree, you know."

"He didn't?" said Hero.

"No. Went off to stay with his uncle in Switzerland."

"His uncle was Swiss?"

"What? Oh, no. His uncle was William Wickham."

Sebastian and Hero exchanged one quick, guarded glance. William Wickham had essentially founded the British foreign secret service during the French Revolution. From his position at the British embassy in Switzerland he established an extensive network of spies that operated throughout southern Europe, schemed with the French royalists, and helped foment the disastrous uprising against the Republic in the Vendée.

"Interesting," said Hero. "Did he stay in Switzerland long?"

"Oh, yes; fifteen years, at least—far longer than his uncle. To be frank, I never quite understood what he was doing there. I mean, he said he was studying the Swiss witch burnings—the Swiss were terrible about it, you know. The small cantons of Valais and Vaud alone executed something like three and a half thousand 'witches' and 'werewolves,' while at one point Geneva burned over five hundred in just three months. I think the last one they killed was a young girl from Canton Glarus, who was tortured into confessing she was a witch just over thirty years ago and beheaded."

"How horrible," murmured Hero. "So what makes you think that wasn't the only reason Tiptoff went there?"

Dunn shrugged. "I don't know. I suppose people change over the course of ten or fifteen years. But he just seemed . . . different when he came back."

"Different in what way?"

"I don't know," he said again, with all the confusion of a man accustomed to analyzing stones, not people. "But it was more than just the limp."

"He didn't limp before?"

"No. I've heard people say it's some kind of birth defect, but that's not true. He never had it when we were up at Cambridge. In fact, he was quite athletic in those days. I remember he could run like the wind."

"What do you know of his family?" said Sebastian. "I gather Wickham was his mother's brother?"

"No, his father's—the father's younger half brother, as I understand it. Tiptoff's mother was French."

"Was she?" said Hero, sitting forward with an encouraging smile.

"Oh, yes. They actually lived in France until he was fourteen or so. His mother and father were both killed in the Terror, but Tiptoff and his sister managed to escape and came here."

"How awful," said Hero. "I didn't know he had a sister."

"He did, but she died some time ago, I believe. He had an older brother, too, but he stayed in France. From what I remember, he was in the French Army."

"Is he still alive?" said Sebastian.

"I've no idea." Dunn looked at him, his eyes narrowing. "Why are you so interested in Tiptoff anyway?"

"It would be perhaps best if you didn't ask. The interest is that of my father, Lord Jarvis," lied Hero. "I've no doubt you'll understand our inability to elaborate further." She rose to her feet as all the color drained from Dunn's face and he began to stammer. "Thank you so much for your time. Your assistance has been invaluable."

"I don't like where this is going," said Hero as Sebastian handed her up into their waiting carriage.

He hopped up to sit beside her. "Neither do I."

"The problem is, how to prove any of it?"

Sebastian stared out the window for a moment, his attention seemingly all for the ragged little boy sweeping the nearby crossing. Then he turned his head to meet her gaze. "I have an idea."

꒰

The execution of Sebastian's plan was complicated.

It required, first of all, finding a likeness of Miles Sedgewick. But since both the dead man's wife and his brother were refusing to speak to them, they were forced to turn to Isabella McPherson.

After first insisting that she possessed no likeness, Isabella finally admitted to having in her possession a miniature of the man she'd secretly loved, skillfully painted on a gilt-framed ivory oval. But she refused to allow it out of her sight, even briefly. So Hero was forced to take drawing paper and pencils to Norfolk Street and make a sketch of it there, while Isabella stood at the drawing room window, anxiously keeping an eye out for Monty's return lest she be forced into having to make some awkward explanations.

Hero was a better artist than she tended to believe herself to be, and within an hour or so had reproduced a good pencil likeness of the portrait.

Returning to Brook Street, Sebastian sent for Tom.

"I have an assignment for you," he told the boy, handing him Hero's sketch.

"This that first cove what got hisself killed?" said Tom, turning the sketch to the light.

"It is. I want you to take this to Whitehall and see if you can find someone who saw Sedgewick there the night he was killed—probably somewhere between eight and ten."

Tom looked up, a wide grin splitting his face. "Reckon I can do that, gov'nor!"

꒰

After that, Sebastian went in search of Mr. Dudley Tiptoff.

The streets were becoming increasingly clogged as people kept gathering in the parks, on bridges, and in places like Pall Mall and Fleet Street, hoping to be amongst the first to hear word of the arrival of Wellington's official messenger from Belgium. It was late afternoon by the time Sebastian finally traced the folklore scholar to a small old-fashioned pub in a quiet side street near Covent Garden, where he was eating a simple dinner of roast beef and potatoes at a table near one of the darkly paneled room's leaded front windows.

"Good evening, my lord," said the scholar when he looked up and saw Sebastian. "Won't you have a seat and join me?"

Sebastian ordered a pint of ale, then went to pull out one of the table's stools and sit. "Thank you."

"Have you heard the latest? A couple of Irishmen—a knight and some earl's son—have now arrived from Belgium, and everything they're saying contradicts the report brought by that fellow Sutton. They say Wellington actually retreated before Marshal Ney's troops at Quatre Bras, while Napoléon utterly routed the Prussians at Ligny. And as of last Sunday morning, Wellington had his troops drawn up to meet Napoléon himself near some village called Waterloo. The stock market has crashed, and now no one knows what to believe. What the devil is wrong with Wellington, taking so long to send official word of the battles' outcomes? It's now Wednesday! Surely he knows we are all waiting with bated breath?"

"He was used to taking his time composing his dispatches from Spain," said Sebastian. "Perhaps he simply doesn't realize how important everyone considers this battle."

"So it would seem!"

Sebastian took a slow sip of his ale and watched as Tiptoff sawed off another piece of his roast beef. If the image of a disheveled, preoccupied scholar was assumed, it was done well. His hair was uncut and disarrayed, his rumpled clothes loose and baggy enough to disguise what could easily be a trim, athletic figure beneath. After all, it wasn't difficult to wrap padding around one's middle to suggest an expanding waistline. Hadn't Sebastian done it himself many times?

Now he said, "Someone was telling me that William Wickham is your uncle."

Tiptoff glanced up, but his expression remained unchanged. "He is, yes. Do you know him?"

"Only by repute."

Tiptoff chewed his slice of beef, then swallowed. "He's a complicated man. Helped send Despard and Emmet to the gallows as traitors, then resigned from the government in protest over their treatment of the Irish and Catholics."

"So he's true to his convictions."

"He is, yes. I've always thought he'd have made a splendid medieval knight."

Sebastian took another swallow of ale. "I can't recall—was he ever in the Army?"

"No; he studied law. His brother's the one who was always army mad—like my brother." Tiptoff took a mouthful of potato, then swallowed. "He died in Spain."

"Your brother? I'm sorry," said Sebastian, choosing his words carefully. "We lost a lot of good men in the Peninsula. As did France."

"So true," said Tiptoff, an enigmatic smile touching his lips. And Sebastian thought, *He knows. He knows I suspect him.*

Tiptoff said, "And have you made any progress in finding Sedgewick's killer?"

"Some. What time was it you said you saw him in Whitehall?"

"Ten o'clock."

"Not nine?"

"Not unless I miscounted when the clock in the bell tower struck the hour—which I suppose is possible. Is the time critical for some reason?"

"Probably not. I've simply been finding it difficult to pin down all of Sedgewick's movements that day."

Tiptoff rested his fork on the side of his plate, then looked up, a speculative expression on his face. "I heard that Sibil Wilde was shot and killed yesterday, and one of her sisters murdered just a day or so before. Is there some link between all these killings, do you think?"

Sebastian met the other man's seemingly limpid gray gaze. "It's difficult to say." He took a deep swallow of ale. "I've been wondering, do you know exactly when Sedgewick's interest in the persecution of witches and werewolves began?"

"I do, actually. It was after a visit to Würzburg. They burned children as young as nine there, you know, and boys as little as three and four were thrown in prison as consorts of the devil. It both troubled and intrigued him, and after that he started looking into it more."

"Good God. I had no idea they went after children that young."

Tiptoff nodded. "And Würzburg wasn't even the worst, I'm afraid. The prince-bishop of Cologne burned over two thousand poor souls back in the 1630s, while the tiny town of Ellwangen burned three hundred and eighty-three in just seven years; they essentially killed every woman and girl child in town. Lately I've seen some scholars trying to argue that the number of witch burnings has been grossly exaggerated, that the records don't substantiate the figures. But the truth is, most witch and werewolf burnings were never recorded. And even when they were, many—if not most—of the records have since been destroyed, either deliberately or by war or fire. Anyone who thinks they can count the few records we do have left and come up with an accurate tally is willfully deluding himself."

Tiptoff took another mouthful of his dinner, chewed thoughtfully, then swallowed and said, "But as to why Sedgewick was so

fascinated by the subject, I don't exactly know. I've sometimes wondered if perhaps one of his ancestors was burned as a witch. Most of
those who suffered in the witch hysterias were poor, but not all."

"Atrocities frequently do make more of an impact when they are
personal."

"So true," said Tiptoff with a tight smile.

Sebastian pushed back his stool and rose to his feet. "Thank you
for your help."

"Any time."

Sebastian started to turn away, then paused. "I almost forgot:
Did you ever stop by Sedgewick's house the day after you met him
in Whitehall, to see that witch's ladder?"

"No, I didn't. I was delayed at the museum and ended up sending him a note, telling him I'd need to postpone until later in the
week."

If it was an excuse, it was a good one. In all the household confusion that had surely followed Sedgewick's disappearance and death,
the staff would never remember whether they'd received such a note
or not.

Tiptoff sighed. "It's a pity. I would like to have seen it. But I've no
doubt his widow has destroyed it by now. I know she never shared
her husband's interest in such things, and her dear friend the Reverend would no doubt see such an artifact as satanic."

"Undoubtedly," said Sebastian, and left it at that.

☙

Sebastian was walking down Southampton Street toward the river
when he heard a high-pitched cockney voice shouting, "Gov'nor!
Oy! Gov'nor!"

Sebastian turned to find Tom pelting down the street behind

him, dodging an organ-grinder, an old woman selling ribbons from a tray, and a big copper-colored dog.

"I found somebody!" said Tom, gasping for breath as he skidded to a halt beside him. "It's a pickpocket by the name o' Dilly. She swears she was in Whitehall that night, and wait till ye 'ear what she's got t' say!"

Chapter 51

This time—after his experience with Phoebe Cox—Sebastian took Hero with him.

"I usually try to dress a little less extravagantly for my interviews," said Hero as their carriage worked its way through the crowded streets toward Whitehall. She'd just finished dressing for dinner when he'd found her, and she hadn't had time to change out of her gown of pale yellow *batiste de soie* festooned at the neck, puffed sleeves, and scalloped hem with rows of knotted lilac ribbons.

"I've no doubt Dilly will be dazzled," said Sebastian with a soft laugh, then laughed again when Hero wrinkled her nose at him.

They found the young pickpocket sitting on the steps of an old chapel across from the Horse Guards, waiting for them. She looked to be perhaps eleven or twelve, but her light brown hair was chopped off to just above her shoulders, and she wore a pair of ragged trousers with a boy's blue smock that hung loosely about her small frame. The streets were hard for little girls on their own, and most turned to prostitution by the age of thirteen. Dilly was obviously determined that wasn't going to happen to her.

"You the nobs what wanted t' hear 'bout what happened that night?" she said, pushing to her feet as they approached. Her eyes cut sideways to where Tom was waiting by the carriage. "He said ye'd give me a crown if'n I told you what I saw."

Sebastian handed her a half guinea. "That's right. You get the rest when you've finished telling us what you know."

The girl pocketed the coin and sniffed. "What if ye stiff me?"

"And what if you have no real information to tell?"

She sniffed again and tapped the folded sketch Hero was holding. "You're wantin' to know if I saw this cove, and I did."

"A week ago Saturday night?" Hero asked gently.

Dilly nodded. "I'm not likely to forget him. Caught me tryin' t' lift his purse, he did. Only he just laughed, told me I needed more practice, and let me go."

"What time was this?"

"'Bout nine, I suppose. It weren't dark yet."

"Did you see where he went after that?"

Dilly nodded. "I was afraid maybe he meant t' set the constables on me after all, so I ducked out o' sight real quick. But then I watched him, just t' be sure."

"And?"

"He set off walkin' that way." She jerked her chin toward Downing Street. "But then this other cove hails him."

Sebastian frowned. According to Tiptoff, Sedgewick had hailed *him*. "You're certain it wasn't the other way around?"

Dilly cast him a withering glance. "'Course I'm certain. I said I was watchin' him, didn't I?"

"Yes, of course. I beg your pardon," said Sebastian.

"What did this other 'cove' look like?" said Hero.

"He was maybe a bit older, a bit shorter, and a bit heavier. I'd noticed him before he hailed the first cove, 'cause he was actin' kinda weird."

"Weird in what way?"

"Well, he was dressed all flash—like a nob, ye know? But he wasn't just walkin' along like he was goin' somewhere. At first it was like he was watchin' the other cove, kinda hangin' back. And then he sets off stridin' across the yard and calls out to him."

"So then what happened?" coaxed Hero.

"The first cove turned and walked back toward him, and they jist talked a minute or two."

"Could you hear what they said?"

Dilly shook her head. "Nah. They was too far away. In the end, they turned together and walked toward the river."

"The two of them?" said Sebastian.

Dilly glared at him again. "That's what I said, ain't it?"

He heard Hero smother what sounded suspiciously like a laugh. "Can you tell us anything else about either man?" she said.

Dilly screwed up her face in thought. "Not really. 'Cept there was one other thing kinda weird about the second cove."

"What's that?"

"When I first noticed him, he was walking jist fine. But then right before he hails the first cove, he suddenly starts walking like this . . ." Dilly pantomimed walking away from them, her right foot dragging in a perfect parody of Dudley Tiptoff's halting gait.

Chapter 52

*T*hat evening Kat rode in her town carriage through the crowded streets of London to the theater. She stared unseeingly out the window, her thoughts far, far away, and was jerked back to the present only when they drew up before the short, broad alley that led to the stage door.

"We'll be waiting here for you after the play, Miss Boleyn," said her coachman as the footman opened the carriage door and held out a hand to help her down the steps. "Never you fear."

"Thank you, George," she said with a smile, and turned away.

She let her gaze drift assessingly over the crowd gathered in the streets outside the theater, looking for the man with the distinctively shaped head. But she saw only the usual assortment of half-lit young bucks talking too loudly and laughing uproariously at some crude suggestion or joke. She was dressed in a modest muslin gown topped by a deep forest green spencer, and still she drew catcalls and lewd propositions. Ignoring them, she turned quickly into the alley.

She'd taken perhaps half a dozen steps toward the stage door when she heard a man's footsteps coming up behind her fast. Annoyed, she'd half turned when the man's hand flashed out to close around her arm, his fingers digging deep into the cloth of her spencer. She gasped as he jerked her up against him, and gasped again as something sharp pricked the tender flesh beneath her ribs.

"Don't," he said in a quiet, cultured voice, leaning in so close that his breath ruffled a lock of hair at her temple. "Don't move and don't scream. I assume a woman with your experience recognizes the point of a dagger when it's held against her side?"

Kat swallowed hard. His face was unknown to her, but she recognized him instantly by the shape of his head. "What do you want?" she said, calling upon all her training to keep her voice even. "I've no money on me, and my jewels are paste."

She saw his eyes crinkle with what looked like amusement. "Truly, madam, you cut me to the quick. Do I *look* like a common thief? And here I took such pains to array myself in the guise of a buck on the strut, with no intent beyond imbibing blue ruin and ogling every neatly turned ankle I might chance to spy."

"What do you want from me?" she said again.

His smile widened. "There is a hackney carriage waiting for us at the corner. We will walk to it."

"And if I refuse?"

"Then I will kill you here and now."

"You won't get away with it."

"You think not? A dagger slipped between the ribs is silent. You will collapse, and I will be shocked and horrified and call for help. And then in the resulting crush and confusion, I will simply slip away."

"And if I go with you? Then what? Would you have me believe you won't still kill me?" Her lip curled. "You think me a fool?"

"No. But you have a choice: You can die here and now, or hope that if you come with me, fate may still fall out in your favor. Which is it to be?"

She was painfully aware of the raucous laughter of the men in the street before the theater, of the breath rasping in and out of her lungs and the pounding of her heart, and of the bite of the killer's fingers digging into her arm. She could try to scream but had no doubt that he'd kill her the instant she started to draw a deep breath. There was no choice, really. *While I breathe, I hope . . .*

Kat clenched her jaw and said, "Which corner?"

Chapter 53

I still can't believe Tiptoff is the one who's doing this," said Hero as their carriage swung out into Whitehall and began to slowly weave its way through the crowds to Charing Cross. "I mean, *Dudley Tiptoff?* So he—what? Worked with his uncle Wickham in Switzerland, helping to stir up counterrevolutionary activity in the Vendée and quietly sticking his dagger in anyone the British government wanted eliminated? And then came back to London and set himself up as the epitome of an eccentric, out-of-shape scholar, all the while quietly and efficiently killing people here for the Bourbons?"

"It certainly sounds like it," said Sebastian. He was silent for a moment, his gaze on the stoic mounted guards on duty outside the Horse Guards. "The problem is, there's an alternative, seemingly innocent explanation for everything that implicates him. Sedgewick *could* have told someone else about the role he played in Cabrera. Tiptoff's brother *could* have been killed fighting someplace like Vitoria or Talavera. Dilly *could* have seen him suddenly begin limping simply because his leg started hurting him again. It's even possible he did hail Sedgewick, but then lied about it simply because he was afraid it might make people suspect him."

"And lied about the two of them not walking toward the river for the same reason?"

"That one seems more of a stretch," Sebastian admitted. "What I can't figure out is what the hell Tiptoff could have said to Sedgewick to make him get into a wherry and go down to the McGuire Tannery when the sun was setting."

Hero looked thoughtful for a moment. "That part of Southwark might be an abandoned tannery now, but what if there was something there before—something connected to Sedgewick's interest in witch and werewolf lore? Something Tiptoff could have used to lure Sedgewick there just as the sun was setting?"

Sebastian glanced out the window at the waning daylight, then leaned forward and signaled their coachman to pull up. "The sun is setting now."

❦

They took a wherry rather than their carriage, both to avoid the increasingly crowded streets and to better replicate the events of that fatal night. The setting sun turned the waters of the Thames a fiery orangey pink that faded slowly to a gleaming silver. The evening was cool and sweet, the day's earlier rain having cleansed the air and left it smelling faintly of the distant sea. A row of windmills high on the far bank stood out dark against the pink-streaked sky, with the leafy trees of the Temple Gardens shifting gently in the mellow breeze. It was the time of the summer solstice, so even when the sun finally slipped beyond the distant horizon, the sky remained quite light and would for some time.

"Ye know the tannery is closed now, right?" said their wherryman as they glided under Blackfriars Bridge and he began to turn his boat toward the south bank. "I mean, it has been for years."

"Yes, we know," said Hero.

The man shrugged, as if there was no understanding the ways of the Quality, then pivoted the boat sharply to send the bow knocking against the rotting boards of the tannery's dilapidated old wharf. "I can wait fer ye, if ye want," he said.

"Yes, please," said Sebastian, helping Hero ashore.

"Me rates go up after dark," warned the man, squinting toward the sinking sun.

"That won't be a problem."

The wherryman nodded and turned his head to shoot a stream of tobacco juice into the choppy waves. "Jist so's ye know."

"In my next life," said Hero as they worked their way along the bank, the soft soles of her delicate lilac shoes slipping and sliding on the wet, slime-covered stones at the river's edge, "I'm going to come back as a man and wear nice sturdy boots." Then she thought about it a moment and said, "Although I must admit the thought of wearing nothing but brown, black, and white is rather depressing."

Sebastian laughed and reached back to take her hand. "Here."

They drew up at the point where they had found Sedgewick's boot. The pile of driftwood that once stood there had been torn apart by Lovejoy's constables in their search of the area. But they hadn't found anything else that seemed out of place.

"I wonder what was here before," said Hero, her head falling back as she let her gaze wander to the ruins that stood on the bank above. "Before they built the tannery, I mean."

"You think they might have burned witches here?"

"Perhaps." She nodded to where St. Paul's loomed above the clustered rooftops of the city on the far side of the river, its dome and towers silhouetted black now against the fading sky. "It is across the river from the cathedral. Or they could have used this spot for a 'swimming test' of women accused of being witches. They used to strip

them of their clothes, tie them up, and toss them in the river to see if
they'd float—the idea being that since witches had supposedly re-
jected the sacrament of baptism, the water would then reject them."

"Lovely."

"Isn't it? Although I think I'd rather go through that than have
them strip me and prick me all over to see if I had some 'devil-tainted'
place that didn't bleed."

"Maybe," said Sebastian. "As long as they managed to haul you
out of the river before you drowned."

"Yes, but even if the river didn't 'reject' me, they'd still probably
burn me—on the off chance the river might have made a mistake."

Sebastian was silent for a moment, his gaze on the wide expanse
of the Thames now turning pewter in the dying light. "There's been
a hell of a lot of evil done in God's name."

"Yes," she said simply.

They turned to climb the bank to where the abandoned pits and
half-collapsed buildings of the old tannery stood dark and brooding
in the gathering gloom. The air smelled of rust and dirt and sun-
warmed grass, the long, rank weeds bending softly in the evening
breeze. They'd almost reached the ivy-smothered walls of the old
abandoned warehouse when the clatter of hoofbeats and a jingle of
harness jerked Sebastian's attention toward the lane, where a familiar
hackney drawn by a single horse was turning in through the tannery's old broken gateposts.

"What is it?" said Hero as he caught her arm and drew her back
into the shadows cast by the crumbling brick building.

"A hackney," he said quietly. "And unless I'm mistaken, the jarvey
driving it is the same fellow involved in a certain lethal encounter in
Oxford Street."

They could see it quite clearly now, the horse's head dark against
the purpling sky as the hackney drew up inside the tannery's broken

gates. The near door opened and a gentleman in a round hat and trousers hopped down, dragging with him a young woman in a dashing hat with a curled brim and a fashionably cut high-waisted muslin gown topped by a deep forest green spencer. She stumbled when she hit the uneven ground, and he jerked her arm hard enough that she let out a soft cry, quickly bit off.

"If yer gonna be long," said the jarvey, "how about I go 'ave me somethin' t' drink and come back and get ye when yer done 'ere?"

Turning toward him, the gentleman drew a small pistol from his pocket, wordlessly leveled the muzzle at the hackney driver's head, thumbed back the hammer, and fired.

Hero sucked in her breath in a quiet gasp as the night exploded with a burst of flame and smoke. The bay between the shafts snorted and threw back its head, sidling nervously, while the driver pitched sideways off his seat to hit the hard earth with a quiet *thump*.

"I can't see from this distance," she whispered. "Is that Tiptoff?"

"Yes."

"Who's the woman?"

Slim and well formed, with cascading rich dark hair, the woman had her head turned so that Sebastian couldn't see her face. Then Tiptoff tightened his grip on her arm, jerking her around, and Sebastian felt his heart slam hard up against his ribs.

"It's Kat. Kat Boleyn."

Chapter 54

$\mathscr{D}$oes his pistol have one barrel or two?" whispered Hero.

"One." Sebastian looked at her. "Why?"

"Good. Then he won't be able to shoot me when I walk out there and cheerfully talk to him like an oblivious idiot while you work your way around the back of the building and jump him."

"No," said Sebastian.

She glanced over at him. "Do you have a better idea?"

He thought about it. "No."

Hero straightened her gaily plumed hat. "Then let's do it."

⚜

"Mr. Tiptoff! Good evening! That is you, is it not?"

Sebastian could hear Hero's voice, ringing with a cheerful, hail-fellow-well-met buoyancy, as he quietly slipped around the back of the old warehouse, stepping carefully lest he stumble over rubble hidden in the long, rank weeds. The air was thick with the smell of decay and the loud whine of insects waking up with the approach of nightfall.

"What a pleasant surprise," Hero was saying. "Running into you like this. Whatever are you doing out here? And Miss Kat Boleyn, too. You do remember me, don't you? I believe we met at one of Annabelle Hershey's salons. Or perhaps it was at a scientific lecture at Somerset House. Do you recall?"

Splendid in yellow *batiste de soie*, her lilac ribbons fluttering in the breeze, Hero drew up just before the end of the building, forcing Tiptoff to continue walking toward her. Flattening himself against the wall, Sebastian watched as Hero, a blithe smile curling her lips, waited for Tiptoff and Kat to come to her. Kat's face was a white mask of rigid self-control. Tiptoff still had her by one arm, the fingers of his left hand digging into the cloth of her dark green spencer just above the elbow. His right arm hung straight down at his side, and Sebastian knew by the curve of his fist that he held a knife.

His breath coming hard and fast, Sebastian measured the distance between them. The timing was going to be tight. One betraying sound, any hint of warning, and Tiptoff could instantly shift to hold the edge of that knife to Kat's throat. Creeping around the corner, Sebastian took one step, two, then threw himself forward in a running lunge.

He slammed into the man hard, breaking his hold on Kat and bowling Tiptoff over. The two men went down together, Sebastian grunting as his hip hit the ground. He lost his hold on Tiptoff and felt something sharp slice his arm as he rolled up into a crouch. He saw Tiptoff leap to his feet, then quickly jump back, eyes widening as Kat seized what looked like the broken handle of an old wheelbarrow buried in the weeds and swung it at his head.

"You bloody son of a bitch," she swore, the Irish accent she'd long ago eradicated from her speech now coming through thick and strong.

Tiptoff's eyes cut from Kat to Sebastian to Hero, who was picking up a length of rusty iron.

He turned and ran.

"Take the wherry and get out of here," Sebastian shouted to Hero
and Kat, then tore after the bastard.

Slipping and sliding on the narrow ribbons of bare clay, Tiptoff
cut between the long rows of dye pits, their rainbows of color muted
and dusky in the gathering gloom. He was quick and agile, his body
lean and lithe beneath the deceptive padding that had now slipped
slightly askew. Gone was the limping, eccentric scholar of Bloomsbury. In his place was the man who'd once fomented counterrevolu-
tion in the Vendée for his notorious uncle and who now killed with
lethal purposefulness as the assassin Gabriel.

Casting a quick glance at Sebastian over one shoulder, he leapt a
pile of debris that lay in his path, then careened around one of the
crumbling old gateposts to hit the cobbles of the narrow, winding
lane beyond. This was a wretched part of Southwark dominated by
timber yards and cloth manufactories, the pavements broken or nonexistent, the tightly packed shops and houses old and mean. But even
here, people were milling about in the streets and congregating on
corners, everyone anxious to hear the official word that was, surely,
coming at any moment from Wellington.

Heedless of the mutterings and foul looks he provoked, Tiptoff
plowed through the crowds of shopkeepers and artisans, dockworkers and navvies, servants and barmaids, with Sebastian close behind.
But Sebastian's leg was already on fire, the familiar burning pain from
his half-healed wound ripping through him with each jarring step.
They ducked under a row of ragged, flapping laundry dangling from
a line stretched from one window to the next; dodged a skinny, half-
grown yellow dog nosing a pile of rubbish. Two boys tossing a ball
with split seams stopped to cheer them on, while a white-haired,
stoop-shouldered old woman shouted something as they dashed past
her, her milky white eyes widening blindly.

The light was fading rapidly from the sky now, the streets growing narrower and older as they neared the bridge. Sebastian was starting to suck air badly, his leg a breath-stealing agony, every gasp fouled by the stomach-churning smells of poverty, the reek of decay and rot mingling always with the noisome stench of overflowing bog houses.

The pain was starting to make him clumsy, so that he tripped over an iron boot scrape, then stumbled in the gaping water-filled hole left by a missing sett. Gritting his teeth, he ran on. Up ahead he saw Tiptoff veer around the corner toward Blackfriars Bridge. A coal wagon rumbled past, heading toward the city, and Sebastian saw Tiptoff leap up to hook an elbow over the high tailgate. For a moment he hung there, legs pedaling as he scrambled for purchase. Then his feet found the narrow ledge of the wagon bed and he steadied, half turning to gaze back at Sebastian with a taunting smile.

"*God damn it,*" swore Sebastian as the wagon's driver cracked his whip and the tired team leaned into their collars, picking up speed as the wagon lurched up the approach to the bridge.

But the bridge was thick with a raucous, surging crowd that spilled off the narrow pavements running along the side battlements to block the roadway. The team of bays jibbed at their bits, sidling nervously; the wagon creaked nearly to a halt.

Putting on a burst of speed, Sebastian reached up to close his fists around one of Tiptoff's legs and drag him down into the roadway. The man landed on his back with a grunt but scrambled up fast, throwing a punch that caught Sebastian high on the cheekbone and swung him halfway around. For an instant his wounded leg gave out from under him, and he almost went down. And in that split second Tiptoff was off again, weaving nimbly through the swelling crowd.

Sebastian barreled after him.

Reaching the end of the bridge, Tiptoff plowed through the

crowds gathered in Chatham Place to dart down a narrow street that opened up to one side.

His leg now a howling agony, Sebastian ran on.

This was an ancient part of London's waterfront, an area of decrepit, soot-stained brick warehouses and dilapidated wharves piled with everything from freshly milled timber to barrels of grain, all reduced now to looming shadows as the long midsummer twilight neared its end and the last of the light faded from the sky.

By day the waterfront would be crawling with laborers and watermen, porters and thieves. But now the rickety piers were deserted, the weathered gray planks of the old wharves creaking and groaning underfoot as the two men ran on, dodging piles of crates and lurking coils of rope and dangerously broken boards. Sebastian could hear the roar of the crowds gathered on Fleet Street in hopes of catching news from the battlefield and, nearer, the inrushing tide washing against the stone foundations of a row of long-vanished structures that littered the riverbank far below the high wharves.

He had been gradually falling farther and farther behind. But as darkness closed upon them, his wolflike night vision gave him the advantage. Tiptoff was obviously running almost blind, tripping and stumbling. Then he caught his foot on the unseen long pole of an idle handcart and went down on all fours. He was just pushing up when Sebastian kicked him in the face and sent him flying.

Tiptoff slammed back against a rotting pier, blood streaming from his nose and mouth, his body curling forward. When he pushed away from the pier and bounded up, he had his knife in his hand.

Sebastian kicked again, sending the blade skittering away into the darkness. But as he stepped back, his wounded leg gave out from under him and Sebastian went down, his back slamming hard against the dock's splintered, uneven planking. Tiptoff threw himself on him, his hands closing tight around Sebastian's throat, his elbows locked, his lips curling away from his teeth as he squeezed and squeezed.

"You couldn't leave well enough alone, could you?" said the assassin, squeezing, squeezing. "You bloody fool."

His blood rushing in his ears, Sebastian shot his fists up between the man's outstretched arms to smash into the assassin's chin.

Tiptoff's head snapped back and he went reeling, losing his grip on Sebastian's throat. Rolling away from him, Sebastian yanked his own knife from the sheath in his boot and staggered to his feet just as Tiptoff scrambled up.

The two men circled each other warily, blood dripping from Tiptoff's nose and lips, Sebastian with the knife in his hand but limping badly, both men streaming with sweat and sucking air hard.

"How did you figure it out?" said Tiptoff, his bloody nostrils flaring with each labored breath. "Did Jarvis tell you?"

"That you kill for the Bourbons?" Sebastian shook his head, trying to shake the sweat out of his eyes. "No."

"Is that what you think? That I only kill for the Bourbons?" Tiptoff gave a ragged, breathless laugh. "You haven't realized yet that I kill for Jarvis, too?"

"I don't believe you."

The man's lip curled in derision. "Believe it."

"So why not give him Fouché's list?"

"Because I know him. Jarvis would have had some killed, but he'd insist others be left alive so he could use them."

"And you want them all dead?"

Tiptoff swiped a crooked elbow across his bloody face. "They aided the regime that killed my mother and father."

"Did it never occur to you that at the same time you've been murdering those you hold responsible for your brother's death on

Cabrera, you've also been killing the men and women whose activities here in London might once have helped protect him?"

Tiptoff's eyes narrowed. "How the hell did you know my brother died on Cabrera?"

When Sebastian simply shook his head again, Tiptoff sucked in a harsh breath that shuddered his chest. "He starved to death. Did you know that? *Starved to death.*"

"It was horrible, what was done to those men. No one with any conscience could deny that. But why kill Hamilton Evans? Cabrera was his father's sin, not his."

"And now his father has paid for it, hasn't he?"

"Is that why you didn't mutilate André Ternant the way you did the others? Because he had nothing to do with Cabrera?"

Tiptoff nodded. "Those who spied for Napoléon were misguided, not evil."

"You don't see yourself as evil?"

Something flared in the other man's eyes. "I only kill those who deserve to die."

"The wherryman you killed didn't deserve to die any more than Hamilton Evans. You killed the wherryman to protect yourself, and Evans to hurt someone you hated but couldn't reach. Is that not the height of selfishness—your very definition of evil?" Sebastian paused, then said, "And you call Palmer a hypocrite."

Eyes glittering with rage even as an icy smile curled his bleeding lips, Tiptoff lunged. Sebastian pivoted, blocking the charge, his knife slashing only air as Tiptoff danced nimbly away again. But in the darkness the assassin had miscalculated, unable to see just how near Sebastian was to the end of the wharf. Tiptoff feinted to one side, ready to launch his next attack . . . and stepped back into nothing.

For a moment he teetered at the edge, arms windmilling as he sought to regain his balance. Sebastian stayed where he was and watched as the man pitched backward into the dark void. There was a moment's eerie silence filled only with the damp, briny wind rising off the water and the slap of the inrushing tide. Then came the thumping crunch of bone and sinew as the assassin's body slammed into the stones of the ancient foundations lurking far below. Tiptoff convulsed once, then went still, his eyes wide and staring.

"You bastard," said Sebastian hoarsely, and turned away.

❦

He could hear a growing roar of distant voices as he pushed his way through the crowds in Charing Cross to Pall Mall and then to St. James's Square. At the corner, an old woman was selling hot potatoes from a barrel filled with glowing coals to the crowd that had collected outside the home of Mr. and Mrs. Edmund Boehm, where the Prince Regent and the cream of London society were known to have gathered that night for an exclusive dinner and dance.

The windows of the house had been thrown open, for the night was warm and the rooms within heated by hundreds of blazing beeswax candles; Sebastian could hear the lilting strains of Haydn as he paused beside the old woman and handed her a penny. But rather than take one of her potatoes, he drew a folded paper from his pocket and held it over the glowing embers in her barrow. "May I?" he asked.

She nodded, and without looking at it again, he touched one corner of the paper to the coals.

It caught quickly, the yellow and orange flame flaring up hot and bright, Fouché's deadly list of names disappearing as the blackening paper curled back on itself. At last Sebastian was forced to drop the burning remnant to the pavement at his feet. He watched as the fire consumed the rest, until only a curl of white ash remained. Then he crushed it beneath his boot heel, nodded his thanks to the old woman, and turned to run up the stairs of the gaily lit town house of Mr. and Mrs. Boehm.

Chapter 55

$\mathcal{C}$harles, Lord Jarvis, stood near the entrance to Mrs. Boehm's ballroom, a glass of fine brandy in one hand, a smile touching his lips as he watched the first quadrille forming. It had been a pleasant evening. The Prince Regent, now sprawled at his ease in the wide seat their hostess had provided for him on a dais at one end of the room, was in his cups, of course. Several of the buttons of Prinny's waistcoat had been undone to ease the pressure on his ample belly, but he had a smile on his ruddy, sweat-sheened face. Tonight, surely, they would hear good news from Waterloo. Others such as Liverpool and Hendon might fret, but Jarvis's confidence in their ultimate triumph had never deserted him. Soon Bonaparte would be on his way to St. Helena—or in his grave—and order would be restored to the world.

What had begun as a faint stirring behind him was becoming more intense. Turning, Jarvis recognized his own disreputable son-in-law pushing his way through the elegant throng of silk-and-satin-clad ladies and their gentlemen. He was dressed in muddy high boots, blood-splattered buckskin breeches, and a torn coat. His hat was gone, his hair disheveled, and he had what was probably a knife cut across one cheek.

"What the devil are you doing here?" snapped Jarvis as the Viscount came up to him.

Devlin stopped beside him, his hard eyes narrowing as he watched the Prince Regent reach out to fondle the posterior of a young woman who made the mistake of stopping too close to his chair. "I have something for you."

"Not now, for God's sake. You look like hell."

"Now," said Devlin, his nostrils flaring.

Swallowing an oath, Jarvis turned on his heel and led the way to a small chamber near the top of the steps. "Very well," he said, shutting the door behind them with a snap, then going to stand so that the table in the center of the room lay between them. "What is it?"

Devlin reached one hand, its glove torn and bloodstained, into his pocket. Drawing forth a braided cord knotted at each end with a dowel, he flicked his wrist to send the cord skittering across the table between them. "Your assassin Gabriel is dead."

Jarvis stared down at the professional garrote, then raised his gaze to the Viscount's flinty face. "I don't know what you're talking about."

"Of course not," said Devlin, and turned to go.

He had his hand on the doorknob when Jarvis stopped him. "And Fouché's list? Do you have it?"

Devlin looked back at him, those feral yellow eyes glittering. From somewhere in the distance came a strange commotion, shouts and laughter mixed with huzzahs. "I burned it."

Jarvis knew a powerful surge of annoyance, but he was careful to keep it off his face. "No matter. I've no doubt most of the names it contained are known to us anyway."

A gleam of what might have been amusement flickered in the younger man's eyes. "No doubt."

The disturbance outside the house in the square was growing, cheers and excited voices mingling with the sound of running feet. "What the devil is that?" said Jarvis as Devlin jerked open the door to the hall.

A cavalcade of men was just reaching the top of the stairs, led by a tall, dark-haired officer wearing a mud- and bloodstained red and gold tunic, his dust-covered face creased with lines of extreme exhaustion and yet glowing with pride. In his hands he carried two captured French flags, their gold-fringed tricolors as stained with mud and blood as the dress uniform he must have donned some six days before to attend the Duchess of Richmond's ball. The light from the beeswax candles in the chandeliers overhead gleamed on the gilt of two famous Imperial Eagles.

Behind the major came various members of the cabinet—Liverpool and Bathurst and Hendon amongst them. The music stopped abruptly, the dancers breaking apart to clear a path as Wellington's triumphant aide-de-camp strode across the glittering ballroom to drop to one knee before his drunken Prince.

"Victory, sir!" the major shouted as a cheer went up around the room, echoing the cheering in the street outside. "Victory!"

The babble of voices became a roar.

The Prince Regent burst into tears; the members of Mrs. Boehm's band looked at one another and began to play "God Save the King."

One voice after another took up the song, joined by those in the street outside. *"God save our gracious King, Long live our noble King . . ."*

"So," said Jarvis quietly. "It's over."

Devlin met his gaze as the voices swelled around them.

"Send him victorious, Happy and glorious, Long to reign over us, God save our King."

"Yes," said Devlin. "This time I believe it truly is over."

Chapter 56

Thursday, 22 June

$\mathcal{E}$arly the next morning, Kat walked through the crowds of revelers thronging the streets of the city. The day had dawned clear and warm, the sun dazzling in its brightness. She was surrounded by noise and people, their faces shiny with joy and laughter. But it had been a long time since she had felt this alone.

The events of the last week had shaken her, taught her things she hadn't known about herself and forced her to reevaluate both the life she was living and the life she wanted to live. She had faced death before. And yet those experiences had been different in ways she couldn't quite articulate, although she suspected it had something to do with the hopes and dreams that had once driven her but were hers no longer.

And she knew now, as she paused beside the worn stone battlements of Blackfriars Bridge to watch a flotilla of gaily decked barges drifting down the sun-dazzled Thames far below, that there would be no going back to the woman she had been before. To the life that had been hers before.

She was still standing there some minutes later when a handsome young Irishman with laughing green eyes and two deceptive dimples came up beside her. "I heard what happened," said Aiden O'Connell, his gaze hard on her face. "Are you all right?"

She looked over at him and smiled. "Probably not. But I will be, eventually."

He nodded, his eyes narrowing as he turned to gaze out over the cheering crowds. "Look at them, celebrating the restoration of a bunch of crowned tyrants who value their lives and those of their children less than those of the sheep and goats of the field."

"Are they celebrating the restoration, do you think? Or simply the end of a war that has bled us all for so long?"

"That I could understand," he said, his jaw tightening as a roar went up from the crowd. "What a useless tragedy it has all been."

Kat nodded, conscious of an ache pulling across her chest. "Napoléon was an imperfect vessel for anyone's hopes and dreams, let alone entire nations."

"That he was, indeed." He fell silent for a moment, the air filling with music as a band on one of the barges below struck up a rousing march. Then he said, "The theater season will be ending soon. What will you do?"

She turned her face into the cool wind rising off the water, letting it buffet her cheeks and grab her hair to stream it out behind her. "Travel, I think. I've always wanted to see Rome and Venice. I might even go back to Paris once things sort themselves out there." She looked over at him. "Have you ever been?"

"To Rome or Venice? I have not. Nor have I been to Paris."

"I suppose the existence of Fouché's list might make Paris problematic," said Kat.

"That it might. I doubt Sedgewick's copy was the only one."

An eddy of wind billowed her hair around her face, and she flung up both hands to catch it back again. "So perhaps not Paris," she said. Then her gaze met his and they shared a smile. "At least not yet."

❧

Shortly before ten that morning, Sebastian and Hero took the boys to St. James's Park to watch a grand victorious display of cavalry and infantry organized by the Prince Regent's brother the Duke of York, who was also the commander in chief of the Army. Bathed in a rich golden light, with a faint breeze that stirred the bright green leaves of the plane trees and ruffled the sky-blue waters of the canal, the park was crowded with men, women, and children from all walks of life, laughing and passing the morning editions of the city's papers from hand to hand, the loose pages flapping in the breeze.

"I somehow can't quite bring myself to believe the wars are finally, truly over," said Hero as Sebastian hoisted Simon up onto his shoulders so the little boy could see better. "What do you think will happen to Bonaparte?"

"I suspect he'll try to abdicate in favor of his son, but I doubt the Allies will accept it. If Marie-Thérèse has her way, he'll be shot—or hanged. Of course, they'll need to catch him first—"

He broke off as someone shouted "Fire!" and the thunderous booms of a double salute sounded from the guns, the clouds of smoke drifting across the grass.

"Wow," said Patrick, his eyes bright, his cheeks ruddy with the morning chill. "Ain't that something?"

"Boom!" said Simon, and Hero laughed.

From their position at the head of the canal, a military band broke into "See, the Conquering Hero Comes," and the crowd roared.

But there was a somber edge to the celebrations, for while Wellington had won an undeniable victory, it had come at a terrible cost. The morning papers all carried a long list of the dead and wounded from two battles they were calling Quatre Bras and Waterloo. And as horrible as those lists were, everyone knew they would only grow longer in the days to come. Amongst the dead was the Duke of Brunswick, first cousin to the Prince Regent and uncle to his daughter, Princess Charlotte. Also dead was one of the Duchess of Claiborne's favorite grandsons, Alexander, although his cousin, Peter, had escaped with only a minor shoulder wound. He was one of the lucky ones.

For a time Hero and Sebastian stood side by side in silence, the boys in their arms as they watched the cavalry wheel and charge. But Sebastian could tell Hero's thoughts were elsewhere, and after a moment she said quietly, "I find it strangely disturbing that Tiptoff discovered the part Sedgewick played in the tragedy of Cabrera as a result of a philosophical discussion on the nature of evil."

Sebastian glanced over at her. "Monty said Sedgewick wasn't ashamed of it. He probably used Cabrera as an example of something that otherwise might be classified as evil, but wasn't since it was for a 'good' cause."

"Except he didn't know the man he was saying it to had lost a brother there," said Hero.

Sebastian nodded. "And who was both willing and able to exact a terrible revenge. Another evil act justified as good."

"How did he find out that Hamilton Evans was fathered by one of the Wellesley brothers?"

Sebastian's eyes narrowed as he watched the cavalry thunder back toward them. "I wouldn't be surprised if Sibil Wilde knew that. It's exactly the sort of thing she would be likely to learn and tuck away as potentially useful. But I have no idea how he learned about Francisco de la Serna."

"So why kill Sibil?"

"I could be wrong, but I suspect he must have decided she'd become a threat to him in some way. After so many killings, what's one more?"

Hero was silent for a moment as the infantrymen cheered and tossed their caps into the air. "How many have died, do you think?" she said. "In the last twenty-five years of war, I mean."

"Altogether? I've heard estimates of between five and seven million. But I don't know if that includes civilians or simply the military."

"Good Lord," she whispered as the crowds around them cheered. "And for what? Here we are, back exactly where we were before, with the same spoiled, dissolute crowned monarchs once more on their thrones. Except that millions of men are dead or broken and millions more are grieving."

"At least, hopefully, we'll now have peace." He reached out to take her hand in his and hold her tight. "For a time."

❧

Paul Gibson was in the stone outbuilding at the base of his garden, about to begin the autopsy of the half-decomposed body of a woman lying on the stone slab before him, when he looked up to see Alexi coming down the garden path toward him. A bird was singing sweetly from someplace out of sight, the morning sun bright and warm on her glorious hair, and she cradled a suspiciously shaped bundle of rags in her arms.

"What's this, then?" he said as she drew up just outside the open door.

He watched in wonder as her face broke into a wide smile that stole his heart all over again. "Meet Miss Amelia Cox," she said, shifting her hold on the bundle so that he could see the babe's blithely sleeping face.

"Lord love us," said Gibson, setting aside his knife with a clatter as he came from behind the granite slab. "However did you find her?"

"I kept thinking about what Devlin had said, about Miles going to Seven Dials after he saw Phoebe. So I went to the Haymarket and started walking to the northeast. The churchyard of St. Anne is right there. Turns out the vicar heard her screaming her head off while he was preparing for the funeral of one of his more important parishioners, and sent his housekeeper to see what the racket was. The woman's daughter had just lost her own babe, so she was able to nurse Amelia."

"Are you telling me Sedgewick abandoned his own child *in a graveyard*?"

"Yes."

"Who would do something like that?" Reaching out, Gibson took the babe from her arms and held her close. Miss Amelia pursed her lips and cooed. Gibson laughed, but sobered quickly. "You had a real bounder for a da, little one," he told her. "But everything is going to be all right now—for you and your poor mother both. I promise."

"Sometimes miracles do happen," said Alexi softly. "If we're willing to try hard enough."

He looked up to meet her gaze and saw there all her worry and hope and fear and, yes, love, glazing her beautiful brown eyes with unshed tears. And he felt humbled and shamed and, oddly, strong.

"You still willing to give your box-and-mirror trick a try with me?" he asked, his voice suddenly hoarse.

She sucked in a quick breath, her lips parting, her expression wary, as if she were afraid to believe what he was saying. "You mean it? Truly?"

Balancing the babe in the crook of one arm, he reached to loop his free elbow around the back of Alexi's neck and draw her close enough that he could press his forehead against hers. "I mean it." And then he said it again in case she still couldn't quite believe him.

"I mean it."

$\mathcal{I}$ have tried to be faithful to what is known of both the way in which news of the Battle of Waterloo reached London and the timing. Because Percy's journey from Wellington to the Prince Regent was rather convoluted, those who write about it often simplify it, with the result that many of the accounts one sees are misleading.

Wellington sent a messenger to London on Friday, the sixteenth of June, telling the British government about the battles of Quatre Bras and Ligny; this is the messenger Hendon comes to tell Sebastian about. Waterloo took place two days later, on Sunday, the eighteenth of June, and its outcome was essentially decided by about eight thirty that evening. Wellington then went back to the inn at the village where he had spent the previous night. As he was about to retire to bed, one of his officers suggested it might be a good idea to send word of the victory to the French King Louis XVIII, then in Ghent. So a messenger was dispatched, and Wellington went to sleep.

The next morning the Duke rode back to Brussels, where he first sat down and wrote to a married (and pregnant) woman named Lady Frances Wedderburn Webster, with whom he was in all likelihood having an affair (he later denied the affair, of course, as was required of a gentleman). He then began writing his dispatches. Such dispatches were traditionally quite long, as they contained the names of some of the dead and wounded as well as officers the commander wished to commend (being "mentioned in the dispatches" was an honor that was good for one's career and therefore important). The dispatches then had to be copied several times. As a result it wasn't until one o'clock Monday afternoon that Wellington's aide-de-camp, Major Henry Percy, finally set out for London.

Percy began his journey by carriage. It was only seventy-five miles to the port of Ostend, but the roads were choked with civilians fleeing Brussels (no one had thought to tell them the French had been defeated), fresh horses were scarce, and mud from the recent rains added to the mayhem. It took Percy twenty-four hours to reach the port. There he found a small but fast two-masted brig-sloop, HMS *Peruvian*, waiting for him, and they set off on what could have been a relatively speedy seventy-mile voyage to Kent. But the winds failed and they were virtually becalmed. It wasn't until the next day— Wednesday—that they were close enough to Kent that the *Peruvian*'s captain could put Percy, his dispatches, and the two captured Imperial Eagles into a boat with four sailors who then spent hours *rowing* him to England.

But by that time at least four other men had arrived in London with news of the battles. The first unauthorized report came from a man named Daniel Sutton, and he got it wrong. Evidently having heard a garbled account of the battles of Quatre Bras and Ligny, he told everyone that the French had been thoroughly defeated on Friday, the city of Charleroi burned, and Napoléon sent fleeing back to Paris.

The stock market soared. But then an Irish knight named Maurice Fitzgerald arrived in London with more authoritative and accurate—although incomplete—news. With him was the MP James Butler, a younger brother of the Marquis of Ormonde. The two men had been traveling as tourists and were present at the Duchess of Richmond's famous ball. On Saturday morning they had visited the scene of the Battle of Quatre Bras and had actually spoken to Wellington at about ten thirty Sunday morning, when the British Army was in position at Waterloo but before fighting had begun. Then, at the request of a British admiral named Malcolm who feared news of Wellington's retreat from Quatre Bras and the Prussian defeat at Ligny might have spooked his countrymen, the two men left Belgium aboard the HMS *Leveret* to carry word to London.

Their more accurate news contradicted Sutton's earlier, flawed report, and the stock market fell. But while authoritative, this report was technically unofficial and thus dangerously close to a serious breach of the sacred dispatches protocol, and in the end most people simply didn't know whom to believe.

The identity of a fourth man to reach London, one "Mr. C. of Dover," is still unknown. He seems to have been present in Ghent when Wellington's messenger delivered word of the victory at Waterloo to the French King Louis XVIII. But he was evidently a rather shifty character (hence his desire for anonymity), and London had already been burned by Sutton's false report, so most of those in the government and the press were disinclined to believe him. Much of the populace took to the streets, waiting together for Wellington's official messenger to finally arrive and sort it all out.

In the meantime, the rowboat containing Major Percy was landing at the small fishing village of Broadstairs. Hiring a post chaise and four, he headed for London. His passage through the English countryside must have attracted considerable attention, since the shafts of the two Imperial Eagles he carried with him were so long that they stuck out the carriage's windows. The dispatches were, as always, addressed to the Secretary of War, so Percy went first to Bathurst's office in Downing Street. Learning there that Bathurst was having dinner in Grosvenor Square with many of the other members of the cabinet, Percy went there. Then Percy, Bathurst, Liverpool, and others all trooped over to St. James's Square, where the Prince Regent was known to be attending a grand dinner given by a wealthy couple named Boehm. By that time dinner was over, the Prince was up on his dais, and dancing was about to begin. Brian Cathcart's *The News from Waterloo* provides by far the best explanation of the tangled saga of how and when London heard about Waterloo. My accounts of the earlier reports to the Palace of Napoléon's departure from Paris and of the battles of Quatre Bras and Ligny are based on other sources.

If you're wondering why they didn't simply use the semaphore system developed during the Napoleonic Wars, it was because the British government had dismantled it in 1814 to save money. Government use of carrier pigeons was not common until the twentieth century.

Most exploring officers (probably the best known being Colquhoun Grant) rode in uniform to keep from being hanged as spies if they were captured. But such a tradition obviously seriously curtailed their ability to gather information, and some (such as John Waters of the Royal Scots) are said to have occasionally adopted local dress when slipping behind enemy lines. It wasn't seen as a "gentlemanly" thing to do, so they tended not to talk about it. Although Dudley Tiptoff is my own invention, William Wickham was a real man. It is widely assumed that Jane Austen named the villain in *Pride and Prejudice* after him. See Elizabeth Sparrow's *Secret Service: British Agents in France, 1792–1815*; Steven Maffeo, *Most Secret and Confidential: Intelligence in the Age of Nelson*; and Mary McGrigor, *Wellington's Spies*.

The early nineteenth century saw a significant increase in the scholarly interest in folklore. The Grimm Brothers first published their collection of fairy tales in December 1812. There was a growing recognition of the fact that many old songs, legends, and sayings were quickly disappearing, provoking a scramble to record them before they were lost forever. The various witch and werewolf tortures and burnings mentioned here are historical; such persecutions were particularly severe in the sixteenth and seventeenth centuries but had ended by the late eighteenth century. Seven Dials was indeed popular with astrologers and cartomancers, and werewolves were a frequent and popular feature in eighteenth- and nineteenth-century romance novels. The more things change, the more they stay the same. . . .

The British did stop the Spanish government from honoring the terms of the French surrender after Bailén. Thousands of the twenty-five thousand prisoners (this figure includes men taken prisoner elsewhere) held for months in appalling conditions in Calais died; no one knows exactly how many. About half of the survivors, women and children amongst them, were eventually crammed into transports, taken to the tiny deserted island of Cabrera, and dumped there without food, shelter, or clothing. For five years, warships of the Royal Navy patrolled offshore to keep them there. The wife of one of the French officers did give birth to twins on the transport ships; I could not find what happened to them but presume they died. Some of the prisoners—especially those who were Italian, Swiss, and French conscripts—eventually managed to get off the island by volunteering to join the Spanish Army, figuring they would have a better chance of surviving the war that way. A few managed to pull off daring and exciting escapes. Most died.

In 1836, a group of survivors who petitioned the French National Assembly listed sixteen thousand dead out of those taken at Bailén. But many of those died in Calais or in transport, and other

French prisoners were also sent to Cabrera. So no one knows exactly how many actually died on Cabrera, although the more conservative modern estimates do not add up. I have based much of the account here on Denis Smith's *The Prisoners of Cabrera: Napoleon's Forgotten Soldiers, 1809–1814*. It makes for harrowing reading.

After his defeat at Waterloo, Napoléon returned to Paris and abdicated in favor of his young son. He then tried to flee to a ship that was to take him to the United States but ultimately surrendered to the captain of the British ship HMS *Bellerophon*. The British refused to hand him over to the French to be hanged, but the French did hang or quietly murder many of the officers who fought with him at Waterloo. The Bourbons then launched a vicious and bloody White Terror against anyone they perceived as their enemies. They were overthrown by the French people again in 1830.

Acknowledgments

$\mathcal{A}$n author always has many people to thank, and that is especially true when a book's path to publication is disrupted by disaster. I was only a few chapters into the writing of *Who Cries for the Lost* when Hurricane Ida slammed ashore on the anniversary of Katrina and wrecked my New Orleans–area home. There were times when I thought this book would never see the light of day. That it did is only due to the many people to whom I am so very grateful.

Thank you to my editor, Michelle Vega, for being so patient, understanding, and supportive; I can't begin to tell you how much that has meant to me. Thank you to my publicist, Dache Rogers; to Elisha Katz, marketing coordinator; and to Jenn Snyder and Claire Zion, for putting up with one very stressed author constantly distracted by evacuation, house repairs, endless drives back and forth between Texas and Louisiana, the sale of two houses, and a multi-segmented move from hell, all in the midst of a pandemic.

Thank you to my agent, Helen Breitwieser, who went through

this with me once before, during Katrina, and has never, ever wavered.

Thank you to Aaron Cook, Carlos Martinez, and Jose Diaz; the repair and sale of our New Orleans house after Ida would have been impossible without you. You guys are the best. Thank you to Carrie Godbold, who did a brilliant job selling our lake house under less-than-ideal circumstances. And thank you to James Coker, who built the bookcases and cabinets we so desperately needed to start getting settled in our new house.

Thank you to my friend Charles Gramlich, whose lovely poem fragment has now inspired the titles for two of my books.

Thank you to my dear friends Pam Ahearn and Farrah Rochon; you will never know how much you helped me get through this. And thank you to Lillian Wegmann, who not only let us sleep at her house for weeks but also fed us and consoled us. If y'all ever need a refuge from future storms, you know exactly where to go.

A huge thank-you to my daughters, Samantha and Danielle, and their husbands, Thomas and Ryan, for being there for us and helping with everything from packing to house painting to cat sitting. We couldn't have done it without you.

And finally, thank you to my husband, Steve. There is no one with whom I'd rather go through two house-wrecking hurricanes. You are my rock.

Keep reading for a sneak peek of

WHAT CANNOT BE SAID

the next riveting Sebastian St. Cyr mystery from USA Today
bestselling author C.S. Harris

Chapter 1

Richmond Park: Sunday, 23 July 1815

"I've figured out what's wrong with women," declared Ben. He lay on his back on the grassy hillside, his face lifted to the wide blue sky, his cheeks ruddy from a heady combination of sunshine, fresh air, and a bota of cheap red wine.

Harry swiveled his head to look at his brother. "So what is it?"

"They're *women!*"

The observation struck both young gentlemen as uproariously funny, and they rolled about in the sun-warmed grass, eyes squeezing shut, bodies convulsing with laughter. Separated in age by only two years, the sons of Thomas Barrows, Esquire, had retreated to Richmond Park on this glorious July afternoon to escape the hubbub surrounding their elder sister's wedding, which was scheduled to take place in three days' time.

"I think," said Ben, "that—" He broke off, his jaw going slack as a loud *cr-rack* echoed across the park.

"What was that?" said Harry, jerking upright.

Ben sat up beside him. "Sounded like a pistol shot."

Cr-rack.

At the second shot, the brothers looked at each other. "Reckon it's a duel?"

Harry pushed to his feet. "Let's go see!"

Snagging the straps of their leather wineskins, the brothers sprinted up the hill. From the top they could look out over the vast royal park's rolling vista of lush green grass and leafy woodland; London was a dirty smudge in the distance.

"Don't see anyone," said Ben.

Harry nodded to the stretch of oak mingled with chestnut near the base of the hill. "Bet it came from there."

They ran down the daisy-strewn grassy slope, laughing as they gained momentum, arms flung wide for balance, botas bouncing against hips. Then they slowed, breath catching as they stumbled to a halt. Harry felt the sun hot on his back, felt his stomach clench and his mouth go dry.

A woman and a girl lay on their backs in the grass beside a picnic rug scattered with sturdy white ironstone plates and the remnants of a genteel nuncheon. Dressed in fine gowns of delicate white muslin, they lay not side by side but in a line, so that the soles of the woman's shoes almost touched the girl's. Their hands were brought together at their chests as if in prayer, their silent faces turned to the sky, the bodices of their gowns shiny red. The stench of freshly spilled blood hung thick in the air, along with the lingering sulfuric stench of burnt gunpowder.

"*Oh, my God,*" whispered Ben.

His breath now coming in gasping pants, the blood rushing in his ears, Harry heard a child's lighthearted trill of laughter.

He wrenched his gaze away from that bloody horror to see a

young girl and boy coming up the path that wound along a small stream, the girl golden haired and rosy cheeked, the boy younger and even fairer. Her arms were filled with a cheerful rainbow of flowers—cornflowers and lilies, daisies and sunflowers, tansy and field poppies—that tumbled to the ground as she drew up, her eyes going wide.

For a long moment she stood rigid, her throat working soundlessly. Then she opened her mouth and Harry tensed, waiting for her scream.

But she simply stood there, her chest shuddering with her ragged breaths, her nostrils flaring and the color draining from her face.

Chapter 2

Sir Henry Lovejoy, one of Bow Street Public Office's three stipendiary magistrates, stood at the base of the grassy hill, his hands tucked up under his armpits, his chin resting against his chest as he gazed at the scene before him. He was a slight, sparse man in his late fifties, barely five feet tall and quite bald. After fourteen years as a magistrate, he should have become inured to the sight of violent death. But *these* deaths . . .

God help him, these deaths.

Swallowing hard, he turned to the full-faced, corpulent squire who stood to one side, the wind ruffling his unruly head of thick ginger hair. "No one's touched anything?"

Squire Adams, the local magistrate, shook his head. When called to the scene by the park's keepers, he'd taken one look at the murdered woman and girl, and sent word straightaway to Bow Street. "No, sir. Made sure of that, I did."

"And we're certain of the victims' identities?"

"Aye, no doubt about that. It's Lady McInnis, all right—wife of Sir Ivo himself. And Miss Emma, one of his daughters."

"How old is she?" *Was she,* thought Lovejoy, mentally correcting himself.

"Sixteen, according to her young cousins. The wife of one of the keepers has them at her cottage—the children, I mean. Seemed best to get them away from here."

"Quite right." Lovejoy felt his throat thicken as he stared down at the winsome young girl. Her dark hair was fashionably cropped to curl around her face, her features even, her nose small and almost childlike, her mouth wide. The shot that killed the girl had been fired so close to her chest that the cloth of her muslin gown was charred.

Lovejoy glanced over to where the two young gentlemen who'd found the bodies now sat in the grass, their forearms resting on bent knees, their heads bowed. The younger lad, Ben, had been sick several times. His older brother was thus far managing to keep down his wine, although he kept puffing up his cheeks and then blowing out his breath, hard.

"You say the brothers just happened upon this?"

"Well, they heard the shots and came to investigate."

"But saw no one?"

"Only Lady McInnis's young niece and nephew, who came along right afterward."

"Those poor children."

"Aye."

Drawing a deep breath, Lovejoy forced himself to look again at the bodies before him. The mother and her daughter hadn't died this way; they'd been posed—carefully, deliberately posed by their killer. Lovejoy had seen such a thing only once before, fourteen years ago.

Oh, Julia, Julia, Julia, he thought. *How can it be? How can it possibly be?*

His head jerked around at the sound of rapid hoofbeats. A gentleman's curricle was approaching at a spanking pace, drawn by a splendidly matched pair of fine chestnuts and driven by a rakish-looking man in a lightweight summer duster with shoulder capes and a stylish beaver hat set at a reckless angle. He drew up where the narrow lane began to curve away again and handed the reins to his young groom, or tiger, before hopping down to the road. He said something to the boy, then turned to walk toward them, his gait slightly marred by the leg wound from which he was still recovering.

A tall, lean man in his early thirties with dark hair, fine features, and the strangest feral-looking yellow eyes Lovejoy had ever seen, Sebastian St. Cyr, Viscount Devlin, was the only surviving son and heir of the powerful Earl of Hendon. He'd returned to England some four or five years before, after serving as a cavalry officer in the wars. There'd been a time when his lordship had been accused of murder and Lovejoy assigned the task of bringing him to justice. But in the years since, the two men had forged a strong friendship, and as soon as Lovejoy heard the identities of today's victims, he had sent for Devlin. Murder investigations involving the aristocracy were always delicate. And this murder . . . Ah, this murder.

"Sir Henry," said Devlin, walking up to him. Then his gaze fell on the dead mother and girl and he said, *"Christ."*

"Did you know Lady McInnis?"

"Not well, although I have met her. She's a friend of Lady Devlin."

"Ah. I am sorry."

Devlin's brows drew together in a disturbed frown. "They were found like this?"

"They were, yes." Lovejoy cleared his throat. "You should know that two other women were killed here in the park fourteen years ago—a woman in her early forties and her young daughter, both shot in the chest and their bodies deliberately positioned exactly like this: feet to feet, hands brought together as if in prayer."

"Good God. Do you know who they were?"

"Oh, yes," said Lovejoy in a voice that sounded strange even to his own ears. "Julia and Madeline Lovejoy." He paused, then somehow managed to add, "My wife and seventeen-year-old daughter."

Chapter 3

$\mathcal{S}$ebastian drew a slow, even breath as he studied the magistrate's tightly held features. He'd known this man for four years. Over the course of more murder investigations than he liked to think about, the two men had talked for endless hours, sharing some of their deepest thoughts and secrets. Sebastian knew Lovejoy's wife and daughter had died suddenly; knew that those deaths had altered the path of his life and profoundly impacted his spiritual beliefs. So how could he not have known *this*?

For a moment, he found himself at a loss for words.

Lovejoy said, "It can't be a coincidence."

"No." Sebastian gazed down at the oddly posed bodies. Their postures reminded him of the stone effigies one often saw atop medieval tombs, and he wondered if the echo was deliberate. "No one was ever arrested for their murders?"

"Oh, yes; someone was arrested—a one-armed ex-soldier named Daniel O'Toole who'd been menacing other people in the area. He was remanded into custody, tried, convicted, and hanged."

Sebastian glanced over at his friend. "You're thinking they hanged the wrong man?"

Lovejoy's small dark eyes were filled with silent anguish. "What else can one think? The man did die shouting his innocence from the scaffold."

"Someone could have learned the details of the previous murders and patterned this after them. We've seen it before."

Lovejoy considered this. "I suppose. But . . . why would he?"

It was a question for which Sebastian had no answer.

He hunkered down beside the still, lifeless husk of what was once Laura McInnis. She'd been an attractive woman probably somewhere in her late thirties, still youthful and slim, with honey-colored hair and delicate features. In death she looked peaceful, serene.

He hoped she was.

"What time did this happen?" he asked. Flies were buzzing around her open mouth and blood-soaked chest, and he batted them away in a spurt of useless rage.

"Half past one or thereabouts, we believe."

It had taken time for the brothers to summon one of the park's keepers, more time for the keepers to call in the local magistrate, and more time still for word to be sent to London some eight miles away. By now, Lady McInnis and her daughter had been dead at least four or five hours.

Sebastian picked up one of her ladyship's limp, still vaguely warm hands and turned it over. The edge of her fine kid glove was stained bright red from where it had rested against the blood-drenched cloth of her bodice. He could see no sign that she had attempted to fight off their attacker. But then, how could a couple of gentlewomen grapple with an armed man?

He shifted to where her daughter lay in a similar pose. Unlike her mother, Emma McInnis's soft brown eyes were open and staring, and she looked so young and innocent that it tore at his heart. He said, *"Christ,"* again and pushed to his feet.

He was intensely aware of a woodlark singing sweetly from the top of a nearby oak, of the restless sighing of the breeze through the leafy branches of the adjacent wood and the late-afternoon sun drenching the long summer grass with a deep golden light. Turning, he let his gaze drift over the nearby picnic rug and hamper. The cheese, bread, and chicken that remained from the women's nuncheon were now dried and crawling with ants.

He said, "Has anyone told Sir Ivo?"

"One of my colleagues has undertaken the task of breaking the news to him, as well as carrying word of the situation to the surviving children's father. But it's difficult to say if he's managed to do so yet."

Sebastian's gaze shifted to where the brothers still sat. "What do we know about those two?"

"Their father is a prosperous barrister—has a small estate not far from Richmond. They say they came here today to escape a house filled with relatives for their sister's wedding."

"And they neither saw nor heard anything?"

"Nothing beyond the pistol shots," said Lovejoy, just as the younger brother pushed to his feet, whirled, and was sick again.

※

Harry Barrows was twenty years old, with lanky brown hair, a thin face, and a long, narrow nose. He sat now with his arms wrapped around his bent knees, his hands locked together so tightly his knuckles were turning white. His face was pale, and a muscle kept twitching beneath his right eye, but Sebastian could tell the young man was gamely fighting to maintain his composure.

"I hear you're down from Cambridge for the summer," said Sebastian, settling in the grass beside him.

Harry nodded. "Yes, sir. Magdalene College."

"I'm an Oxford man, myself."

A faint smile touched Harry's face, then was gone. "Sir Henry said you'd be wanting to talk to us, but I don't know how much we can tell you."

"Where were you when you heard the first shot?"

Harry nodded toward the top of the nearby hill. "Just over there, sir."

"How many shots did you hear?"

"Only two, sir."

"Sir Henry says you think it was a pistol?"

"Yes, sir. No doubt about that. Ben and I've been going shooting with our father since we were breeched."

"Do you remember how much time there was between the first and second shot?"

Harry was silent, as if mentally reconstructing the moment. "Only seconds, sir. I figure it had to have been a double-barreled pistol—there wasn't enough time in between for anyone to reload. Ben thinks so, too." He turned his head to look at his brother, who was now lying on his back in the grass with his eyes closed. "Is he going to be all right? He's been awfully unwell."

"It will pass. How long was it between the last shot and the time you and your brother arrived here?"

"Not long, sir. Not long at all."

"Yet you didn't see anyone running away?"

"No, sir. But then we wouldn't, would we? I mean, not if whoever did that had headed straight into the wood."

"And you didn't hear anything besides the pistol shots?"

"No, sir."

"No voices? No screams?"

The young man pressed his lips together and shook his head.

There was a bleakness to his expression that Sebastian had seen before, the look of someone whose safe, predictable existence has suddenly been touched by evil and horror. The world would never be quite the same for him again.

Harry said, "That girl—the one who'd been picking flowers down by the stream with her little brother. She didn't scream. She opened her mouth, and I kept waiting and waiting for her to scream. But she never did." He swallowed. "In a way, it was almost worse than if she had screamed."

"I suspect she was in shock."

"I should have tried to stop her from seeing it—the bodies and all that blood, I mean. I didn't even think of it."

"Not your fault," said Sebastian, although he knew it would do no good, that this burden of guilt and regret, once picked up, would niggle at Harry Barrows forever. "Had you seen anyone else in the park before you heard the shots?"

Harry stared at him blankly. "I suppose we must have, but I don't recall anyone in particular, if that's what you're asking. We weren't really paying attention, if you know what I mean?"

"I understand."

Harry stared off across the park, the late-afternoon sun shining through the branches overhead to dance a pattern of light and shadow across his face. "Who would do something like that? Shoot a woman and girl having themselves a picnic? And then do that weird thing with their bodies? It makes no sense."

"No," said Sebastian. "No, it doesn't."

Photograph by Samantha Brown

C. S. Harris is the *USA Today* bestselling author of more than two dozen novels, including the Sebastian St. Cyr Mysteries; as C. S. Graham, a thriller series coauthored with former intelligence officer Steven Harris; and seven award-winning historical romances written under the name Candice Proctor. A respected scholar with a PhD in nineteenth-century European history, she is also the author of a nonfiction historical study of the French Revolution. She lives in San Antonio with her husband and has two grown daughters.

VISIT C. S. HARRIS ONLINE

CSHarris.net
❶ CSHarrisAuthor

Ready to find
your next great read?

Let us help.

Visit prh.com/nextread

Penguin
Random
House